Ferryl Shayde

By
Vance Huxley

© 2017 Vance Huxley

Published by Entrada Publishing.

Printed in the United States of America.

Contents

Dedication
To my Noeline and to the Joy of my life

Acknowledgements

Thank you to my editor Sharon Umbaugh,
for turning my words into a book worth reading.

My thanks to Rachel at Entrada
for all her hard work and encouragement.

Out of the Pit

Abel Conroy, fifteen, stood in the library van and chose the three old-fashioned romance novels that would change his life. His mum had to go into work today, library van day, so Abel had been volunteered to pick out three new ones for her. Now he hoped she liked them, or she would have to make a trip into town to the library to swap them again. His mum had enough on her plate just raising Abel on her own. Abel headed back into the little village of Brinsford, nestled in the edges of the Pennines, veering into the road a little as he came past Castle House. The boarded up doors and windows of the big, old, rambling house and the overgrown gardens always gave him a creepy feeling. He sometimes wondered why anyone had bothered to padlock the gate in the fence.

Abel hesitated when he saw Henry Copples coming up the road towards him, then braced himself for the hassle. He hunched his shoulders and kept walking, taking care not to meet Henry's eyes. At 190 centimetres and nearly 80 kilos of muscle, even at fifteen Henry Copples loomed over Abel's 168 centimetres and scrawny 44 kilos, or seven stone as Grandad insisted. "Hey, Squeak, what you got? Porn?"

Abel didn't object to being called squeak or Henry would hurt him until he squeaked to prove the point. "These are from the library van, books for my mum."

"I didn't know the library van stocked porn. Wish my mum read us bedtime stories like that. Let me see." Henry advanced, grinning. "I'll only tear out the good ones."

Abel glanced back down the lane for any possible help, but it was empty now the library van had left. He daren't let Henry get the three books because despite them not being even remotely pornographic, Henry would tear a few pages out anyway. "They're library books. I can't let you rip them up." Abel took a step back, looking round, but the only escape might be over the fence into the garden of Castle House. He hesitated, because the tangled trees and bushes suddenly looked even creepier for some reason. Abel decided he'd be better off trying to get past Henry and hoping someone heard the yelling and came to look.

A voice cut in. "What are you two doing?" Abel's momentary relief died when he recognised Tyson, Henry's big brother, letting his dog out of a car. Until he left school at sixteen, two years ago, Tyson had been an even worse bully than his brother. "Hey, it's a squeaky. Gettim, Cooch." The dog lunged towards Abel, barking and snarling, pulling the chain lead taut.

Abel turned to run, but too late as Henry caught hold of his arm and pulled him back round. Frantic now, Abel struggled, trying to prise Henry's hand off the books. "You want to fight?" Pain exploded as a fist hit Abel's nose and he staggered back, blood dripping as Henry pulled the books free. Abel snatched at them but Henry pulled his prize back out of reach, raising his fist again. As he swung, Abel ducked and turned, lunging for the fence and half-falling over. He scrambled to his feet and staggered towards the trees, holding his nose to stop the blood from pouring out. Behind him Henry sounded jubilant. "Come on Tyson, set Cooch after him."

"Hunting with hounds is illegal, ain't it?" Tyson laughed loudly. "Stop playing with those books and open the bloody gate you idiot, or he'll get away." Behind him Abel could hear excited barking and now splintering sounds as the brothers kicked in the padlocked gate.

Abel ran across the rough grass and down a faint path as fast as possible, holding a wad of tissues to his nose and wondering how to get away from a dog. Climbing a tree wouldn't help because the brothers would pull him down again. Cooch probably wouldn't bite him much, he hoped, but those two would beat seven bells out of him. Glancing down at the overgrown path, and the trail he left through the grass, Abel realised he'd have to get in among the undergrowth at least.

A gap showed him the house off to the side, but all the side windows were boarded. A pity, or Abel might have risked all the rumours of ghosts and monsters. He could have hidden in the huge, sprawling place forever. "Let Cooch go. We'll know when he's caught the squeak by the screaming." Henry's voice made the decision for Abel; he swerved away from the house and off the path, jumping over a low bush and heading for the thickest bushes he could see.

Abel didn't go far, though it felt like forever when he ran out of breath and lost any idea of direction. He pushed through yet more bushes and rampant honeysuckle, between two trees, and burst out into a small glade. Even as he saw the cliff blocking his way, Abel tripped over a huge flat circular slab, falling to his hands and knees. The tissue fell from his hands, blood pouring from his nose onto the stone. A crackling noise surrounded him as if he'd stepped on a giant frozen puddle as lines of dust rose from the worn carvings. Abel jumped back as the dust blew aside in a sudden gust of wind. That noise had to be from the network of cracks zigzagging across the slab! Abel shivered as his blood drained into the cracks. He'd nearly broken through and fallen into whatever lay hidden.

Two hollow thumps sounded, followed by an echoing voice. *"Knock, knock, who be that?"*

Abel spun round but couldn't see anyone. "I'm supposed to ask who you are." He kept his voice down because he didn't want to give that dog any help. He didn't want to play knock-knock jokes either.

"Tis my joke so I make the rules. Who be that?" The voice echoed around Abel from all directions and suddenly sounded stronger. *"Such strong blood, and distant kin to the sorcerer? What do ye need? I been left here too long so I will not be much help."*

Abel ignored the voice for a moment, looking around for someplace to hide from Cooch and the Copples. The cliff face stopped him running any further and stretched out of sight in both directions. The cave straight ahead wasn't deep and mostly filled by a well-worn statue, one of those gargoyle type garden ornaments. This one stood taller than Abel and wide enough to hide behind if there was room. Even as he ran round the slab to get there, fumbling for another tissue to stop his nosebleed, Abel wondered what the voice meant. "Help? You could scare off that dog and the two lunatics chasing me."

"I need more blood if I be going to fight three. Unless ye set me free?"

"Blood? My blood?" Abel had reached the cave and found that the stone figure almost touched the back wall. Now most of his mind turned to wondering if he could hide by scrambling onto the statue's back. "Who are you? Show yourself."

"I be, I be... Wait, I know, let me think.... Pungh Hmmshtfun, Spiritus qui furabatur, Koška Smerti, Braeth Huntian..... I remember! This body be Ferryl Shayde. I cannot come out. I be trapped here."

"Pungh Hmmshtfun? What sort of name is that?" Abel put a foot on the statue's haunch but it promptly slipped off. The stone didn't look that smooth so he tried again, slipping a second time.

"Who gave you my true-name?"

"Which name? Pungh Hmmshtfun? You told me." Abel tried to hold onto one of the stubby horns to pull himself up, but his hand slithered off.

After a short silence the voice answered, quieter and definitely disgruntled. *"Blood-link. Stupid, stupid. If I had my wits..."* It spoke louder. *"Keep quiet, do not tell anyone else that name. 'Tis bad enough with the sorcerer and now you."* A sigh more like a breeze through leaves sounded, though no leaves moved. *"What be your wish?"*

"Can you help me? Please?" Abel had given up on trying to get onto or behind the statue, and couldn't see anywhere else to hide. "Can I hide with you?"

"You would not like it." The voice definitely sounded amused. *"I can help ye fight?"*

"Fight? Me?" Abel would have laughed, but he'd heard crashing in the bushes so he felt more terrified than amused. "There's a dog and two lads bigger than me."

"Give me more blood?"

"For God's sake, stop it with the blood. What are you, a vampire? And keep a bit quieter will you?" Abel realised he'd possibly hissed that a bit louder than he'd meant to.

The voice sounded sulky now. *"Nobody can hear me but you. I am not a blood-leech. I want the blood for the magic in it. Nobody uses blood for glyphs if there's any other way. If you want me to help, pick up a stick and step on the stone."*

"It'll break! It's already cracked."

"In my dreams. Now do it!" The last three words had some snap in them so Abel picked up a stick. He stepped on the stone, right at the edge and very gingerly, but it didn't move or make any noise. *"That be a twig."* Abel glanced down at the stick. It wasn't very big, but better than a twig and the biggest nearby. *"The hound comes. As soon as it do step on the stone, throw the stick."*

"What, and shout fetch?"

"No. Throw at it, you fool. I will deal with the rest." The voice became a little bit hopeful with some wheedling. *"A few more drops of blood would help. Fresh, with the magic still in it?"*

"Here." Abel threw his now sodden tissue on the slab and stared as it turned pure white again. He didn't have time to ask, because Cooch burst from the bushes and headed straight for him. Abel threw the stick, but hopelessly misjudged the dog's speed and the stick flew high and wide, or almost did before looping in mid-air and sticking into Cooch's shoulder! Cooch yelped, swerved aside, and for a moment Abel thought the stick wiggled and pushed itself deeper. Cooch certainly yelped again, louder, before limping back into the bushes as fast as possible.

"Curses. Hardly any magic at all. Dog blood. Thin, weak, and hairy." Abel ignored the voice, staring at the clean stone and the blood trail in the grass. He'd seen Cooch bleed on the slab! *"Can ye hold one of the men on the stone long enough to drain more magic?"*

"What? No! No killing, draining, whatever. What the hell are you?" Abel stared around, then down at his empty hands. "Don't worry, there'll be lots of blood when they beat the crap out of me."

"Tempting, but you used my name, so I must help. Can ye find another stick?"

"Too late."

Henry burst out of the bushes, eyes wild. "You nearly killed Cooch, you nasty little sod. Now it's payback. This for starters." He ripped the book in his other hand in half, letting the pages fall before striding forward.

As Henry pulled back his fist, a voice snapped, *"Hit him."* The voice didn't ask, it commanded, or Abel would never have tried punching Henry in the chin. His hand barely moved before something caught hold of it and jerked it forward to strike Henry just below the eye. To Abel's utter astonishment Henry staggered back before stumbling off to the side, clutching his face!

Abel didn't have time to savour that because blinding pain from his hand doubled him up. Even as he cradled the injury, the voice berated him. *"Not in the head, fool. The head is made of bone. Hit the next one in the body."*

"I can't. I broke my hand." Abel barely whispered, but the mystery woman heard him. He felt sure the voice was a woman because she sounded like Miss Eddings, a particularly waspy teacher at primary school.

"Use the other hand. Remember, in the body."

Tyson burst from the bushes, stopping to stare at Henry. "What's the matter with you?" Tyson's eyes moved to Abel, then back again. "Why didn't you flatten the squeak?"

Abel took the chance to straighten up and try to look ready. He daren't look at the state of his left hand. Henry mumbled the reply, pointing at Abel. "Watch out. He's learned boxing or some bullshit martial arts."

"Got you with a sucker shot you mean. Serves you right." Tyson might have sneered but he moved in slowly and held both hands up in defence, fists clenched.

"Now." Abel didn't think Tyson had come near enough, but as his right hand started forward it pulled the rest of him with it. Tyson grinned as the punch started, moving his arm to block. Instead Abel's fist dropped as it sped up, hitting the larger youth solidly just below his ribs. Tyson's breath whooshed out as he doubled up, staggered two steps backwards and sat in the grass. He fell over on his side, both hands holding his belly, gasping for air while Abel shook his numb hand and forearm. *"You really are weak. Be you sick, or a scholar?"*

Abel didn't answer, concentrating on not crying out because now his other hand hurt like hell. If he'd dared he might have laughed at the sight of the two brothers, one laid out and the other hunched over holding his face. Unfortunately, if either of them tried again he'd got nothing left for the voice to use. Abel skittered away from that thought, that something used his hand, but he certainly didn't throw either punch.

"Told you," Henry mumbled. He still had a hand to his face, glaring at Abel but making no attempt to attack again.

"Just leave me alone, all right? I don't want trouble." Abel didn't. He'd already started worrying that these two would get some payback sooner or later. Unless Abel persuaded his mum that she wanted the voice as a very shy lodger, so it could protect him?

"For now. It's not finished." Henry kept glaring but he moved to where Tyson had now sat back up, and reached down to help his brother stand. Both looked at a defiant Abel for long moments before turning to leave. As a final gesture, Henry stamped on the pieces of the book, grinding them into the dirt.

As soon as the pair disappeared Abel sat down and curled up around his left hand. "Who or what are you and why didn't you come out and hit them?" Another thought hit him. "Why didn't they hear you?" Dead silence answered him. "Pung Humstfun? No, that's wrong. Pungh Hmmshtfun?"

"Stop saying that name!"

"Well answer me then."

"If you swear to stop saying my true-name. Use another, any other."

"Why?"

"Because they are not my true-name so I will ignore them if I wish." Abel could almost hear the 'of course, idiot' at the end of that.

"Can we start again, please? I'm Abel Conroy, and in spite of you crippling me, I'm pleased you helped. If you helped. However you helped?"

"I be Ferryl Shayde when the sorcerer put me in the pit." The voice sharpened. *"Where is he? He should have heard when ye cracked the seal!"*

"What pit?" Abel put the big cracked stone slab and pit together, he'd been right to jump back off it. "Nobody lives here. The house has been empty forever. The place is boarded up and there's rumours of ghosts and monsters and a ghastly death at some time. It must have been a long time ago because Grandad says the place was empty when he was a nipper. Oh, er, blimey, are you a ghost or a monster?" Some odd part of Abel's head reminded him not to swear in front of an adult, because Ferryl Shayde definitely sounded adult.

"I be someone who made a mistake. I lost a.....a sort of contest with the sorcerer and he put me under the stone. He took my wits to keep me helpless, then used me for testing dangerous glyphs. The type that may fight back. Describe the house and garden, and the village." After a short pause

the voice added, *"If ye please?"*

*　　*　　*

Abel described Brinsford as best he could; Main Street with older houses and the pub and village shop, the Village Green, Brinn Lane with a few posh new houses at one side and older ones on the other, and Riverside Close with a dozen old council houses. The voice asked more questions and her comments showed she really had been in that hole a long time. The old house, Castle House, had been rebuilt or added to since Ferryl Shayde last saw it, and several houses Abel thought of as old were new to her.

Ferryl recognised his description of most of Main Street with the Green at one end and Castle Road at the other, running past Castle House to the road into town. She also knew Brinn's Lane, leading out of the village over the bridge and up the valley, but not all the houses. Ferryl knew the Copples owned one farm, but thought the other one belonged to a Lord. She'd never heard of Riverside Close, the council housing where Abel lived with his mum.

Abel had suspended any sort of belief at the moment, especially after Ferryl explained she, definitely she, wasn't talking at all. They were communicating by blood-link after he dripped on the stone above her prison. Ferryl was a magician of some sort, but kept skirting round an exact description. By now Abel wondered if the blood loss and pain were making him hallucinate, or perhaps he'd passed out and imagined most of it.

"I've got to go. I'll have to go to the hospital with my hand." Abel looked down at himself. "That'll be fun, explaining, because I don't think mentioning you is a good idea. Mum will be mad about the blood all over my clothes because these are new jeans and they'll stain." He glanced at the stone slab, allegedly where Ferryl Shayde lived. "I'll come back when I can."

"Once you leave, you will find many reasons not to come back onto the grounds. You did well to manage it this time. Perhaps the boundary has faded." The voice sounded truly desolate now.

"Henry and Tyson managed, so did Cooch."

"Hunters on a blood trail are very hard to stop. You are the first to

come, ever, since the sorcerer stopped using my skills. I cannot survive that long again, not on the whispers of power in worms and insects. I will fade."

"Die?" Abel frowned. "How, I mean if you've been under here for a hundred years or whatever you're dead already, yes?" Definitely blood loss, Abel thought, to even think that let alone say it.

"Let me out, please? I can reward you."

Abel giggled; he had to. "Let me guess, I get three wishes. Eternal life, a palace full of gold and a harem full of women."

A matching giggle answered him. *"You have heard that tale as well. Not quite, but I will protect and serve you."*

"Then once you are out, you'll laugh and drain my blood or rip out my soul before flying, galloping or slithering off." Abel wasn't giggling now. He'd started thinking properly and a being still alive after a hundred years under a rock wasn't good news even if it was human.

"I will swear. I, Ferryl Shayde, swear to honour my promise and do you no harm."

"Nice try. You can ignore that name, you said so. You said your true-name commands you, so tell me the truth, Pungh Hmmshtfun. What can you promise if I can get you out?" Abel didn't like the idea of leaving this whatever under a stone until it faded. It had already served at least one life sentence, and had definitely helped him out of a really bad spot. On the other hand, even thinking of letting it out proved he must be concussed or off his rocker.

"I wish I had never told you that name. You caught me at a bad time." From the resignation in her voice, Abel thought that must be true. *"Gold, eternal life and women? I cannot promise eternal life, only that I will do my best to make sure you endure as long as I do."*

"I don't like the sound of endure so I'll settle for protection until I hit a hundred, if I last that long. Maybe, because none of it makes sense right now. I've got to think about this for a bit. If I go for it, how would I get you out?" Abel eyed up the stone slab. "A sledgehammer?"

"No! Breaking the stone will release enough power to destroy your village! The stone is a store, draining the magic from half the garden and storing the power. It has not been tapped for many, many years, and is

straining the containment glyphs. Worse, you have already cracked one set of glyphs, the ones holding me in here." Her voice suddenly perked up. "*Is the guardian still there?*"

Abel looked around, startled. "A guardian? Where?"

"*A large stone creature. It will be set where it can sense if I break free, and will be strong enough to stop me.*" Dust stirred briefly as Ferryl sighed. "*You are fortunate that cracking the glyph did not rouse it. The guardian would have destroyed you and those who followed.*"

Abel looked all around, but only one thing came close to the description. "There's a big stone garden ornament, all claws and ugly expression, but I don't think it will be dangerous. Even protected by that hollow in the cliff, most of the features have weathered away and the claws and horns are nearly gone."

"*That will not make any difference if it wakes. There is a glyph, magic stored deep inside that will not wear out.*"

"I could hit it with the hammer, break it up? Will a glyph, whatever that is, break?" Though he'd have to wait until his hands felt better.

"*You would not harm the guardian. Any attempt to seriously damage the stone will slide off or awaken it.*" Unfortunately, in his present state of suspended belief, that made sense because Abel had slipped off when he tried to climb aboard. "*A glyph is a symbol that directs magic and can only be released, not broken. You really will free me?*"

The mixture of hope and real relief in her voice decided Abel. "Yes, if I can work out how to stop you from hurting me or the village afterwards."

"*I will swear whatever you ask, on my true-name, as long as it is not eternal slavery. I would not allow the sorcerer to bind me, which is why I am under here.*" Abel heard distinct pride in that. "*You will need two solid glyphs to free me, now that you have cracked the seal. Remember these so that you can inscribe them on two pebbles.*" Dust shivered and moved then settled into two complicated designs. "*The rounded glyph will allow you back into the gardens, the sharper edged glyph must be thrown at the guardian once it is awake. Not before.*"

"Remember those? You are joking." Abel searched the ruin of the library book and found a half-blank page without much mud. "I'll draw them on here," he sniggered as his nose dripped, "with blood which you should appreciate."

"No! That will activate them. Do not scribe the whole glyph, just most of it and do not use blood." Ferryl's voice dropped, mumbling, *"Typical young fool, straight into blood magic,"* which Abel ignored. He spat into the dirt and drew with the mud and a bit of twig, careful to leave a break in a line so Ferryl didn't bend his ear again. The drawing wasn't exactly brilliant, due at least partly to the pain in his hand.

After a final round of instructions Abel came out of the gate and walked down the street in some sort of daze. He could have dismissed most of it as a nasty nightmare after Henry beat him unconscious, except for his shirt and jeans. Ferryl had somehow sucked the blood off them while he stood on the slab. Unfortunately, the mud remained so his mum would still give him earache, but they wouldn't be ruined. Abel picked up the two library books laid on the road where Henry must have dropped them, so at least he'd only have to pay for one.

*   *   *

Half an hour later after an ear-bashing for the clothes, a hug because of his nose and hands, and some sort of mixture of proud and exasperated over how they happened, Abel sat in the car on the way to hospital. Mum couldn't wait to get back and tell her friends that her boy had finally punched Henry Copples and his big brother. She always called him her boy when he'd done something she felt proud of, even if Abel cringed a bit at the version she'd give out. Abel daren't mention things in holes under the ground, so his mum thought he'd beat the pair of them. Henry really would be looking for payback once it got around.

His mum babbled away while Abel tried to get his head straight. He couldn't explain the library book or his mum would try to get in the garden for the evidence to confront Mr. Copples about his sons. Abel didn't think a spell would deter Mum once she'd got wound up, but he did worry about what Ferryl might do. He certainly had no intention of mentioning Ferryl Shayde, but wanted to be really careful in how he freed her. A part of him still wondered if he should let her out, but She Who Must Not be Named had seemed downright cheerful when Abel left. It would be cruel to just leave her to fade.

The Accident and Emergency wasn't too crowded on a Thursday afternoon, which Abel considered a blessing because his left hand really, really hurt now. His right hand had swelled, but not as much. The nurse took a look at his hands and nose and rolled her eyes, and his mum promptly launched into her version of how the hands were defensive injuries.

The x-rays that followed hurt all over again when Abel had to straighten his fingers. Abel had a cracked knuckle on his little finger and a clean crack across the bone in his ring finger, both on his left hand. Abel's right hand would be a lovely colour as the bruising came out but wasn't seriously damaged, and his nose wasn't broken. He endured a lecture about learning how to box if he wanted to hit things, while wondering just how the doctor would deal with Henry. Eventually, Abel left outpatients with his ring and little finger strapped together, a list of instructions, and painkillers to tide him over.

On the way back Abel chewed over his next problem, how to scratch patterns on two pebbles with both hands swollen up like boxer's mitts. One hand would be useable in days, but as a left-hander Abel didn't want to risk proper drawing with his right. While his mum fussed around and cooked tea, Abel sat with his right hand in a bowl of cold water and a bag of frozen peas on his left and thought about it. He could only come up with one solution, which meant involving someone else.

Abel managed to talk Mum out of spoon feeding him, then as she fussed around after the meal he took a deep breath. "I'll just nip round and see Rob and Kelis for a bit if that's all right, Mum?"

"You should rest those hands. Unless you want to brag a bit?" Her smile took the sting out of it, because two swollen hands and a swollen nose wasn't much to brag about. "You'll not be able to play computer games like that."

"No, but you know we've been working on a new game, or a different way of playing an old board game anyway." Abel smiled, hopefully innocently. "I've got a new idea and want to talk it through while it's fresh." He raised his hands. "I can't text or write it down."

"You're round there or those two are here nearly every day and most nights anyway, even now you're on holiday. I'm beginning to think you've got a girlfriend." She grinned. "Or a boyfriend?"

Abel laughed. "Stop it. If I even looked sideways at a girl or boy the whole village would be hammering on the door to let you know." The laughter hid a less palatable truth; few girls or boys were going to look twice at short, skinny Abel. Rob might have more luck once he reached sixteen. Kelis more or less ran away from any lad but Abel and Rob, founding members of the geek squeaks. Kelis, a tall, pale, skinny and intensely shy girl with long light brown hair, quickly became the third squeak after her family moved into the village a couple of years ago.

"Don't be late. You'll heal faster if you sleep properly." Abel agreed, even though the doctor had told him three weeks and never mentioned sleep patterns, and got out sharpish. He had a good look down the street and then didn't hang about because he really didn't fancy meeting either of the Copples brothers. They lived four miles away, but would have had time to recover and decide on payback. Somehow, after today, the undergrowth on the riverbank at the end of the road seemed sort of threatening, maybe a bit creepy.

*   *   *

When he tapped on the back door of Rob's house with his toe to save his hands, Abel braced himself. Sure enough, he had to endure cross-questioning about his injuries from Rob's mum while his dad and two sisters, one nineteen and one thirteen, listened with interest. "You should have run away." Abel agreed and let it wash over him until he could get upstairs to Rob's bedroom. As usual, Kelis had beaten him to it; she seemed to spend most of her spare time at Rob's or Abel's house.

"Mum's right, you should have run away." Rob inspected Abel's face. "No broken teeth? What did they do after you hit them?"

Abel grinned. "Fell over. Then they left me alone."

"Hellfire." Rob looked at Abel's swollen hands. "I hope those heal up quick, or they'll kill you next time."

"Nah, they think I've learned Kung Fu or something like that. Though I did learn one thing, never hit someone on the head."

"You needed a broken hand to learn that Henry's head is solid rock?" Kelis inspected Abel's bandaged and swollen digits and sighed. "You'll not be able to work on the game tonight."

"You two can and I've got an idea for it, for the magic part. How about casting runes for spells?" Abel pulled out the piece of paper, very gingerly with finger and thumb. "Like these but firm lines, not like I've drawn it."

"What did you draw this with?" Kelis inspected the paper, careful to only touch the clean parts.

"Mud and a twig. I didn't have a pencil."

Rob laughed. "You, my man, are truly weird."

"He's a male, of course he's weird." Kelis smirked, then looked closer at the drawings. "What do they mean?"

"It doesn't matter, we'll make something up. I just wanted to try a couple to see how much work they'd be. I thought we could use something like pebbles if you can engrave them?" Abel eased the two pebbles out of his pocket. He'd rather have left it until his hands felt better, but he really didn't like the idea of leaving Ferryl under the stone until then. He felt responsible, somehow, because he'd woken her up. "That'll give us an idea of how long a set would take, and then we can design some more."

"There's already runes, with proper meanings. We can buy plastic sets." Rob looked at the drawing. "Though I suppose we can make up our own. Let me get the file up on the computer and we'll try to work out how many it'll take for the spells we want."

"Can you make these two first, to try it?" Abel shrugged, not trying to hide that he felt embarrassed at asking. "I'd ask to use your engraving kit, but I'd drop it. I just fancy seeing what they look like."

Rob sighed. "I'd tell you to wait, but for the man who thumped both of the Copples?" He slapped Abel on the shoulder. "Freedom of the village tonight, buddy." He glanced at Kelis. "Can you draw them on the pebbles for me, Kelis? You're better at the arty stuff. At least this is a better use for that engraving kit than putting postcodes on TVs and kettles."

"OK. I like the idea of putting them on pebbles, because then Saint Georgeous can carry spells or just draw on the nearest bit of rock." Kelis smirked. "Butch Musclebound will be stuffed, there's no room in that tee-shirt and jeans for anything but muscle. Can he write? Can he talk?" At the moment none of the game characters had set names, which meant all three of them kept changing the ones they'd started with.

"It's leather and he's the barbarian so he's supposed to look like that. Hah, wait until you see the armour we design for your paladin."

Kelis thumped Rob on the shoulder. "You are not putting Saint Georgeous in some sort of schoolboy fantasy armour." Abel relaxed as the two bickered over character names and how they'd be dressed, because they were more interested in that than the glyphs.

*   *   *

A half hour later, the three of them inspected the result. "They're pretty?" Kelis didn't seem convinced.

"But complicated so by the time the hero," Abel grinned at Kelis, "or heroine manage to draw one, the orc or slime monster will have started digesting them."

"I still like the idea. Maybe we should go back to runes?" Rob turned back to the computer, and a few moments later the screen filled with angular characters. "Some of these look a bit complicated if time's short."

"They've already got meanings. We should make up our own symbols for each spell." Kelis glanced from the pebbles to the screen. "Our characters can carry a limited number for immediate use, with a delay of one turn or a penalty if they need an extra spell to allow for drawing or scratching them. We'd better make the basic spells simple for Butch and the other males."

"But with a little twirly bit for the girls?" Rob inspected the two pebbles again. "These were a waste of time."

"Not really. I'll keep them because I still like them, they're just not practical." Abel picked the pair up, wrapping each one in a tissue so they didn't get scratched.

Kelis nudged him. "Ooh, is one of them a love spell? Is it for Jenny or Arabelle?"

"I do not fancy Jenny! Or Arabelle."

"All the boys fancy all the Acro dancers, especially when they team up for those double throws." Kelis did a quick impression of an Acro dancer, carefully so she didn't thump anyone or hit the computer.

"You should join up, add a bit of class and double the collective brainpower." The three of them reverted to insulting the mental capacities of the Acro dancers and the school rugby team. Completely unfairly as they all knew, especially the Acro dancers considering the effortless way the dancers, mainly girls, ran through their complicated routines. At other times, in a more forgiving mood, all three agreed the Acros would give any of those American cheerleaders a run for their money.

Nearly two hours later, Abel walked home well pleased with the stones in his pocket, even if he doubted they were magic. The glyphs, as Ferryl called them, really were quite pretty, maybe just because he'd picked a white quartz pebble for one and a multi-coloured banded stone for the other. Despite being deep in thought, Abel checked the road for lurking Copples and almost trotted home. The day's exertions or medication finally caught up with him so he called out goodnight to his mum and went to bed.

*   *   *

When he woke up Abel laid for a long time thinking about yesterday. His hands proved it had happened but the rest seemed unreal now. Something under a stone used his hands to thump the Copples? The swelling in his right hand had mostly gone down so at least getting dressed hurt less than getting his clothes off last night. Downstairs Abel found a short note. Mum had been called in for extra work again today and would be back this afternoon. His mum often made extra money from her part-time job in the summer, while the full-time staff were on holiday.

After a quick bowl of cereal, Abel took out the two pebbles and inspected them. He still wasn't happy about the next bit even if Ferryl had explained it. Everyone had magic, they sort of sucked it out of the air just by walking about which Abel really wanted to ask more questions about. Unfortunately most people, including Abel, couldn't use magic because they'd never been trained. Abel would need a drop of his blood on each stone to transfer some magic and activate them. All this blood stuff freaked Abel a bit so he wanted to check that part again, but just in case he rummaged in his mum's sewing box and took a long pin.

A quick check showed that the street wasn't full of vengeful Copples, so Abel set off for Castle House at a brisk pace. It didn't take long to walk through Brinsford, even if the building lay on the outskirts. As he approached Castle House, Abel had second thoughts. After all, Ferryl had been in the hole for over a hundred years, so another couple of days didn't matter. He should wait a bit, probably until his hands had healed.

Abel turned away and started back home before he realised what had happened. Ferryl told him the second glyph, the one inscribed on the white pebble, had to be activated to get him back inside the garden. The barrier or enchantment didn't physically stop anyone, just persuaded them they didn't want to go in there. That made some sort of sense because Abel didn't know anyone who'd ever trespassed. Yesterday he'd hesitated and decided against going over the fence until Henry hit him and Tyson threatened him with the dog. Abel took out the stone and pin before walking back towards the gate.

By the time he'd taken a few steps, Abel had decided the whole thing must be concussion, or maybe a trick to get his blood and then he'd be enchanted. Even as he turned away again Abel remembered that Ferryl had taken a lot more than a pinprick of blood yesterday, so that didn't make sense. Before he could talk himself out of it again Abel stabbed his finger, sticking the pin safely back in the sleeve of his shirt before smudging blood on the stone. He stared, gobsmacked, when the innocent white pebble absorbed every trace of red.

Even while his mind tried to get round that, Abel looked up at a creaking noise to find a dead tree looking back! Two slits opened in the weathered trunk, and pale mauve orbs stared at Abel. The massive, gnarled, leafless tree sat on a bit of grass opposite Castle House, or it had because now it lurched forward, grass and dirt flying outwards as the roots ripped clear of the ground.

Abel might have stayed frozen too long, but a clod of grass smacked into his chest and with a startled squawk he turned, bolting through the gate towards Castle House. A look back showed a thick limb curved round and down, with the smaller branches at the end buried in the road where he'd been stood. As the last root came clear and the creature started across the road, Abel bounced off a tree onto his backside for a moment. Just a moment, panic drove him to his feet but this time he kept looking where he was going. Afterwards he would feel embarrassed, but at the time squealing and waving his arms in panic seemed perfectly reasonable.

"Ferryl, Ferryl, there's a tree chasing me. Help! Ferryl!" Abel skidded to a halt on the slab, any worries about it collapsing thoroughly forgotten. "What can I do? Help me!"

"Did it come into the garden?" A crashing and splintering, not very far away, answered the question for him. *"Did ye bring the glyph?"*

"Yes, should I throw it at the tree?" Abel took out the striped pebble with trembling hands and poised the pin, any reluctance long gone.

"No! That one will not work on wood or flesh. I have been testing and you broke the sealing glyphs, so I can start to come out. The guardian is attracted to magical beings so it will awaken, and should attack this tree creature first. Activate the pebble just in case it doesn't. Don't let the glyph touch anything but your skin."

"What do I do then?"

"Throw it at the guardian but only if it attacks you, then run away from the other one very fast. If you can get home it might be frightened off with a burning log from your hearth. Quickly!" Abel scuttled to the side and stabbed his finger, blood spurting onto the stone and immediately disappearing. A tree at the edge of the glade shuddered, then leant aside as a thick gnarled limb pushed it.

"It's here!"

"Calm down. Is the guardian waking?"

Abel looked at the worn statue, only a little surprised when its eyes opened. Blue eyes this time, but they sort of flickered and sparked like lightning. "Its eyes are open."

"I be going down deep again. Keep out of the way." Abel didn't answer because only a lunatic would get close to that tree. He watched transfixed as light blue scales appeared in a smooth ripple across the stone creature's body, its claws and horns lengthened and sharpened, and its mouth opened to show an impressive set of fangs. The creature, definitely not a statue now, surged off its haunches and launched itself but not at Abel! With huge relief he saw it bite a second thick limb, the one reaching for Abel, tearing a huge bite out of the wood.

Not just wood because dark purple liquid bubbled out of the rent.

A thin screech from the bushes heralded the arrival of the main trunk or body. A third limb clubbed the stone guardian and scales flew off, but claws and teeth struck back tearing more splinters and chunks away. Another limb smashed down, breaking off a horn while a dozen smaller branches stabbed at the guardian's chest. Most shattered, but two penetrated and a bone-trembling rumble answered as thick white liquid oozed out.

Up until then, Abel had assumed a stone creature would beat a wooden one, but now he started to worry. "Ferryl? They're fighting, but what happens if the tree thing wins?"

"You might run fast enough to find a fire, and fire might frighten it off. The best way to kill it would be to throw the glyph onto the stone over my hole, when it crosses over so it gets the full effect." Ferryl sounded resigned, and Abel remembered why.

"You said breaking the stone would destroy the village."

"Possibly. It will kill anything nearer. Probably. Maybe the Bound Shade will absorb everything, and we will live? Or maybe you would rather it caught you in your home?" Ferryl didn't sound happy, but her words definitely stiffened Abel's spine. He didn't want either of these things crashing into the village and finding Mum, or Rob and Kelis. Meanwhile, the two beings stabbed and clubbed and tore and clawed at each other, spattering the whole glade with white and purple.

The creatures closed on each other, the guardian ripping at the main trunk while the branches curled around it, trying to pull it in and crush it. With a sharp crack one of the front limbs fell off the guardian, crumbling as it bounced on the grass, and again that deep grumble echoed right through Abel. The guardian surged forward and up, clinging to the main trunk while it bit and clawed and tried to dig in between the eyes. Both of those were weeping ruins, but neither fighter needed to see now. The remaining four thick tree limbs clamped around the guardian, crushing it closer, and dozens of smaller branches wove a mesh to hold it firmly.

As its limbs were constricted, the stone beast bit harder, but with another sharp crack the other horn fell free. Abel braced to run, because it looked all over, but the guardian's tail started to stretch. He'd paid no attention to the tail, a stubby thing with one of those devil-style points,

27

but now it stretched to about two metres, curled, and drove up beneath the guardian's body! From the high screech and the thrashing, it also drove into the tree-thing.

Now the tree-creature wanted to let go, to free the guardian so it could pull the barb free but the guardian gripped on tight. No tearing now, the creature held on with its fangs and claws dug in deep. Thick boughs beat frantically at the stone body while smaller branches pulled or stabbed at the guardian's limbs. Even as they did a flood of purple poured out onto the grass, some of it draining away under the round stone slab.

"That tastes disgusting!" Abel jumped as Ferryl's voice broke into his concentration.

"Don't knock it, I think it means the tree-thing is dying." More scales flew from the guardian, and white splashed. "Maybe, because the guardian thing doesn't look good."

"Even crippled, either will try to kill you. Worse, either of them will heal in time and must feed now that they are active. Be ready." Abel didn't even ask what they'd feed on. It wouldn't be grass which left him and the rest of the village. He doubted old Stan's shotgun would even slow up the incredible rock-hulk or a rabid tree.

The guardian's tail must have dug deep enough because the screeches from the tree-thing faltered. Its big limbs gripped the nearby real trees, trying to drag itself back towards the road but in vain. Another limb faltered and slumped with a last screech that set Abel's teeth on edge the creature finally toppled. The trunk made one last attempt to roll over onto the guardian before the last branches and the final big limb stilled, one after the other. For long seconds after the main trunk lay still and silent the tail kept thrusting, until finally the weapon tore itself free.

Abel barely breathed, but the guardian hadn't forgotten him. It turned, ponderously on three legs but Abel could see a new, slimmer limb already sprouting. It limped forward, and the tail rose up above its head, pointing at Abel. He waited because as a lefty, a right-handed throw wouldn't be accurate. In a moment of cold calculation he didn't know he had in him, Abel waited until the creature stepped on the stone slab. If he missed, the pebble would break that and take them all out. The beast crouched to spring, haunches bunching, and Abel threw.

He'd never be sure if he hit the moving paw or the creature swatted at the pebble, but the two connected. Moments later Abel dropped down to sit like a puppet with the strings cut, trembling all over. The result was a complete anti-climax, when in a soft whoosh a cloud of white dust spread out from the pebble. Creature dust, because as it fell the guardian had completely disintegrated. "Good glyph, Ferryl." Abel mumbled it but Ferryl caught the gist.

"It worked? Does that mean they are both dead?" She sounded cautious, ready for bad news.

"I thought they were both dead to start with!" Abel realised that came out a bit sharp. "Sorry."

"Not quite dead. So I can come out now?" Ferryl suddenly sounded downright cheerful. *"Did you decide on how much gold and how many women?"*

Abel realised he hadn't got a firm agreement! "Pungh Hmmshtfun, I command you to stay there!" He'd practiced the name for a while last night and this morning, alone in his room, and got it right first time. "You aren't coming out until we have an agreement, one you've sworn to, that means I keep my own brains and body. I've thought about the usual options and want something a little bit different." Abel took a deep breath. "I'll still want the hundred year's protection, but instead of the riches and women I want you to show me how to do magic, properly like you and without stabbing myself."

The silence went on and on, but Abel let it because he knew how to make her answer if he had to. *"I can, but there is danger. If you wish to learn how to use magic, you must obey me. Only work the glyphs I show you, when I show you, until you are strong enough to stand more."* Ferryl's voice strengthened. *"For this prize, there will be a price. You must let me ride with you for a while, inside you, until I gather strength."*

"Possession? Not a chance. Grand theft schoolboy? You get to drive my body around like a stolen car until you wreck it, then trade up? Think again."

"I cannot possess anyone without their consent, not without mind damage that leaves them nearly useless. I usually cure them of something and agree to leave after a score of years." The voice took on a wheedling

tone. *"I will leave your body in excellent condition? Much better than it is now?"*

"I'm not handing my brain over to you." Abel snorted. "Improving my body wouldn't be hard."

"I don't have to be in control. Just like a rider on a horse." Before Abel could respond, Ferryl spoke again. *"You must exercise and strengthen your body anyway, to stand the strain of magic."*

"I might agree to a rider with no reins or spurs." Abel tried to work out how that would feel. "No rooting through my brain and listening to thoughts?" He really didn't want someone, even a something, eavesdropping in his head.

"That is possible. In return you must let me take magic from your blood when the time comes to leave, enough for me to survive the first transfer. Will your woman, wife, ask questions?"

"What! I'm fifteen! Magic from blood? Do you tie me to a stone slab and fill a mug?" Abel was horrified. First this thing about possession, then blood? He began to wonder just what was under the stone, while a part of him wondered if being under a stone for a hundred years had sent her crackers.

"It isn't the blood, you young fool. It is the power in the blood, the magic that you have been soaking up and never used. Taken straight from a willing body, that is truly powerful. Too young at fifteen? How old must you be? You are not sworn to a church, are you?"

"Marriage is illegal until sixteen at least. In some places it's eighteen. I haven't even got a girlfriend, so forget that part."

"Excellent. I will take what magic there is as I leave, in payment, though there may not be as much by then. If I am to teach you properly and protect you I must insist on a proper bond while I ride with you, to the bone. I must be able draw on your magic at will, because I have little of my own left." Abel sighed, sat on the stone and set into another round of explanation and bargaining. At least Ferryl never mentioned blood again. After a last argument on the placement and maximum size of the tattoo, Abel took a deep breath.

"You, Pungh Hmmshtfun, now called Ferryl Shayde, will protect me to the best of your ability for ninety years. You will also teach me how to control magic, slowly and safely. If I refuse to obey you about the magic instruction, you are absolved of teaching me any further until I obey. In return I will help you escape from your prison, and allow you to live within the tattoo you provide. Once you are strong enough you will leave my body, taking the magic you need to survive, but leaving me unharmed. You will not have any control of my body or mind unless I permit it temporarily while learning magic, or to save me from serious harm when you will release me as soon as possible. You will be allowed to tap the magic I hold, but must never drain my levels dangerously low." Abel reran it in his head. "Swear it on your true-name, spoken clearly."

After a pause, Ferryl repeated everything and swore on her true-name, though she changed "if you help me escape" to "when you allow me to leave" which seemed fair. *It is done. Let me out. Please.*

"Pungh Hmmshtfun, you may leave your prison." A cloud of guardian-dust rose from the stone slab and Abel turned away, covering his eyes and mouth.

"Greetings. What do you think of me?" The possibly human thing wore a loose woman's dress, ragged, filthy, long-sleeved and down to the ground which might be a blessing. The hands and face were almost skeletal, covered in little more than leathery looking skin and when it looked at him Abel couldn't see anything but black holes where its eyes should be. Long black hair, tangled and dusty, hung over its shoulders but as it looked down at itself the worst part showed. A huge hole gaped in the top of its skull, filled with black nothing. *"I think this body is past repair."*

She started to move towards Abel and he flinched away, he couldn't help it. That wanted to live inside him? "Hang on."

"You wish to break our agreement?"

Abel almost nodded, but realised that would release this thing to grab a body, maybe his. Even if she didn't, Ferryl could leave a certain schoolboy to be hammered by the Copples brothers. "No, but how does that, you, get in here?" He gestured to his upper arm, the agreed tattoo location.

"This body is the best I can manage as a temporary home. It will fall into dust when I leave." She glided closer. *"You are marked by a God,*

though it seems very weak. I cannot come in if you believe in its protection." She touched her forehead.

"No problem, I don't believe in all that anyway. The mark will be from my christening but I've only been to church once since then, to Grandad's funeral. Christ, is God real?"

"All of them are, as long as one worshipper still lives. Nobody knows what happens then. Now, quickly before I lose control." Abel pulled up his shirt sleeve and turned his left side towards her, shutting his eyes as the ruined face began to disintegrate.

A moment later Abel screamed, dropping to the floor holding his shoulder and rolling around in the dust. "What did you do?"

"Burned the magic connection into your bone, as you agreed. It will stop hurting soon." True enough the pain receded quickly, though not as quickly as it arrived. *"Do you like your tattoo?"*

Abel realised that gruesome creature must now be a tattoo, yeuk. He looked at his arm, just above his bicep, and looked away again. "Christ, can you change it? Could she, it, have clothes or turn round or something? Mum will kill me if she sees that." He gritted his teeth. "Change it, even if it hurts again." He'd never actually discussed the picture, and now Abel wondered what else the agreement had missed.

"Like that? It might be wise to stop calling on Gods if you are not sworn to them."

Abel took a quick look at the tattoo. Not a cat despite the ears and tail, and the dappled fur covering her. A young woman in a furry onesie, maybe, now half-knelt, half-sat almost facing away with her tail curled around and over her leg. She turned her head further towards him and winked a big, green, decidedly cat-like eye. "Don't let her, it, you, do that. Tattoos don't move." The tail waved and her whiskers moved when her definitely human face smiled.

"They do with sufficient muscle control. If I still had a body I could show you." A giggle echoed in Abel's head. *"This is wonderful. I had almost forgotten the light, the colours, the scents. Ooh, flowers, smell the flowers!"* Abel obliged, then made his slow way through the garden to the front smelling and touching every different plant and tree. He didn't have to struggle through undergrowth because the tree-thing had smashed a

wide, curving swathe through the smaller trees and shrubs.

Abel stood on the overgrown lawn for a while so that Ferryl could look at the house, then walked up to the front door and reached out to touch it. "Ow. I'm guessing that was magic." Abel shook his hand, still stinging from the zap he got just before making contact with the wood.

"Yes, and shaped to repel anything even slightly magically active. A human who had never used magic might walk straight in if they had a key, except the garden boundary would stop them getting this far. Walk through the village now so that I can see it."

"In a minute. Is there anything we can do about this?" Abel waved a hand at the hole smashed through the fence, the torn grass and trampled woodland. Outside the garden the tarmac road now had several gouges and grooves, and the patch of grass the other side had a big hole torn out of it. "That hole is where the dead tree, that wasn't, used to stand."

"Clever. The sorcerer left a guard outside, in case someone used a glyph to get through the boundary. Though he must have made a mistake because it should have detected your glyph coming along the track and caught you before the gate."

Abel felt slightly guilty and then confessed. "I didn't do the blood thing at first. I tried to get in twice before I stabbed myself. I don't like the blood stuff, it's creepy."

"You will never need it again. I must use your hand to strengthen the boundary."

"All right." Abel's hand moved by itself and rested on the gatepost. He suddenly staggered and felt weak though the feeling passed, leaving him feeling tired. "What was that?"

"I used some of your magic, quite a lot, to strengthen this barrier. I doubt anyone else will enter now."

"Isn't is dangerous to use up all my magic? There might be something else." Though Abel's worries had more to do with Henry than magical creatures.

"Not all of it and you are already collecting more just by walking around. I will explain back in your home. Are all tracks like this, smooth? Where do you live? This surface is wonderful." Abel gave up because Ferryl

descended into almost babbling as they came past the first houses.

*　　*　　*

Except for her being invisible, the walk through the village with Ferryl felt like escorting a lively, excited, inquisitive little sister or talkative puppy. A dozen steps after leaving the gate she'd persuaded Abel to bend down and touch the tarmac road, then take off his trainers and socks so Ferryl could enjoy how smooth and warm it felt. The last time she saw it, the road had been a rutted track connecting the village to the post road. The whole walk turned out like that, with Abel touching walls, lamp posts, and glass. Ferryl seemed stunned by the amount of metal, whole carriages made of it, and the lack of horses.

"Too much time has passed. Let me look inside your head, to see what you know." For the tenth time Abel refused but this time, instead of pushing harder, Ferryl changed tack entirely. *"Put out your hand to the cat."* After a pause she added, *"Please?"*

"I appreciate the please for a change, but I'm not getting too near. That one isn't always friendly." Abel held out his hand and to his surprise the black and white neutered tom came towards him instead of hissing or backing off.

"May I use your hand, to say hello?"

"You've got to stop if he scratches." Even as he said that, the cat stretched and rubbed his head along Abel's hand, purring. The answering purr startled Abel since it came from inside his head, and his fingers stroked and scratched. The cat lay down, arching his back happily while Ferryl murmured something Abel didn't understand. After a few moments the cat stood, stretched, butted his head against Abel's hand and leapt up and over the low wall.

"Your world has become too complicated for such creatures. He will worship, in the way of cats, but cannot help me this time."

"The cat talked to you? Were you speaking cat?"

Ferryl sounded amused. *"No, fool, but he let me see his world. Many strange things he does not understand, and a few he does. I spoke in an old language."*

"When you told me names you spoke Latin, I think. Spiritus or something like that?"

"I speak Latin and Greek, but I do not read very well. What is that?"

Abel shelved the idea of a Latin and Greek speaking tattoo for now. He should have taken ancient languages as a study option. "The bus shelter? It's to keep the rain off while people wait for transport to town."

"All that metal and good glass just to keep the rain off a few coach passengers? Why is it cursed? Even with no sorcerer in the village, your local witch should have cleansed it." Abel heard a dismissive sniff. *"Or at least chased off the Globhoblin."*

"We don't have a witch, how can a bus stop be cursed and why, and where and what on earth is a Globhoblin?" Abel's vision blurred and cleared again. "Yeuk. The slimy football thing with too many legs and warts is a Globhoblin? Not a Hobgoblin?"

"Hobgoblins are bigger, greener and can be good or bad. Globhoblins have as many legs as they wish and are always unpleasant. How do you stop creatures like this from drooling in milk pails and stealing kittens? I don't remember seeing any hexes on the doors. The witch should keep your village clean even if another sorcerer or sorceress hasn't moved in." Ferryl sounded really worried now.

"Can you do that? Get rid of the globlin thing, and the curse, and protect the village?" Abel didn't even try to make sense of the rest of her answer. That warped toad-like thing in the bus stop had just stuck out a warty tongue and given him a grin with too many teeth.

"Give me your hand. For one glyph." Abel agreed without thinking because the thing freaked him, and a vague, smoky shape flew from his finger to hit the football sized creature. It popped, the gloop bubbling briefly before disappearing. *"Let me look at the curse."* Abel walked a bit closer, cautiously, seeing a vague reddish glow appear around some of the graffiti. Someone had been crudely unhappy about the bus being late.

"That's a curse?"

"Whoever scribed it had enough intent to give it life, or maybe something else found it funny to activate the letters." Ferryl snorted. *"If I were to activate that other one, there, the man might need a witch very quickly before anything really dropped off."* Ferryl paused. *"I cannot read*

some, or understand others. I must look in your head!"

"Break that curse, please, then let's go home and we'll think about it?" Another glyph made of smoke or vapour drifted from Abel's finger and the glow around the writing died away. He headed straight home and by the time they arrived Ferryl had reverted to childish wonder at almost everything. Abel had become a lot more worried because things, creatures, seemed to be everywhere. Not many of them, and not large, but he really didn't like the idea of them slithering, hopping or flitting about without being seen.

*   *   *

"Hand, quickly." Abel had barely come through the back door into the kitchen, and stared around in alarm even as he agreed. His hand gestured and a wispy shape flew towards the kettle, then the microwave. A little creature came out of each, both smoking slightly. These were the first even vaguely humanoid types Abel had seen up to now, reminding him of a toothless old man in overalls. The creatures had no actual clothes, but the shape looked eerily similar.

"What are they?"

"Gremlins. You have so many homes for them in here. Luckily some of your mechanicals are already protected by hexes." Ferryl pointed Abel's hand at the fridge and cooker, but after a quick inspection couldn't find any protection on the water taps or the freezer. The two singed gremlins scuttled outside, and Ferryl confirmed the kitchen didn't have any more in residence right now.

Abel didn't need an explanation of a gremlin, an unexplained fault in equipment, though finding out they were real came as a shock. He would have liked an explanation for the creatures flying and scuttling around the kitchen. Some were rooting in the rubbish bin, while others were clustered on the dirty dishes in the sink. Though first, "Where are the hexes?" Abel glanced around, wondering why anything had them, or if the cooker did why didn't the microwave? Did some people know about the magic life around them?

"There, the scribed shape attached to the front."

"The brand logo?" Abel touched the one on the fridge and Ferryl agreed that was an active hex to repel gremlins. All the brand logos on the protected items were hexes, but neither of them could work out why the logos on others weren't activated. "We'd better check the other equipment. Mum keeps complaining the digibox records the wrong TV channel now and then." The other creatures could wait for now, since a good few were leaving.

"I do not understand, but I can check for a gremlin." Ten minutes later another three slightly singed gremlins had left the house. According to Ferryl the digibox should work better even if she still had no idea what it was.

Abel followed the last gremlin through the kitchen to make sure it left. "Why didn't you splat them?" Ferryl didn't strike Abel as the merciful type.

"If I destroy it in the machine the gremlin will wreck what it can as it dies. The gremlins understand the glyph's warning. If they leave and stay away, I will not kill them. If they stay or come back, I can and will." Abel could hear the sheer frustration in the next part. *"I must learn what all these things in your house are, what they do, or I may damage them by mistake."* Abel's hand moved and a slug-like creature near the rubbish bin splattered and evaporated.

"Is that dangerous?"

"No, but it has been too long since I could do this." Another two creatures, one scuttling and one flying, exploded into slime that evaporated.

"That's not hygienic. Won't the bits leave slime over everything?"

"No, the creature reverts to pure magic." Another one died. *"You must let me into your head!"*

"No, and I'd like my hand back if you're done, please." Abel waited, ready to use her name, but his hand suddenly started obeying. "I'd like to check upstairs now, and you can take my hand to remove gremlins and dangerous creatures. Then you give me it back, and we'll try to work out a way for you to get what you need."

Ferryl sniggered. *"You are learning."*

They checked all the rooms upstairs, which definitely felt a bit weird as Abel never went into Mum's bedroom. Ferryl evicted two more gremlins, one from Mum's laptop and the other from the bathroom scales. The second one might explain why Mum complained about her diet only working sometimes. Once they'd done, Abel sat down for a talk to his tattoo about how long she had been out of touch. As they talked, he noticed several flying and scuttling creatures left the room.

Unfortunately, Ferryl didn't consider the numbering of years, dates, to be important because people kept changing the system. Eventually Abel used his computer to search for when various things happened, people and facts Ferryl remembered. They concluded that Ferryl went in the hole, literally she insisted, nearly two hundred years ago in the early eighteen hundreds. From a few things the sorcerer told her, and her own estimate, the visits stopped in the late eighteen hundreds. Victoria had definitely still been on the throne the last time the sorcerer used Ferryl's skills.

Ferryl's memory really did seem patchy, and she kept blaming the sorcerer for stealing her wits. Physically, she swore, and insisted they would be hidden away, probably in Castle House. Though even her wits, whatever they were, couldn't fill in two hundred years of missing information on how the world worked, day to day. Not rocket science but what a car was, zips and electric lights, reading modern English, why milk went in a fridge. Some questions seemed more surreal, like why Brinsford didn't have a witch to deal with the curses and globhoblins.

Abel agreed that Ferryl had to find a way of catching up, of learning how the modern world worked, before she lashed out thinking something normal had threatened her. The two of them went round and round the problem and either Ferryl had to look inside Abel's head, properly, or she had to look in someone else's. Abel insisted on someone else's, because he could use her true-name to stop Ferryl from taking any other person over. At least the tattoo promised she could take all she needed from a sleeping person without leaving more than a few odd dreams.

"Not my mother."

"She sleeps here so it would be easy. Why do you have a room each and a whole house for two? Are you rich? Why don't you hire bully-boys to beat those two peasants?"

Abel ignored most of that as the usual way 'talking' to Ferryl strayed off course. "She's my mother. If there is a problem, I don't want her waking up brain dead or with a spooky passenger."

"I told you this will not damage her. Once I have my wits back I could gift her a glyph to attract a strong young man, or a rich one? To thank her." Ferryl paused. *"I could find her man and bring him back?"*

"I'm not risking Mum, and she doesn't want or need another man. You can't bring Dad back because his ashes were scattered out at sea." Abel didn't need reminding of standing on a boat in the rain one grey November day, or Mum sobbing, not being able to speak properly when she scattered the contents of a plastic pot then dropped it in the sea. Then six year old Abel had to throw his flowers followed by Grandad. "Please keep quiet while I try to work out where I can find someone asleep." Abel cudgelled his brain but unless he found a drunk in Brinsford, it wouldn't be easy. He vetoed Ferryl's suggestion of using a glyph to knock someone out. He had to find an answer because the constant torrent of ill-informed and downright dangerous or illegal suggestions from Ferryl were driving him crackers.

His tattoo talking stopped when Mum came home, because Abel didn't fancy trying to talk to anyone else with Ferryl's voice rattling on inside him. Mercifully, the silence also stopped Ferryl complaining about all the information she needed. Unfortunately keeping her quiet meant Abel couldn't ask her to get rid of creatures. Several appeared and scuttled about in the food while Mum made tea. Abel found that if he stood near enough either he or probably Ferryl scared them away.

Abel repeated his instructions on the way round to see Rob and Kelis. He felt a bit mean because Ferryl hadn't had anyone to talk to for a long time, but until she managed to catch up with modern life her comments really were either hilarious or scary. At least Abel could walk down the street in the open, with his cat-lady aboard the Copples brothers were the least of Abel's problems.

Abel could feel her interest and frustration as he and his friends discussed the board game that might, hopefully, make their fortune. She really did try to keep quiet but occasional comments, and the feel of her moving in his skin under his sleeve, were both distracting. She seized control of Abel's hand once but neither Rob nor Kelis saw the smoky glyph or the slightly singed gremlin scurrying out of Robs' computer, though Rob sniffed at the air and looked around. When Abel left to go home, Rob's front door had barely shut behind them when she started. *"Now may I talk?"*

"Yes Ferryl. I can answer quietly and nobody will hear while we are on the street."

"Could we walk to your house across the fields where I can check for wards or hexes?"

"No. I'll arrive home muddy again, a really bad idea, and anyone looking out of a window will wonder why someone is in the field." Abel looked at the edges of the light cast by the street lamps and could see odd creatures moving about. "I'm not keen on getting out of the light and giving that lot a chance to get me."

"Those beings are not frightened of the light, they are staying out there because they are frightened of me, or us. They sense the magic, but are not sure what you are." Ferryl's tone became a little bit plaintive, and once again Abel wondered if she was playing for sympathy. *"It has been so long since I walked in the open countryside, day or night. I can show you the different fairies, and you can explain how those portraits and words on paper are a magical world?"*

Abel immediately turned back to cut up the side of Rob's house and over his back fence. He really did want to see a proper Tinkerbell after all the ugly looking things he'd seen so far. "I'll walk along the grass just outside the garden fences, and slowly so I don't get home looking like a tramp. If anyone sees me I'll tell them I'm hiding from Henry." Abel tried to work out how to explain gameplay to a complete newcomer. "The idea of the game is for those who play to imagine they are casting spells and fighting monsters, rescuing maidens and finding treasure."

"Why not make the glyphs real, then the magic would be real, the monsters would come to investigate, and maybe the survivors would find treasure and maidens." After a pause, Ferryl laughed. *"Though maybe you would lose too many players, and then a sorcerer would be sent to stamp out the problem."*

"I really hope that was a joke." Abel left a pause but Ferryl's agreement took a while coming, so maybe not. "Where are the fairies?" There were creatures here, ugly little flying ones with long, thin horny wings, but no bright colours or pretty fluttery types. Everything he could see had patches or whorls of muddy greens, browns and a few splashes of white or black. He hoped these were moth equivalents, and the daylight version would be prettier. The creatures flitted between the bushes in the gardens and the nettles along the edge of the fields but as Ferryl promised they gave Abel a wide berth.

"These be faerie, and fae. The faerie live off grass, fruit and leaves, mainly the magic from them but they eat tiny amounts to help them to keep a shape. The small fae prey on midges, flies, and similar small pests or weak faerie, but leave anything larger alone. The larger fae have stings, prey on faerie or the likes of wasps and butterflies, and drain small amounts from larger magical creatures. Their stings will drain a little magic from humans, leaving a red mark that will irritate, and too many will weaken the young or ill. Stop here." Abel stopped for a while. *"Nothing, no sign of hexes or wards, not even a fae-trap. Your witch or warlock, whoever it be, must be very weak or lazy."*

Abel gave up trying to explain Brinsford had no witch or warlock, in fact he'd started to wonder who might be one. Ferryl launched into a description of each type of creature they saw, so at least by the time he climbed into his own garden Abel knew the difference between some fae and faerie. The fae were longer and sleeker, and really did look more predatory, but all the fliers were dull colours and often mottled to blend in even better. It might have been the medication, or the excitement, but all Abel wanted to do when he arrived home was sleep.

*   *   *

Abel opened his eyes the following morning and could sense Ferryl's satisfaction. *"I have discovered what I need to know."* She sniggered. *"Your mother had lovely dreams. I wish I had my wits, then I could gift her a small glyph to stop her hip hurting as much. You are right, she does not want a man while you are still at home."*

"I told you not to do that!" Abel pulled up his pyjama sleeve to be met by a smug smile.

"But you did not order me, and I did not go far away and leave you unguarded. Now the problem is solved. You must learn to subvocalize."

"What?"

"Your mother told me the word for speaking without noise, so we can

talk in public. I still need to get my wits back because they contain much of my magical knowledge. We must find a way to break the wards and get inside Castle House, but until then we can use the gardens to teach you magic." Ferryl paused while Abel wondered about these wits. *"Until I gain my wits, I can only remember a few glyphs. I memorised the one for the guardian, for if the stone holding me ever failed."*

Abel thought about that while he cleaned his teeth and got dressed. "It'll probably be a week before we can go back to the gardens. After all there's that big hole and missing tree, and a clear trail inside the garden. The place will be knee deep in coppers and maybe a reporter with a camera by now. They'll be trying to work out how that tree got over there and why it's in bits and covered in purple gunk." Abel flinched at a sudden thought. "I hope they don't break that stone slab to see what's underneath."

"Only a few bones though they'll never find out. None of them will go into the garden. I told you, your pursuers were hunting wounded prey or they would have been dissuaded. I strengthened the barrier at the front as we left and now non-magical humans will only go inside if it is that or death, and maybe not then. Any magic users will be badly hurt if they try." Ferryl seemed very sure. *"The Bound Shade will have reverted to its natural state, long dead, and rotted away. The fluid energised it and will dissipate without a host, losing colour and any power. Your local militia, policeman, will look from the road and decide there is no need to go inside."*

Exactly why a dead tree would be called a Bound Shade went onto Abel's list for later. "What about the big hole beside the road and the ripped tarmac?"

"I do not know. If someone brings in a sorcerer or priest that could cause a problem, though I have learned nobody believes in witches or magic any more. Unless the police retain a magic user or contact the church, our only danger is if another sorcerer finds out. If a sorcerer or priest tries to get inside the garden we will need solids glyphs, several of them." Ferryl paused. *"Someone may be curious about the bones in the hole. Have any children gone missing?"*

"Christ, no."

"Will you please stop calling on a God you have just rejected! Are you

trying to attract attention? It will not be amused."

"Sorry. It's a habit. Lots of people say my, er, the G word, or the C word, without really believing in them. The English are well known for not being very religious." Abel didn't feel too comfortable with the idea now. He'd been taking names in vain all his life, and something might have been listening? "I didn't reject God. My parents put that on me and I've never believed in religion and all that." Or magic Abel thought, and quickly shelved the subject for now. He went back to Ferryl's other question. "Why would there be missing children?"

"If it has been there so long, the Bound Shade will have fed now and then. They are known to take whatever is convenient, which can be a child or vagrant though the instructions would have bid it be discreet. It probably ate stray dogs or foolish birds since neither see any harm in a dead tree. How long will your police be there? I must teach you some basic magic straight away, so you are at least capable of warding your home."

"Can't you do it, ward the house? Not that I don't want to learn, I just don't want to wait." As Abel came downstairs two little crawling things stared in surprise and scuttled out under the door through a crack that should be too small. That had to be magic. "To stop those."

"They will eat pests, ants and flies. Much better hunters than spiders and pictsies don't leave dusty webs." Ferryl tutted, which in Abel's head seemed even worse than out loud. *"Laziness is not a good trait in a student, and it will be easier to keep the wards strong if you lay them."*

"Surely we can get rid of the ones that crawl in the food? Tell me about pixies while I have breakfast, because I'm fairly sure I'm going to need all my strength today." As he listened Abel wished he'd waited until after eating. Ferryl gave him a lecture on pictsies versus piskies and pixies, brownies, sprites, haunts, various sorts of goblins and hoblins, and a multitude of creepies and crawlies that definitely made Abel queasy. The lecture included eating more meat and exercising so he could stand the strain of wielding glyphs. Abel agreed if only to shut her up and set into persuading Ferryl to ward the house, right now, promising to learn how as quickly as possible. He could have ordered her, but wanted to save that for when he needed to. Ferryl Shayde didn't seem the sort to like orders very much.

Eventually Ferryl agreed, and they worked around the windows and doors while Abel's hand drew invisible glyphs. *"These should be incised. They would be much stronger. You have a cat!"* Ferryl sounded delighted when Mrs. Tabitha, a fat tortoiseshell cat, sauntered over to exchange purrs. After having her tummy stroked, Mrs. Tabitha left to sunbathe, probably. *"She will let me know if something unpleasant tries to enter. Unless it is small enough, then she will kill it herself."*

"Cats can see creatures?" Abel stared after Mrs. Tabitha. "They hunt them?"

"Not hunt, kill, because the creatures are made of magic and are not edible. Cats can only kill those without strong venom. They cannot see the magical creatures clearly, but I have gifted Mrs. Tabitha knowledge of magic so she can see the creatures properly and she will be a very efficient lookout. Cats have more sense than to attack the seriously dangerous types." Abel added that to the list of things to think through once he had a spare week to sit in a dark room and make sense of it all. Hopefully, he wouldn't start finding dead creatures outside the back door where Mrs. Tabitha usually left her mice and birds. Right now, Abel needed to concentrate on learning magic.

A Glyph from the Gods

From the look of it Abel wouldn't be having magic lessons today at least, and he doubted he'd get any tomorrow either. Two strips of police tape and traffic cones marked off the worst damaged section of the road outside Castle House, also blocking access to the hole where the Bound Shade had lived. A police panda car and a council van were parked further along the road, the other side of the big hole in Castle House's fence. A bored looking copper directed the occasional car past the cones. Another copper and a workman in an orange jacket peered into the garden, but they weren't crossing the boundary. Abel joined the half-dozen villagers who stood by the tape, some of them taking pictures with their phones. "What happened?"

Kelis turned. "Hi Abel. Nobody knows. Someone must have called the coppers because of all the mess and damage. There's no sign of that dead tree, unless it's at the end of that mess." She pointed at the trail of damage in the gardens.

"You think it ran off?"

She giggled. "Yeah, or maybe it fancied some company and the trees over there threw a party. It's probably laid in there, drunk as a skunk. Tomorrow it'll be back in place but with a lousy hangover."

"That will worry the coppers more than some gyppo nicking it for firewood." The speaker's smile died as he saw Abel's face. "Did they run over you on the way through?"

"No Stan. He got into a fight with Henry." Kelis sounded happy about that, probably because her hands and face didn't hurt. "Have you seen Henry?" Last night both Kelis and Rob had speculated on what Henry's face might look like.

"Yes. Did you do that, Abel, give him that black eye?" Stan, a pensioner and allegedly an ex-poacher, inspected Abel's face and hands. "His face is swollen as well, but not as badly as yours. You lost, but well done anyway."

Since one hand had straps on it, the other was bruised and scratched, and running into a tree hadn't improved his already swollen and bruised nose and face, Abel could only agree. "I always lose, though I knocked Tyson down as well."

"Really? I'll loan you my shotgun to make it fairer next time, if you wipe off the fingerprints afterwards." They all laughed because Stan really would like to see the Copples knocked back, but never let anyone near his shotgun. "Something happened to that bloody dog as well because its shoulder is all strapped up. At least the thing will leave Bugsy alone for a bit." The ancient Jack Russell wagged his tail. Cooch harassed the smaller dog, but Tyson never let it get serious because Stan had threatened to shoot Cooch if he bit Bugsy.

"Maybe the Gyppos ran Cooch down." After a bit more talk while watching the policemen and council worker scratch their heads, Abel more or less gave up on visiting the garden today.

"Your policemen are diligent, and slow. We must go around to the back gate." Abel opened his mouth to point out he'd never heard of a back gate, then realised if anyone knew it would be Ferryl.

*   *   *

After a long walk out in the fields, and into a small wood Abel never knew existed, they approached a gate in a stone wall. "Will it be locked, or have a guardian?"

"Nobody comes into this wood."

Abel looked around him and nothing scuttled or slithered in the shadows, or nothing creepy anyway. Conversely, a perfectly normal squirrel looked at him from high in a tree and birds were flitting about, singing merrily. "Not the little crittur things, but animals do. Does that mean people can wander in here as well?"

"They will not do so without good reason, and will be stopped by the main spell on the fence and wall."

"Does that mean you could put a barrier around the whole village?" The place wasn't exactly overrun but the magic creatures gave Abel the heebie-jeebies. Despite them allegedly being made of magic he didn't like them in his food, clothes and bed. "Then I wouldn't have to ward the houses." He didn't fancy that, explaining to everyone in the village why he wanted to draw invisible shapes with his finger on windowsills and doorsteps.

"*A witch should be doing that, unless you want to become the local warlock? The villagers should be paying for hexes against whatever causes them trouble.*"

"But they aren't, probably because they've no idea they need hexes. I've thought about it and there isn't a witch, I'm sure. So back to the first question. Can we ward the village, because that would be easier to explain? We could do it outside the fences." Abel waved a hand to indicate the wood. "This seems to work."

"*The boundary here is powered by magic from trees. We could build a magical deterrent anywhere there are enough trees in the right places, trees without a resident, but it will take a long time.*" Her voice suddenly became more urgent. "*I didn't expect another one, not with such a wide barrier. Let me have control!*" A crackling and creaking heralded a dead tree wrenching roots from the ground, its pale mauve eyes fixed on Abel.

"Ok. Can you deal with it? Or make me run faster?"

"*I can teach it respect, so that we can get into the garden and construct a solid glyph to threaten it in the future.*" Abel watched his finger wiggle a bit and a smoky shape flew across the gap to strike the Bound Shade. At least Abel knew what a Bound Shade was now, a creature's essence captured at the moment of dying and used to keep a semblance of life. According to Ferryl there would be something inside the tree, a glyph of some sort, to strengthen the captured being and force it to obey a set of instructions.

"Is it meant to do that?" Flame gouted from the trunk and an unearthly screech set Abel's teeth on edge. The Bound Shade moved back, stumbling and in obvious pain.

"*Not really. That should have burned it just enough to ensure respect. Air-drawn glyphs don't have the power of carved glyphs.*" Ferryl sounded puzzled. "*I shouldn't be able to hurt it that badly without using a solid glyph.*"

"Can you get rid of it? You know, just in case some kid is frightened by something else and runs in here? Worse, the Bound Shade might get loose." The last one had frightened Abel badly, at least partly because it took too much damage before it quit.

"There will be nothing to stop anything magical that can overcome their discomfort long enough to reach the gate. They may try to break through the inner barrier."

"We can make something else, or strengthen the barrier like you said you did at the front? A stronger warning rather than a killer tree?" The creature had stopped making any movement or noise, but Abel thought it only wanted him to turn his back.

"As you wish. I will try since it seems susceptible to air-drawn glyphs. We can adapt the barrier." The smoky glyph looked bigger this time, and Abel felt a sensation as if something flowed out of his hand. He got an impression of shape as well, a wobbly pyramid with something in the middle. The Bound Spirit stirred as if to try and avoid the glyph but much too slowly, and the innocuous puff of smoke struck right between its eyes. Flame gushed out, followed by purple liquid but not for long. This time the noise cut out mid-screech. The limbs flopped, much quicker than the last time Abel saw one die, while the main trunk slumped before slowly keeling over. "Very strange. I will look for the glyph when we come back, in case it is stone or iron and didn't burn."

"Can we go in now? Is that thing finished?" Abel tried to turn and couldn't.

"Yes. Would you like control back now? I do not need it to pass through the gate." He could hear the humour in Ferryl's voice, but didn't trust it. Not being able to move had come as a hell of a shock and once again Abel had given her control without a second thought.

"Yes please." Abel poised to use her true-name, but suddenly his limbs were back under control. The snigger as he wobbled for a moment didn't help his peace of mind.

*   *   *

The cliff face hadn't been the garden boundary at all, the grounds went back much further. If he'd run the right way and found the steps up the cliff Abel might have still been wandering, lost in the untended semi-jungle. Ferryl knew the way and directed him to the stone slab. True to her prediction the remains of the fight looked like dust and scraps of rotten wood, with no signs of liquid. At least the Bound Shade had taken a curved path to the glade, following Abel, so they were out of sight of the road. As asked, Abel rooted around where the trunk had fallen until he uncovered a yellowish piece of stone.

"That is the glyph. Typical of the sorcerer. He put nothing in there to lead back to him, only me. This is an insult, using my wits to animate a dead tree!"

Abel inspected the yellowish rock with something burned into it. "Your wits are rock?"

"No, burned into the bone. It is the best way. He cut them out, all of them." Abel stared at the little nub of bone in horror. He had absolutely no idea of how much pain digging out lumps of bone must inflict, and never wanted to find out. *"The one on my head hurt the most."* Now Abel remembered the hole in her skull. *"If he used another in the Bound Shade guarding the back that explains why it died so easily. My wits will have little defense against me, not when I have your magic to use."*

"Can you use these now?" Abel tossed the little bit of bone up and down. "This one anyway?"

"Not yet. I would like to check the other Bound Shade, then we can hide them until I have flesh again. First, you must learn magic so that I can leave and find a body. You will complain, and be bored, and try to go too fast, and I will laugh." Finding some of her wits seemed to cheer Ferryl up.

*   *   *

Though she wasn't joking. Hours later Abel looked at yet another demonstration, dust jiggling up and down just clear of his palm. He picked up a leaf instead, and moments later it hovered, motionless. When the leaf suddenly burst into flame he couldn't keep quiet any longer. "You keep doing that and saying I can, then I try and can't. Why am I even trying? It's not exactly deadly if another Bound Shade turns up, is it?"

"I warned you. You must learn how to do this, under control or you will try to lift a stick and pull up a tree. You will try to blow a fae or goblin away, and blast the thatch off a roof. The tiles off a roof. Worse, the strain of doing so while you are still weak may break something, a hand or arm." Abel tried again but the dust just laid in his hand. *"You must direct the flow, channel the magic inside and feed it to the glyph. Draw it on your hand again and try until it works. I will check the rest of the boundary."*

"You are leaving?"

"You are safe here. These trees have no guardians. Sooner or later you will recognise the feeling and know how to activate the glyph and then it will be easier, but watching this part is boring."

"What if another Bound Shade or even a fae, a flying stinger, comes?" Abel felt decidedly nervous about either. "If I can't make dust dance I'm not going to put up much of a fight."

"So learn to make dust dance, then how to throw glyphs. I will remain if you wish, but nothing will come through the barrier. I wanted a little freedom to fly on the wind. It has been a long time."

Abel wasn't sure if the wistful tone in the last bit had been added deliberately or not, but either way he could see her point. "All right. As long as you come back if a tree decides to have a stroll around." He heard a little giggle, and felt an odd sensation as if something flowed out of his arm. The air rippled in front of him, lifting the dust in little whirlwinds, then the rippling left the clearing raising a trail of dancing leaves.

Abel suddenly felt very alone. He looked at the tattoo and although very well drawn, he could see the difference. The picture looked flatter, and he even touched it to see if she responded. No, Ferryl really had gone. He concentrated on his hand again, drawing the glyph with a finger on the palm of the other hand. A coil, an overlapping circle, with a smaller version going the other way inside. Since Abel only used his finger there wasn't a mark on his palm, but allegedly he only had to imagine the shape there. Abel placed a leaf on his palm and concentrated. Once again the leaf wasn't impressed.

*   *   *

Ferryl had it exactly right, watching hours of fruitless training over the following days would have been really boring. She spent most of Abel's spare time wandering, or rather floating and flying, around the garden and revelling in being out of the hole. Abel tolerated the jokes about his lack of progress, because he could feel the sheer joy in his tattoo when Ferryl flowed back in. After two hundred years, being free again must be a terrific buzz. Unfortunately, despite the time Abel spent stood, sat or laid in the cave, staring at his palm, neither the dust nor leaf stirred.

Though Ferryl didn't just have fun, she reported that the side and rear boundaries seemed intact and as strong as they had ever been. Once Abel could help, she would strengthen the deterrence to knock out anyone who still came inside. Despite finding evidence that small magical creatures had tried to approach the barrier, several times, Abel still refused to let her make the spell lethal. He didn't want anything killed accidentally. He encouraged her to kill the larger creatures they saw in the village, such as globhoblins, as well as the types he'd seen in the food at home. They had to be careful because according to Ferryl, non-magical humans could see the killing. The raw magical gloop when one died became visible until it evaporated.

When he wasn't staring at his hand Abel jogged around the property and did his best at sit-ups, but begged off heaving small logs like a pathetic rip-off of a Rocky movie. Ferryl insisted the physical training would help, but agreed his left hand should heal first. Abel started lifting increasingly heavy bits of wood with his right hand as the bruising faded, to build up the muscles for casting stronger glyphs. Since they were only smoke that made no sense, but even if he wasn't totally convinced Abel could see a benefit in being fitter. He'd be able to run away faster and further.

Keeping quiet about what he did half the day bugged Abel, but he wasn't involving Kelis or Rob until he knew this could be done. He didn't want his friends seeing all those critturs and not being able to do anything about them. He met the pair of them for a few hours each day and most evenings at his house or Rob's, usually to work on the game since without his left hand Abel couldn't play computer games. At least Henry and Tyson didn't show up, though a couple of people commented on the state of Henry's face and asked if Abel really did that.

Abel came home clean each day so he didn't get any earache from Mum. Mrs. Tabitha allegedly purred reports, or from what Ferryl said bragged how many nasty little intruders she had nobbled. Meanwhile, the wards seemed to be keeping critturs out of the house. Abel still couldn't figure out how to surreptitiously ward Rob's house or Kelis's but his resident cat-lady found a partial solution. After Abel kept complaining Ferryl had a purring session with the cat next door to Kelis, and the young ginger and white cat called Rusty who lived at Rob's. Ferryl also placed glyphs on Rob's house when they had a few moments waiting for someone to answer the door, but would never get near Kelis's home.

Abel had never been through the electronically locked gates to Kelis's house, let alone up to the door. Despite it being a huge, almost new two story residence with extensive gardens, nobody local ever visited. Mr. Ventner, Kelis's dad, never spoke to his neighbours. His job, something big in the city, kept him away during the week and he only appeared occasionally at weekends to cut the grass on a big sit-on mower. A cleaner came from the town twice a week, and a gardener periodically trimmed bushes and trees and replanted flower beds. The Ventners never employed locals and Mrs. Ventner never socialised, even having the milk left in the big mail box. Kelis absolutely and definitely wasn't allowed to bring friends home, but spent as much time as possible with Rob and Abel.

While Abel took breaks from training to eat, or just clear his head, Ferryl answered questions. Sometimes she asked them. *"I still do not understand why some items bear hexes, and some do not. Some of the hexes are very weak, and need replenishing so who does that?"*

"You mean like Stan's old Land Rover logo? I suppose it's worn out and nobody renews anything magical because we've got no witch. I've sort of figured out how it all works. Mr. Ventner's BMW is new and you said it has a strong hex so the logos must be magicked, hexed, when they're made. Some of the older and especially the cheaper cars have no working hexes. I reckon the reason is price. The ones with hexes are mostly brand names known to be reliable, and also expensive, so the hexing costs." Abel wondered just how BMW or Land Rover put that on the tax returns, unless HM Inspector of Taxes accepted Hexing as a justifiable expense. He also wondered briefly about his sanity, but he did that every day. "Now you can explain why some houses have no creatures on them, or very few."

"Those villagers are true believers, and have sworn themselves to their God. Their personal marks provide protection and are renewed each time they go to church and worship. As a result their houses are uncomfortable for any magical being to live in, especially if they have tokens of the God in there, such as crosses."

Abel thought about that. "True. Most of those families drive to the church in Stourton every Sunday. There's at least two that don't go, so what about them?"

"They must be sworn to a different God, but hiding to prevent

persecution."

"We don't do that in England." Abel hesitated. "Not really persecute but yes, sometimes people don't like different religions."

"They would not live here if your church still had a cross and priest. I still do not understand that and it worries me."

*   *   *

Ferryl returned to that worry time after time until Abel went to see Stan, leaning on his front fence as usual and watching the world go by. Nobody knew his age exactly, but the pensioner had supposedly lived in the village all his life. "Hi Stan. Is Cooch still leaving Bugsy alone?"

"I haven't seen that animal in the village since it got hurt. Good riddance. Why aren't you locked in a bedroom staring at a computer?" Stan grinned. "You'll get a suntan at this rate and none of the other kids will talk to you."

Abel laughed, because Stan always reckoned modern youth didn't get enough sun and fresh air. "I'm doing a sort of project on the history of Brinsford. Why is the church closed?"

Stan looked along the main street towards the small village church, surrounded by a stone wall enclosing an overgrown graveyard. "Economy I reckon. There weren't enough of the faithful putting their hard-earned cash in the collection plate to pay for a vicar." He frowned, thinking a bit harder. "Probably something like that. The vicar who lived here moved out, and we had one coming every three weeks for services but then it stopped and the windows were boarded up." He smirked and waved a hand to encompass most of the village. "Us heathens finally scared them off."

"That may be right, in a way. I understand now, I believe."

"Thanks Stan, though I reckon saying the heathen drove the priest out might not get a very good grade at school." Abel almost reached down to pat Bugsy, then remembered the wagging tail didn't mean the little git wouldn't nip him. "Now I've got to work out when the ford turned into a bridge."

"Before my time. Before planning permission as well so good luck with that." Stan laughed, tapping his chest. "Let me know if you find out, or I'll lose my reputation as the local know-it-all." As Abel walked away Ferryl explained what she'd realised. An occupied and well supported church would have spread its protection to cover most of the original village, directing the prayers of the faithful through their mark, the cross. Without enough worshippers, the priest would be unable to protect the whole village. The unbelievers didn't drive the church out, but they didn't pay for protection.

Abel thought he'd got it. "A church powers a barrier with faith."

"Yes, any active church protects the surrounding area." Ferryl's tone turned humorous. *"Though that doesn't work for Castle House. Nobody worships sorcerers. That barrier is deliberately constructed with magic, not faith. All the mature trees in Castle House garden are tied into either gathering magic to store in the stone slab, or to power the boundary spell."*

"So how much magic in a tree?" Abel stopped walking as he rethought, "No, first, how come a tree has magic?"

"As I told you, all living things collect magic, but are usually unable to use it. Animals, fish, birds and even insects move around and absorb more but leak some, while plants absorb less but store all of it. Nettles, grass and even small bushes only collect a negligible amount, and even a young tree can't store enough magic to feed a section of a village boundary." Abel listened but the next bit really grabbed his attention. *"The Castle House trees are particularly good suppliers because they don't have guardians, dryads."*

"Dryads? I haven't seen any trees looking like women, so are they half-person, half-deer?"

Laughter echoed in his head, until Ferryl spoke again. *"Dryads are only barely attractive to their own kind, as gnarled as their homes, suspicious, rude, and fiercely protective of the stored power in their tree."*

"So which trees have one? When can I see one? Will a barrier drive them out?"

"Every mature tree has a dryad, a guardian, so we can't use it to power a barrier. A dryad can live inside a village barrier, but will use all the magic in the tree to avoid being driven out." Ferryl laughed again. *"I doubt you will enjoy it if you meet one."*

"Please?" Abel kept pestering until Ferryl agreed he could meet a dryad socially.

*   *   *

Ferryl warned Abel not to expect dryads to give him any magic to protect the village, but the creature might fill in some of what happened in Brinsford while Ferryl languished. After parting with some of his meagre savings to buy a little pot of honey Abel sat down on the village green, facing the trunk of a big old horse chestnut. "Greetings, tree and guardian." Abel resisted a glance around to see who might be watching. "May I speak to you, please? I bring a gift."

The tree bark didn't move, but a creaky, impatient voice came from somewhere in there. "Manners at least. What do you want? What is that under your shirt?"

"It already knows but lift your shirt sleeve so it can see me clearly." Abel rolled up the short sleeve and glanced down to find his tattoo looking towards the tree. It didn't even seem weird any more and he turned slightly to give her, and the tree, a better view.

"Braith Huntian. The excitement must have been you breaking free." Two bright eyes opened in the bark facing Abel, chestnut brown eyes which seemed appropriate even if eyes in trees brought back some bad memories. "Who is your new host?"

"Not a host. I am bound, by my true-name." Ferryl sighed and this time the grass nearby swayed in a very local breeze. *"Not truly bound, a bargain in exchange for my freedom. I am Ferryl Shayde now."*

The dryad's eyes shifted back to Abel. "Take care, young human. Riches, eternity and females are not always what you expect."

Abel laughed, and Ferryl joined in. "No riches, no women, but I want to learn magic."

"Strange. Most human students run away from magic these days. Why do you want to learn?" As it moved, just slightly, Abel could see that the eyes weren't in the tree at all. A stout, wrinkled creature stood between him and the trunk but marked and coloured to match perfectly. He glanced down and where its feet should be, roots spread out and dived into the soil.

"Because now I know magic exists, and don't fancy trying to outrun another Bound Shade or Guardian." Abel remembered his lines, and used the plastic spoon to scoop out some honey. "I am willing to pay for answers."

"I prefer honeycomb." A jagged rent near the top of the creature opened briefly. "Or I do when I can persuade bees to nest. Since it has been such a long time that will suffice."

"An answer for each spoonful?"

"Miser. Agreed."

"What happened to the witch in Brinsford?"

"She died." A small shoot grew outwards and waved gently, but Abel hesitated. "One answer. Pay." Abel glanced around. The brown eyes moved to the sides and back to him. "You did not veil to hide us? Why? Your passenger should know better."

"Since this is your ground, I thought it would be rude to work a glyph." Even if Abel only heard her in his head, the dryad heard Ferryl perfectly well.

"Rude? When did you learn some manners? You had none when you arrived."

"I spent a long time in a hole." Ferryl laughed. *"This human is very polite, so maybe living in here is having an effect."*

"It won't last, not with you." The brown eyes moved from the tattoo to the human. "Since we are all being polite, I will provide the veil." The dryad paused briefly and a slight chill swept over Abel. "It is done, only magical creatures can see us, and not all of them. My honey, now!" The last bit wasn't even close to polite and Abel quickly held out the spoon. The very supple shoot grew further and sucked every scrap of honey from the spoon. "A very small spoonful."

Abel glanced round but the two kids kicking a football across the grass weren't paying attention. "A small spoonful for a very short answer. A bigger spoonful for bigger answers." He grinned. "I could try a different tree."

"I am the friendly one. Though for honey, who knows? Very well, bigger answers."

The next question didn't take much thinking about. "Why isn't there another witch?"

"None came." With a sigh Abel scraped the spoon as it came out of the jar, leaving very little honey on it. "Very well. Her apprentice ran away, because she did not want to be a witch. No others have turned up since then. Enough?"

"Definitely, thank you." Abel heaped the spoon and held it out, waiting as the supple shoot neatly absorbed the lot. "How long has there been no witch, and why did the apprentice run off?"

"Two questions." The brown eyes dropped to the jar. "One big spoonful?" Abel nodded. "I lose track of time passed, but she died some years after the sorcerer disappeared. Her apprentice did not want to live as the witch did, eating scraps and living in a hovel. She wanted a decent home such as the rest of the village have, and went to the sea to sell fortunes and charms."

"Ask no more about that. I understand. Many despise witches, and if belief has faded she would be very poor. Tied to the village and the land, she would not be able to gain more wealth as others do, travelling to town and serving masters there."

Abel dished out a big spoonful, glancing round as the shoot slurped it up but even though one of the lads with a football looked straight at Abel and the dryad, he didn't react. Abel looked at the tattoo and tried to subvocalize. "Is that enough? Do I ask about the barrier now?"

A creaky, impatient voice answered. "Yes, ask your questions. How else do I get the honey?"

"Do as it says, but do not pay for that answer. It is rude to eavesdrop."

Abel looked at the shoot, waving hopefully. "I will not pay for that answer because I didn't ask you. It is bad manners to listen in to other conversations." The brown eyes narrowed, definitely annoyed. "I will pay well for the next answers if you don't try to cheat me or eavesdrop."

"Dryads eavesdrop on everything, even the rustle of grasses and those never say anything useful. Ask away, sometimes polite human." Honey seemed to be cheering the dryad up a bit.

"I wish to place a barrier all around the village to keep out unwanted creatures. To do that I will need to use the power of older trees, as the sorcerer did." Abel stopped and looked up, flinching a little as a couple of branches thrashed briefly and leaves fluttered down. "I do not want to drive out the dryads, as he did."

"You are not strong enough."

Ferryl had already told Abel that, so he pushed on. "But one day I might be, or I might be annoyed enough to buy a chainsaw to persuade you. I want to avoid conflict, so how do I persuade dryads to share? Not all the strength of a tree, but enough to help me make a barrier."

"A dryad will only protect their tree." A long silence followed and Abel began to scoop a small portion of honey. "I am not giving you a short answer, I am thinking. We think slowly." The dryad closed its eyes.

"Wait. Dryads do not usually think before answering humans. This might be worth waiting for." Ferryl sounded curious.

Abel sat for what must have been an hour, shifting a little now and then as he stiffened. When he glanced down Ferryl Shayde or her tattoo had curled up as if asleep, so she didn't want to disturb the dryad. Abel realised it had to be more than an hour by how far the tree's shadow moved round towards him, startled when the same glance showed he had no shadow at all. At least that reassured him the veil worked.

Ferryl sent a little tingle to warn Abel the dryad had opened its eyes again. "There may be a way. It is difficult for any dryad to find an empty tree, because there are fewer every year. You understand that trees gather power, magic?" Abel nodded. "Until the trees are old enough there is not enough for the dryad to use as a defence. Young dryads take a young tree and hope to survive long enough." The next bit had a tinge of bitterness. "There are creatures who prey on the weak, and others who imprison or enslave them. If you find a suitable tree and provide protection to the young of a dryad, that dryad might help you with a share of its tree. At least enough to protect an area nearby, and perhaps the area containing the young."

That didn't quite answer so Abel asked. "When the young grow, would they help to supply the barrier?"

"Possibly. You could make that a part of the bargain. Though first you must prove you can protect a young tree. It must be strong proof, because there is a long history of sorcerers cheating and enslaving dryads." This dryad certainly sounded suspicious. "How much honey is that worth?"

Abel smiled. "This question isn't for you." He looked down at the tattoo. "Is that enough?"

The tattoo smiled. *"Enough to work with. I had not thought of how young dryads find a strong tree. How much honey will you give it?"*

Abel grinned at the dryad and put the open jar of honey on the grass. "All of it. Thank you for the answers. How do I break the veil once you have finished?"

"I will allow the extra question." Even as the dryad answered the shoot slithered into the jar and the amount of honey quickly shrank. "Stand up and walk away. When you break the edge, it will break the veil. The pot is empty. Thank you." The last bit sounded downright jovial. "I must remember my manners next time."

Abel picked up the pot and stood. On his second step he felt a slight chill and when he looked back the dryad had blended into the tree so he couldn't see it. "Blimey, where did you spring from?" Abel stared at Kelis, trying to come up with a sensible answer, but she rattled on. "You shouldn't jump out from behind trees when some unsuspecting innocent is walking past. What's that?" Abel held out the jar and Kelis smiled. "Honey? You've been hiding behind a tree scoffing honey? You should have told me and I'd have hidden with you."

"No, it was on the grass, empty, so I picked it up." Abel glanced around, worried because he should have checked for spectators before breaking the veil. The few other people in sight didn't seem to have noticed him pop into sight.

"When did we get litter louts in Brinsford? What's that?" Abel looked back, hoping the dryad hadn't followed him. "On your arm, idiot. What does your mum think to it?" Kelis leant closer, looking at the tattoo. "It's a really good tattoo but I don't think you thought it through. The girls aren't going to cluster round admiring her, so unless you want a boyfriend?"

"Don't you start." Abel's head ran round in circles and gave up, so he sort of went for the truth. "That's Ferryl Shayde the cat-sorceress, and I got it done in a moment of weakness or madness."

"That's our sorceress? You'll have to give her clothes for the adverts, or the whole game will be X-rated." Bursting into laughter, Kelis managed to get out, "Unless she fights while running away."

Abel could hear Ferryl giggling in his head, which didn't help. "We could give her clothes for that. What do you think would suit her?"

"Were there medieval Acro dancers? Though that would depend on if she can fight in a leotard. Her claws solve one problem, she can scratch symbols on anything to make spells. Does Rob know?" Kelis grinned. "Has he got a tattoo of Butch, or maybe Saint Georgeous in lacy armour?"

"I've been keeping it a secret because it wasn't really planned." Abel looked past Kelis to where a pair of women had stopped walking to stare at him, and his arm. "I guess that won't work now. Those two will tell Mum."

"Your mum doesn't know? That'll be fun. You could tell her all game players have to wear their identity?" Kelis blushed slightly. "On second thoughts, no, or it'll get round, and my mum will want to check in case I got one. How come you could afford a tattoo? You keep saying you're skint."

"I've been buying a lottery ticket every week and got a rush of blood when I won a couple of quid." Abel's mind ran on with that. "I'm going to blame you two. We had a bet, the first one to win anything on the lottery had to have a tattoo of their favourite character."

"Ok, we were joking but you were stupid enough to actually do it. What are friends for, if not to lie to mothers? I'm going to run away and hide now, until the dust settles, but then I'll lie like a trooper. I'll warn Rob so the lies match." Kelis ran off, still laughing while Abel looked ruefully at his rolled-up sleeve. He'd been wearing shirts with sleeves or a light jacket but now he'd blown it. The tattoo blurred and then wore a little skirt and top.

"Better?"

Abel turned so nobody could see his arm. "Stop moving about where people can see! Why didn't you wear clothes before?"

"I didn't know it mattered. I can't keep these clothes all the time, they are just seeming, an illusion." Ferryl sounded a breath away from laughing. *"I*

will try to remember to put on clothes when your mother is looking. I could wear less in summer and more in winter, or if young women are admiring you? Though showing my tail didn't stop that young woman from looking closer."

"Just stop, all right? You know tattoos don't alter. Let me think." Abel did, all the way home and there wasn't a solution. Ferryl would forget to put on the skirt or wear something different, probably on purpose, and then the questions would be a lot more awkward. He reluctantly conceded she should only wear fur, but had to keep exactly the same modest pose every time others could see her.

Abel managed to stop worrying for long enough to ask one question. "You said you were being polite. Does that mean you can veil us, hide us, at any time?" Abel had lots of uses for that, from wandering around school unseen to avoid bullies through to having a laugh with Kelis and Rob.

"No, but I am embarrassed, because I should." Ferryl really did sound embarrassed. *"I should have set the veil, but how to do so is in my wits. I lied so that dryad Chestnut does not realise I have forgotten so much. Dryads do not usually gossip, but if rumours spread about me it might be best if they do not include me being almost helpless."*

"You're not helpless." Abel hoped not. "What about disintegrating that guardian and zapping globhoblins and fae?" Ferryl regularly zapped creatures as Abel walked through the village.

"I memorised the one for destroying the guardian, really memorised it. The rest is just wind or fire, variations on two glyphs that I have used for… for a very long time. Seeing in the dark and the contacting cats are a part of me in a way. The barrier spell is the same set of glyphs the sorcerer had me use time and again to protect his property, often enough so I could get you through it." Grass waved and litter fluttered as Ferryl sighed. *"I try so hard to remember, but without my wits…."*

"Well, I'm impressed. The village is safer with less globhoblins and similar nasties sucking magic from kids and pets. I've sure those in the rubbish can't be hygienic, and stopping them means less litter. You've protected our house, and we'll protect more from things like gremlins. After all, you've got an apprentice to help you remember now." At least cheering Ferryl up took Abel's mind off the next problem, telling Mum about the tattoo.

*   *   *

Mum wouldn't be home until later so Abel peeled some spuds for chips and washed up the dirty pots. That might put her in a better mood. He couldn't settle, and ended up having a bash at the game. At least he had something to work on, because the next time he met Rob and Kelis they'd want to know all about the newly invented character Ferryl Shayde. As a leftie with broken fingers strapped to the undamaged ones, Abel struggled with writing and drawing right-handed until Ferryl offered to help. With her in charge of his right hand it went better though he had to insist she redrew the character several times, to get something that could go on public display.

Ferryl seemed to be teasing him especially after Abel showed her some pictures of superheroines on the computer. When he explained the game should be medieval, sort of, so lycra was out, she dressed her tattoo in real medieval. They agreed that all-enveloping sacking didn't work either. Eventually they had four drawings, all of which should appeal to games players without upsetting any censor. Abel shuffled them together as he heard the car pull onto the drive, stuffed them in a folder, pulled down his shirt sleeve and braced himself.

"You've washed up. What have you done this time?" His mum looked in the bowl on the draining board. "And spud peeling? I'm starting to get worried." She sounded it, the jovial tone of the first comment had gone. "Let me hang my coat up, and then I don't want to have to prise whatever it is out of you."

Abel put his file on the table and waited. *"I thought peeling vegetables should help."*

"Shush, and stay very, very still even if Mum touches you."

"What if it tickles?" After a very short pause Ferryl giggled. *"I promise."*

Abel sighed, and put the kettle on. That didn't help either. "Brewing a cuppa? Out with it, now."

"I came up with a new character for the game." Abel pulled out the drawings.

"And?"

"I won a few pounds on the lottery?"

"You aren't supposed to buy tickets. You're too young." Mum stopped. "All this isn't because you won money, or you'd have bought chocolates."

Abel turned his left arm towards her, took a deep breath, and pulled up the sleeve. "I got a rush of blood and had this done."

The next half hour didn't go well, and Abel began to wonder if his mum would drag him round Stourton looking for the tattooist to chew him out. Later he had to concede, privately to Ferryl, that showing Mum a clothed drawing was a mistake. After that Abel couldn't really justify the unclothed version even by pointing out the tattoo just looked like someone wearing a furry onesie. He did his best to be apologetic and truly repentant, while all the time hysterical laughter echoed in his head. At least the tattoo didn't roll about with the laughter, not until he shut the bedroom door.

The front door slammed, hard enough to rattle the windows upstairs. "She'll be going to tell Rob's mum. I bet he'll have to prove he didn't get one." Abel sighed. "Grounded for a fortnight, and double that if I do the slightest thing wrong. I suppose I'll get my school project done and compared to that the grounding is fair. Homework in the summer holidays is definitely not fair, especially since I'm getting a different teacher after the summer holidays. One teacher setting work for another is an evil conspiracy to stop kids enjoying themselves."

"I can help you to write? What did the tutor ask for?"

"A comparison of village life in eleventh century England under Alfred and William the Conqueror because it will ground us for the rest of the course. It'll be a total pain because I've already looked on the internet and at least half of what's there is guesswork." The giggle in his head startled him, and Abel glanced down at the tattoo. Halfway through the clothes show Abel realised, and started to smile. "When did you come to England, or have you always been here?"

"I came with what you call the Danes. There is a big difference before and after the Normans, in the north. Many villages died." The tattoo flipped onto her back with a big sword stuck in her. "Others were spared to serve their local lords. I was not in this village, but Brinn's Keep would have been built about that time to keep the local lands under control." Ferryl's tattoo now wore chain mail and a helmet, and waved a sword.

"What are we waiting for? I've never been that keen on history, but suddenly it seems a lot more fun." Abel sighed. "Still, a whole fortnight? I wanted to practice magic."

"Open the window a moment, please." Abel did, and a leaf floated in followed by a handful of gravel from next door's drive. "Practice. The house is warded, so I'll be able to fly around the garden while you stare at these."

"Super."

*   *   *

The fortnight dragged by, as expected. The homework, interesting as it was with the running pictorial commentary on his arm, only kept Abel going for six days. It only took that long because he had to keep breaking off to rest his hand. Despite Ferryl guiding him, the fingers on Abel's right hand were unused to writing and cramped after a while.

He practiced the dust dance and leaf floating for hours, unsuccessfully, jogged on the spot, did sit-ups and went through the notes and drawings for the game. Abel didn't exchange emails with Rob and Kelis except one to say he'd been grounded, because part of being grounded included emails and texts. At least Mum should be impressed by the historical sites on his internet surfing history, though most of them either annoyed or amused Ferryl.

Ferryl didn't always fly off around the garden, sometimes spending Abel's exercise time explaining more about magic. Abel learned more about the larger magical creatures sometimes seen browsing among the crops, taking a little magic from each leaf or blade of grass. There were hunters out there according to Ferryl, but the only predators Abel saw were clouds of larger fae around any groups of grazers. During one of the sessions they 'talked' about finding safe young trees for dryads, or empty old ones. "How did the sorcerer keep the dryads away from the trees in the garden, or did he imprison or enslave them?"

"The boundary stops them coming back, or new ones arriving. I don't know what he did with the ones already living there. From experience, he probably enslaved them until they died." Ferryl's tattoo winked. *"Why do*

you think I am so happy stuck in this? I doubt any of his other captives survived."

"What about the trees outside the wall at the back? They're not inside the boundary, but there's no creatures living there."

"No magical creatures. Squirrels, birds, all the small, unthinking life, can come and go the same as in the gardens. That part, the wood before the wall and real boundary, has no dryads either. It is a wider, less intense version of the real barrier, to make it hard for reasoning or magical creatures to get close enough to break the real spell." The tattoo sprouted branches and leaves, becoming a tree with a waving tail. *"I believe young dryads would think too much, so it would repel them."*

"We could give them glyphs?"

"That would mean a lot of glyphs, and we must set them inside the tree so they are not stolen." Ferryl sighed, and leaves blew off her tree and disappeared. *"Something might destroy the tree before it grew strong enough to resist."* A tattoo goat ate several tattoo branches.

"We could plant young trees in Mum's garden, just to get a couple started. Then maybe we, you, could drain a bit of magic from the empty ones in the wood to the ground nearby. We could use that to protect a couple more." Abel groaned. "Then we'd have to wait until they were large enough to give up some magic. Though we could get part of the village protected?"

The tree on his arm produced big colourful flowers and danced. *"Hooray!"* It hunched over and grew a big white beard. *"One day."*

"You'll have to stop that once I'm outside again." While Abel had been grounded, Ferryl had turned the thing into a permanent animated cartoon of how she felt. Abel wore a jacket or long sleeves downstairs but could feel her moving underneath it.

"I will, but I've never actually had fun with a tattoo before. They are usually very dangerous to alter. Most are glyphs." Ferryl sounded serious now and her tattoo had stopped messing about. *"It is best not to play with the gift of the Gods."*

"Glyphs or tattoos?"

"Glyphs."

"Are they really gifts from Gods, or is that like the legend of Prometheus stealing fire? For that matter, are they real gods? I know one is because the churches protect people, but you said something about all Gods being real." Abel sniggered. "I became a bit distracted at the time because a dead woman wanted to climb into my body."

"All creatures with true worshippers become what is called gods, using the magic given to them by the worship to make themselves immortal and all-powerful. Well, all-powerful except for other gods. Some deep thinkers wonder if they are all the same one, others don't care because it doesn't alter reality." Ferryl paced around his arm, periodically disappearing from sight and appearing round the other side, her brow furrowed in thought. *"The gods gather magic and create miracles by using glyphs. All their followers have marks which feed gods the magic to power the glyphs through prayer. When the follower dies, the god receives all the rest of the magic in them and the spirit disappears to an afterlife. If they are not sworn to a god, the spirit wanders until it fades away."*

"So my christening mark feeds magic to God?" Abel touched his forehead but couldn't feel anything.

"No, that was a mark of intent to stop another god claiming you. You must swear fealty when you are old enough to understand, then the mark creates a real link. Yours is gone now, as soon as you allowed me to enter."

"You're another God? Hang on, you said you came here with the Danes. Are you immortal?" Abel stared, horrified. He'd let some immortal cat-goddess with a strange sense of humour invade him!

Definitely a strange sense of humour. The tattoo twirled round, dressed in a long white frock with a halo and big wings though the tail still waved at him through a slit. *"I have managed to survive because I have never been human, but I am not a God or immortal. Just a free spirit, an old one who tries very hard to never ever annoy a god or even be noticed."* A mouse tattoo scuttled into a tattoo hole, and peeked nervously out.

"So that wavery shape in the air when you go out the window, that's the real you? The truth, Pungh Hmmshtfun." Abel hadn't used her name for ages, but he had to know.

The mouse scowled. *"My pure form, but I need flesh to hold much magic and to wield glyphs. I spent too long in the hole and almost faded back to a puff of wind. Now you have given me a chance to build myself up so that I can find flesh, a body, once again.*" The original cat-woman sat and looked at him, arms crossed and wearing a definite pout. "*No need to say that name out loud.*"

"I had to be sure." Abel felt relieved when she nodded and smiled. Never mind Ferryl keeping the tattoo still, he had to stop looking at it and talking. At least her appearance didn't embarrass him now because he'd sort of persuaded himself that Ferryl really did wear a furry onesie. He thought back over what she'd said. "So were the glyphs stolen or is it a myth?"

"*Perhaps a myth, but humans and one or two other creatures found out how to use glyphs somehow. Perhaps several found out, or one who didn't understand what they did? Now nobody, except maybe a god or two, knows when it started.*"

"Bloody hell. How many found out?"

"*Do not curse. If you wield magic, curses can become reality and a bloody hell does not sound pleasant.*"

"Er, crikey? Sugar? Flipping heck? I'll be good." Abel smiled for a moment. "Stan would be in trouble."

"*You'll be good?*" Ferryl shook her head in mock despair. "*I can only hope. Nobody knows how many use glyphs, but very few become gods and those are shy about how they do so. Those who are gods are now very old and try to destroy anyone trying to join them. Do not ever be tempted.*"

"Not a chance." Abel sniggered. "Weren't you tempted to be one? You know, like the Egyptian cat-goddess, Bastet."

Ferryl cowered and actually looked over her shoulder. "*Don't say that! She might still be aware enough to hear you.*"

Abel doubted it after five or six thousand years, or however long it had been, but cast around for something to divert her because the tattoo looked and sounded terrified. "Since you know so much about magic, how about helping with our new game? Not real glyphs, but to make sure the system makes sense."

"*Not real but making sense?*" Ferryl sounded scornful but her tattoo cheered up. Abel read through his copy of the scenarios so far, and showed her the files on the computer, though it took a while. A whole afternoon passed just explaining the world of board games, and computer spinoffs, and why certain characters were expected. Ferryl found the characters really funny because she'd seen the real thing in a way. Certainly mages and barbarians, though she swore Elves and Dwarves weren't really like the games portrayed them. The magical creatures that inspired both were wiped out long ago. Once she started Ferryl really threw herself into the design of both characters and the world.

Though she wasn't so sure about one human character. *"What is a Paladin supposed to be?"*

"A holy knight, probably a crusader, very pure and usually handsome or in this case, Kelis insists on beautiful." Abel put the two sketches side by side. Kelis's drawing showed a severe, haughty woman with plate armour carrying a selection of lethal weaponry. The other, less skilful drawing showed a rather less well covered version with big lips, eye makeup and plenty of curves. "Kelis and Rob are arguing about beauty versus pure."

"Like this?" Abel looked down to see a tattoo of a woman with a black eye, a missing tooth, scratched, dirty mismatched armour and a tankard in her hand. Behind her stood a scruffy, hairy horse festooned with dirty, notched weapons, two dead geese, a jewel-encrusted goblet, wineskins and a bag with bread and cheese peeking out. The woman staggered and sat down, scratched her backside and took a big swig.

"That's a mercenary." Abel looked closer at the tattoo. "We could use her, because that's another character and Kelis keeps complaining there aren't enough women."

"That is a real Paladin, a crusader. Most women followed the armies in the baggage train, or hid when the knights came past." Ferryl sounded serious now. *"There were true knights, believers with proper armour, but those usually lived at court training to kill or praying. A few went on each crusade, but most of the army were like this or a lot worse."*

"Not in a game, there we have idealistic versions. We really can use the character though."

"May I use your hand, please?" Ferryl tried much harder with her manners since the meeting with the dryad. She drew the woman and horse, much better than Abel would ever do even when his left hand

recovered.

"That's brilliant, thank you. When you leave, I'll have to try and explain why I can't draw any more."

"You will improve after drawing enough glyphs. Every glyph must be created with firm lines, clearly showing intent." Which, when Abel thought about it, was how Ferryl drew pictures. *"Time to go to the crusade."* Abel glanced down and started chuckling as the tattoo began to get up and tripped over her sword. By the time she'd crammed on her helmet, backwards at first, and crawled onto the horse Abel had collapsed on his bed, howling with laughter.

The fist hammering on the door shut him up. "Who have you got in there, Abel? You are supposed to be grounded, young man."

"Mum?" Abel stopped laughing. "I'm on my own."

"Open up please." Abel grimaced, because Mum didn't usually insist. He opened the door after pulling on a jacket to cover Ferryl, because Mum scowled every time she saw the tattoo. "Move aside, Abel. I'm coming in."

Abel stared because his mum left him his own space, on the clear understanding that Abel kept it reasonably clean and tidy. "But…" Abel stood aside, because the look on her face wasn't going to be persuaded. In some sort of shock, he watched her actually look under the bed and in his wardrobe. "I'm on my own, I told you."

Mum looked at the computer showing a picture of Saint Georgeous, the Kelis serious version. "That wasn't making you laugh, and before that you were talking to someone."

"To myself, Mum, I swear. It helps to make up dialogue for characters." Inspiration struck. "I tried to get a different version of the Paladin, because Kelis and Rob can't agree." He held out the two versions. "I ended up drawing this, and I was laughing at what Kelis and Rob will say." Fingers crossed he offered Ferryl's sketch.

Mum stared at it for a few moments. "Who drew this?" She looked very pointedly at his left hand, still with two fingers strapped together.

Abel rolled his eyes. "I did. For some reason, I can draw better with my right hand than my left." He held her eyes, "if I hadn't bust my fingers, I'd never have known." Abel tried for an innocent smile. "I can even write, look." He pulled out the school project, not at all worried about that looking too good. Ferry couldn't write anything like as well as she could draw.

At least the title and amount of schoolwork finally wiped away the suspicion in his mum's eyes. "You did all this? I should ground you more often." She read a bit of it. "I suppose your browsing history will be full of odd historical sites."

Abel objected, with justification. "I do schoolwork even when I'm not grounded." He did plenty and his grades were good enough to prove it.

His mum took a last glance around. "Since there's no rude pictures on the back of the door, no magazines under the bed, and a complete lack of young ladies in the wardrobe I suppose I have to believe you." Abel tried to suppress the sigh of relief because that had quite a bit of humour in it, though the next bit didn't. "I hope the next time I see that picture it isn't tattooed on your other arm?"

"No Mum, honest."

"Good. It won't be on Rob's either, after I had a word with Mrs. Tyler. Though Mrs. Ventner didn't seem very interested. Is Kelis all right?"

Abel stared. His mum wanted gossip about his friends? Kelis preferred not to talk about home, but let slip that her Dad frightened her. Rob and Abel both thought that explained why she spent her spare time with them. For a moment Abel debated telling his mum about the finger marks, bruises, on Kelis's arm, but she'd sworn them to silence. "As far as I know Mum. She's just shy."

"And you three are thick as thieves and telling the adults nothing." She sighed. "I'm sorry. It was just the voices, and laughing, and that..." She gestured at Abel's arm, "but I suppose I'll have to get used to the tattoo. Just try not to flaunt the thing where the rest of the village can see." She mock-scowled. "Idiot." Abel stood for a while after she left, then heaved a big sigh of relief.

"I think you are right. I must be more careful, we both must. If word of me spreads there are people and creatures who may be interested."

"Moving tattoos are something people will recognise?"

"They might recognise a description of me though most who would are

dead now. A tattoo is usually a bound creature and never has this amount of freedom. Such a bound creature is already dead, a Shade, captured and held as protection. Only a sorcerer can do that, and you are not nearly strong enough to stand against something powerful enough to investigate sorcerers." The rustling noise of a sigh echoed in Abel's head. *"It has been too long since I just had fun, and I forgot. Perhaps we should concentrate on training for a while?"*

Abel could only agree, but he still couldn't make the gravel dance or the leaf float.

*   *   *

At least the episode seemed to have cleared the air a bit about the tattoo and Abel's mum stopped frowning at his covered arm. On the last day of his grounding she actually asked him to uncover Ferryl to have a proper look, and agreed he'd gone to a decent artist. Rob's mum stared at his jacket arm the first time Abel went round, but didn't ask to see the offending picture. Both of Rob's sisters, Melanie and Samantha, were hanging around and trying to get a look so word had spread.

As soon as Rob's bedroom door almost-closed behind him Abel took off his jacket, because he could see he'd get no sense out of Rob otherwise. "Bloody hell. Kelis said it was a bit like the anime ones, a person with cat features and ears and tail, and a bit sexy without going over the top. That's a character? She'll need clothes."

"I can show him?" While Abel tried to concentrate to sub-vocalise no, Ferryl chuckled. *"Just teasing. I will try to be good now."*

"It's only like a onesie, no worse than Catwoman in a Batman film in fur instead of leather or rubber. I've got pictures with clothes, and another character, and I've been working on the rules for magic. We need a lot of other creatures in the world, Hobgoblins and that sort of thing. Annoying or disgusting rather than dangerous, and then a few really dangerous types." Voices downstairs interrupted Abel and a few moments later Kelis came in, leaving the door ajar. Rob and Abel had negotiated the same deal for bedrooms, door ajar if a female is inside though so far only Kelis had visited either.

She came straight over to look at Ferryl. "I told you, Rob. Now give, Abel, was alcohol involved?"

"No, just a momentary rush of blood after coming up with her." Eventually Rob and Kelis had finished cross-examining and teasing about Ferryl, so Abel went through the bit about extra creatures. Neither seemed convinced. "We have to make a rounded, believable world. Look, I've got another character. You've got to find a name." He pulled out the sheaf of writing and sketches. "This is our mercenary, a sort of counterpoint to Saint Georgeous?" Abel sniggered. "We'll have to sort out real names sometimes."

"I like that name. Better than the real saints, either sanctimonious or drunken lechers."

Rob stared at the pictures. "Did you draw these?" Abel explained the right hand drawing thing. He really had to learn how to do that before Ferryl left. Oddly, the thought of losing his voice and tattoo left a little pang of regret, quickly buried in apprehension because he'd have to replace her with a real tattoo. With the notes to show how it all fitted together, Abel finally persuaded the other two their game world needed these creatures and rules. The mercenary had to be called Robyn, but Rob's suggestion, Rich, wasn't quite right for a second name even if it sort of summed her up. Ferryl kept quiet and her tattoo stayed still all the way through, which must have been a strain.

Though once again she wanted to check the back fences. As soon as Abel climbed over Rob's fence she started. *"Why do you make the creatures less ugly?"* Kelis had insisted the original drawings were gross, and had smoothed them out a bit.

"So they are less frightening. Kids will play this game if we get it right, and we don't want to give them nightmares."

"It will prepare them to meet the real ones."

Actually, Ferryl would have been right except for one thing. "But most people will never see one, according to you. I hope not. Anyway, Kelis is right, we needed a few pretty ones as well to counter all the real ones."

"Pretty ones are real. Not looking like that but there are what you call pretty fairies. I think there are?" Ferryl chuckled. *"Unless they have all been eaten. Most of them are weak, and bright colours are hard to hide."*

"Can we let a few into the village, the pretty ones? Keep them safe?"

"You want a zoo? I saw a zoo in your mother's head. A small space to keep creatures who should be roaming, so that your kind do not kill the last ones." Abel couldn't argue because that probably summed it up for some species. *"Perhaps some would choose a zoo instead of death. You have decided to become a sorcerer?"*

"What? No, not a chance. I'd rather not be a warlock either. I don't fancy starving in a hovel any more than the witch's apprentice did." Abel picked his way through a patch of nettles, still thinking about that. "I just want to protect the village. Maybe we can find a witch to take over?"

"You can train Kelis? She likes the magic in your game, and she can already draw better than you. Charms and hexes would be easy."

"I don't want Kelis starving either, thanks. We might find a candidate in town, when school starts again. Someone must be keeping Stourton and Stourton Comprehensive clear of creatures."

That distracted Ferryl from the lack of a witch. *"Free learning without the church. I still don't believe that. Can I use a hand, please?"*

"Yes, why?" Even as he spoke, Abel's hand wiggled and a pale shape flew out to hit one of the flying creatures. It crashed to the ground, bubbled and disappeared, and the rest gave Abel a lot more space.

"That fae has a really nasty sting."

Abel waggled his hand to check he could control it again. All the way home he turned it over in his head. Would he, could he, become the local warlock and protect the village while earning a living at something else? Maybe, if he could find work through the internet, though Abel didn't really fancy living in Brinsford all his life. He gave up in the end because he'd never decided what sort of career to aim for anyway.

As they came nearer to home Ferryl used his hand several more times to zap flying creatures, larger fae with particularly nasty stings. This trip she also popped a creature covered in spines, a thorny. It liked to rummage in rubbish bins or kitchens for spoiled food, which put it on Abel's hit list. Able saw the vague shapes of several larger creatures in the field, ranging from cat to sheep size, but they all moved away as he came closer.

* * *

Whether Abel wanted to be a warlock or not, it wouldn't happen until he could make a glyph work. Finally getting the strapping off his fingers meant he could switch hands while practicing, but still couldn't make the gravel dance or the leaf stir, let alone float. Getting his strapping off also signalled an increase in Ferryl's attempts to make him fitter, and did include a Rocky-style regime of running while carrying logs. Not big ones, nor did the larger logs he lifted up and down weigh much, but Abel found he could already run further. He still didn't think he could run faster than the guardian, or further than the Bound Shade, which encouraged him to keep going.

"Can't we help the trees to grow back or something? The grass and bushes at least, so it doesn't look as bad. I'd fix the fence but I'd cut my hand off with the saw." The broad swathe of destruction through Castle House gardens still worried Abel. Despite Ferryl's confidence Abel still felt sure someone would eventually become curious enough to overcome their reluctance and investigate. There wasn't anything to see, but Abel knew just how curious he would have been if he'd found that round carved slab without Cooch after him. According to Ferryl there would be bones under there if someone tunnelled under the edge and shone a light. That would definitely mean police, and someone either moving or breaking the stone.

Ferryl considered while they walked along the trampled path and out of sight of the road. The gardens were much larger, but Abel felt comfortable in this clearing so he used it for practice. *"We can help the bushes. The trees will grow at those angles unless a dryad teaches them to straighten."* Unmistakable pride shone through the next part. *"A dryad will not pass my barrier, not even an old, strong one such as Horse Chestnut."*

Abel suggested letting a dryad through to fix the trees. After a short verbal tussle in which Ferryl objected to anything getting inside as it might weaken the whole protection, Abel let it drop. He wasn't confident enough to order Ferryl with her true-name, and tried not to anyway. The bit about creatures being bound into tattoos came too near to the truth for his peace of mind, because he'd trapped Ferryl in a way. Instead he concentrated on the bushes and grass. Abel knelt down as instructed, feeling grateful that the road running past only led out of the village so few people walked it and the occasional car drivers probably wouldn't notice him.

*   *   *

An hour later Abel wished he'd kept quiet. Crawling around on the overgrown lawn and among the trampled bushes stopped being fun after three or four minutes, as did drawing lines in the dirt with his fingers. Connecting the whirls and loops and leading them to a tree at least raised his interest, and Abel tried hard to remember the glyph on the tree root to power the spell. It wasn't easy, because nothing showed. Ferryl swore the glyph would be marked into the live-wood, the heart of the thick root, but assured Abel the tree didn't feel it. Abel hoped not, he still remembered the pain when she connected into his bone.

"Is that it?" Abel straightened his aching back.

"That should speed recovery of the grass and bushes, though the bushes will grow more shoots rather than straighten. They will look better."

"Good. Then the trees will look like old damage and not as interesting." The council still hadn't fixed the road but someone had filled in the holes and gouges with gravel, and shovelled earth into the hole where the Bound Shade had stood. Village rumour blamed gypsies, travellers, who had allegedly used a lorry to drag the dead tree down, causing the damage through the fence and into the gardens. They had then cut the tree up and probably sold it as firewood in town. A total lack of tyre marks or sawdust didn't seem to make any difference.

"We can repair bushes along the rest of the path another day. I am enjoying this, helping something to grow for a change." Abel opened his mouth to ask if that meant she usually damaged them, and shut it. He still skirted round just what his hitchhiker was.

"But not today, please? I'd rather practice."

Abel didn't have to look at the tattoo to know it was laughing, he could hear it in her voice. *"You want to practice? We should repair plants more often."*

"Practice. Now. Please?"

*   *   *

Abel wore a happy smile when they finally set off home. He felt sure the leaf trembled, once, though Ferryl blamed his breath because he had his face too near. "Hello squeaky." Henry came out of a doorway where he must have been lurking. "I saw you crawling about in that garden, and thought you'd be along soon." He smacked his fist into the palm of the other hand. Abel felt definitely torn because he'd love Ferryl to do something awful to the nasty git, but not in the main street. Not that anybody seemed to be about to care either way.

"Henry rang me, because it's time to squeak. No running away or tricks this time." Abel turned to see Tyson behind him, climbing over the fence from a garden. "No sucker punch." Tyson copied his brother's thump, fist against palm with a distinct smack. "After all the stories about how you beat us up, we've been looking forward to this."

"Let me use your hands, please."

Abel heard the eagerness in Ferryl's voice, which worried him as much as the Copples did. "What did you have in mind?"

"I can crush them, or burn them, or throw them along the road? Would you like them as Bound Shades?"

"No!"

"No? Yes, little squeak. Come on, put up your hands and make it interesting." The brothers closed in from each side. Tyson spat on the pavement. "You ruined Cooch. He won't come into the village now."

Damaging both his hands again, even if he knocked the pair down, wasn't really a good idea. Worse, if they got up again Ferryl didn't seem to understand the consequences of mayhem. "Can you frighten them? Something discreet." Abel wondered if Ferryl understood discreet.

"Frightened? You should be." Abel's sub-vocalisation needed work because Henry had heard some of it.

"A show of power? Hit them with a car?" Ferryl giggled and then a wicked edge came into her voice. "If they hit you, I am allowed to take over."

That sounded like a blood-bath in waiting, which made broken hands seem a better option. "Please?"

"Begging, squeak? It'll have to be louder, and you've got to bleed a little bit." Henry grinned and his brother laughed. Abel started to wonder why he cared, the pair of them flying down the street bouncing off cars suddenly seemed appealing.

"*Tell them to watch your left hand, then let me have control. Please.*" Abel considered asking why because of the anticipation in that, but the pair were too close to speak.

"Watch my left hand, please." He held it up, trying not to laugh at the puzzled look on Henry's face.

Even as Tyson said "I'll break it again if you…" Ferryl brought the hand down and Abel felt his fingers wiggle. The tip of his second finger tapped a brick in the garden wall next to him. Abel felt a little surge down along his hand and the brick blew out into the garden in dust and gravel!

Both brothers stared, until Tyson found his voice. "What the hell was that?"

"I told you, just leave me alone, all right?" Abel backed against the low wall so he could keep an eye on both of them. "Unless you fancy a tap like that?"

"That wasn't Kung Fu or karate, I've seen them. When did you learn that? Where?" Tyson looked at the oblong hole in the wall. "You picked a rotten brick." Though he didn't come any closer, neither of them did.

"Choose another one? Not the whole wall, unless you pay to get it fixed." Abel watched as both of them considered it and looked at the brick-shaped hole.

"We'll leave it this time." Tyson looked up the street. "Too many witnesses." Abel glanced up the street, still empty but he could recognise an excuse. He'd made plenty.

"That's why it's just one brick. Next time it could be ribs. Then my teacher would be annoyed because I'm not supposed to hurt anyone unless I have to." There, a clear warning without a challenge to a fight. Neither of these two could resist a real challenge.

Abel still didn't trust Ferryl if she got control because his teacher actually thought hurting both brothers would be a lot of fun. "*One rib? Now? One each?*" He doubted Ferryl would stick to one rib, not without careful instructions.

"Come on Henry." Tyson scowled at Abel. "I'll be asking around at the club. Someone will recognise a trick like that." Abel didn't think so because even if Henry's club had all sorts of martial arts types, he doubted they'd seen a Ferryl Shayde move. He kept his smart mouth shut and watched Tyson walk out into the road to pass before the pair of them left.

"They did not learn so you will have to break a rib eventually. One rib? Maybe I can push it through his heart and out the back?"

Being right about Ferryl's tendency to violence didn't make Abel feel better, so he tried to explain. "No. Do not kill humans because there will be a really big investigation and I'll end up in jail."

"I can get you out. A prison wall is just more bricks."

"Then my picture will be on the TV and everyone in the country will be looking for me. If I'm attacked, just hurt whoever it is so they stop."

"I will be discreet." Abel didn't trust her tone but just had to hope nobody threw a punch. Instead of worrying about that, he set off home thinking about how Ferryl had pulverised the brick. He'd felt the something, the magic, as it went through his finger and he'd felt the same swoosh when Ferryl threw the fire glyph at the Bound Shade. With mounting excitement Abel realised he'd felt a low-level version as Ferryl drew the lines in the dirt and activated them with the glyph. If he could copy that, get the feeling, the gravel should dance!

Abel heard the hissing and screech from two houses away. *"The guardian is under attack. Quickly!"* Abel didn't need encouragement, even if Mrs. Tabitha being a guardian came as a surprise. He started running, cutting across the front lawn to go round into the back garden. Mrs. Tabitha crouched in the middle of the grass at the back, slowly retreating towards the house. Three somethings were stalking her, two of them trying to outflank her with fangs bared.

Mrs. Tabitha bared her own impressive fangs, but she wasn't stopping the trio. "What are they Ferryl? Get them!" His hand wrenched up, a swirly glyph smoked across and into the first, and the furred shape crumpled. Even as Ferryl moved Abel's hand, Mrs. Tabitha ran towards him before turning to defend herself again. Both the low, slim creatures had closed rapidly as she ran and as the cat leapt back and forth, threatening them, Abel's hand hesitated.

"I may hit her."

Abel pulled up a garden cane, wincing as a Chrysanthemum flopped over. "Can you do the Cooch thing?"

"*Yes.*" Abel threw, right handed because Ferryl had his left, so the cane spun uselessly across the garden. Abel's left hand moved and, just like the stick thrown at Cooch, the cane straightened and arrowed in. Not a kill, despite the creature being pinned to the ground it writhed and snapped at the thin shaft. Abel looked around for something tougher. He ran the few steps to Mum's pride and joy, her Japanese Maple with the pink-edged leaves, and ripped out the stake holding it upright. Abel spun round, throwing in the general direction of the last creature which turned and started to run.

Too late, the stake nailed it firmly to the ground but the other one splintered its cane and lurched to its feet. With a burbling hiss it scurried under the fruit bushes and Abel saw it wriggle up and over the fence, a bit of cane still stuck out of one side. "Get it!"

"*It's gone. It will be too frightened to come near here again.*"

"It might get someone else's cat. Burn it, Ferryl!" Though Abel thought she'd be too late because he could barely see the shadow scurrying through the stubble in the field. His hand came up of its own accord and once again Abel felt that flow, out through his palm this time. After a pause, a spark of light appeared in the field. "Did you get it?"

"*Of course. A glyph cannot miss while you are looking at the target. I keep telling you, intent is what matters.*" Abel looked down as Mrs. Tabitha rubbed round his ankles and bent to stroke her, but Ferryl continued, "*I would like to question that one.*"

Abel stared at the third creature, still firmly pinned despite clawing and chewing at the stake. "You can talk to it?" He moved closer, getting a proper look now he wasn't busy reacting. The thing's body, covered in long, matted dirty brown fur, looked only a little longer than Mrs. Tabitha but lower to the ground. At one end a bald tail nearly the length of Abel's forearm lashed at the ground, while the head and snout at the other end were nearly as long. Tiny, red eyes glared from an almost bald skull but most of its head consisted of a thin pointed snout, now showing several rows of sharp teeth. As Abel came nearer he gave up trying to count the little legs with wicked claws still scratching at the grass and stake.

"*It cannot talk, but I will understand the Skurrit once it is bound.*"

"Bound? How?"

"*To you, to serve and protect you. It will be more powerful than a live Skurrit, but completely obedient. We can wait until it dies or I can kill and bind it now.*"

"Whoa, not another tattoo and burning. I don't fancy that thing in me anyway, dead or alive, and it might not be keen."

"*A tattoo, but no burning into the bone, because giving it access to all that power might be dangerous. Bound Shade will be better for the Skurrit than dying completely.*"

Abel thought about that, and looked into those glaring red dots. The screeching had died down, as had its struggling, and the Skurrit's tail finally gave up as well. "Can you ask it? If it prefers that, and will be useful, I'll go for it but only with a very small, innocent looking tattoo."

"*I can try.*" Abel knew the answer as soon as Ferryl spoke because the creature began to struggle again, weakly but the fire in its eyes blazed bright. "*It recognises intent and does not wish to be bound. Few wild creatures do.*"

"So kill it clean, please." Abel concentrated this time, waiting, and felt the flow into his hand before a dim swirly glyph struck the Skurrit. It stilled, quickly turning to a bubbling mess that started evaporating.

"What are you playing at out here? What's the matter with Mrs. Tabitha?" Mum had heard!

Abel moved in front of the stake and mess, though a glance confirmed the last scraps were almost gone. "A fox tried to get her, but I frightened it off."

"Foxes usually have more sense than to tackle a grown cat. What did you do to my tree?"

"Sorry. I needed something to throw. I'll put it back." Abel found himself speaking to his mum's behind as she bent over to inspect her plant.

"It's split. If it dies you will be buying a new one, young man. Give me that stake. I'll do it or you'll snap the poor thing in half." Abel retrieved the stake and passed it to her, keeping his big mouth shut. He still hadn't enough money to pay for the library book, let alone a new tree, and the library van would be back in a couple of days. "Go and get the gaffer tape. If I bind it up you might get lucky."

Abel went to the shed, which gave him a chance to ask one burning question. "Why did you want to ask why that Skurrit thing came here? I thought creatures like that just wandered about?"

"There have been more large fae, flying stingers, coming into your garden lately. I have also killed several hoplins and similar minor hunters while patrolling when you are practicing. Worse, the guardians report more in the village and there is evidence of persistent efforts to breach the barrier around Castle House. They are being attracted by the release of magic when the Bound Shade and guardian were destroyed at the same time, but I hoped nothing stronger felt it. Hunters like packs of skurrits usually prey on the creatures out in the fields and prefer not to come near human habitation. I wanted to check if something stronger had sent them. If a strong magic user comes here before you are ready, my glyphs may not be able to stop them." A wind lifted dust in the shed as Ferryl sighed. *"You must learn to use your magic."*

"But you can use it through my fingers." Abel wiggled a few.

"I am only tapping your magic. If you form the glyph, it will be more powerful."

Abel thought of a glaring discrepancy in that. "But my fingers make the glyph anyway."

"But not with intent. I keep telling you that." Abel could hear her annoyance now. *"This is why I never wanted to teach anyone."*

Abel looked through the heap on the bench in the shed, finally spotting a roll of tape. "What did you use to kill the first Skurrit, and the last? It wasn't burning."

"Someone nearby might have seen a flame. There are many glyphs." The humour this time came as a welcome relief to Abel. *"You will wish there were fewer."*

"How many?"

"I do not know because they can be combined, though only a sorcerer would risk it. A strong sorcerer, preferably using a captive as a buffer, perhaps a witless Ferryl Shayde."

Abel skipped round what had to be a bad memory from her bitter tone. "So wind and flame as a flamethrower."

"Possibly. The result is not exact because intent as well as the relative strength of each aspect in the glyph matters. Do not try it while I am trapped in here, please." Her sigh blew dust again. *"I knew some combined glyphs but they are trapped in my wits. If you do not experiment, I will teach you once I have them."*

"I promise." Abel shut up as he returned to the garden because he couldn't talk silently yet. He stood by and took his ear-bashing while Mum taped up the tree and set up the stake, then in a fit of remorse made her a cuppa and gave her a hand fixing tea.

*   *   *

Eventually, after washing up, Abel finally headed for his room. He immediately took out his saucer with the handful of gravel, and after drawing the glyph on his palm with a finger, spread half the gravel on his hand.

"I thought you had done enough practicing?"

"Hush please. No help." Abel tried to empty his mind of everything but that flowing feeling. After a while he thought he had a hint of it, then lost it by trying to sort of grab it. The next time he sneaked up on it, mentally, and directed it towards where he'd drawn the glyph. The picture, the position and shape of the invisible glyph, had burned into his memory by now. He felt a flow down his arm and Abel got behind it, pushing and encouraging. He jumped a mile when the gravel shot off his palm and smacked into the ceiling! "Yes!"

"No. You threw it instead of lifting gently. No control." Though Abel could feel the excitement in Ferryl's voice.

"That gravel was definitely lifted. I didn't know what to do with the flow, whatever it's called so I just pushed it." Abel looked up at the ceiling where three bits of gravel were stuck in the plaster. The rest must be scattered everywhere. "Blimey. Good job I'm not under the light. We'll need more gravel."

"Give me your hand, please, and I will show you control." Abel agreed, intrigued. His hand twisted and the fingers moved, but too fast for him

to follow, then stopped with the palm cupped. A cloud of tiny glyphs spread out. Bits of gravel began to float in from every direction until the last three pulled out of the ceiling with a distinct grinding noise. His hand tipped the gravel back into the saucer followed by a distinctly smug, *"That is control."*

"What was that? It looked like more than one glyph and you sort of gestured." Abel waved his other hand about, then found he'd regained control of both.

"Just a combination of wind glyphs, with control and intent. You must learn to control one glyph first. That sort of combination takes many years to learn." Ferryl couldn't hide the distinct pride in that. With that as example Abel kept practicing the same old move for a good hour without complaint. Bashing skurrits looked impressive, but that last demonstration really hooked him.

Since Ferryl seemed to be in a happy mood, he asked about some sort of protection around the garden. If there were more and stronger creatures coming, and they seemed to like his garden, Abel didn't want to rely on Mrs. Tabitha. What Ferryl had said about the trees feeding the barrier around Castle House led to him suggesting drawing lines in the dirt and using the fruit bushes. According to the expert that wouldn't work without a big tree to provide more raw magic. At least Ferryl agreed to think of ways to knit the fruit bushes into a magical barrier, even a relatively weak one.

*   *   *

A couple of days later Abel stood up and straightened his aching back. He picked up the bucket of weeds, the excuse for crawling about the end of the garden, and headed for the green wheelie bin. *"We should have left the weeds. They are strong plants, and could have helped."*

"Try explaining that to anyone else." Abel stopped by the Japanese Maple. "I really hope this recovers because I can't afford a new one. I should have asked for some riches after all."

"Pick up a stone and let me use your hands, please." Abel did and Ferryl giggled. *"Riches, Lord."*

Abel looked at the now faceted, shiny stone. "What is that?"

"*A diamond.*"

"A big one. Can I sell it?"

"*Yes, but quickly.*"

Abel sighed in resignation. "It doesn't last."

"*Not for long. To do that needs a glyph inscribed in the centre of the stone. That is slow, skilled work, and doesn't work for diamonds because it shows. I could do that with a piece of rock and make it into gold? If we trap enough magic in there it will not revert.*" The giggle gave her away.

"You mean like the guardian? Though that lasted for a very long time so what's the snag?" Abel wasn't against fool's gold if it didn't turn to dust in his lifetime.

"*When a goldsmith tries to work the gold, he will destroy the glyph and the stone will revert.*"

"So how were you going to give me riches?"

"*Steal them. If you take me to a place where riches are stored, I will remove them and place them in your treasury.*"

"The crown jewels won't fit in my piggy bank. Can I get money legally?"

"*Fortune telling and selling charms? Sorcerers are not known for caring about human laws.*" Ferryl sniggered, then her voice sobered. "*Perhaps I can find old money, precious metal that has been hidden?*"

"A treasure hunt? Then I'd have to wait for years while some old duffers in a museum decided what I was entitled to." Abel tossed the stone down, then picked it back up. "Mum would have a fit if she found this. I'll have to think about money. I'd get a job, but there aren't any in the village."

They talked about it and couldn't come up with anything that worked quickly. Abel was tempted by gambling, but although Ferryl swore she could control dice she also claimed a gambling house would have protective glyphs. Abel settled for more glyph practice until Rob and Kelis arrived to work on their game. Tonight he'd tried the leaf, but although it moved he couldn't stop it fluttering off across the room.

He quickly shelved thoughts of glyphs when Kelis spotted the diamond, sat on the desk next to the computer. "Wow, what's that?"

Abel pointed at Kelis's arm as she reached for the stone, because her sleeve rode up and he saw three distinct round bruises. "Was that Henry?" He thought the Copples might have picked an easier target.

"No." Kelis blushed and pulled her sleeve down. "You know Dad doesn't always realise how strong he is, not when he's had a couple. Forget it, please?"

Rob and Abel looked at each other. This wasn't the first time Dad had misjudged, but Kelis never wanted to talk about it. "All right but if it gets bad, come and visit. Any time. I mean it." Abel smiled, making a joke of it. "You'll have to sleep on the settee, or leave the door ajar."

"Hah, a feeble attempt to steal my girlfriend. Hard luck, her heart is already spoken for." Rob blew on his nails and polished them on his chest.

"You pair of losers? Please! I'd rather run off with Roughly Hewn." Kelis had renamed the barbarian, again.

"I thought you preferred Saint Georgeous." The three of them set into their usual round of mutual insults, and then worked on the game.

After a while Kelis returned to the stone. "Do you want this?"

"It's just an enchanted stone and will turn to dust in daylight." Abel laughed. "You'd be better off with a bit of glass or cheap crystal."

Both Rob and Kelis laughed, but she didn't give up. "Can I keep it then? Please? Unless it's sentimental or something?"

"It will not fade if I put a glyph and more magic inside. You must hold it for a long time because the work is slow and difficult." Abel jumped a bit because Ferryl usually kept quiet.

"Blurglyph?" Abel tried to sub-vocalise but both the others looked.

"What? Was that a yes, because it sounded a lot more like a frog choking?" Kelis grinned and held the stone against an ear. "What do you think?"

"You'd get a crick in your neck wearing that as an earring." Rob snatched the diamond and they wrestled briefly before he gave it back.

Abel took his chance to murmur. "Blurred so glyph can't be read."

"I can blur the centre, which would be useless as a ruse but will not

matter now. Are you trying to attract this woman? Never mind. You can tell me later. May I have control of one hand while I work? Please?"

Abel held out his hand for the stone. "Yes."

"Why should I hand it over if the answer is yes?" Kelis narrowed her eyes. "Will you give me it back?"

"Yes, but I have to hold it for a while to strengthen the spell." Abel grinned. "Otherwise, come morning?" He threw one hand up, because the other wasn't obeying any more. "Puff, gone, lump of useless rock."

"Go on then, idiot, if you insist. We could add that in, a way to make false diamonds and gold. Then we can have a way to detect them. Players would have to earn or discover the spell to avoid being cheated." Kelis handed the stone over and began writing, more interested in the idea than why Abel really wanted the stone back. She remembered before leaving but by then Abel had the use of his hand back, and Ferryl had reported it finished.

He spent an amusing few minutes after Rob and Kelis left explaining why he wasn't wooing Kelis. Ferryl couldn't see why friend and something more personal had to be separate, but gave up after a while. There were plenty of other puzzles and problems to keep her occupied.

Learning Curve

When the library van visited again Abel volunteered to exchange his mum's two books. He asked the librarian to renew the loan of the destroyed one so he didn't have to produce it. Hopefully he could keep doing that, and explaining to his mum he couldn't find a third suitable book, until he could find the money. At the moment returning to school came a lot higher up Abel's list of worries. He wanted good marks in History, IT and Graphic Art so he could choose them as his main options next year. Abel still had no idea of what he'd do for a living, except that concentrated Maths or English just didn't appeal.

At least his Graphic Art marks would improve with Ferryl helping, though Abel had already started practicing drawing on his own. Oddly enough the more sketching Ferryl did the more his hand seemed used to the idea, and he could draw nearly as well with either hand now. Both were rubbish, but he had time to work on it.

Glyph practice became a refuge from everything; money, school or the possibility that Henry might bushwhack him. Even with Ferryl on board Abel worried that either Henry would be too quick, or she would do something that brought police and TV cameras, then possibly jail. Abel could empty his mind and sit in peace in Castle House garden just looking at his hand or drawing precise shapes. Not full glyphs as that would be dangerous, just portions, trying to get them as crisp and neat as Ferryl's example. Ferryl had advanced his training now. Sometimes he trotted around while levitating a leaf or a few tiny pieces of stone because, as she pointed out, he couldn't sit down in every emergency. Abel didn't mind the running, because he still preferred to run away from trouble if possible.

Despite promising himself to tell Kelis and Rob about magic, Abel just couldn't find the right time. He had a good excuse, Ferryl kept saying learning about magic might be dangerous. His friends still didn't know about it when the holidays ended and the three of them walked past Castle House, down to the main road to catch the school bus for the first day of term. Rob, Kelis and Abel looked around the bus, claimed three seats together, and talked quietly to each other for the rest of the journey.

At least none of the snooty types came on the school bus. Any that had parents with a spare car, and time to drive them, arrived by car. Many of the other pupils came from town or on other buses.

Abel kept his eyes towards the window most of the time because Ferryl wanted to see how everything had changed. The bus seemed to be the equivalent of a roller-coaster to her, because horses didn't run this fast let alone coaches. Abel more or less managed to separate the excited babble in his head from the conversation he tried to have with the other two. The occasional lapse when he reacted to Ferryl or missed what was said Abel put down to worrying about classes. From her comments, Ferryl had suddenly realised that what she'd read from Abel's mum's head didn't completely prepare her for the wider world.

Abel had a few wobbles when he saw large herds of creatures in some fields, more than he'd seen near Brinsford. Despite Ferryl's claiming that Brinsford had so many because of having no witch or warlock, magic creatures seemed to be widespread in the fields and hedgerows all the way to town. To Abel's relief they all looked like the grazer types, sucking magic from greenery, though Ferryl's indignant *"they are killing the crops"* meant this wasn't usual. He wasn't sure how the grazers killed crops, but some patches definitely looked brown.

Abel hoped the town had better protection, and specifically the comprehensive, but as the bus drove through the streets his hopes plummeted. Some sections had few or no magical creatures, which according to Ferryl's meant they were protected, while others were overrun. Abel soon realised that he could tell the unprotected areas without seeing the creatures. They had the most litter and graffiti. Ferryl broke off from exclaiming over the buildings, vehicles and pedestrians to complain, and ask what the local sorcerers were doing. From her comments the witches and sorcerers should be protecting the whole town. With a sinking feeling Abel remembered Ferryl had expected Brinsford to be protected as well.

She switched to excitement at the school, and Abel had to reassess his opinion of the somewhat tired old concrete and glass structure. Ferryl thought the place was wonderful, especially for a college giving free education. The scuffed floors and slightly chipped and stained furniture meant wealth and luxury, and the sheer cleanliness probably impressed her most. Personally, Abel felt happier about the lack of creatures. The school seemed to have protective hexes even if Ferryl couldn't detect them.

The three of them and Abel's hitchhiker found the rest of the geeks, the squeakies as Henry called them, and claimed an empty table in the canteen until school started. The elite claimed their usual couple of tables by the door, ejecting a few new kids who didn't know the rules, and set into insulting the rest as they came in. Business as usual, as Kelis put it.

Ferryl didn't care. She'd switched to drooling over the amount and variety of food on offer. Mentally drooling, luckily, or Abel's ears would have been oozing. He tuned her out and caught up with the people he knew. Unsurprisingly almost all of them were in the IT class, and some in either History or Graphic Art.

Ferryl calmed down a little when classes finally started, and after half an hour declared that the pace of learning bored her. Abel managed to tune out the feel of her tattoo moving under his shirt and jacket as she kept herself amused, until her voice burst back into his head. *"The defensive glyphs aren't working! I still can't feel any and now there is a Globhoblin at the window! There are sprites and thornies. Who do we warn?"*

Abel scribbled on a piece of paper so she could read it. "I don't know. Nobody can see them."

"The Lord of the Manor will have a sorcerer. Curses, you don't have one, do you, a Lord? Who took over?"

"Wait until break." Abel crumpled up the paper as the tutor scowled suspiciously at him, and concentrated on history.

"How long? This is ridiculous! I will send a seeker to find the resident magic user, there must be one. Please let me use a hand, for a moment." His hand moved a little and Ferryl quietened. Abel managed to ignore the occasional flyer since they were the smaller, harmless types. He concentrated on schoolwork until break despite Ferryl's growing concern. Her seeker had failed to find a single hex, and had disappeared on the third trip. She became more and more baffled by the complete lack of any reaction to an increasing number of small creeping and slithering things.

* * *

One look at the rain outside and Abel abandoned his first plan, to wander off alone so he could talk to Ferryl. The crowded canteen wouldn't work so Abel gave up on a drink and snack and went to the library, skirting a group of the little spikey creatures called thornies. Sure enough the place looked almost deserted. "No food or drink in the library."

"I know." Abel glanced down at his lunch box. "Sorry. I'll put it away." He sat down well away from the librarian and put the box into his backpack, pulling out his notes from the History lesson. "Hi Ferryl. I'm worried as well so talk slowly and we'll work it out." Since his sub-vocalisation attempts weren't really quiet yet, Abel sat behind a few bookshelves with his back to anyone else.

"*All these manuscripts, books. More than in the library van. Is this where the van collects them from?*"

"Calm down. No, there is a bigger library. These are for students. Can we talk about protection?"

"*There is none, anywhere. Why not?*"

Abel had been worried, but Ferryl's concern made it much worse. "Isn't there any sign of a witch at least?"

"*No, none and I saw little sign of one anywhere on the way here. Even in the clear areas there were no visible hexes, protective glyphs. I dare not send another seeker in case it is noticed and followed.*"

"What is a seeker?"

"*May I catch one? Please?*" Moments later a house fly landed on Abel's hand. "*It is now bound as a seeker. It cannot tell me much, just if it finds places where a glyph stops it from flying. There are no such places in the college, except one or two hints in here.*"

Following the fly, not something Abel ever expected to do, led to several books it wouldn't go near. Investigating the books proved that pictures of some heraldic devices, Celtic crosses, and illuminated manuscripts contained protective glyphs. "Let it go, please." Abel didn't like the idea of binding things, even flies. "These are old books, so people knew about glyphs way back then."

"*There are glyphs in the pyramids.*"

"But why have people stopped using them?" Abel sighed, packed up his books and headed towards his Graphic Art class. He stopped in the library doorway as two students walked past with what Ferryl had claimed were harmless fae on their heads. "Bloo... blimey."

"They are hunting lice."

Abel stared at the pair, chattering away without a care in the world, and decided that on balance maybe those fae were a good thing. The Globhoblin through the big glass doors at the end of the corridor wasn't, and several of the others didn't look terribly beneficial. "We should stop those coming in." The buzzer rang. "After this lesson." He headed for the computer room.

"ABC, Abel Bernard Conroy. Why do you bother? You'll always be a waste of space so you may as well go home now and save the taxpayers some money." Abel glanced at the speaker, Seraph Bellamy-Courts, and for once she made perfect sense. He turned towards the door.

"Stop!"

Abel shrugged, not even bothering to lower his voice. "She's right. I can struggle for three years and get a crap job, or go home now and get a crap job."

"Be quiet! She has enchanted you, influenced, a type of binding but without true intent. Break it, Abel Bernard Conroy." The urgency in Ferryl's voice got through and Abel began to think properly again.

"The bitch! Is she a witch, or a sorceress?" Abel glared at the young woman's retreating back. Seraph Angelique Bellamy-Courts, at seventeen the elite of the elite. A combination of wealth, looks, charisma, intelligence and her implacable will meant she dominated the select group sometimes referred to as the seraphims.

"I think not. She did not attempt to bind or control you, so perhaps she does not realise her ability. I will think on this. Now you know, fight any suggestions from her."

"Not hard, because she rarely speaks to the likes of me. I'm more worried about finding a way of warding the school and Brinsford." Abel couldn't see how one untrained boy, even with a Ferryl Shayde to help, could do it. He accepted a ticking off for being late and settled down to the IT lesson, determined to do his best. The four gremlins Ferryl sent scurrying off, trailing smoke, underlined the school's problem.

*　　*　　*

Abel didn't have a way to protect the whole school by the time he climbed on the bus to go home, but at least a couple of classrooms were safer. He'd nicked a wax crayon from the art supplies and, coached by Ferryl, drawn glyphs on any entrance he could get near. With luck the cleaners would miss them, though they'd probably scrub the ones off the walls and windows in the toilets. Abel had been horrified by the number of creatures clustered in there.

Kelis nudged him. "Are you all right, Abel? You went missing at break and lunch-time, and you look dead miserable when you should be pleased we're going home."

Abel managed a smile for her. "Bad belly, and I'm worried about money."

"We all worry about money. You could cast a spell and make some?" Kelis made several extravagant gestures. "Make more diamonds. Pow, riches beyond your wildest dreams."

"A bad belly explains why someone reckoned you were lurking in the toilets." Rob tried to look sympathetic but a smile broke through. "You'll get talked about doing that."

"I'm better now." Abel had spent most of lunch-time there, putting glyphs on the door and windows and killing the creatures already inside whenever he could without being seen. He'd been careful to only kill anything when nobody could see the bubbling mess as they evaporated. Abel insisted on killing every one so they couldn't carry germs from the toilets to the canteen. "I must have picked up a bug from someplace."

"With luck Seraph, Henry and that crowd will get it, because they all eat canteen food." Kelis grinned. "Us poor folk wot only have dry crusts and water will be safe." She might be right after what Abel saw crawling over and in the food on display. Abel would never complain at taking packed lunches - not now.

"Will you have time to come round tonight?" The disgusted look on Rob's face spoke volumes. "After homework, anyway. They could have left it a couple of days, just to let us get settled back in."

"Yes, I'll be fine once I get a proper meal at home." Better yet, working on the game might stop Abel worrying.

*   *   *

Though after tea, before she let him go anywhere, Ferryl had a really serious problem to discuss. *"Abel Bernard Conroy is your true-name, given by a God, yes?"*

"At my christening? I suppose so, though I'd not thought about it. True-name? Is that why Seraph got me to believe her? Surely everyone isn't commanded by their Christian and surname?" Abel thought about that. "That would be like using the name I have for you, which can't be right or nobody would disobey teachers for starters. They always use full names when they're telling someone off."

"Magical creatures with enough sentience to know their names can be bound by it. Humans cannot be bound by names, not normally, but I think that must have changed when you began to use magic. Not truly bound, but it seems that if another person with some magic talent speaks your name you are influenced. If they speak with true intent, you might be unable to resist. Human witches and sorcerers are usually warded, but none of them explained why it was necessary. Now I know why they were so shy." Ferryl chuckled. *"There are times I wish I'd known an un-warded human awakened to magic could be commanded by their name."*

"I'm convinced. Ward me please, Ferryl, whatever that means."

"I cannot. Firstly I am part of you, bound in a way, and more importantly you must ward yourself. Your ward must be a protective magical sign you create, without help." She hesitated. *"Then you must draw it on your skin."*

"A glyph?" Abel flinched. "Another burning tattoo? The pain is bad enough but Mum will go crackers."

"No, not a glyph. You must create something unique because every human ward I ever saw looked different."

"Wrong person. I'll get Kelis to help me." Abel stood up, ready to go. "I'm still not convinced about another tattoo."

"Stop! Please, listen. If someone controls you, they will control me. I am not yet strong enough to live without this tattoo, and they would bind me properly. At the very least they would make you give up my name, and

I am still sworn to serve you." Ferryl sounded panic-stricken. *"You must do this, now."*

"Not a chance. Not another tattoo. I'll be grounded for a year."

"Make it a part of mine. Your mother never looks closely, so add a little bit."

"A tiny one? Is it really that important?" Abel thought about it and his mum avoided looking at Ferryl's tattoo if it accidentally showed. "What would have happened if Seraph had known what she was doing, and used real intent?"

"I believe you would have come home, and never gone to the school again." Abel couldn't ignore the total sincerity in that.

Though he still worried about his mum's reaction. "Maybe a tattoo on your tattoo's arm? What happens when you leave?"

"Not on me. You could put it close, as if it belongs. Intent matters more than size, so it can be small. Please?"

Abel gave up. He didn't know enough to argue, and Seraph really had an effect. A chill went up his spine at the idea of someone like her ordering him about. "I'll try." He pulled out the sketch pad and a pencil, but coming up with a design wasn't easy because Ferryl insisted she couldn't help. Worse, she flew out of the tattoo so he had to draw without any help. Half an hour later Abel sat back to inspect the latest result. "What do you think?"

The sense of something flowing into his arm heralded Ferryl coming home. *"Very good. Soft, gentle curves, to reflect your nature, with a small solid centre for strength and surrounded by sharp edges proving you will protect you and yours. Why is it a plant, a flower with roots?"*

Abel stared at the drawing because he hadn't actually tried for all that but could see it now, sort of. "So it fits with your tattoo. I could have put it in a pot but prefer this. We all have roots."

Barely an echo of a whisper, Ferryl replied, *"Not all of us."*

Abel didn't think he should have heard that, so he moved on. "I'm not sure I can draw this on my arm." He chuckled. "I can't keep rubbing a tattoo out and trying again. Not only that, but I can't stand the pain of several attempts. I'm not keen on suffering once. Will it hurt every time I draw a line, or when it's done?"

"No drawing for this. Memorise your ward, really memorise it, then place your finger and imagine it in place before activating. Pushing magic as you call it." Ferryl chuckled. *"The pain will be less because this is welcomed, your magic to your magic. Try not to scream."*

"That was a surprise." And pain, Abel admitted privately, and braced himself. After a moment's thought he wadded up a few tissues to bite on. He took his time, making sure he'd got the little picture memorised perfectly, then took a deep breath and held out his arm so he could see it clearly. Abel hesitated again, but finally put his finger down firmly, near to Ferryl's cat-woman. He imagined the flower growing there, protecting him from the likes of Seraph. The magic pushing, which is how it really did feel, came easier after all his practice and then Abel snatched his finger away and bit hard on the tissues.

"Very good. A solid connection with crisp clear lines and real intent." Abel looked at his arm and Ferryl's tattoo leant over to sniff at the little plant. Two tattoo butterflies fluttered round it before landing on her ears. *"It smells welcoming, calming, but too spikey for butterflies."*

Abel couldn't smell a thing but he thought the tattoo came out much better than his drawing. The blue and purple flower looked almost alive, and the roots really seemed to disappear into his arm. He touched it. "Oh! That feels strange."

"You are touching your own magic. What does it feel like?"

"Soothing. Calming, as if everything is all right." He stroked the flower gently. "Should it feel like that?"

"I don't know. I have warded the bodies I am in, but the magic is theirs so I have never been able to touch my own." Ferryl sounded sad and Abel almost asked why not, but he still worried he might not like the answers.

"Can we go out now?"

"Oh yes. The next time Seraph tries to bind you, she will be rebuffed. Hopefully it will hurt her." Ferryl's tattoo beamed happily and more butterflies appeared. *"I feel much safer."*

"That's me protected. Just the village and school to go." Abel braced himself before asking because he might not like the answer. "Have the extra magical creatures stopped arriving?"

"*No. There have been none strong enough to get past Mrs. Tabitha, but now they are testing all around the village. I fear something or someone is testing. For that reason I will burn the paper with the drawing. I do not know if it can be used against you but it is your own ward, drawn by your own hand, so better to be safe.*"

"Will you show me how?" Ferryl must have been in a terrific mood because on the way to Rob's she allowed Abel to create a tiny flame glyph all by himself. The wobbly pyramid he'd glimpsed Ferryl using turned out to look like a cartoon flame with a smaller one inside. Abel used his first attempt to burn his drawing, though first he had to suffer a litany of warnings about burning haystacks and houses.

*   *   *

Four days later, on Saturday, Abel still hadn't been able to protect the school. He spent part of Saturday afternoon grubbing about in a hedgerow at the opposite side of the field behind the council houses, binding them all into a deterrent for part of the village. Not a strong one, because once again the dryads in the trees here and there along the hedgerow refused to part with any magic. None of them believed he could or would guard the young.

Even if small magical creatures could go around the ends of this stretch and stronger ones would walk right through, the barrier wouldn't be useless. According to Ferryl, passing across it would be uncomfortable and many would wander off elsewhere. Better yet it might catch some. Abel had already despatched one creature caught in the magical mesh between his mum's fruit bushes. The number of flyers in Abel's back garden had decreased dramatically even if they could still get in from the gardens each side.

The effort of creating glyphs for this whole stretch tired Abel, so despite a slight drizzle he headed to Castle House gardens. Part of the fatigue, according to Ferryl, would be the lowering of his personal magic levels. She suggested sitting on the stone slab because he seemed to recover faster there. Ferryl thought he might be picking up some leakage from the magic trap, because his blood cracked the holding glyphs.

The alternative might be that his distant blood connection to the sorcerer allowed Abel to connect with the stored magic. Abel didn't understand that part, but Ferryl insisted she could taste the connection in the first drops to land on the slab. While discussing it, Ferryl came to the conclusion that only Abel's connection to the sorcerer let him crack the glyphs. Abel went around it with her several times, but his tattoo insisted. He wasn't keen on her reasoning, that the sorcerer probably used magic to seduce local women and Abel's ancestral blood-link came through a discarded bastard. If he'd been a direct descendant, Ferryl's relentless logic insisted, Abel would have inherited Castle House.

After sitting on the slab for a while the slight drizzle increased to light rain. Abel moved into the shallow cave where the guardian used to sit, while Ferryl went off to inspect the boundary. If anything had tried too hard to get in, she would use Abel's hand to strengthen the place. Abel didn't mind, he sat quietly practicing making dust hover and a leaf float. He couldn't keep the leaf still but had found that when he became frustrated, stroking his little flower calmed him down. "I've looked and looked but there's no wires. How are you doing that?"

Abel jumped to his feet, then calmed a bit because he recognised Kelis's voice. Even so, he wondered why Ferryl hadn't detected her arriving. "Do what? What did you think you saw?" He'd sat on his jacket, but picked it up to put on and hide the tattoo.

"Hah, nice try. I've been stood here for a while, watching. You did it with dust and a leaf, made them sort of dance about. Why do you keep touching that tattoo in between? That's downright kinky, now that I think about it." Kelis had been walking closer as she talked and her eyes narrowed. "That's new."

"What is?" Abel casually pulled the jacket sleeve up over his tattoo. "You've seen Ferryl Shayde before."

"There's more." Kelis had come close enough to tug on his sleeve now. "Come on. Is this why you come here?" She cupped her hand and jiggled it.

"I come for peace and quiet. Why are *you* here?" Because according to Ferryl, Kelis shouldn't be able to walk through the boundary.

"For peace and quiet." Kelis touched her arm then snatched her hand away and a faint blush stained her cheeks. "Dad's home."

Which, Abel assumed, meant drunk and he'd hurt Kelis, though she'd be embarrassed if Abel mentioned it. "I've not seen you here before."

"No, I've never liked the place but then a strange thing happened a couple of weeks back. I wanted to see what happened at the end of the trail, where the tree got drunk or the gypsies stopped the truck. I set off a couple of times but changed my mind." Kelis stopped talking and frowned as if struck by a thought before continuing. "Have you still got those pebbles, the ones with the pretty symbols on?"

"Not on me."

"You haven't got the white one at all, and I've just realised something else. The strange thing I just mentioned is that I suddenly found the garden quite inviting, and came inside to have a look. I liked it so I come back when I want privacy." Kelis pulled something from her pocket and held it up. "The something else I've just realised is that it happened right after I picked this up off the road." Abel stared at the white pebble with the glyph on. "How much of that complicated magic system you produced is real, Abel?"

"It's a game, Kelis, just a game. Magic isn't real."

"What we do in your room or Rob's isn't magic, but dancing leaves might be. Now show me your tattoo, Abel, please, the one you stroke before making leaves dance?" If she'd been mocking or demanding Abel could have stormed off in a huff but Kelis just stood there, smiling quietly and holding up the pebble.

Abel peeled off his jacket and turned his shoulder towards her and away again. "See, furry babe with strategically placed tail."

"She's been planting a garden, a very strange one. Did it grow or did you win a few quid on the lottery again, Abel?" Abel's mind ran around in circles because another tattoo wouldn't fly, not after the trouble with the first one. "You may as well turn your shoulder this way so I can see properly."

With a sigh, Abel let her have a proper look. "It's to help my concentration. Stroking the tattoo helps me calm down."

Kelis giggled. "Stroking which tattoo? I'm sure stroking one of them is illegal, or kinky at the very least."

"Stop it." Abel had to laugh. "The flower you idiot. I don't suppose the other one feels furry anyway."

"Hang on." Kelis touched his arm, then again. "Nope, not furry. The flower isn't spikey either. What is it?"

"A tattoo?" Abel pretended to cower away from her glare. "I don't know. An Abel-flower."

"Does it really work, calm you down?" Kelis looked closer. "It's really good, realistic in spite of the colour and odd petals."

"It works if I just relax and let it. All my stress floats away and I feel really peaceful. It's probably nothing to do with the flower." He tried, but Abel already knew his attempt at acting innocent didn't have a chance.

"And coming into this garden has nothing to do with the pebble, except now I'm realising the couple of times I've changed my mind I wasn't wearing this jacket. The one with the pebble in the pocket?" Kelis's eyes narrowed and she stopped smiling. "Now give. This is magic, hallucinogenic gas, or very strange and I'd love to hear your explanation." She bent down and picked up a leaf. "Make this dance again, and use any wires you like."

Abel looked at the leaf, and Kelis, and gave up. He'd been dying to tell someone, or Kelis and Rob at least. "All right." He put the leaf on his palm, touched the flower for a moment with the other hand, and let the magic flow. The leaf danced up, jerking about and then fluttering off to the side. "Magic."

"I knew it! All right, maybe I didn't, but wow!" Kelis glanced around, suddenly not so sure. "Real magic? Hang on, are those other things real, the ones you introduced into the game?" Her eyes widened. "Is Ferryl Shayde real?"

"The creatures are real but you can't see them unless you can use magic. They really are gross. Ferryl Shayde is a tattoo." She was, sort of, Abel thought.

"So show me. Magic first, then the creatures. You can stop them, can't you? You must be able to because you aren't worried about them. You said a lot of them are harmless." Kelis picked up a leaf and put it on her palm, eyes alight with excitement. "Come on, what do I do next? Do I need a tattoo?" Her face dropped. "I daren't have one like that."

This had all happened too fast, and without Ferryl here to advise. Abel didn't know if Kelis had already been awakened to magic as Ferryl put it, just by knowing it worked. A chill ran up his back because in that case Kelis could be controlled by her name, by someone like Seraph. She needed a ward! "You need your version of the flower, a ward, before you learn any magic. Otherwise you'll attract creatures and you'll see them now. Worse, someone who knows how might try to control you." Abel tried to make his voice as grave as possible. "I daren't show you magic until then. Your ward doesn't have to be where mine is."

They went around that a bit, because Kelis thought he just didn't want to show her. Eventually she accepted she had to wear a mark, a ward, but then started to worry what it had to be. "Does it have to be a tattoo? How about a drawing in indelible felt tip? Then if Dad or Mum see it I can swear it'll wear off. I can keep renewing it." Kelis grinned, eyes still alight with excitement. "Come on, try it, draw one. Will you be able to tell if it's worked?"

"You can. You'll feel it when you touch it." Abel sighed and gave up. "You are supposed to make up your own."

"No, I like the flower. It works for you, so that's what I want as well." Kelis inspected it. "Without that creepy root. I'll put it someplace private so Dad won't spot it. Oh. Not too private." She sniggered. "Not if you're drawing it."

"You could draw it." Abel sniggered as well. "Even then remember you might want to stroke the flower in public."

"Ooh yes." Kelis rummaged in her pocket and pulled out a marker pen. "Good thing I'm an art nut." She took off her jacket and rolled up her sleeve, debating. Abel realised Kelis must be distracted because she'd bared the finger-mark bruises on her arm, something Kelis never did except by accident. "Not on the outside, like yours. On the inside of my arm I think, then I can cross my arms and my hand will tuck under and," she tucked one hand out of sight under the other arm, "just there. A bit below my armpit where I can reach it inside my jacket." Kelis held out the pen. "Come on. I can't draw there." She held her arm straight up. "Don't tickle."

Abel hesitated for long moments, then gave up and took the indelible pen. It would wear off eventually, and Kelis could make her own. "Hold still." Firm strokes, with intent, Abel reminded himself. The intent came easily; to ward Kelis from control and magic creatures and to stop the pain, the stress when her Dad acted up, make her feel safe. He drew a slightly stylised version of the flower which would look the same upside down, and thought it looked pretty good.

As he finished, Kelis jerked a little, then twisted her head and arm to see the result. "Hey, pretty good. I'll leave it a minute to dry." She held up the pebble again. "Do I have to buy an engraving kit and run around with a pocket full of pebbles, or is it like the game?"

"A bit like the game. I drew the glyph for the leaf and dust on my hand with my finger ages ago. Not actually draw because a finger doesn't leave a mark, so you have to picture where it is. This is a very weak spell." Abel remembered what Ferryl could do with concentrated wind. "You have to be gentle and learn real control before trying anything else. Promise?"

"I'd promise pretty much anything if you really teach me to do magic. Can't I draw the symbol on my palm with my pen?"

"No because there will be more glyphs eventually, or so I believe." Abel daren't tell her he already knew another or Kelis would want it now. Remembering his first success with wind, Abel didn't want that sudden surge to happen with fire. "But they only come after mastering this one."

"Like levelling up in a game? When do I see the creatures?" Kelis looked round. "I can't see any yet."

"There aren't any inside this garden. You get in through the fence because of the pebble, I get in because of magic, and everyone else finds a reason not to come here." Abel smiled. "Unless they really are motivated. Tyson and Henry were chasing me when they came in here."

"When you hit them?" Kelis inspected the trampled trail to the clearing, not as bad as it had been now the bushes were growing. "What really made that mess? You said something about a tree running in here and I thought you were being funny." Her smile faded. "Just how serious were you, and are trees likely to chase me?"

"Very serious, but it was a special tree and the stone statue that lived in this cave killed it. Neither survived the fight." Kelis stared, eyes wide.

"There aren't any more trees or statues like that." Abel kept near enough to the truth or he'd get mixed up. More than that, he didn't want to scare Kelis too much to start with. Once again he wondered why Ferryl hadn't heard or sensed something and come back.

Kelis relaxed again. "You and I are going to have a long talk about keeping secrets like running trees and statues that fight." Her smile belied her chiding tone and she lifted her arm. "This should be dry." She stroked it gently. "Oh! It really works!" Abel jumped because he felt a tingle in his own tattoo, the plant. What was that? "Like a trickle down my arm." She stroked it again, gently. "I can see how that can be soothing, once I'm used to it. Now how do I magic a leaf to dance?"

"Slow up. The idea is to make the leaf hover. It's dancing because I haven't got it right. Until you can manage control, anything else is dangerous." Abel really needed to talk to Ferryl about this, if she'd just come back. "The magic is a feeling like you just described, down your arm but into the glyph. They are called glyphs, the real ones, not symbols." Abel drew the version for leaf hovering, the two coils, in the dust on the cave floor. "Draw this on your palm with one finger, firm strokes with real intent. The intent matters."

"Oh, I intend floating a leaf, believe me." Kelis looked at the dust drawing and copied the marks onto her palm with her finger. "I can't see it."

"Memorise it, picture it there." Abel nearly giggled, remembering how impatient Ferryl had been as he struggled through this.

Kelis held out her hand and sure enough, three seconds later, sighed. "Nothing. Are you sure this is magic. Not some windup? No, because I felt that drawing which is impossible. Unless magic works. So magic works." She giggled. "I should be screaming and running about. Maybe it's because we've been pretending to do magic for a year and this is just the proper version?"

"Time, patience, intent, and you must be calm."

"Yes sensei." Kelis giggled then tried to be serious. "Have you found one? An old oriental geezer with a little white beard?"

Staying serious wasn't easy with Kelis in this mood. "No oriental anyone. Stop talking, calm down and concentrate. It took me days, but I hadn't learned the flower stroking trick."

"So how did you find out about magic?"

"Tree chasing me? Stone statue fighting? They were a really big hint. I saw the glyphs on the stone, and the statue and tree had one." Abel glanced at the stone slab. "Do not copy anything on that slab, please. If you break the holding spell it will destroy the house, and probably the village." Abel locked eyes. "Please? I really do mean that."

Unfortunately Kelis stopped giggling and started thinking. "How did you learn this stuff?"

"Later, grasshopper. What comes first?" Abel kept his voice light, and Kelis laughed.

"One leaf, floating. I hear and obey." Kelis straightened her face, stroked her arm three times, then stopped and stared at her hand. "Nope. Days?"

"Yup."

"At least it's peaceful here, and that mark makes me feel really calm and somehow safe. I can sit here and forget…" Kelis stopped, tensing a little and moving as if to cover the bruises. "Too late now."

"We know about your Dad drinking, me and Rob." Abel sighed. "We'd both find you a spot on a settee."

Kelis relaxed. "Dad would go crazy if I did that. Though I might if I could be sure it gave him a bloody heart attack. Ah, sorry." A faint blush stained Kelis's cheeks. "Anyway, you say he can't get in this garden so it's safer than your settee. Better yet?" She smiled, stoking her mark and Abel felt the little tingle. "I might camp here. If it gets worse, I can bring Mum." Kelis stopped, stiffening. "Can you sort of forget that, all of what I just said? I won't bring anyone, I swear."

Abel opened his mouth to answer but leaves and dust swirled and he felt Ferryl pour back into her tattoo, or rather she stormed back in. *"Why is she here? Why did you bring her? You fool! She'll tell everyone! Men always want to impress women! Typical!"*

"I'll leave you in peace. Ignore the gross things you see on the way home." Abel began to leave and thought of something else. "Don't tell Rob until I can explain properly, please?"

"Not a chance. We'll tell him once I've sorted out this leaf thing. I want to see him try and explain it away as a trick the first time." Kelis giggled. "I stood there for ages trying to work it out before I gave up." She went back to staring at the leaf and Abel left as quickly as possible so he could answer Ferryl, still ranting in his head.

Abel didn't fancy walking through the village arguing with himself so he went around to the far side of the house. "I didn't bring her in."

"You didn't?" At least Ferryl stopped ranting for a moment, startled. *"She followed you?"*

"No, she found the pebble with the glyph in the road, and was already curious about all the damage. I must have dropped it when the Bound Shade attacked. By then sheer terror probably outweighed your barrier, and I never even realised I'd lost the glyph. The barrier hasn't been a problem since then." Abel found a stone bench and sat, explaining the whole thing. Apart from giving him an ear-bashing for dropping the stone, Ferryl agreed he hadn't done much wrong. Abel finished with, "So I've got to teach her to protect her from the nastier creatures. At least she's got a ward to protect her from Seraph."

"Good. You had me as a warning, but a real ward she drew herself will be better." Abel kept his mouth shut. He could still feel the occasional tingle from Kelis. *"She must learn about me, but not immediately. Eventually, as her magic develops, she will realise I am different and not just a tattoo. It is best to tell her first."*

"Put some clothes on before you turn round and introduce yourself."

Ferryl giggled. *"You are worse than the Puritans, though I could tell you a few things about them."*

"Not until I'm older. Probably about thirty years older." A sudden thought struck Abel. "At least we can get her house protected. It's a good job you remembered the protection glyph."

"Only because it is a part of the garden protection glyph, the barrier. Kelis can help with the school and village. Perhaps she could be the witch and you the sorcerer? That would be better than usual because the two types usually argue." Abel relaxed because Ferryl seemed to have accepted Kelis, but Ferryl continued, *"There have been more attempts to breach the barrier."*

"Who?"

"*Not a who, an it. Humans are deterred and simply don't test the barrier. Magical creatures are barred, painfully if they push hard. There is no woodland at the sides, so hidden intruders can come closer and that is where someone is testing.*"

"You just said not a human."

"*The testing is creatures. The intent behind them, the driving force might be human because some were pushed to where I'm sure the barrier killed them.*"

"I said no killing!"

"*If something pushes past pain, past damage, then perhaps it is a good job they die. Do you want something that determined inside here?* Ferryl paused to let Abel think and no, he didn't. "*To push that far, the creatures are either terrified or bound.*"

"What can you do?"

"*Use you to strengthen the spell, now you can use your own intent. Better yet, some of the trees were too young to use when I built it, but are strong enough now and completely untapped. If you draw the glyphs without me controlling your hand, so the binding is stronger, we can tie those trees into the rest of the garden. I will instruct you.*" Abel would have argued about binding a tree that couldn't object but it made sense because this also protected the tree. He spent the rest of the afternoon crouching in the rain, drawing lines in mud and glyphs on roots. Ferryl insisted he buried the roots again to hide the glyphs, because Abel didn't have the control to burn into the live-wood under the bark. Kelis must have stayed in the cave because even when he went home Abel could feel the occasional tingle from his flower.

*   *   *

Abel felt a lot of tingling in his flower over the rest of the weekend so Kelis really did want to make her leaf float. Now he'd thought about it, Abel should have insisted both Kelis and Rob were told right at the beginning. Having three in on the secret would make protecting the village and school easier, because one could draw while another covered what she did. Abel thought Kelis should be the one drawing because her glyphs would be strong, firm clear lines. According to Ferryl that would work better. He debated with himself about telling Ferryl he could feel Kelis's mark, but she had enough worries.

On Sunday evening, Abel had to concentrate on his homework or he'd be in trouble at school. Maths bored Ferryl so she went off for a float around the garden. He looked up as Ferryl's wind form shimmered in through the barely open window and settled back into her tattoo. *"Something is testing our barrier, the one in the garden. Probably the same something that tested Castle House."*

"Is this barrier strong enough?" Abel closed the page, because he wouldn't be able to concentrate until he knew.

"Not strong enough to stop whatever came, and the testing is deliberate. It came part-way through the barrier in the bushes, which means it could have come all the way if it wished. Instead it withdrew, which probably means whatever sent it will come next."

"We have to strengthen the bushes. Can't we make a sort of trip-wire, or maybe a trap, a magical snare? Those two little hoplins were snared." The little creatures looked like a miniature armadillo that hopped like a kangaroo, and had a mildly poisonous bite. Not terribly dangerous to people or even Mrs. Tabitha, but two of them could take a kitten. Ferryl considered them useful for dealing with rats and mice, but neither were a serious problem in Brinsford so she killed them.

"Hoplins are weak. We could set a trap, but to kill or wound rather than catch. We will find it easier to defeat a wounded opponent, and if it runs we might be able to capture it. Even if it escapes I might track it or work out what came from the traces." Ferryl stayed silent for a while but Abel didn't interrupt her as she paced around his arm, deep in thought. When she 'spoke' again, Ferryl sounded hesitant. *"If we strengthen barriers using your ward that will tell you if they are breached, and maybe some idea of direction. Though I am not sure how that works, if perhaps you could be attacked through the link, because I have never had a personal ward."* She paced again, wrestling with some problem. *"No, we cannot risk it until you are stronger, until you can defend using your own intent instead of mine."*

"But we can set a trap, a strong one?" If something or someone might sneak up on his mum, Abel didn't mind how lethal Ferryl wanted to make it. "A trap won't catch Mrs. Tabitha, will it?"

"She is too smart, but in any case our surprise will only catch an intruder using direct magical power. I will use a version of the barrier around Castle House, but concentrated because there is less magic to use. This will kill rather than catch, or wound if whoever comes is stronger than expected." Her harsh laugh had no humour at all. *"There are things and people we do not want to capture unless they are already wounded."*

"Tonight, or can we leave it until tomorrow night because I'd prefer to finish my homework. You can help me?" At least that made Ferryl laugh, though she reassured Abel that whoever had been testing would wait to assess whatever its servant had found out. She left to keep an eye on the back fence, and purr with Mrs. Tabitha because cats made more sense than mathematics.

*   *   *

Over the next week Abel added glyphs as instructed to the net among the bushes behind his house. He daren't try to snare a creature elsewhere because he wouldn't be able to go and deal with it. Ferryl agreed to recruit more local guardians, and exchanged purrs with more village cats. Abel couldn't do much more during the week because it grew dark at seven. He couldn't go wandering around the neighbouring fields, setting up more deterrence in the hedges, without someone wondering why.

Kelis kept giving him little looks, her eyes alight with mischief, and he could feel his flower tingle regularly. They could only meet in the week on Tuesday and Thursday evenings now, because of homework, and at Rob's on the Thursday Kelis introduced protection marks to the game. By the time Abel came into the room the damage had been done. The sign outside her drawing of the Tavern held a picture of his flower in a shield, to protect the building from unwelcome magical creatures. Rob liked it, and Abel simply didn't dare say too much about the design because while she explained, Kelis put her hand on her arm and grinned. Abel still didn't want Ferryl seeing his mark on Kelis, especially after her reluctance to put it on traps.

Kelis must be practicing in her room at home, because Abel could feel her while he did his homework or practiced control. He daren't say he knew, and now began to worry about keeping a secret from his tattoo. His own control improved to where the gravel hovered even if it rippled, and the leaf stayed above his hand but still fluttered and danced a little. Twice on the way back from Rob's, Ferryl allowed him to form a glyph to burn down flying stingers. He missed one on the first try, but hit it after she reminded him to watch the target. As long as he kept his eye on the creature, the glyph acted like a homing missile.

Abel worried that the mystery tester would come in the day and catch his mum, but Ferryl scoffed at that. Magical creatures, especially those up to no good, much preferred darkness. Although few humans could see them, some caught hints of movement so darkness really did help. Though Ferryl felt more and more certain there would be a serious visit because the testing dropped off. Whoever it was, they believed they had enough information. Ferryl directed Abel to add a few more lines, and redraw some of the lines Ferryl had put in using Abel's hand.

At school the week passed quickly, between trying to get to grips with the new term's curriculum and warding as many places as possible. Unfortunately, the cleaners who came in after the students went home kept rubbing them off. Abel moved the locations, finding places they didn't clean, or didn't scrub hard enough to shift the wax crayon. Ferryl insisted the marks had to be physical, not like the invisible ones on his hand. At least Seraph and her entourage seemed to be just as occupied with the new lessons, barely harassing the other pupils.

Abel shouldn't have felt relieved as he took his coat from his locker Friday evening, because that more or less invited trouble. Seraph's voice rang out behind him. "Abel Bernard Conroy, since you won't take a hint and stay away you could at least have the decency to stay out of my way. You will move aside in future, and hide until I have passed. Ow!"

Abel turned to see Seraph and several of her acolytes. The corridor had plenty of room for them to pass, but she had obviously decided to have some fun on the way home. Now she stared at her hand, still pointing at him, and flexed the fingers as if they were stiff. Another voice asked, "What happened?" Abel rolled his eyes and groaned, because Henry had attached himself to the group and had now pushed to the front. Seraph usually allowed him to join them when she wanted someone chastised.

"I have no idea. Something stung my hand and I suspect this

disgusting little boy is involved in some way. Move him aside, Henry."

Henry took the step so he could reach out and catch hold of Abel's arm. "Poor squeaky, your locker will be left wide open. Anything might happen in there." Henry pushed.

Abel's mind whirled. He could swing, and with Ferryl's help probably knock Henry down but end up with a broken hand again. "I told you to leave me alone." That wouldn't work, so Abel braced himself for a punch.

"No. Now what are you going to do?" Henry lowered his voice. "Make a hole in a wall? Tyson asked at the club, and no martial arts can do that so it was a trick."

"You could put your hand on his and use the flame glyph, with or without control. Unless you want me to do it? I do not care if I burn his arm off but you keep telling me too much strength might bring unwanted attention."

Abel stifled a giggle, and put his hand on the one holding his other arm. "Let go Henry. Last chance."

"Or what? I knew it was a bluff." Henry pushed Abel away from the locker and two of the others moved towards it, smirking. "Aah!" As Abel pictured the glyph and pushed a little magic into it Henry snatched his hand away and shook it. "What was that?"

"Less than a brick, Henry." Abel moved back towards his locker and the two who'd started that way backed off, confused. Abel raised his voice. "As I keep saying, just leave me alone."

"We haven't time for this. I will be dealing with you next week, little boy." Seraph had lowered her hand, and looked a little less certain than usual. The rest were undecided, looking from Seraph to Henry, now inspecting the blister on the back of his hand with a scowl on his face. "Since you seem unable to deal with this nuisance, Henry, I see no point in you coming to the party this weekend. Father will have hired competent security." Seraph swept off with the rest, leaving Henry and Abel.

"There's something weird about you, squeak, and I'm gonna find out what. Then I'm gonna hammer you." Abel didn't bother to answer as Henry stalked off, still shaking and inspecting his hand.

"Whew. What did you do, use a Vulcan Death grip or a good manners spell?" Rob, only five lockers away, had obviously heard the whole thing even if he hadn't seen what Abel did.

"It's a Vulcan nerve pinch, idiot, but Abel probably used a club because nothing else works on Henry." Kelis's eyes danced with excitement and laughter, because she'd guessed what had happened or at least that magic must be involved. "Come on Abel, get your coat and let's go or we'll miss the bus."

All the way home Kelis had the question in her eyes, and as they walked up the main street from the bus stop she tugged Abel's sleeve to let Rob get ahead. "You used magic! What did you do?"

"Something very little, that needs control."

"Show me?"

"Not until you have control, grasshopper." Kelis pouted, but Rob turned back before she could try again.

"Hey, are you two plotting something back there?"

Kelis stuck her nose in the air. "With wimp here? Fat chance. I might be plotting, but neither of you two will know until it's too late." They wrangled until she headed home down Brinn's Lane while Rob and Abel turned up the road to Riverside Close. Not much of a name, but the small river going past one end had been enough of an excuse for planners needing a name for the street. To be honest, the council houses themselves weren't very imaginative. There were four pairs and four single plain brick two or three bedroom houses, all built to the same basic plan with the same colour paintwork.

"So what was that about?" Rob didn't seem bothered, just nosy.

"She still wants to know how I managed an A- for the project." The tutor had only marked Abel down for assuming too much about pre-Norman England from the evidence. Ferryl had wanted to fry the poor man, because the assumptions were solid truth. "You know how Kelis is about schoolwork and she only managed a B+."

"Oh yes. I had to share your ear-bending on the way home when she found out and I don't even take history." Rob turned into his gate. "See you tonight?"

"After tea." Abel waited until he had moved out of earshot. "Will that cause trouble? Using the glyph at school?"

"No, the magic used wouldn't be noticed outside the building. You were very controlled." Abel preened a little. *"For a student. Now you can start to learn how to increase the strength of the wind and fire."*

"The gravel and leaf really is just wind?"

"Yes, because I can only remember a very few glyphs after nearly fading. Wind and fire are very versatile with control and intent. As I keep telling you." Abel rolled his eyes and shut up, because he'd reached home and Mum would hear him.

*   *   *

Kelis couldn't press Abel when they met Friday evening because of Rob. He spent Saturday out in the fields weaving magic traps into bushes, hopefully strong enough to deter the mystery person or creature. On Sunday afternoon, Kelis burst into the little clearing in Castle House garden with a huge smile all over her face, and began to dance around the slab. "I did it, I did it, I did it. I made magic and it worked!"

"You managed to keep the leaf floating?" That impressed Abel because it had taken him a lot longer.

"No, I stopped those nasty little creepies from coming into my room." Kelis hugged Abel and danced off round the stone again. "They gross me out, but now they stay out of my room. I made my own ward. Hah! Zap, Pow, intent is my middle name, beware the mighty sorceress Kelis Glyphwielder." She waved her hands about in extravagant gestures.

Abel knew Kelis had been practicing because he could feel his tattoo tingling, but she'd made a ward? He tried to concentrate on a question to stop the flood from Kelis and the tirade about reckless young fools echoing inside his head. "How did you make a ward?"

"I based it on the flower. I've drawn it on the inside of my bedroom door and the window pane and hidden them with posters." She twirled, hands in the air and singing "I can do magic."

"Shut up, stop it a moment. That stops the creatures?"

"Intent. I keep telling you. But how did she activate a drawing of your mark? I could understand if she'd used her own." Ferryl sounded thoroughly confused as well as really ticked off.

"You used the one on the Tavern sign? Not this one?" Abel tapped his jacket sleeve above the tattoo.

"No and yes. I copied the one you drew on my arm."

Abel cringed as dead silence echoed in his head, before an explosive, *"Men!"*

"Hasn't it faded?"

Any hope Abel still had died in the beaming smile as Kelis answered. "You really are joking. That thing works! Not only does it make me feel calm and safe, I can make the leaf flutter away even if it's not floating yet. I renew your flower every night with the marker pen to make sure I don't lose it."

"You drew your mark on her arm. Personally, with your own hand?" Abel tried really hard to work out how to answer that, but Ferryl saved him the bother. *"You must have, if she has used it to activate a glyph. Not a glyph, the protecting marks on houses are hexes designed for a fixed purpose, and anyway..... I must think about this."* Blessed silence fell in Abel's head, even if Kelis hadn't finished.

"You look serious. Are you mad about me not waiting? I'm sorry, but the things were crawling over my bed, but wouldn't come near me. There were slimies on my pillow! Everything moved further away when I touched the flower, so I thought?" Kelis shrugged. "I thought it had to be worth a try?"

Abel smiled at her. "Sorry. You didn't see that tree charging across the road, or that stone statue produce teeth and claws and leap out of this cave. I'm a bit wary about magic." He grinned. "Though even if your door had opened its eyes it would be firmly fastened to the frame."

"My door has eyes?" Kelis looked shocked, then recognised the grin on Abel's face and began to laugh. "That would be a bit Disney, furniture dancing around. Could I get the vacuum cleaner and duster to clean my room up?"

"Don't try, please." Abel did his best to be serious but Kelis looked so happy. "I really don't know how things get animated, though I'm sure your door is safe."

"Not necessarily, but that would need many glyphs and considerable

skill and intent." Ferryl didn't sound even slightly humorous. *"What was your intent when you drew the mark?"* The exasperated snort after that meant Abel wasn't off the hook yet.

Abel tried to keep his tone soft, because Kelis would be embarrassed. "Does the flower still make you feel safer, Kelis? Did it make you feel better, hurt less? I'm sorry if it's a bit embarrassing, but I'd like to know." He tried for reassuring in his smile. "That ward shouldn't have worked, not drawn by you."

"Yes, I feel safe and calm, and now you've mentioned it my elbow hurts less." Kelis blushed, then recovered enough for a little smile though she'd stopped bouncing around. "Don't tell Rob that Dad twisted my elbow. Please?"

"No, but maybe you should tell someone." From the way Kelis hunched in on herself, that wasn't going to happen.

"Protection and reassurance. That makes sense because you would have real intent." An edge of humour entered Ferryl's tone. *"Those are not the usual reasons for binding a young woman."*

"Bound? I haven't bound Kelis! I wouldn't. Undo it!" Abel froze, his mouth still open as Kelis stared, then her eyes narrowed.

"Who are you talking to?" She whirled, looking all around. "Come on out, sensei or whatever. What did Abel mean, bound?" Kelis turned back to Abel, her face pale. "Is it a bad thing?"

"I don't know. I didn't mean to, honest. You were upset, and frightened." Abel knew he wasn't answering the main question, who he'd been talking to.

"I should have known. Young men and women. No patience, no control, and too much intent." This time when Ferryl sighed dust and leaves blew about the clearing. *"Introduce us, please."* She giggled. *"I will wear clothes."*

Kelis stared at the dust and leaves and whirled towards Abel. "He's here, isn't he? He or she," she paused, eyes wide, "or it?"

"Definitely she." Abel took off his jacket, rolled up his shirt sleeve, and turned enough for Kelis to see his tattoo clearly. "Kelis, meet Ferryl Shayde. Ferryl Shayde, please say hello to Kelis Glyphmistress."

"Hah, not a Glyphmistress yet." Abel glanced down and choked back

an exclamation. Ferryl Shayde wore a long cloak that completely covered her, including a hood so only her green eyes showed. A moment later her tail appeared from behind her to wave hello. *"Ask Kelis to put out a hand so that I can speak, please."*

Abel looked back at Kelis, utterly transfixed with her mouth forming an almost perfect O. "If you put a hand out Ferryl can contact you." Kelis didn't alter a muscle of her expression, but she stretched out a hand. A definitely wary look greeted the thin tendril of mist that reached out towards her. "Ferryl won't hurt you."

Kelis's quiet reply wavered just a little. "I trust you, Abel." Her eyes didn't totally trust the mist as it curled around her hand, and her other hand tucked across and up under her jacket to touch her mark. Abel felt the tingle.

"Hello Kelis. I am Ferryl Shayde and will not harm anyone protected by Abel Bernard Conroy. I am bound to protect him, and you wear his mark."

"Bound. What does that mean?" Abel felt proud of Kelis, because she managed that with barely a tremble in her voice.

"Not truly bound. I promised by my true-name, and he placed your ward to protect and reassure. Abel did not know what he did. He even makes me release bound houseflies."

"So what does bound mean?" Kelis looked at Abel and definitely nervously this time. "Can Abel control me?"

"No, or I do not think so."

Abel jumped in sharpish at that. "Make sure please. I'm sorry Kelis, I didn't know and you were worried. I said make your own…"

"And I said yours would do the job. It has." Kelis seemed to be calming down. "Why is Ferryl wearing a cloak? I've seen her before. How is a tattoo suddenly wearing a cloak? Oh God, you've turned round. Is that why you've got clothes?"

"He insists when I turn round."

"Can you change them? So you look like the game? You really can move? Of course you can, your tail just waved. Sorry, it's a bit much all at once." Kelis seemed to be losing her worries, engrossed in the idea of a mobile, talking tattoo. Abel kept quiet, sitting down when Kelis joined them in the cave and letting his tattoo and friend get to know each other. He relaxed when Ferryl broke the ice by showing Kelis several clothes changes including Robyn D'Ritche the mercenary and her horse. Once the laughter stopped all three of them talked about the mark, and what it had done or meant.

Ferryl didn't know what a mark without compulsion meant, because she'd never seen it happen. The usual reason for binding anyone or anything was to compel them, control their actions. An embarrassed Kelis took off her jacket and raised her arm, while Ferryl ran a tendril of mist over the flower. *"Give Kelis an order, one you really mean."*

"Kelis, punch my arm, hard." Abel meant it, because he deserved that at least, but Kelis laughed.

"Not a chance. Does that mean I'm not really bound?"

"There is no compulsion so not bound in any sense I know of. Perhaps it is not active, just a drawing. No, it taps your magic because you somehow activated a copy as a hex." The tattoo paced back and forth a little. *"The mark seems harmless but you should change it, create your own ward."*

"No chance. It's harmless and it works. If it ain't bust, don't fix it." Kelis smiled happily as she stroked underneath her arm. "I like this one." Abel kept quiet about the tingle in his flower, because that didn't do any harm either.

Eventually Kelis and Abel sat side by side, both trying to float a leaf, while Ferryl went flying off around the garden, *"To see how many other strays you let in."*

The two of them sat for a while, but neither were doing well with their leaves, and eventually Kelis started with, "So what happens now?"

"Nothing?" Apprehensively, because Abel really wasn't sure how she felt.

"Something might because you bound me."

"I didn't know!"

"Not a defence in law. Does magic have law? I mean apart from the way it's done." Kelis didn't sound annoyed, just curious.

"You could make some laws?" Abel thought Kelis might, if nobody else had. "Maybe not bound, because it didn't compel you?"

"Incompetence isn't a defence either." Kelis suddenly giggled. "And I did ask for it, literally." Her voice gentled. "It didn't work because of intent."

"Lack of intent."

"No, Ferryl said intent." Now Kelis spoke very softly, barely above a whisper. "Intent to protect me and make me feel better." She leaned across, quickly kissing Abel on the cheek before sitting straight up, facing forward. Abel looked at her, surprised, and two spots of red grew on her cheeks. "If you tell Rob I kissed you I'll kill you. It was just thank you."

"If you tell him I'll commit suicide in embarrassment."

"Is there a glyph for that?"

"I don't know. You could make a new one. You already did it once." Abel smiled happily. Ferryl really felt intimidating at times and Kelis had completely flummoxed her.

An answering smile broke on Kelis's face. "I told you." She waved her hands about. "Kelis Glyphmistress." She leant sideways and nudged Abel with her shoulder. "So watch it."

"I'll hide behind my tattoo Glyphmistress."

"You still owe me for that, keeping Ferryl Shayde a secret." Kelis picked up her leaf, placed it on her palm and straightened her face. She put one hand across to her arm and Abel felt the tingle, then a few moments later her leaf trembled and fluttered up briefly before slipping sideways and falling. Undeterred she picked it up and tried again. Abel didn't need his tattoo, knowing that Kelis had forgiven him brought perfect peace though that wasn't enough to stop his leaf dancing about a bit.

Ferryl seemed happier when she came back, though she vetoed using Glyphmistress in the game. That would be a big hint to anyone out there this wasn't strictly a game now.

* * *

For the next couple of weeks, while Kelis perfected her leaf and dust moving, Abel worked on using the fire and wind glyphs to affect more than leaves. Ferryl had him trying to knock creatures off fences or out of the air with puffs of wind. Despite all the warnings, whoever had been testing didn't turn up though the trap in the fruit bushes caught several unwary creatures. Ferryl thoroughly examined the broken twigs or fallen leaves each time. The tally came to a pair of hoplins, two thornies, and a sprite she couldn't classify because they were basically shapeless. None of them were strong enough to penetrate, though they might have been sent in an attempt to gauge the strength of the defences.

Though the intrusions led to Abel's training advancing another two steps. The second time something magical died, Ferryl used Abel's hand to check. *"A thorny. You should learn to do this."*

"I can't even see where to check." Abel tried, but although he thought there might be a slight disturbance of the soil, and a scattering of brown spots on some leaves, those might be imagination. The two fallen twigs and a broken twig were definite signs, but Ferryl had been testing something else.

"I apologise, I had been thinking you were clumsy, not blind. Usually any creature I…. ride with can see as I do. Close your eyes because this will sting."

There wasn't time to wonder what Ferryl had been going to say instead of ride. No sooner were his eyes shut than they began to sting, feeling the same as after chopping two or three onions. "I hope I'm not expected to look at anything just now. We should have done this where I could splash them with water." Abel rubbed at his eyelids, feeling the wetness of tears.

"It will clear quickly. I forget you are not my usual host. Altering your body causes discomfort because I am not fully a part of you. A rider without reins."

At least that answered the part about what Ferryl had started to stay, host sounded a lot more personal than rider. Alarm jolted through Abel. "You changed my eyes? What did you do? Do they look the same?" He rubbed again. "Can I open my eyes yet?"

"Calm down, the way the front covering of your eyes filters what you see has been altered. Your mother's memories had some words." Ferryl paused for a few moments, during which the stinging in Abel's eyes almost faded. *"In your words, I slightly altered the composition of your lens or pupil, and increased the sensitivity and range of your retina. Abel, your mother is not sure of what everything in there is called."*

"Nor me. Sensitivity? Can I see in the dark?" Suddenly the stinging didn't seem such a bad deal, not if it meant bat-vision.

"You can see clearer in faint light, and will see magical creatures better. Keep your eyes closed!" Ferryl sounded alarmed and Abel scrunched his eyes as tightly closed as possible. *"Just a moment."* His eyes stung again, but just a tiny irritation. *"Blinding you would have been embarrassing because I'm not sure I could fix it."*

"Blinding!"

"Increased sensitivity to light. I had forgotten to adjust how your eyes adapt. Working from memory is much harder than being able to feel how everything works. You are safe now."

When Abel opened his eyes, cautiously, everything looked about the same. Not quite, when he looked properly. The shadows weren't quite as dark, and as he concentrated a faint web of shimmering, smoky lines appeared. "That sort of spider's web of smoke, is that magic?"

"Spider's web? That is very flattering, spiders are very good spinners." Abel's right hand, the one Ferryl had been using to check the trap, moved and pointed. *"Look for where the web is broken."*

"Got it. There's a gap and something on the leaves and ground. Oh, there are little lines in the leaves."

"Later, that is their stored magic. Bring your magic to your hand without forming a glyph, and touch this trace here."

"Could you fix Kelis's eyes as well, please, because that would make learning a lot easier."

"Once I am sure yours work properly, and that she has some control. Now hurry up and test these traces before they revert to pure magic." Abel tried. He destroyed the first three traces because, according to Ferryl, he let the magic leak from his hand. Abel thought it might be because he kept worrying about the comment about his eyes working properly. Eventually he persuaded himself Ferryl could fix small problems, and concentrated enough to feel some sort of tingle. Ferryl claimed that each creature left a different trace and he could learn the difference, but Abel doubted it. Obtaining different types of creature traces for him to test led to another step in glyph training.

The wind training meant Abel could knock fae out of the air. This time Ferryl allowed him to burn the grounded stingers. Not incinerate them, because that would cause a flare of light and heat and might not leave enough of a trace. Abel sighed, and concentrated on producing small, controlled heat glyphs. He really fancied letting go, blasting a great big fireball into something, but couldn't sneak away from his own tattoo. A couple of fae flew off streaming smoke, but Ferryl considered too little much better than too much when practicing. Though even after touching the traces from the ones he hit properly, Abel couldn't tell the difference.

*   *   *

Some evenings, while Abel completed his homework, Ferryl experimented with the new sign, the mark within a shield. Eventually she concluded that Kelis had produced a new protection hex. Not a strong one, but Ferryl thought it might be similar to the signs on churches, the protection depended on how many believed in it working. Alternatively, the Tavern signs were more like the hexes on cars and cookers, in which case the protection depended on the amount of magic put into them. As an experiment, Ferryl asked Abel to draw a Tavern sign, while pushing magic through the pencil. Despite his less than perfect artwork, the result glowed afterwards.

Kelis caught Abel alone to tell him she had put signs on all the doors and windows at home, but they were rubbed off by the cleaner. Abel still had the same trouble at school, where the cleaners periodically removed the original hexes Ferryl taught him to draw. Noticing when one had been removed became a lot easier now Abel could see the faint reddish glow, the same one he'd seen on the bus stop curse, from the active protection.

At school Kelis warded the female toilets, using Tavern signs, but had to shepherd all the creatures out first. They tried to avoid her so she'd used herself to force them out of the window after warding the door, and then sealed it. Ferryl still wasn't sure how effective that would be, but creatures were deterred so Kelis's and Abel's belief seemed to be enough as yet. Either that or Kelis had enough intent to properly infuse her hexes with magic. Finding out would have been easier if Ferryl had agreed to teach Kelis more about magic, but she refused until the new trainee had control. Abel drew wax hexes on as many outside walls as possible, to help the interior ones.

According to Ferryl, Abel and then Kelis had to learn to put the glyph beneath the surface where it didn't show. Abel had done so several times now but with Ferryl in charge of his hand. His only solo attempt, on a small tree in Castle House gardens, left a definite burn showing on the surface of the root. Ferryl had been right about one thing, drawing the glyphs and lines to connect the newer trees to Castle House's protection became easier when Abel could see them. He could also see the soft glow of bluish power in the stone slab over the pit, and brighter lines where his blood had cracked some glyphs.

At least Rob's room had protection now, because Kelis insisted on hanging the new Tavern sign on his door and in his window. She claimed that both Rob's and Abel's rooms counted as Taverns, where players met to start their game, so Abel hung up signs as well. He really wanted Kelis to see the result, a fine web of magic lines connecting the signs and enclosing the room. Despite Abel's improved eyesight not causing any problems, Ferryl still refused to touch Kelis's. As a result, Abel had to remember not to comment on what he could see in the evenings after dusk drew in. He couldn't see quite as well after dark, except on clear nights when moonlight worked as well as sunlight.

Seraph glared at Abel every time he passed her, but didn't try to order him about again. Abel could hear his name sometimes, and muttered insults from her group as he passed, but those were more or less normal for any passing geek. Henry worried him more, because Abel didn't expect much conversation or even warning so he took care to never be alone anyplace Henry might find him. On the plus side, more of the geeks, the computer and art students, began to experiment with the game Abel and his friends were creating. The unpaid beta testers took the new rules and characters home, adding them to the original version. Several had now tried playing the Tavern game as if they had bought it, and came back with suggestions for improving the flow.

School in general settled down, and although the creatures roamed the school grounds Abel and Kelis cleared more and more of the inside. The biggest failures were the staff rooms and the canteen, and especially the food. Now Abel knew the creatures left traces when they died, he felt sure the ones crawling in the food weren't hygienic.

Abel still felt the tingle on a regular basis, especially late evening when Kelis must practice after her homework. The muttered, "Tomorrow morning at ten, cave, Glyphmistress" as the three of them walked home on Friday, followed by a big smile, didn't come as a huge surprise.

*　*　*

Abel arrived a little early, but still later than Kelis. *"Perhaps I picked the wrong apprentice."* Abel opened his mouth to reply before he registered the humour in Ferryl's voice, though he couldn't really argue the point. As he came into the clearing Kelis sat in the cave with a leaf dancing above her outstretched palm. She'd certainly managed it a lot faster than he had.

Kelis looked up and as her concentration wavered the leaf fell off to one side. "Glyphmistress!"

"Definitely. How are you getting on with the dust?"

Kelis lost her smile. "Not as well because I can't take dust into my bedroom. I could, but the cleaner would probably complain because it would go everywhere."

"Ferryl brought me gravel for indoors." Abel laughed. "The first time I got it right three bits were embedded in the ceiling."

"Crikey! What did your mum say? Though she doesn't clean your room does she? I wish my room could be private." Kelis sighed. "The cleaner moved my pictures, and there were things crawling all over my room when she'd gone. I shooed the gross little critturs out and hung the signs back up, so I'm all right for another week."

"Ferryl cleaned up the gravel the first time. I'll warn you, this will make you feel a bit inadequate." Abel glanced at his jacket arm. "Will you collect up a lot of twigs if I scatter them, Ferryl, please?"

"A teacher's work is never done." Though from the ripple of amusement Ferryl enjoyed this part. Abel broke several small sticks into much smaller pieces and scattered them before she took over his hand and collected them back in a neat heap. *"Glyphmistress."* Once again he heard the distinct pride in her voice afterwards, while Kelis looked crestfallen.

Not for long, her smile soon came back. "I don't care. This is good enough to stump Rob. If I try to keep quiet any longer while he's arguing how magic should work, I'll burst." She made the usual extravagant gesture. "Tonight the Glyphmistress is revealed. I want my moment of glory before Ferryl squishes me. Sorry Ferryl."

"Not me, not yet. He may be frightened and reject magic or denounce you both as witches. I would be considered a devil, a familiar."

"Ferryl agrees she should stay a secret for now. She doesn't want to upset her star pupil."

Kelis giggled and promised to only show Rob the leaf. "You can juggle gravel the next time, then if you get it wrong Ferryl can clear up. Sorry, I meant if you would, please, Ferryl?"

"You two really are polite." A tendril of mist drifted out and this time Kelis had no hesitation in stretching out her hand. *"A pleasure. I like to encourage Abel to try harder."*

*   *   *

The Tavern met in Abel's room tonight, and Rob had barely arrived when Kelis burst in with, "Look Rob, I've got a new trick for the game." Kelis placed the leaf on her palm and put her other hand on her jacket sleeve, and moments later the leaf fluttered upwards. "It's a training exercise for an apprentice sorceress."

"Roll up your sleeve and do it again." Kelis took off her jacket and, after hesitating, rolled up her shirt sleeve. That showed faint marks where bruises had faded, but didn't uncover her mark. Abel still felt the tingle when she touched the cloth over it. Rob looked over, under, and even blew on the leaf, which sent it tumbling to the ground. Kelis replaced it on her palm, and up it fluttered. "I give in. How are you doing it?"

"I told you. Magic training."

Rob looked from one grinning face to the other so Abel put a leaf on his palm, careful to let it flutter a bit more than Kelis's. "That is very noble." Kelis grinned because she knew he'd done it on purpose, and her leaf jumped a bit more then flew off her hand.

Rob looked at them both, and went around and around it. "How?"

"You know how. We've been telling you, but you keep insisting magic doesn't work like that." Kelis's leaf fluttered up again. "Ta-da. Yes, it does."

"So the concentrating on those symbols makes a leaf float. Really?" He shook his head. "Throwing fire, shrinking, levitation, all those powers in the game?"

"Magic. This is wind, and I'm told there are more."

"If I can find my wits and remember them!"

Kelis wasn't connected so she didn't hear, still smiling proudly. "It's all down to practice and intent but you need a mark first, to protect you the same way the Tavern is protected." Rob looked at the picture hung on the door, and then the one on the window.

Abel tried very hard to stay serious when he wanted to howl with laughter. Rob still couldn't decide if this was a windup. "Those are real. You have to make up your own protection, a personal symbol, and draw it on your skin. It's called a ward."

"A tattoo is best." Kelis laughed at the mixture of shock and speculation in Rob's look. "No, mine is in permanent marker in case Mum or Dad see it." She paused a moment. "I'll show you if this sleeve will go up far enough." She struggled, but managed to get it pushed up far enough with her arm straight upwards.

"There's no shield."

"No roots either. Abel's has roots." Kelis giggled. "This tickled when he drew it, but not much. You'll love it, it's really amazing."

"Give the poor guy a minute, Kelis." Abel interrupted because Rob looked as if he needed oxygen or possibly a resuscitation unit, not just a minute. He'd sagged back in the chair, mouth open as if gasping for air, unable to speak. "Remember how you were? I mean how long you watched, not the dancing about later."

"The Glyphmistress victory dance. You'll have to learn the steps for when you are a Glyphmaster."

Rob looked beseechingly at Abel, who explained. "She means the first time the leaf moves, or you make a symbol work."

"Or some idiot tries to bind him." Nobody else heard Ferryl, and Abel ignored her.

"Glyphs, they are glyphs, not symbols. This rotten git cheated with that magical world because it's real. Though the creatures really are gross. Don't worry." Abel sat back and let Kelis rattle on. She explained the whole thing, sort of, before Rob managed to get a word in. Then she went through it all again, and a third time but much slower and actually answering questions.

"It's like the game, but I need a mark before I start?" Rob looked straight at Abel, probably trying to avoid a fourth repeat of the whole thing.

"A ward. Something you design." Abel wasn't binding anyone else!

"Can I see yours, please?"

Abel smiled and took off his jacket, because he knew Ferryl would have to sit still now. He usually kept her covered around Rob, so that she could move but also so he didn't notice the addition. Rob stared at the flower. "You got another tattoo? He glanced down to where Abel's mum would be watching TV. "Which makes you a lot braver than me."

"An addition that I'll swear has always been there. Mum tries to not look anyway, if she sees me with my arms bare." Abel glanced at Kelis. "Though you can use permanent marker as well."

"Not unless you or Kelis draws it. I think. Perhaps you just need to touch and activate it. An apprentice usually lives with the sorcerer or witch, so they are protected until they learn to apply a mark properly." Abel felt a slight twitch as Ferryl started to move then remembered not to. *"It really is best if Rob creates his own."*

Rob looked at the flower, then at Kelis's arm where the mark had now been covered up again. "I can put it someplace Mum or Dad will never see it."

"Someplace you can touch in public, without blushing. Believe me, you will want to touch it whenever you need to calm down." Kelis blushed, just a little bit. "Abel warned me, and anyway he drew mine so it had to be a safe spot. Though you'll be able to feel it through clothes, which I didn't know at the time."

"So who draws mine?" Rob smiled hopefully at Kelis. "You'll do a better job."

Abel saw the shock on her face so Kelis had remembered the binding part. "In your dreams, buster."

Abel didn't wait to be asked. "You have to draw it."

"Definitely, unless you wish to bind him." Ferryl sniggered. *"Kelis*

doesn't."

"Does it have to be something made up? Yours is the same as Abel's." Rob inspected the flower. "Without the roots."

Abel had his instructions from Ferryl. "Different, so make up your own."

"That one." Rob pointed to the Tavern protection shield. "If you designed it to protect the tavern, I'll bet it protects me."

"Kelis designed it, but it does protect the area from small creatures." Abel played for time because he felt sure Ferryl would object but needed a reason.

Though the answer from a thoughtful-sounding Ferryl surprised him. *"That might be a good idea. When he truly understands Rob can make his own, down to the bone, as can Kelis, though hers seems to be very firmly embedded. Take care not to bind him."*

Abel almost suggested Kelis activate it, but she might bind Rob by accident and probably wouldn't do it anyway. Rob must have been thinking, because he hooked his thumb in his belt, with his hand on the outside of his hip. "Just here."

Kelis jumped to her feet. "I feel a sudden urge to spend what, ten minutes? Yes, ten minutes in the toilet. Just until you've got your jeans back on." She left the room with a giggle and "I hope your mum doesn't come in."

"You've got to actually draw it. Firm lines, with clear intent to protect yourself. I hope I can actually activate it, because I'm not really expert."

"I will instruct you, so there is no binding." Abel suppressed his sigh of relief.

*   *   *

Ten minutes later Kelis knocked gently. "Can an innocent maid enter without getting an eyeful?"

"No eyeful, idiot, because much to my relief Rob doesn't go commando. Not that it matters because he just turned down the top of the waistband on his jeans." Abel tapped his waist, at the side. "It's there."

Kelis eyed Rob. "Did yours burn as well?"

"Yes, just when his finger touched it for a second, but Abel said yours didn't."

"It did, but I don't think I said anything because I was more interested in the magic." Kelis turned to Abel. "Well, sensei? Why does it burn right at the beginning?"

Ferryl knew who Kelis had asked. *"It will be the connection to their magic. To the flesh, not to the bone. It certainly confirms that the glyph works, and the Tavern mark should be stronger connected directly to Rob."* Abel explained, and the rest of the evening passed in discussing magic and instructing Rob in leaf floating. Rob also promised to make a glyph pebble so he could come into the garden, once Kelis redrew the shape from hers.

Ten minutes after Rob left to go home, a text arrived from his phone. "Gross!" He must have started seeing creatures. At least the game had warned him which ones might be dangerous, and they'd avoid his ward.

At the Tuesday meeting in Rob's room, his dad called up to tell them to keep the noise down. That happened after Ferryl Shayde had been introduced and just completed introducing the mercenary game character, Robyn D'Ritche, complete with the tankard and scruffy horse. At least the rest of the explanation became much simpler with Ferryl sending out her little mist tendrils so she could answer either Rob or Kelis directly. Abel showed how he could float gravel, Kelis showed how to scatter it while trying, and Ferryl showed how a true Glyphmistress could collect it again.

With both Abel's friends in on the secret, the Taverners made a big decision. Some people out there might be magically aware but not realise. They would be vulnerable to the likes of Seraphim. After some serious discussion with Ferryl, one real glyph went into The Tavern game instructions, the wind glyph. Instead of drawing on a hand with a finger, the players were to try and float a leaf by imagining the glyph.

"Can that be done, Ferryl?" Rob looked at his hand, but the leaf stayed still. Kelis tried and hers moved slightly.

"Only if they are already active, if they have already discovered how to push magic, as Abel calls it. Telling them to make the leaf float, hover, should stop any accidents. Nobody will blow off a roof while concentrating

on a leaf and using pure imagination. Not hovering gravel, because that could be dangerous."

Abel explained about gravel stuck into his ceiling, and tried moving a leaf just thinking about it. The leaf moved up, but fluttered to the side. "Do we still need to draw an invisible glyph with a finger?"

"Yes. You will need very good control to control the strength and intent without drawing the shape first."

"If we put in a moment of meditation before starting the game, some people won't bother." Abel chuckled. "The rest probably won't move the leaf, but if one can we need to talk to them."

"I can give you a contact email, I've got three spare inboxes that came with the domain Mum and Dad bought me for my birthday." Rob sniggered. "We can tell them to email Ferryl Shayde."

Kelis started scribbling, adding to her notes. "Just in case, they contact?" She looked at Rob and he gave her the address. He logged on immediately and started setting it up while Kelis continued. "Any player who moves a leaf must email Ferryl Shayde at Dragon Toast." They all laughed about that because as far as the game and betas were concerned, Ferryl Shayde was a generic game character. Ferryl herself found the idea of having her own contact address fascinating.

Within the week Rob had found places to put Tavern marks here and there in his home to drive most of the creatures out. Ferryl thought they would need renewing as he gained better control of magic, but there would be plenty of intent behind them. Rob had a lot of leaf-floating intent, but Abel wasn't sure how often Rob practiced because he couldn't feel any different tingles. He felt a lot happier now that both his friends were in on the secret, because Abel knew he'd need all the help he could get to ward the village.

He even managed to persuade Ferryl that Kelis needed bat-vision. Abel insisted at least partly because of how disgusted Kelis seemed around the creatures. Now he could see their magic glowing like a dim amber light inside them, most didn't seem quite as gross to Abel. With her experience fixing Abel, including another minor adaptation he'd never even known about, Ferryl had perfected the procedure. Abel spent half that evening answering texts from Kelis as she watched glowing creatures fly and scuttle past her window. They still weren't exactly pretty, but some of the browns became almost orange.

Despite or maybe due to their muddy green glow, Kelis still considered the slimy types utterly gross and wanted to learn how to squish them as soon as possible.

Unwelcome Attention

The following Saturday brought a completely unexpected visitor. A man in a black suit stood by the gate into Castle House garden, not quite touching the remaining fence and inspecting the broken section. As he turned, Abel stopped, because the little white collar meant a vicar had come to investigate. Ferryl had worried about that, and a formless yelp in his head told Abel she wasn't happy.

"You are going to enter the garden?" The vicar inspected Abel before continuing. "Yes, you fit the description. I could enter, but that might disturb something unpleasant."

"It would! Don't let him!"

Abel passed the message. "I'm told that would be a bad idea."

"As bad as that was?" The churchman gestured towards the patch of bare earth and the gravel-filled holes in the road. "A dead tree, so a Bound Shade I would think. What activated it?" He frowned, inspecting Abel again. "More to the point what stopped it because, no offence intended, you do not seem to be capable."

"Tell him worse than that."

"I'm told what you would wake up is worse than a Bound Shade." Abel decided there wasn't any point beating around the bush if this bloke knew about Bound Shades and the barrier. "I had a pebble, a glyph for the barrier, and that woke up the tree. A stone guardian, a big one, stopped it. Luckily, I had a pebble glyph for the guardian."

At that the vicar straightened, suddenly more intent. "Luck or planning?"

"Planning. I had very precise instructions, from the same person who warned me about what you will wake up." Abel wanted to ask Ferryl some questions about that, as soon as he had a chance.

Now the man looked curious, and just a little bit wary. "May I test, to see if you have been bound? If something is using you to gain access to that house, I must interfere regardless of what I rouse."

Abel braced himself for whatever came next. "Yes, if you agree to leave me exactly as I am now, and answer some questions afterwards."

"Careful. I do not have to ask. Though since you have been courteous so far, I will agree." The vicar pulled out a cross, and made some tiny hand gestures. The crucifix glowed gently, white or a very faint blue, and several small tendrils drifted out towards Abel. Abel felt a gentle wave of warmth, turning to icy cold as the feeling reached his ward before retreating. "You have a shy passenger, and a ward strong enough to hide it. Take care what you allow inside your defences."

"My passenger has sworn by her true-name not to harm me, and to protect me. She needed a safe place." Abel looked the vicar straight in the eye. "She has been a great help. More help than the church."

"Perhaps it is lucky I asked before presuming. Your appearance is deceptive. Be very, very careful before entering that house because our records show that a great evil lived there in the past. If it persists and you release it, we may have to return."

"Fair enough, but can we cut out some of the mystery please? Why isn't the church looking after this place?" Abel pointed to a couple of fliers in the trees. "The village is overrun by creatures."

"Your church closed because the believers dropped below the number needed to keep the ward, the cross, working effectively. At the same time, the reduction in their tithes meant the church could not support a vicar. That should mean there are enough unbelievers to support a witch and a local sorcerer usually deals with larger problems." He cocked his head, suddenly very curious. "You understand the pact betwixt believer and unbeliever, magic and faith?"

"No. I've never heard of it."

"Education today is going to the dogs. Worse, the magic users are not instructing new practitioners." The churchman pursed his lips, thinking for a moment. "The church fights what you would perhaps think of as God wars, against other faiths. In return for their faith, prayers and tithes our believers are warded against magic, although we don't tell them that. Magical creatures usually avoid the faithful, though such creatures can still cause physical harm if they overcome their fear. The church announced there was no magic, nor witches or sorcerers, and in return the magic wielders agreed to guard the unbelievers and stop the worst infestations." His eyes drifted past Abel to Brinsford. "The fields near here are definitely infested. You have warded these homes?"

"Some, and I'm trying to protect the village and school. There's no protection there either."

"Stourton Comprehensive? State schools will not pay tithes or insist on prayers, so they are not protected. The lack of magical infestations is why Church Schools tend to do better academically. Coincidentally that means the faithful are better equipped to do well in their chosen career." The little smile looked just a bit smug, while Abel knew he looked horrified.

"What about the faithful who go to the comprehensive? The food in the canteen is crawling with the things and students can't get near it to draw a ward." Abel frowned because he wasn't sure about the next bit. "It can't be hygienic."

The vicar frowned and considered that for a moment. "I will make that point, but doubt it will have any effect. I will also report that this area has a warlock at least, unless you are the sorcerer and this is the witch?" His eyes narrowed. "Perhaps a bound apprentice?" Abel turned to where the vicar's eyes were looking, to see Kelis approaching.

"Hi Abel. Is there a problem?"

"I don't think so." Turning back, Abel smiled at the man. "Kelis is definitely in charge of herself, and more likely to be the sorceress. She draws a mean glyph and learns faster than me."

"Don't learn too fast because if you turn loose something you can't control, we will stop it. Your village will be badly damaged at the very least."

"Can you stop the riddles please? Who is we?" Abel paused as he saw the slight frown. This vicar wasn't used to that sort of tone. "Sorry, but we need to know what's happening."

"You, along with this young woman, are filling in a gap in the magical protection of England. That is a relief because there are too many gaps these days, especially outside the cities." He bowed very slightly. "I represent the arm of mother church that deals with creatures such as

Bound Shades if they are not stopped by the local practitioners. Such creatures are not deterred by a cross."

"So if we get something we can't handle, we call on you?" Abel could hear the relief in Kelis's voice.

"Only in an extreme emergency because we are a very blunt instrument. There will be considerable collateral." The churchman glanced at Castle House. "I came when a strange report mentioned this house, just in case it had been breached." He seemed to be considering something. "Since this house is involved I will leave a card. Think very carefully before using it. Now, since this village does not need my attention I really must go. You should repair that fence to reinforce the barrier, to increase any reluctance to trespass."

"Neither of us can afford it." Abel shrugged. "And neither of us is very good with a hammer and nails."

The vicar brought out a wallet, and extracted several banknotes. "This should cover it. Mother church's contribution to the safety of the local faithful." He smiled. "I am sure your very shy passenger will know how to let the workmen enter to carry out the work."

Ferryl didn't make a sound while Abel accepted the money and a business card. "Thank you, Mr. or Reverend?"

"Vicar covers it. Thank you and goodbye, Abel and Kelis." He turned, walked to a car nearby, and drove off.

"I had about a thousand questions left." Kelis nudged Abel. "How much did he cough up? Is it enough for Rob's tattoo?"

"What? Rob wants a tattoo?" Completely thrown, Abel looked from the notes to the fence. "What about the fence?"

"We'll get cheap workmen. You can pay for that library book as well. Come on," Kelis tugged Abel's arm, "I want to know everything his holiness Mysterio Creepio said. He sounded like God's SAS, or MI5."

As Abel followed Kelis into the garden a very quiet voice asked,"*Has he gone yet?*" Once settled in the cave, on the milk crates they'd brought for seats, Ferryl explained that the church frightened her. The cross put out something that repelled her, though hiding behind Abel's flower had stopped it, and the search spell. The three of them discussed the visit but it seemed that they were on their own again. None of them fancied calling in what the business card called a Peripatetic Archbishop, not if it could be avoided.

Abel finally remembered to ask, and Ferryl didn't know what would respond if the church entered the grounds. Whatever roused would be much more violent and powerful than the guardian or Bound Shade. Ferryl had been badly hurt by the backlash when the sorcerer contained it, because he'd used her as a buffer. Whatever it was hated the church, a deep hatred, and she didn't think it would care who else it hurt.

*   *   *

The mystery churchman must have spoken to someone because on Monday morning a cross hung from the wall of the canteen, behind the counter over the food, and nothing magical went near. As the geeks had their lunches, Rob passed round the new details of the Tavern game for the betas to try out. They included the meditation before a game with exercises for making a leaf float, and instructions on how to contact their sorcerer.

Though that puzzled Una, a beta who lived in town. "Where does this email go?"

"Ferryl Shayde, so don't send spam." Rob grinned while everyone else laughed at Una. Anyone knowing Rob's email would recognise the domain, and assume he'd answer. Una shook her head in disgust and dropped the subject.

"Players might want someone to contact, to ask questions. We should have permanent bar staff at the Tavern." Warren, one of the betas, smiled. "All Taverns have a barmaid."

"She wouldn't give out her email. If any of the staff do, I want a barman." Una paused. "There aren't actually drinks but we do need a help menu. When it goes out in the computer version the bar staff could answer queries."

"Medieval, or sort of, so a barmaid and a bouncer as beefcake for Una?" Warren looked hopefully at Rob, who tended to be the hardest to convince.

"Probably, because it makes sense. We'll try and work it in." The rest of the betas seemed to like the idea. There were eleven of them now, five in town and six in various villages.

Warren wasn't done. "The five of us in town want to get together and play, rather than use phones and emails or Skype. My parents have half agreed to let us use the front room if we keep the noise down. We probably won't want to come in costume, not yet."

"You've got costumes?" Abel stared as three of the betas looked a bit shamefaced.

Una didn't, she grinned. "Robyn D'Ritche, at your service. Throats cut, tenants terrified, small easy wars fought cheaply, males in distress rescued." Her grin faded a little. "We'll need a Tavern sign of our own. Do we just draw one, or we could print one off if you send it in an email?"

"The Tavern sign has to come from the original Tavern, though of course yours will be free." Kelis smirked. "Then when the game is sold, we get a little earner every time someone sets up an actual Tavern." Abel wanted to applaud, because it also meant the Taverns would be really protected from magical creatures.

"Neat. How near are you to selling it?" Petra, one of the betas living in a village, inspected the sketch of the sign. "You'll want something more than The Tavern. There must be thousands of places called that."

Justin, another one from town, smirked. "Rachel, my sister, will want to call it after the barmaid. That will also attract more girls to play."

"She'll be Robyn's half-sister which is why a mercenary would support the place instead of robbing it." Una laughed at the looks from the rest. "Well I would, rob the Tavern I mean if it wasn't for my half-sister."

"I hope Santa doesn't bring you a real sword." Petra cowered away, then grinned, "If he does, I'm volunteering as barmaid to keep safe."

"That's agreed then?" Rob waited for everyone to nod and wrote it down.

"I've got another puzzle for you all." Kelis winked at Abel. "May as well make them work for their money." Everyone laughed since nobody had been paid. "A Tavern should protect their village. To do that they must ask their local dryads to supply magic from their trees." She passed a sheet of paper to each beta. "In return you must persuade the dryads you can keep their young safe. This paper shows you all the problems, because we wouldn't want it to be too easy."

The buzzer went for lessons, and Rob collected up his notes and drawings. Abel had one last word for them all. "Good thinking on the barmaid and Tavern name. Everyone come up with a default name for the barmaid and we'll choose the best at the end of the week."

Various names came in over the next few days, though none had many supporters. Midweek, as the seraphims pushed past him, Abel felt one stuff something in his pocket. He looked, very carefully, but could only see a piece of paper. When he unfolded it, instead of an insult it read "Bonny the Barmaid" with a roughly drawn Tavern sign!

The seraphims sneered at anything the geeks did. Since there'd been no rude comments about the Tavern the betas assumed the seraphims didn't know about the game. Now one of them had suggested a character. Neither Kelis nor Rob could figure out which of the seraphims knew about the game, but the name seemed to stick. Rob tried for Blousy after Kelis drew her, but Bonny she became as the betas voted during the rest of the week, and definitely the half-sister of Robyn the mercenary. Kelis even made them look a bit alike.

* * *

By then the original Tavern, in Brinsford, had another problem. Abel looked up from his homework as a distinct bell-like noise echoed in the night. Moments later Ferryl flew in through the window and poured into the tattoo. *"Quickly, the trap. We killed or damaged something big."*

Abel dashed downstairs as quietly as possible, hoping the TV masked the noise, and ran up the garden. He could see where the trap had been sprung because several fruit bushes had broken branches, but he couldn't see a creature. "Where is it?" The sound of Mrs. Tabitha, sat on a fence post spitting and hissing out into the darkness, answered him. "It got away."

His right hand moved on its own, pointing to spatters of rapidly disappearing magic glowing on the bushes and fence. *"It has left a trail. Quickly, after it."*

Half-way over the fence Abel thought to ask "What is it? Is this a good idea?"

"No time to test the residue. Maybe our mystery watcher, or a really strong test. The trap hurt it so not too tough. Better yet, it is injured and leaving a trail, but we must follow before the leakage evaporates."

With his bat-vision Abel could see well enough in the dark to avoid stumbling. By the time he reached the other side of the field and scrambled through the hedge, Abel felt pleased he'd built up his stamina. Though now he wished he'd picked up something warm to wear while on the way out of the house. The running wasn't quite keeping him warm enough, and his hands were definitely getting numb. "If we keep going my hands will be too cold to form a glyph."

"Create a small flame glyph, very small. It will warm your hands. I told you the practice while moving would be useful." Ferryl sounded excited, caught up in the chase, and a fierce exhilaration filled the next words. *"It is close, and weakening. We have it!"*

Sure enough the trail looked thicker, clearer, and Abel finally saw a stumbling centaur-like shape ahead, four-legged with an upright front half. He pushed himself hard and a pale, desperate face glanced back as the creature heard his pounding feet. A mistake, the creature stumbled and fell, rolling back to its feet but instead of running it turned. Four long thin arms unfolded to each side and Abel stopped. "A spider?"

"No, but similar in shape at first glance. Try to break its arms, but be careful. The fangs are not poisonous, but it eats carrion and will infect you."

"Its arms? Why don't I just kill it?" Abel formed a tight wind glyph and knocked one of the creature's legs away so it stumbled. As the creature rose he could see one of the other legs bent sideways. It wasn't supporting any weight, which explained why the creature stopped running.

"May I have your hand, please, to find out what it is? We have finally cornered a servant because these creatures should hide in dark places. Something drove it to invade Brinsford." Ferryl had lost that excited edge now, and sounded cold and calculating. *"If you break its arms we can capture it and make sure it gives up its secrets."*

"No binding."

"Agreed. I do not understand some of the magic involved here, so you do not want it inside you." A little bit of impatience crept in. *"If I could have the hand, please? You could break another leg with the other hand to*

make sure it stays?"

Abel used his left hand to knock the creature over again with a wind glyph, because breaking a leg seemed too much like torture. As he did, his right hand moved and he saw a glyph reach out. Not fly, the glyph left a trail very like the mist link Ferryl used to talk to Rob and Kelis, and attached itself to the creature's pale chest. Abel could now see the upper torso looked close to human, but with the details smoothed out as if wrapped in thick bandages. The long, multi-jointed arms, fanged mouth and four eyes in a row across its forehead weren't even close to human.

"Kill it, now!"

Ferryl's voice seemed strained so Abel didn't ask why, just lashed out with a fire glyph without worrying about control. A flare of flame swathed the creature and it collapsed, the long upper limbs thrashing briefly until they stilled. As the fire died the remains smoked and bubbled, rapidly disappearing. The smoky link had gone. "What happened?"

"A trap. I should have expected it in one of Aryadne's hounds. She tended to spin more than one web. It is too long since I saw them and this one should not exist." Ferryl seemed to be talking to herself now. *"The wrong place and the wrong creature. The last were supposed to have died in Greece, and it had strange magic infusing it."*

"Can I have that in English please, Ferryl, and perhaps go home? I'm freezing." Abel turned to look back, surprised at how far he'd come. "Wonderful, I've run halfway to Stourton."

"The town is the other way because the hound headed towards the hills. It will have been living in a cave." Ferryl sighed and grass rustled. *"I will explain as you walk home. You did well to run it down."*

Abel thought the deep gouges where the fruit bush trap had torn at it probably helped. Still, he had run a hell of a way, maybe a couple of miles cross-country though as he trudged back it seemed more like ten. As Abel plodded along Ferryl explained that Aryadne the spider-woman goddess in Greece had trapped and enchanted men as guards and hunters, her hounds. Aryadne had faded, long ago, and all her hounds were supposed to have died as well. Someone had kept one alive, not an easy task, or preserved a body and raised it which should be impossible as magical bodies dissolved with death.

"*Whatever or whoever sent it is testing both the barriers and you. If you or I had been alone and tried to investigate as I did, we would have been snared and possibly died. I'm not sure what the snare would have done, but I couldn't break it.*" Ferryl stayed silent for a little while. "*Our opponent does not know about me, because if I had my wits I would have broken that easily and followed the magic back. You are the target. Someone wonders who you are, how strong or experienced.*" The next pause went on for longer. "*You cannot control proper protection yet.*"

"So I just keep hoping the thing doesn't get me?"

"*Better than just hope. There are three of you now, and I am your hidden surprise. I promised to protect you.*" Though Ferryl wasn't relying on that. "*Trying to get free has reminded me of another glyph, a very minor one. It may help.*" On the way back Abel practiced the new glyph, one to make it harder for another spell to attach itself. It wouldn't stop such attacks entirely, but made him slippery to magic as near as Abel could understand.

Abel had to knock on the door to get back in because he'd forgotten the spring catch on the door and it had locked behind him. At least his mum had no idea how long he'd been out there, but didn't seem convinced by Abel's claim that he'd seen the fox again. Abel spent time practicing really controlled fire glyphs to help warm up his feet and hands and then tried to get back to French homework. Ferryl could have done it, but he wanted to actually learn some of the language even if it wasn't his main option.

The following day Abel told Kelis and Rob, and both promised to call for help before chasing anything. Kelis pushed again for some sort of offensive glyph, and this time Ferryl promised to start training at the weekend.

*   *   *

As much as Kelis wanted and needed protection in her garden, Abel couldn't take Ferryl in there to bind the bushes together. Kelis's parents seemed a bit paranoid and there were security lights fixed in among the trees and bushes which would react to anybody trespassing. Kelis had taken to walking around along the edges to get her parents used to the lights coming on, but she found security cameras so she couldn't even pin up signs. Inside the house she'd hidden drawings of the Tavern shield in the kitchen and pantry, laminated so they didn't get damp, and drawn one on the underside of the dining table.

Meanwhile the betas worked on the game and another new character. Champ, a retired bareknuckle fighter, became the Tavern bouncer. Answers came in for the other question, with some suggesting marking trees with the Tavern symbol to protect a village, without asking. Could a dryad prevent it, and would the symbol use tree magic to become more powerful? With a little smile, Abel promised a reply on Monday because he'd have to ask a tree. Everyone laughed of course. On the way home Kelis offered to try it on a tree at home, but Abel told her to be patient. She still wasn't totally convinced that dryads existed, because none of the ones in her garden would respond when she spoke.

All three of them were busy for the rest of the week, because the school cleaners went on a purge and removed at least half the protection along with a lot of other graffiti. That meant lurking in corridors and near entrances until there weren't many people about, not easy without skipping a lesson and then they'd be conspicuous. The three of them decided to keep trying during breaks and not risk being caught skiving. The school forbade eating anywhere but in the canteen, or the three of them might have missed a rare challenge to Seraph's authority.

"Get your hands off!" The entire canteen turned to see Jenny jump to her feet and glare at Henry, sat next to her. "I've told you, I don't want a boyfriend, and definitely not you. Hold Claris's hand, she might even like it." Claris, a bubbly redhead, shrugged and smiled so apparently she might.

Henry flushed as he saw everyone watching. "But Seraph said you liked me."

"I said you were cute in a sort of pet bull way. That is not wanting to hold hands."

"Jennifer Tremain, you should sit next to Henry and be sociable. As an Acro dancer it would be right to have one of the rugby team as a boyfriend." Seraph smiled. "Now the two of you should smile, hold hands and make up."

Jenny stood for long moments and Abel could see her hesitating. Jenny couldn't have much awareness of magic if any, or that tone would have made her sit straight down. The whole canteen had quietened, watching, until Rob suddenly spoke up. "I can't understand you telling Jenny to sit. Henry yes, because he really is a bad dog and needs housetraining at least. Hey, Jenny, I know it's a really bad choice but you could sit here if you like and you don't even have to look at me." The canteen dissolved in laughter and the moment had been broken.

"Thank you Rob, but I'll just sit at the next table. They won't insist I take up IT as an option and play weird board games." Though Jenny smiled, so she meant it as a joke. Someone pointed to an empty chair and she sat down at the next table. Seraph and Henry, and most of those at their table, glared at a completely unfazed Rob. After a few moments, everyone else in the canteen returned to eating or their own little conversations.

"I knew it. Another sucker has fallen to a leotard, a big smile and a well-practiced athletics routine." Kelis's grin widened as Rob slowly blushed scarlet.

"I have not, didn't. I just wanted to wind Henry up and that Seraph is a pig. Anyway, I've spoken to Jenny's sister a couple of times and she seems all right so Jenny probably is." He grinned. "She's not too stuck-up to talk to me."

"Diane? Cradle-robber, she's only fourteen." Kelis glanced at a group across the canteen, at the infant in question.

"I said I talked to her. She asked what we were all looking at, who the pictures are so I told her about the game. She wants to try it if we want more betas." Rob shrugged. "I said I'd keep her in mind."

"But then her sister would know the details, and tell that Seraph about it and the whole lot of them would start taking the mickey." Abel held up his hands as everyone looked at him in incredulity or humour. "All right, they already do. We'll see."

"We could do with some betas who aren't geeks." Rob left it at that.

Seraph didn't wait. She stood by the canteen door until Rob, Kelis and Abel left. "Robert Tyler, you should be ashamed of yourself, embarrassing Jenny like that." She frowned a little and lowered her hand before rubbing it with the other one.

Rob knew all about the binding thing now, and the truth of Abel's arguments with Henry. "Seraphim, or is it Cherrybum? I always get them mixed up. You shouldn't talk to people like that. Henry, yes. People, no." Henry pushed forward, as expected, and Rob held up his hand and waggled a finger. "One brick, Henry?" Behind him Abel and Kelis recognised a cue, and raised their hands to waggle a finger.

Henry hesitated, obviously trying to figure out if all three could have learned whatever Abel did, and then a voice cut in. "Perhaps if you cleared the doorway, any students who actually wanted to go to lessons could get through?" Mr Beresford, the PE instructor, didn't look even slightly amused.

Rob smiled happily. "Come along children, our work is done." He headed off down the corridor with Abel and Kelis pressing in on each side.

As soon as he thought they were out of hearing, Abel whispered, "What are you doing, idiot, trying to get thumped?"

"I found it very funny."

Rob didn't hear Ferryl, luckily because he certainly didn't need encouragement. Though his face had now lost the smile, almost. "Do you know how many years I've been putting up with Henry or his brother pushing me into puddles or hedges, making me squeak, or stuffing frogspawn down my back? It's so long I can't remember him not doing it. Well, you saw how he just backed off from one wiggly finger." His smile grew again. "Better yet, Seraph looked as if she'd been sucking frogspawn."

"You do remember Abel ended up with a broken hand, Rob?" Kelis thumped him gently, "You put years on me just then even if yes, Henry backing away from waggling fingers has made my day."

"Just don't walk down empty corridors on your own, Rob. You have to get control before you can learn," Abel grinned, "wiggly finger-fighting."

"So I can learn?" Kelis forgot all about tweaking Rob. "I've already got control."

"It might be a good idea after that. I cannot protect all three. Not unless I break Henry's legs first?"

Abel had opened his mouth to put Rob off, but put like that? "Ferryl says yes, but you've got to promise not to burn off his arm or throw him down the road."

Rob stared. "Bl.. curses, I really must work on that control thing. Throw Henry down the road?"

The other side of him Kelis now wore a wicked smile. "I can be controlled as long I get to inflict excruciating pain."

*   *   *

Some of Rob's euphoria wore off by the time school finished. More disappeared when Tyson stopped his car to let Henry talk through the open window. "I'm watching you three from now on. There's something weird about all of you, and I'm going to find out what. Then I'm gonna feed him a brick." He pointed at Rob, wound up the window and Tyson drove off.

"I could burn a wheel."

"No." That would leave Henry and Tyson on foot between them and the village, and could end up with Ferryl finally getting her excuse.

"What?"

Rather than mention Ferryl's reaction, and give Kelis ideas, Abel stuck to Henry's comment. "No, Henry can't feed anyone a brick. Well he can, but only if he catches one of you outside the village on your own."

"Or at night. You should escort Kelis and Rob home after Tavern meetings until they can defend themselves." When Abel passed that on he had to suffer Rob accusing him of wanting to walk Kelis home to kiss her goodnight, and Kelis insisting it was Rob that Abel had designs on. In spite of the humour, both of them seemed relieved. Rob even admitted that perhaps he'd gone over the top, but still enjoyed it.

*   *   *

Sunday morning Abel found out just how much trouble Henry could be. A stretch of hedge he'd spent long hours magically weaving into a barrier had been damaged by creatures. Only grazers so not a probe according to Ferryl. Even so the sheep-sized, multi-legged egg shapes had blundered into the glyphs and wrecked them. Abel had barely started repairs when a familiar voice called out. "Oy, squeak, sod off."

Abel stood up and carefully erased the few lines he'd drawn in the dirt. Despite Ferryl's assurances, years of being thumped meant Abel felt nervous as Henry made his way across the field. "Just walking in the countryside. It's a free country."

"Not here it isn't. You are trespassing because this is Dad's land." The youth hesitated, staying well back and his hand moved to stroke the other one where Abel had burned him. "I saw someone out here the other day, but didn't recognise you. I'll know in future, and I'll let Tyson know. Now sod off, and stay away." Despite Ferryl frantically pleading to be allowed to singe just a couple of Henry's fingers, Abel left without a word. The land belonged to the Copples so nothing he said or did would make any difference. Ferryl's anger came from frustration as much as anything, because without any repairs the traps and barriers would quickly break down.

Abel cheered up a bit after dinner, because this would be fun. He'd arranged to meet Kelis at her gate, but refused to say why. "Would you like to talk to a tree?"

"I've got trees here, and believe me they aren't conversationalists." Her eyes narrowed suspiciously, then opened wide in delight. "A dryad? Where? Now?"

On the way to the village green Abel suffered the torrent of questions and complaints that trees never talked to her. He tried to smile enigmatically, refusing to say more than "patience, grasshopper" which just made Kelis worse. They sat down on the plastic sheet he'd brought, because it had been raining, and Abel produced his secret weapon.

Torn between a scowl and excitement about the dryad, Kelis restricted herself to punching Abel's arm, being careful to miss Ferryl. "Honey! I should have known. You didn't find that pot last time, did you?"

Answering while laughing might not be diplomatic, but Abel couldn't help himself. "Hush. When meeting dryads be polite and respectful, and bring honey. Ferryl, do you need me to take off my jacket so you can talk to the dryad or Kelis?"

"No Abel. I can look through your eyes." The tendril of mist that

connected to Kelis came through Abel's jacket sleeve.

Facing the tree, Abel wiped the smile from his face. "In that case, let's get started. Greetings, Dryad Horse Chestnut. This is Kelis, and Ferryl is here of course. I would like to trade honey for answers."

Two brown eyes opened and Kelis gasped. "About time. I have almost forgotten the taste. Why do you call me after my tree?"

"I don't know any other name, and using names is polite. That is a free answer." Abel heard a little giggle from Kelis. "Would you create the veil, please? I will pay with one spoonful."

"Still polite. Very well, one large spoonful. Please. Abel." The chill swept over Abel so he knew the veil had been put in place, and told Kelis. As the shoot grew out to empty the spoon, bringing another gasp from Kelis, the dryad continued. "We rarely speak, so have little use for names. I will not give you mine, because a sorcerer might be able to use it. Chestnut will suffice for good manners. The spoon is empty."

"Kelis would like to ask a question."

"Hello Chestnut. Why won't the trees in my garden talk to me? Oh, er, bother, that wasn't the question." Kelis glanced at Abel and shrugged slightly.

"It was a question. You have not approached them politely, and spoken to them with enough respect. More important, you did not offer them honey. They will be unhappy because you have driven iron into them, and cut away limbs." The brown eyes switched back to Abel. "One answer."

Abel proffered the honey then blurted out "How? How do you know about cut limbs and iron, when you tell me dryads don't talk to each other?"

"Sometimes my branches brush against the nearest tree, or my kin come out to talk in the quiet times. We all hear whispers, hints and rumours from the creatures that pass through and around us. There are six of us close together here so we can gradually piece together what is happening. A large answer." The last bit sounded decidedly smug, though suddenly the dryad's voice had more edge in it. "I still don't really trust you, because you damaged a tree and will not heal it."

"What tree?" Abel sighed and once the spoon had been emptied he scooped a small amount of honey. "A small question."

"The one in your garden. It is a young tree, which you claim you will protect, in which case you should start with that one."

Abel had fixed bushes, but Ferryl claimed the trees in Castle House gardens couldn't be straightened. "This is not a question for you. Ferryl, can we do that?"

"The tree is small enough to grow straight if held. Unfortunately there is nothing nearby that we can tap, even in the summer when the flowers grow."

"There is wood." An odd creaking might have been humour from the tone of the next part. "It must be catching, I am speaking without thought."

Abel waved the spoon. "If you say which wood, that is definitely worth honey."

The dryad's eyes followed the spoon. "Cut wood driven into the ground. Use magic stored in there."

"The fence? Not a question." Abel turned and saw Kelis staring at him.

"So does that mean...?" Kelis turned to the tree. "Not a question for you, Dryad Chestnut." She turned back. "There's magic in fence posts? Did you know that, Ferryl?

"No, though some sorcerers used wood for magical constructs so maybe they did know. The knowledge may be.... elsewhere." Abel remembered that Ferryl didn't want the dryad knowing she had lost her wits. *"Any magic in dead wood must be buried deep, or I would sense it."*

"For just a little honey I can tell you." Kelis and Abel looked at the pot, now half empty.

"We should ask the main question first. The one we actually came for, if any of us remembers." Both Kelis and Abel winced at the sarcasm.

"Sorry." Abel gestured towards the tree. "Kelis?"

She chuckled. "You still trust me to ask? All right then." Kelis took a deep breath. "Dryad Chestnut, if a sorcerer put a glyph on a tree without consulting the dryad, what would happen? I would like to know what the dryad would think of that, what the dryad would do about it, and if the glyph would work."

"Please note none of us have tried this without asking you first." Abel had seen the brown eyes narrowing as Kelis spoke. Now they relaxed again.

"Still polite. A very big answer?" Abel heaped the spoon. "The dryad would be angry. First it would try to drop a branch on the sorcerer before the glyph could be completed. Then the tree would be encouraged to reject the glyph. Removal could be difficult." Branches rustled and a few leaves drifted down. "That might mean growing a short branch beneath the glyph to push it off the trunk, then allowing the limb to die and fall off. Depending on how strong the sorcerer were, and how deep the glyph had been anchored, this could take years. During that time the glyph would work, and take magic from the tree." The brown eyes narrowed. "The sorcerer would not be safe walking under a local tree, ever."

"Annoying many dryads is not a good idea."

Abel sat thinking about it while the dryad slurped honey. He might have risked annoying one dryad to fill a gap in the boundary, but now he knew dryads corresponded or at least gathered news about the area. "Question for Ferryl and Kelis only. Do we have our answer? Shall we ask about fences?"

"Yes and yes, but I've got another one, about transferring baby dryads in potted trees." Kelis pointed to the two small trees in pots outside one of the houses near the Green. "I sat looking at those, and wondered."

"To keep them safe in transit? I wonder about a protection glyph on a young tree helping to protect the young dryad as they both grow."

"Magic in cut wood could be useful elsewhere."

"There is enough honey for answers." Dryad Chestnut had run out of patience.

"Magic in cut wood, transport of young, protecting young and tree with protection glyph, all three would have to be answered." Abel stirred the remaining honey a little.

"Yes, yes. Wood retains some magic when cut, though most is lost. The last dregs drain slowly, and once gone the wood rots but before then wood accepts magic very easily. The larger the piece the easier to put magic in, and the better it will be retained. Put magic in a fence post and then carve a healing glyph before leading that to the tree." The odd creaking sounded again. "A very big answer as it will heal a young tree. I am becoming sentimental. Shorter answers now. A protection glyph on a strong, healthy young tree should work and will not harm it, but will slow the building of a magic reserve. I do not know about a young dryad travelling in a captive tree. It is possible but we must trust you more before we test that." The shoot hung out, hopefully swaying back and forth.

"That is enough for now."

"For me as well." Kelis sighed. "Now I've got to persuade Mum to feed my sudden craving for honey."

Abel laughed and put the pot on the grass near the tree. "All yours, Dryad Chestnut. I would be obliged if you could move enough for Kelis to see you, because she is curious, but too polite to ask." The sharp intake of breath from Kelis meant she could now actually see the dryad's shape. As soon as the shoot had polished the honey jar Abel stood up and all three of them said goodbye before he broke the veil. This time Abel had a good look round first so he didn't surprise anyone.

*   *   *

The betas were impressed by the answer to their question, but preoccupied with Halloween and Guy Fawkes. Those living in the town were keener on Halloween, because trick and treat wasn't as much fun in a village when everyone knew everyone else from birth. Privately, Kelis, Abel and Rob were unanimous. If there might be some truth to Halloween or Samhain, they were staying at home. Ferryl couldn't be sure, because how dangerous that one night became varied from place to place and time to time.

"The old gods had the best festivals, and some really did walk among their followers." They could all hear her humour through the mist links. *"Many humans blamed their mischief on gods, of course."*

"Did you get up to mischief, Ferryl?" Rob's half-smile had a good idea of the answer.

"Of course, but so do children now. Though mine might not have

been childish mischief." Abel's right hand, under Ferryl's control for the evening, sucked a fae out of the gloom into the streetlight, a reverse wind glyph. Abel nailed it with a fire glyph, using his left hand. The three of them, four with Ferryl, were braving the cold by sitting at Abel's open bedroom window.

"My turn." Kelis knocked a scuttling creature off the garden wall on the opposite side of the street. "Curses, I didn't get it tight enough to squish the thing." Kelis, Rob and Abel were trying to adopt Ferryl's habit of saying curses instead of hell or similar sayings. Nobody liked Ferryl's suggestion that their supposedly innocuous words could become something unpleasant.

"When can I do that?" Rob leant out, looking up and down the deserted street. "I could try? If it's a bit sloppy nobody would notice."

"It will be noticed if you blast a garden wall down, or smash in a car window. You must have better control." Kelis sounded just a bit smug.

Though Rob didn't sound convinced. "I want to squish a nasty. A thorny or a fae at least."

"There is no sign of any of the larger, more dangerous creatures tonight. Maybe they truly are extinct, maybe the church really did destroy them all." All three of the humans stared at the tattoo. *"There is very little protection in Brinsford. If one were prowling, it would have been attracted by the tempting targets earlier. The young children and mothers."*

Kelis scowled. "I thought you just wanted to watch to learn about trick or treat?"

"I did, because nobody would have risked that before I went into that hole." Ferryl's voice cheered up. *"Since nothing appeared, we can go out there and knock a few fae down for Rob to beat with a stick. Though magical creatures are hard to damage with non-magical weapons so Abel should cut a glyph into a big stick, a club."*

"Seriously? On Halloween, or Samhain, or whatever? What about gods wandering about?" Rob glanced out of the window, hopeful.

"Not for a long, long time. The church definitely stopped the gods. Though we should be disguised, just in case?" That had a lot of humour in, and the tattoo ran through a bewildering series of disguises that would

have taken a team of makeup artists and a full theatrical wardrobe to produce.

"Roughly Hewn only needs jeans and a shirt, and his club of course." Kelis giggled. "I could ask your mum if she'd lend me her slinky dressing gown Abel, that long one, the bath robe. Glyphmistress robe?" She looked Abel over. "We've got no costume for you."

"How about this?" Rob and Kelis stared at him so Abel looked down at his suddenly furry hand. Striped fur?

"A male cat-sorcerer? Your jeans don't look magical, but I like the ears." Kelis frowned and reached out tentatively. "You don't feel furry. Weird."

"Just a seeming, a type of illusion." The fur disappeared. *"I will put it on again after we leave. Then the Tavern can hunt monsters, since I don't think there are any."* Ferryl sounded really excited. *"A real hunt! There has been no Wild Hunt for many long years, but this will suffice. We can drive the globhoblins and fae out of Brinsford, or many of them, because nobody will see them die in the dark."*

"Globhoblins, skurrits, gremlins, hoplins, thornies, fae and anything slimy. I don't care if those are good or bad." Kelis shuddered. "How can slimy be good?" She jumped up. "I'll go and ask your mum, Abel."

While she did, Abel looked in his wardrobe for his old rounders bat. "It's a pity none of us took up baseball, then we'd have a decent sized club."

Rob took the small stick and swung it, carefully in the small bedroom. "Good enough as long as I can get near enough." Abel kept searching, and found elbow and knee protectors from when he'd tried roller skating. Rob took them with a big grin. "Brilliant, armour. Is there a helmet?" Once Abel found that, Rob rolled up his sleeves and jeans legs and considered himself a properly kitted out barbarian. "As long as we stay on the street or I'll trip over."

"Ferryl? Is it time?" Abel ignored Rob's curious look.

"I believe so. We can't have a barbarian falling all over the place." Abel explained, Rob shut his eyes, and moments later tears trickled out from beneath the eyelids. Abel nipped to the bathroom, coming back with

a wet flannel for Rob to ease the irritation. While they waited for the stinging to stop, he got back to arming Rob properly.

"What glyph do we put on the bat, Ferryl" Abel poised, a marker pen ready. "Do you want to draw it with my hand?"

Some of the excitement left Ferryl's voice. *"No, because I cannot remember the glyphs for enhancing weapons. They are in my wits, somewhere. We could use the Tavern hex, but that would work better cut into the wood. Why do none of you carry a knife?"* Ferryl's exasperation showed. *"Then you could cut solid glyphs into wood instead of drawing on wood or pebbles. The result is much stronger."*

"I'll nip down and get a kitchen knife, a little one, but you do the cutting. I'd end up with a glyph carved into my hand." At the top of the stairs Abel had to wait for his mum and Kelis, coming up.

"I thought you weren't going out?" She glanced at Kelis. "And no dragging this young lady anywhere muddy while she's wearing my dressing gown. Glyphmistress? I don't know where you come up with them." Though Abel's mum had a little smile as she wagged a finger. "Definitely no banging on doors and running away, or moving garden gates."

"I only did it one year." Abel sighed. "I promise." While Kelis kept his mum occupied with robing the Glyphmistress he took a small, sharp knife from the kitchen, one with a plastic cover over the blade. Back upstairs Kelis drew the Tavern mark on the bat. Abel carefully cut it into the wood and then pushed magic into the carving because Ferryl insisted on his unaided hand.

When the three of them set off Abel wore his dressing gown over his shirt and jeans, a short terry towelling one. His clothes looked ridiculous, unlike the long, silky-looking white robe Kelis wore, but Ferryl promised to fix it. Sure enough, once outside Kelis and Rob started laughing. Abel glanced down at a long blue silky jacket, something like silky pyjama trousers, and two furry feet sticking out at the bottom.

* * *

By the time the three of had cleared Riverside Close and the end of Main Street nearest Castle House they were having a ball. Ferryl had sucked several fae, two thornies and eventually a globhoblin in reach of

Rob's bat, which worked perfectly. Better yet, all the gunk they spattered on the road and fences evaporated. Kelis and Abel worked as a team. She knocked them over or out of the air and he finished them with either a tight wind glyph or a small fire one. It gave Abel a great sense of satisfaction to really clear out part of the village and already magical creatures were fleeing out into the countryside as the trio approached.

"The Village Green next. If we'd brought honey Rob could have met the dryad. If they are out he will be able to see one through the veil now." Kelis blew a fae against a house wall and it popped before bubbling away. "There's more houses down there. Do you think they'll notice the disappearing bodies?"

"The appearing bodies." Rob waited a moment as a stunned fae tumbled downwards, then swung as if hitting a rounder's ball. The mess flew across the road, dissolving before hitting the ground.

"They'll think we are hitting plastic toys." Abel hit a thorny with a fire glyph but it ran off smoking. "As long as we don't set fire to a bush, or blow tiles off a roof."

"We can stop if someone comes out to look, or carry on but just pretending." A hoplin flew off a car and rolled down the street before hopping at full speed over a fence and heading for the fields. "Hah, precision, Kelis is thy name."

"*Time to start pretending, someone is coming.*" Ferryl chuckled. "*Though I had better keep up Abel's seeming or he will look very silly.*"

"Sillier than cat ears and whiskers, and wearing silk pyjamas?" Rob stopped suddenly. "Er, sorry Ferryl. Cat ears and whiskers aren't silly on some people, well, not people."

"Cat-sorceress, Glyphmistress and barbarian." Kelis danced a few steps along the road, waving her hands about as four young kids with three mothers came out of Brinn's Lane. "Zap, pow, die, creatures of darkness."

The children looked startled but the mothers laughed. "What are you three idiots?"

"Hello Mrs. Turner. We're on a quest. A Barbarian, a Sorceress and a Cat-wizard, dealing death and destruction to the evil beasts that roam on

Halloween." Kelis beamed.

"It's certainly cheered you up." Mrs. Tomlins looked them over. "Nice tail Abel." From the laughs, Abel assumed he had a real tail.

"Try not to look surprised." Abel's right hand, Ferryl's for tonight, glowed a bright emerald green and drew lines of light in the air that glowed for a few moments before disappearing. The four kids watched, entranced.

"All battery powered, Mrs. Turner." Abel really hoped Mrs. Turner didn't say anything to Mum. He couldn't even talk to Ferryl with so many people here.

"Well I think that deserves some sweets." Mrs. Turner took a few from each of the bags the children carried. "Come on kids. The magicians are keeping us safe tonight, so pay your protection money." In a quiet voice she added, "A few less sweets might stop these four being sick."

Everyone laughed, and the three of them thanked the mothers and headed off. As soon as the trick or treat group turned up towards Riverside Close, the Taverners swung into action again. "How will you explain that to your mum?" Kelis grinned. "You could blame your tattoo?"

Even though Ferryl found that amusing, Abel didn't. "I'd rather not mention it to her, but that lot will be banging on Mum's door demanding sweets in a few minutes."

"Tell her you used a sparkler. They leave lines in the air, just for a moment."

Kelis stared at Rob in feigned shock. "Oh no, a Barbarian with brains. The magical world will never recover." She stopped laughing and whirled round at a voice from the trees on the Green.

"About time you got rid of some of those pests. You can't expect us to do it." Dryad Chestnut had stepped out from his tree, clearly visible. "I wondered if you really were a sorcerer, if your passenger had taught you anything or only made promises. Just be careful with fire near my leaves."

"Always, Dryad Chestnut."

"Dryad?" Rob looked from Kelis to Abel, his face dropping. "I know you said, but, well…" He sighed. "I still sort of hoped those old books and the internet were right, you know?" He looked at the other trees and all five of their dryads were clearly visible tonight, all of them gnarled, wrinkly, and definitely ugly.

"You mean all those pretty young tree-ladies?" Kelis sniggered. "You could get a tattoo."

Dryad Chestnut inspected Rob. "Another one with some magic. Has he brought honey?"

"No." Abel grinned. "That was a free answer. Will this do?" He unwrapped a humbug and threw it onto the grass near the dryad. "It is sweet?"

The mobile shoot came from almost directly between dryad's eyes, and stroked the confectionery. "It is sweet enough. The children sometimes drop similar treats on the grass. Not honey, and I am old enough to prefer that." Abel noticed the humbug shrinking, so it hadn't been rejected. "If your friend wants to meet a dryad who is younger, cross the bridge to the young willows. They are less crinkled."

"Are they women dryads?" Rob shrugged at the looks from the other two. "Just curious."

"All dryads are what you would term female. We all create seedlings if there is an opportunity to find them homes."

"Our thanks, Dryad Chestnut." Kelis threw another unwrapped sweet. "For the answer. Come on Rob, let's find you a willowy friend."

"Really, I can talk to one?"

"Not if you eat all your sweets. You'll need bribery." Kelis sighed. "The trees at home still barely talk, even after scoffing pots of honey. They really do blame me for the iron spikes holding the lights and cameras, and the branches the gardener trimmed." She shot out a glyph, catching a Hoplin against a wall and squishing it. "There, I feel better again. Onward, Taverneers. Taverners?"

"To the bridge. We haven't cleared Brinn's Lane yet, and you live along here so it's only right." Abel led the way. A score of creatures later the three of them stopped just short of the humpbacked bridge.

"Will there be a troll under here, Ferryl?" Rob hefted his bat. "I'm not exactly Billy-goat Gruff."

"*No, I checked when Abel crossed to try and create a barrier outside the*

153

village." Ferryl sounded unworried, but she'd startled Abel because he'd never even thought of that.

"I think Rob was joking, Ferryl. Are there real trolls elsewhere?

"Yes, but usually cave trolls as far as I remember. I think most of the bridge trolls and water serpents were removed by the church or sorcerers. My wits would be more certain."

Abel had started to think of Ferryl's wits as some sort of memory storage, from the way she spoke about them. "Will that information be on the two we found?"

"I can't tell unless I have a body. Then I can put them back into bone." Her sigh rustled. *"The sorcerer would put a wit back in when he wanted a skill, my knowledge, and I would try to remember when he took it away but the knowledge faded."* She sounded downright desolate now.

"Don't worry, we'll get them back. We'll have to or Kelis will be taking the Glyphmistress title."

"Hah, I think not. Control, you still need control." Ferryl plucked three fae from the sky with one hand-wriggle which definitely cheered her up. The three humans squished them, with two of them trying for control and one just swinging as hard as possible. Targets were getting scarce because the magical creatures of Brinsford, the unpleasant types at least, had definitely got the message and were scattering across the fields. Some of the more benign weren't running, but they were crouched down in shadows and keeping very still.

The three of them crossed the bridge, and paused. "Pick a tree, Rob, and offer her a sweetie." Kelis eyed up the young willow trees. "Do these class as children?"

"Greetings, Dryad Willows. We bring sweet things, but no honey." Abel had barely finished before all three of the willow trees started rustling their leaves, and decidedly human faces appeared in the bark. The two female ones smiled at Rob and Abel, the male one smiled at Kelis.

"Yes, that's what I meant! What do I do now?" Rob looked triumphant.

"Offer her sweets. Then you might get a better look."

Rob didn't seem to notice the definite humour in Ferryl's reply. "Right. Here, do you have a preference?" He held out a hand with half a dozen sweets on it.

"We wouldn't know. We never get anything here, across the river. The old trees over there find sweet things left by human children, or are old enough to have holes for bees." The woman's head came out a little further, long hair falling to mingle back in with the trunk. "Let me see?" Rob took a step nearer.

"Ferryl? Is he safe?"

"Yes, and this way he will see the dryad himself. The mark will protect him from a young dryad, but I would like to see how well it works." Abel thought about it a moment, but Ferryl wouldn't risk Rob. She had given him the same assurance as Kelis about not harming anyone bearing Abel's mark. Meanwhile a long limb, looking very much like a slim arm, reached for Rob's hand.

"May I look at your sweets, please?" The male version smiled at Kelis. "If you step a little closer, we can talk properly?"

"Yeah, right, said the wolf to the little piggy. Let's just see..." Kelis's words were cut off by a sharp screech, and when Abel and Kelis looked at Rob a little puff of smoke drifted up from near his hand.

The limb reaching for Rob quickly withdrew, trailing smoke, and the face on the tree trunk suddenly looked craggier. Anger blazed from the pale yellowish-green eyes, and a jagged rent opened where the mouth had been. "Why did you do that?" The dryad became clearly visible, long and willowy but not remotely human.

"What did you try to do?" Ferryl's voice had some definite edge to it. She continued in a voice Abel barely heard, almost the swish of a gentle breeze, *"Exactly what I expected and the mark worked very well."*

"Just tried to take a little magic." The willow dryad sounded petulant. "Humans have so much, and leak magic all the time."

"The older dryad in the horse chestnut is polite and enjoys the rewards. Good manners work much better." Abel remembered what Kelis had asked about age. "Are you children, young dryads?"

"Not old, but the three of us together manage to survive. A little more magic from anywhere will help. We do not get much chance for either sweetness or magic here." Her branches rustled. "I suppose that means I get no sweetness."

"You answered a question. Give her a sweet please, Rob." Rob glanced and Abel nodded, so he unwrapped one and threw it on the ground near the tree. A slim, definitely not human shoot reached out and explored the treat.

"This is good!" After a long pause, the dryad's eyes went to each human in turn. "Thank you?"

"I could answer a question?" Both of the other dryads were clearly visible now, and the one that had looked male moved a little closer. "I have only heard of sweet, never tried it."

"I know as much as you do." The third dryad looked straight at Abel. "I did not try to get you closer."

"One sweet each, then we will ask questions."

Although the dryads didn't exactly crowd anyone all three moved a little closer, a definite answer. None of them bargained well. The three of them had moved here together, and there had been four. That one had been taken by a creature they did not have a name for, because the fourth tree stood too far away for them to help. The fourth tree, another willow tree a little smaller than these three, remained empty. When Abel asked about the village barrier none of them could spare magic for anything just now, not until the trees were stronger.

Abel turned at a new, gloating voice from the fields. "This will be a bonus for my mistress. Three young dryads, in trees without enough magic to protect them." A harsh laugh followed. "She had been told this village would be unprotected, and thought that at Samhain we would not be noticed. She sent us to see what might be taken." A ragged human and a huge rough-looking dog stood in the nearby field, watching. "Stand back, humans. We will not try to enter your village."

The mist connections from Ferryl to Rob and Kelis disappeared. *"Best if I am invisible."* Though Abel's fur stayed intact.

"The dog talked." Abel tried to sub-vocalise, but needn't have bothered.

"Ferr... Abel, why is the dog doing the talking?" Rob took a step back towards the bridge. "Not talking, but the voice comes from there."

"Tell him neither is talking, their mistress is and she has a stronger link to the wolf. They are Bound Shades, but not like the tree. These are linked to their mistress's tattoos, and have no life outside that." Abel opened his mouth to ask if the two intruders frightened Ferryl like the vicar had, but she answered after a fashion. *"They may not realise I am here, so I will be a surprise if they attack you."*

"We're not giving up the dryads are we, Abel?" Kelis glanced over, then went back to watching the Shades with one hand poised for glyph-throwing.

"No." Abel quickly explained what the two creatures were and Kelis looked a little less certain. Rob looked definitely worried now.

"Do not be foolish. Our mistress is content with three dryads for one night's work. If you fight she may decide on three bound humans, especially a warlock and two trainees with some magic skills." The dog and the man moved a little closer, and the man raised his hand.

"If he starts to form a glyph, hit his leg with wind, hard."

"I'll have to make a wind glyph and he'll have started." Abel barely breathed the words and hoped the pair couldn't hear him. "My finger drew fire on my hand for hunting."

"Can you remember the glyph for wind?" Abel laughed out loud because that one had imprinted on his brain after all the times he'd imagined it under the dust or gravel. *"Advanced glyph wielding, first lesson. If you can imagine the glyph well enough, you can use it. Size is the amount of magic and intent, not the size you draw it."* Ferryl chuckled. *"The training has uses though we might need a solid glyph for the wolf."*

"How?" Abel meant the glyph but everyone looked at him so he smiled at Kelis and Rob. "I'm wondering how these two are going to bind anyone when they'll be scuttling back home."

"Carve one on Rob's club?"

"We have time?

"No, now!" The man's hand had started to move and Abel lashed out, trying to keep the glyph tight. Perhaps the tension wound Abel up because he put a lot more than expected into the magic, and the man's leg flew out from under him. He stumbled, and before he could recover a less

concentrated blast of wind from behind Abel struck and the Shade fell. Ferryl sent a concentrated blast of something straight into the sprawled Shade, and he called out in a woman's voice and began to shrivel.

"Yeah....." Kelis's shout of triumph tailed off as the wolf leapt forward, its eyes shining and a glyph forming in the air in front of it. Abel tried for a leg, but although the animal stumbled it kept coming. The wolf's glyph shot forward straight at Abel, but his right hand wriggled just in time though he felt the shock as Ferryl's defence absorbed the hit.

The wolf felt the shock as well, slowing, then it fastened its jaws on Abel's right arm. He could feel pressure, but the teeth didn't go in. A paw came up and tried to claw at Abel's left arm before sliding off without damaging his sleeve. Abel felt a stab of cold as his mark deflected whatever the distant sorceress did. Wind from the side battered at the wolf and Abel but it clung on, though its teeth still didn't go into Abel's arm. *"Knife. Non-magical attack."* Ferryl sounded strained, pre-occupied, but Abel heard the urgency.

Abel grabbed the knife, but it took him three tries to scrape the plastic cover off against his leg because Ferryl still had his right hand. Abel began to worry as he felt the pressure on his arm increase and now the teeth were sinking into his dressing gown arm. More wind, a double hit and better concentrated, smashed into the wolf and knocked it sideways a little. Abel took his chance. He didn't think the short blade would do much damage, then a little smile touched his lips because Abel had memorised two glyphs.

Kelis had moved right up close now, trying to throw glyphs two-handed to keep the pressure on, but she had started to tire. Another blast, scattered and not very strong, must have been Rob trying to help. Abel slashed at the head trying to bite off his arm, because a thrust wouldn't go deep. Smoke billowed, stinking of burned hair and meat while the wolf stopped trying to bite and screamed. Abel dropped the knife before the glowing blade melted through the handle to his fingers. The jaws on his arm drew back a little allowing Abel to place his palm on the wolf's head, while mentally forming another fire glyph.

As smoke gushed out under his fingers a loud crack sounded, light flashed, and the wolf staggered back on three legs. Rob followed the beast, taking another swing and another flash lit up the rounders bat as it hit the wolf, staggering it again. *"Get him back. Quickly."*

"Rob, back, now!" Rob hesitated but stepped back, just in time as the wolf rallied and lunged low at his legs. It pulled its head back again, avoiding another blow and stood, head low, one front leg up and a long bubbling slash across its face right through one eye. Smoke still rose from the charred stump of an ear, where Abel had placed his hand for the second fire glyph. Rob stood by Abel's shoulder, bat raised, and Kelis moved up on the other side, hands outstretched to throw glyphs.

No pretence now, a woman's voice came from the wolf. "You can't protect the dryads for ever."

"Wind, leg." Abel understood immediately, hitting the unwounded front leg as hard as he could. The wolf went down on its knee, then Ferryl took over completely and Abel leapt forward, scooping up the little knife. The wounded creature fought back onto three legs but another blast from Kelis caught it, not a strong blast but enough to stop it recovering fast enough. Abel, or Ferryl controlling Abel, hit the unwounded leg with a fire glyph and then thrust with the knife. Abel saw the knife glow again as she drove it into the wolf's head between its eyes and twisted, scooping as she did. Another, louder scream split the night and the wolf dropped, starting to shrivel.

Abel, or Ferryl in Abel, straightened and dropped the glowing knife. "Is that it?" Kelis sounded tired, and very cautious.

"Yes, tell her yes. You had to send a warning to the sorceress." Ferryl sounded really wary, unsure. *"Now the sorceress will be in great pain and will not be back for some time, if ever."*

"What did you do? Can you let the other two know as well, please?" Abel turned, realising as he did that Ferryl had given him back control of everything. "All over, Kelis." A moment later they were in a three-way hug.

"Did we kill it?" Rob sounded jubilant. "Did you see what this little bat did?" He hesitated. "How did it do that?"

The mist tendrils reconnected all three. *"The ward. It was carved into the wood by Abel's hand and direct will, not drawn with a finger or with paint. What I told you about glyphs works very well with hexes. Better than expected. Belief and intent."*

Abel remembered what Ferryl said about taking him over. "So why did you stabbing it have such an effect?"

"Ferryl did that?" Rob's shock turned to humour. "That explains why you didn't fall over."

"I know why Ferryl took over, to kill that thing. She sure hurt it, going by the scream though that didn't sound like a wolf. Too human." Kelis sounded shaken. "I kept throwing air but the glyphs were getting weaker. I want to learn fire."

"You used up your spare magic so you would have no fire either. The magic will come back with a little rest. I'm not sure if what I did worked properly, not until the body has gone." All three turned to watch the last of the wolf bubbling away.

Kelis stared at the shrinking mess. "Body? So we did kill it?"

"No, neither of them because both are already dead. Repairing them will cost the sorceress magic and time, but…. Good, it worked. May I have a hand, please?"

"Yes."

Abel's hand pointed. *"There, the small piece of stone, or possibly bone. Bone! I have taken one of her wits!"* Ferryl sounded triumphant. *"I may not have all my wits, but I remembered that!"*

"What?" Three voices sounded as one.

"Sorry. A Bound Shade is just that, a shade, a dead spirit. Unless bound within something else, with magic to sustain it, a shade must always be attached to the sorceress. For the Shade to throw magic she, the sorceress, must feed magic through the connection. To cause physical damage she must use a little of her physical self."

"That biting seemed physical enough. Though the claws slid off." Abel tried to work that out. "Surely clawing is physical?"

"A typical sorcerer mistake." Ferryl chuckled. *"If she had left the claws to do their work they would have drawn blood, and the wolf would have bit into your arm. Most sorcerers automatically add magical enhancement to physical attacks, which means your ward could help repel them."*

"What about that glyph it used? You stopped throwing magic after that." Kelis shrugged. "I'm sure you could have, even with Abel's arm in its mouth."

"*The wolf glyph tried to attach to Abel but the slippery spell helped me to resist, more than I expected.*" Ferryl sounded puzzled. "*I could not throw glyphs because I had to fight the wolf glyph, stop it invading. Though that gave me time to think, to work out what she did, that she had to be vulnerable.*"

"It didn't look very vulnerable." Abel inspected the small tear marks on his sleeve where the teeth had gone in.

"*The glyph from the wolf had no hand forming it. It could be a memorised glyph directly from the sorceress or a solid glyph placed within the Shade. Similar to the glyphs in the dead tree Bound Shades.*" All three humans nodded, though still struggling to understand. "*I realised she would not risk trying to remember such a complicated glyph while controlling two Shades in a fight.*"

"That carved glyph there, she sent it inside the wolf? Put it inside that thing before it left? Kelis stared at the tiny piece of what Ferryl said might be bone.

"*Not put inside, it physically stayed with her but linked directly to the Shade, a very close, tight link. It is hard to explain, difficult to accomplish, and rarely done because there is a weakness. Even the physical must remain attached to her, as does the wolf unless killed. Killing the Shades will hurt her because of the tiny part of herself included in them. In addition, she has lost the magic used to form them, so she will be weakened.*"

"How badly hurt? I hope it really stings, and hopefully bleeds!" Kelis glared at the wisps of wolf still evaporating.

"*Serious burning at least, but that is the least of her worries now. That glyph is literally cut out of her bone, and anything else will pale in comparison. Seeing Abel's knife glowing brought the knowledge back because only a red-hot knife will reach through the Shade link to the origin.*" Ferryl suddenly became very formal. "*I ask forgiveness for taking control despite the promise I made by my true-name. There was no time to explain or ask. I know I should only do that when you are in danger, and the wolf was about to leave.*"

"No problem. I understand, and that really was brilliant." Abel glanced sideways and smiled at Kelis. "Still the true Glyphmistress." Kelis stuck out her tongue and relaxed a little.

"Maybe. It helped that the sorceress and Shade were distracted." Ferryl's laugh echoed in their heads. *"Distracted? She will not understand how a little bat hurt a Shade, Kelis kept throwing air blasts too fast to dodge or stop, and then Abel gouged out an eye, all while she had her magic locked in battle with me."*

"Not a real eye!"

"No, probably, though she will be in great pain and not seeing properly just now." Ferryl sobered. *"She may still send something for the dryads. Sorceresses are well known for keeping threats, it is a matter of both pride and status."*

A plaintive voice interrupted the explanation. "Help us. Please? We are sorry for being rude. Here are some sweets back again. Do you have a tree somewhere else we can go to? Even a little one?" All three dryads had come right out from under their trees, limbs extended with partly dissolved sweets resting on tangles of tiny twigs.

"Will the trees on the Village Green help, or in Kelis's garden?" Abel eyed up the distance. "It's a long way to lay a feed for magic. Can we go through the water or must it go over the bridge?"

Kelis knew he was talking to Ferryl, but tugged Abel's arm. "We could put them in a potted plant? Take them to the wood or your mum's garden, to the maple?"

"I doubt it. Look at the size of them." Rob scowled at the one that had tried to fool him.

"I doubt they will fit in a plant much smaller than those trees. Certainly not in the damaged maple, and it is only one tree." Ferryl's sigh rustled. *"We are too far from a large tree, even if they would help another dryad's seedlings."*

"We can walk a little way. Across the bridge?" Away from their trees Abel had lost track which belonged where, but one now seemed to be spokes-dryad.

Abel shook his head. "Sorry, the vacant trees are much further than that."

The three dryads conferred, "What about the protection you offered at the start? In return for some magic?"

"You can spare some magic now you've been frightened?"

Abel knew he'd spoken sharply, but didn't expect all three dryads to droop, their whole forms hunching over. "No, we have none to spare yet. We could promise?"

"Your ward, the Tavern ward, might be enough to keep them safe because the sorceress will see they are part of the village. The magic in the tree will be more effective with the protection hex helping, though the protection would be even stronger if the dryads allow you to link the trees."

Abel passed that on. "Perhaps we can give you some help, if you allow us to link your trees."

"No binding!" All three dryads flinched back.

From their reactions, Abel realised this binding business must be well known and very unpleasant. "No binding. Only a protection hex and a magical connection to each other. If one is attacked, the strength of all three trees will be available for defence." The more Abel thought about it the better the idea sounded, but the dryads seemed unsure.

"Give magic to another tree? What about my tree?" The dryad moved back towards its own willow.

"Or mine? It barely has enough." Another moved away a little.

"Then something comes along and takes you." Kelis pointed at the first to move away. "Then you, then you, because none of you can stop it, not on your own." She swept her hands together, as if joining the dryads. "Or something attacks one, and three trees smack it back, and it crawls away and never comes near you again."

"Dryads rarely share." Ferryl's laughter echoed. *"Dryads never share, unless the memory is in my wits."* Though the three dryads had moved closer to each other again, and were conferring. Eventually the spokes-dryad moved towards Abel.

"Could you link the fourth tree to us as well? To help? It has no dryad so losing some magic will not hurt it. Not as much." The dryad looked from Abel to Kelis to Rob, making no attempt to be appealing or even vaguely human. "Please?"

"Yes, and we could ward the fourth tree as well. That would make the

group much stronger."

"Strong enough for all of them to live?" Kelis whirled to look at Rob and Abel. "When the fourth tree grows, it would be a home for another dryad, a protected home we could gift in exchange for magic elsewhere."

"Probably, unless something strong and really determined came and we would know if that happened. Even then the trees might last long enough for us to help."

Kelis turned back to the dryads. "If we protect the fourth tree, we will bring a young dryad to live there sometime in the future. You must allow that. You must also swear to give us some magic when you are strong enough, a small amount of magic we can use to ward the village."

"Yes, yes, we promise." The dryads crowded forward. "We will not try to trick any other humans."

Half an hour later the very subdued Taverners walked back down Brinn's Lane. The four trees and three dryads were linked and the trees protected, using the little kitchen knife to cut the hexes deep into the wood. In a few years the trees would grow big enough, and store enough magic, to be safe from most threats. As they grew even bigger, the trees would accumulate spare magic, some of which could be siphoned off. Even taking just a fraction of what a large tree absorbed, the amount available for powering the village barrier would grow every year after that.

"You may as well go home now, rather than us walking you back later." Rob looked up at the big wrought iron gates. "We'll watch you down the drive."

"Ok, but one of you has to text me, let me know what Chestnut has to say about the bone thing, the wit." Kelis shuddered. "I can't be upset if the sorceress has been hurt, but losing a bit of bone? That's gotta hurt."

"It does. Putting it into another creature to see what it contains hurts more. The sorcerer did that and I had to tell him what each one contained. Then he took them out again." Ferryl's voice held bleak certainty. *"You do not ever want to put in a bone glyph from another creature to read it, or cut it out again."*

Abel kept his tone deliberately light. "Which is why we are never going to do that. I'd rather whack it with a hammer."

"I'm hiding behind Rob when you do. Ferryl said there's magic inside it." Kelis peered suspiciously at the tissue wrapping the bone, with Abel's hand only holding the corners together to avoid contact. "I'm off. Please let me know?" A little smile touched her mouth, "Especially if you need honey."

"Of course."

"The Glyphmistress returns to her hidden identity, the innocent schoolgirl, Kelis." Kelis took off the dressing gown with a flourish and passed it to Abel. "Thank your mum, please."

*　　*　　*

Abel didn't beat around the bushes when he reached the Horse Chestnut. "Dryad Chestnut, I have a question."

"You have honey?"

"Not right now, but…" Abel explained, with Rob and Ferryl helping. "So what we want to know is, can you tell if this is dangerous?" He put the captured bone on the grass near the tree, unwrapped it and moved back.

The usual shoot extruded and moved all around the tiny lump without touching, then shot back into the tree. "If you bring this near my tree again, I will drop a branch on you! A large one!"

"Why?"

"How much honey?"

"A full pot if you give us everything you know." Rob stared but Abel shrugged. If it frightened a dryad, they needed to know. "Delivered tomorrow."

After a long wait, the dryad stirred. "I will risk being cheated because you helped the dryads, and to stop you using this. The combined glyphs in that bone will kill and bind, create a Bound Shade, by following a magical attack or defence back to the source. Do not activate it unless you wish to bind something, do not put it into any other creature or it may bind you. The Bound Shades you met were only sent for one purpose, to take a magic user. Possibly a dryad, but we only redirect tree magic." Chestnut's eyes centred on Abel.

"You were lucky."

"The sorceress made a mistake, she aimed the glyph at Abel but I countered. I could not be drawn out and Bound, because I had his protection to help anchor me." Ferryl sounded shaken. *"My wits would already know this, and possibly how to prevent it. Can we destroy it safely?"* Abel realised Ferryl really must be upset, to mention her wits in front of Chestnut.

"Best not to. Save it for if the sorceress attacks again, then launch it at her. It is her bone so she will have no defence if it comes in through her own magic." The dryad's eyes narrowed. "Bound Shade is a fitting end for one who binds dryads."

"I'm not keen on binding." Abel ignored the looks from Rob and the dryad.

"Then I will study the glyph and work out a defence. You need one, we all do. I need my wits!" Abel shrugged and picked up the wrapped bone, very gingerly, because he agreed but couldn't do much about it. On the way back the three of them discussed it, but couldn't think of anything else to do.

According to Ferryl, the sorceress should know she had no defence against the glyph, so she might stay completely clear. For now the bit of bone would go into Castle House grounds, and be buried on its own a long way from Ferryl's wits.

Abel apologised for a little bit of mud and dust on his mum's robe, but she had apparently expected some. He kept waiting for some comment about furry tails or lights, but all he got were a few digs about a gang of sorcerers scaring kids. Kelis delivered the honey to Dryad Chestnut the following day. It came from the stash she had persuaded her mum to buy because of the tremendous health benefits.

Despite thrashing it out when all three were together, nobody could come up with a way of finding out if the sorceress would leave them be. Dryad Chestnut's comment about her having no defence against her own bone seemed encouraging.

All the Taverners relaxed, because Ferryl felt sure the sorceress had to be the one sending creatures to test the barriers. Better yet, in the five days leading up to Guy Fawkes, very few of the less savoury creatures came back into Brinsford. Even without the barrier, the Halloween Hunt had definitely made the village safer. In addition, without thornies and globhoblins rooting in rubbish and then houses, the whole place looked tidier.

The Taverners were in just the right mood for the Guy Fawkes celebrations.

Troubled Times

Nothing very magical happened at Guy Fawkes, except the usual magic of lots of fireworks banging and flashing and zooming across the sky. Rob and Abel went with their parents to the big bonfire and display in Stourton, which had plenty of thornies and other small creatures attracted by the spilled and discarded food but nothing really dangerous. Even the globhoblins had plenty of discarded food to concentrate on without trying to steal magic from young or drunk humans. Kelis went to a bigger display someplace near where her Dad worked and sponsored by his firm.

Both Abel and Rob relaxed and enjoyed themselves wandering around the stalls, especially when their parents bought candy floss and toffee apples. There were quite a few people there that both of them knew, especially from school so it turned into a bit of a social occasion. Abel had just been competing with Rob's sisters and Una, bobbing apples, when he saw Rob stagger out from between the parked cars.

He headed that way, and as he came closer Abel could see Rob's black eye and split lip, and the way he favoured one leg. Rob lisped one word. "Henry."

Abel looked round, ready to show Henry some real Ferryl Shayde moves. *"Where?"* Ferryl seemed eager as well.

"Don't know." Rob winced and gingerly touched his lip. "He left."

"Your Dad will get involved now. There's no way you picked a fight."

"Can't tell them." Abel realised Rob kept moving so Abel hid him from his family.

Abel stared at him. "You can't hide it."

"Mystery mugger."

"Why are you covering for him?" Abel glanced back to where his mum was looking around for him. "He shouldn't keep getting away with it."

"Arabelle."

"Arabelle?"

"She wanted me to win her something on the grabby machine." Which made sense because Rob had a knack with the coin-operated cranes, already winning a toy for each of his sisters. Rob sighed. "Then she pulled me between the stalls, out of the light, and kissed me."

"Henry was waiting."

"Yes. She laughed when he dragged me among the cars and beat me up. After he smacked me in the face I couldn't concentrate enough for a glyph. They left together. Arabelle says if I blab she'll swear I tried to, you know, and Henry rescued her."

"Idiot."

"I didn't have time to think. Then it was too late." Rob straightened. "Here we go." Moments later his older sister, Samantha, called out and began to ask questions. Just as he'd said, Rob stuck to mystery mugger who had run off when someone came near. The two families spent some time at the Accident and Emergency, but Rob's leg only had a nasty bruise and wasn't seriously damaged. After a trip to the police station, where Rob couldn't give a description because it was dark, they all went home.

*   *   *

Rob's face took a while to heal, with Seraph, Arabelle, Claris and Henry smirking whenever they went past. Only a few other seraphims smirked, so Seraph hadn't told them all. There wasn't anything Rob or his friends could actually do except fume silently and invent retributions they daren't carry out. Abel wasn't sure if Kelis or Ferryl came up with the most bloodthirsty solutions to the problem, but Henry would definitely get badly hurt if he ever cornered Kelis. She still didn't have very good control, but probably wouldn't care about who saw the magic.

Everyone at the squeak table understood what had happened regardless of the public story. They put it down to Rob showing Henry up and then getting cornered. Arabelle sat next to Henry at breaks now, while Jenny carried on sitting at the next table with the athletes, rich, and favoured who were not invited to Seraph's table.

"I'm going to ask for a real sword for Christmas. Then if Henry or any of the seraphims gives me trouble again I can stick them like a real mercenary would." Una smirked. "My Dad has already sort of promised boots, long leather ones but without high heels."

"Blimey. When do we get to see this outfit?" Warren asked but everyone looked interested.

"I won't have the boots until Christmas, but I can manage the rest with a plastic sword so I'll be wearing it to any Christmas parties. How many others have costumes that are near enough for public?" Seven put up their hands with varying amounts of confidence. "Warren, you are slacking, because if you get sorted out, we can have a full-dress meeting for the town Tavern. Rachel's Tavern because we usually meet at Justin's house and she'll cry if we call it anything else." Una kept her eyes on Justin, winding him up a bit but then sighed. "I'm sorry Petra, but unless you can get a lift into town?"

"Not a chance, not dressed up in a onesie with cat ears and a tail. Dad would go crackers." Petra turned to Kelis. "How come you three haven't got something yet? You designed the game."

Abel, Rob and Kelis kept them all laughing with descriptions of the costumes at Halloween. "You wore those when you asked the trees about banding together for protection?" Warren chuckled. "It's a wonder they took you seriously, dressed like that." The whole table found that funny because none of them thought Abel actually asked a tree.

Though afterwards some betas were more thoughtful. "I reckon a long dressing gown, bath robe would make a great sorceress robe. I'm going to try and nobble my mum's."

"I'm going for barbarian, but with a baseball bat and maybe a pair of those leather shorts. Lederhosen?"

"My Dad has loads of thin plywood. Covered in tinfoil it would make great armour. I could ask for a sword for Christmas as well?"

"I'd try for Bonny, but Dad would kill me."

"A ninja warrior, bodyguard to Petra the Ferryl Shayde, with lots of daggers and my judo gear. I can put the Tavern mark on my headband." Warren made some sort of martial arts-style moves with his hands. The table broke up into discussions on how to make costumes that just had to be better than Rob's or Abel's.

*   *   *

Henry, or Seraph, seemed satisfied with their revenge, school settled back to routine, and so did life in Brinsford for Abel, Kelis and Rob. Rob began to get control of his leaf, while Kelis definitely mastered keeping the wind glyph tight and focused and started on fire glyphs. Abel could now fry a fae without the slightest danger to the surrounding countryside and would soon start on reverse wind glyphs. Better yet, the clearance of the creatures from Brinsford at Halloween seemed to have a permanent effect, with fewer about. Rob managed to fully ward his house with glyphs scratched into bricks or frames, as Abel now had. Kelis cleared her kitchen, pantry, bedroom and bathroom, with occasional relapses when the cleaner found and cleaned off or moved the hexes.

The result wasn't completely beneficial. "My mum is complaining about the amount of muck we all trek in. She reckons we've got worse." Rob sat on Abel's bed, inspecting his shoes. "I have to stand on the doormat until I've scrubbed these clean."

"My mum complains about more dust and flies, but she reckons it's either winter or Mrs. Tabitha." Abel sniggered. "Finding a dead mouse under the settee didn't help. It's a good job magic creatures dissolve."

"This is your fault. I told you at the beginning, and then again, but you ignored me so I've kept quiet." The three of them looked at a decidedly smug looking tattoo. *"You have banished all magical creatures from the houses."*

"Yeuk. Too true." Kelis mimed being sick. "They were crawling all over my bed, and my breakfast."

"But some didn't. What types of creatures are there in houses, usually? The beneficial ones." All three groaned at the clothes Ferryl now wore; she liked a picture of a university professor and now wore a mortarboard and black robe when teaching.

"Pictsies hunt insects such as flies and lice, and like a drop of warm milk. Pixies live on magic leaking from humans and clean magic residues and stuff like dandruff from clothes. Leaving Pixies a little sugar stops them playing tricks. Piskies prefer outside and stockyards, will remove animal parasites if given milk, and will play tricks if trapped inside." Abel spoke in a sing-song voice, reciting the answers, then sat back.

Kelis used the same tone. "Faeries eat magic from fruit and vegetation, and leave little marks as they do. A few can be allowed in if there are potted plants, as they will frighten away pests and encourage the plant to be healthy. Small fae will kill plant pests and clear infestations of flies, lice or midges, and will be attracted to a little bit of lard. Larger fae hunt insects, faeries, and fairies, attack larger magical creatures in swarms, and will sting humans or animals to feed. Fairies are harmless, love flowers, are prettier, and probably extinct."

Rob sighed. "Hoplins can be allowed to clear large numbers of rats or mice, but should be kept out otherwise or they'll take kittens, hamsters and caged birds. Thornies like discarded food, but will scatter rubbish while foraging and invade kitchens if hungry. Brownies are the best house creatures, if not annoyed. Brownies like everything clean and tidy, and will strive to keep their surroundings that way. If they are allowed a small area to keep pristine, and left milk now and then, they will also clean up the rest of the house. If the house is too messy, or they are not appreciated, the Brownie tribe will wreck the place before leaving." He frowned as he finished. "How do we manage that? Let some in and not the rest?"

"Top student." A yellow star floated across to Rob and stuck itself to his forehead, glowing softly as it slowly disappeared. *"None of you asked. It was all yeuk, nasty, get rid of it."* Kelis blushed a little because Ferryl managed to copy her voice almost exactly. *"Now students, here is your homework."* They all groaned. *"I will not be helping Abel, to make everything fair. You must trap Brownies, Pictsies and Pixies. Or maybe not Pixies, if Kelis really can't stand them on her clothes."*

"Trap? I don't like that idea." Abel scowled. "I don't want prisoners."

"These want to be inside, foolish boy, where they are safe from fae and hoplins. You must make a gap in the hexes, then judge when you have enough. None of those will touch your plate of food, and your parents do not spill enough to need thornies. Nor do they allow livestock in the house so Piskies are not required." Ferryl smile happily. *"Your parents will be surprised when the house is much cleaner."*

"My mum wouldn't notice, and the cleaner deserves what she gets. I keep telling her to leave my hexes alone." Kelis threw up her hands in surrender. "Let a few good ones in and trap them, I hear and obey Sensei.

What if bad ones get in as well?"

Ferryl turned into a leopard that leapt onto a tattoo thorny. *"Bug hunt!"* The humans smiled. *"Without fire or breaking windows."* Rob and Kelis laughed at Abel, though he hadn't actually broken the window. Abel had set off a house alarm being a bit enthusiastic with a wind glyph aimed at a goblin, once he had finally seen one of the little green-skinned munchkins. Ferryl insisted he couldn't use fire, since most goblins were really flammable once they ignited. They had been hunted to near extinction to stop them causing house fires when sleeping too near to hearths.

"Remember to check for gremlins sneaking in." Kelis had been really annoyed when one wiped out her homework after she left her laptop on the table in the breakfast room.

"I've fixed Dad's car now. There's a drawn hex under the bonnet, and a laminated one under the carpet in the boot." Rob grinned at Kelis. "Have you fixed your Dad's car yet?"

"Hah! I wish Ferryl could find me a glyph to attract gremlins. Then he could break down on the way home, time after time, and not get here until Sunday teatime." She glanced at the other two. "Sorry."

"We'd help you fix the glyph if Ferryl found one." Rob sniggered. "You could collect the slimy critters instead of zapping them, and shove them in his pockets. He wouldn't know but you would."

"A ward on a person, a hex on a building or object, though what Kelis wants is a curse."

"I wish. I'm going to invent a creature-attracting curse in the game. Robyn or Bonny can put them on annoying customers. Something to get the victim stung by hordes of fae while being slimed all over." She opened her sketch pad and started, and the rest set to helping her.

"I must concentrate on my own homework, getting into that glyph, the one from the sorceress. I cannot see how to use it without immediately killing and binding something, and attempts to destroy it could activate a part. That might bind something or someone to the nearest object such as a tree, or kill them and leave a wandering Shade, unable to move on." All three knew what Ferryl would say next. *"I need my wits!"*

* * *

By the time the three students had trapped enough beneficial creatures in their houses, Ferryl had bad news about the glyph. *"I cannot work out how to destroy the bone glyph, or make it safe."*

"We could ask for help." Kelis didn't look convinced. "From Vicar Mysterio Creepio?"

"Collateral? Blunt instrument? Do we really want God's SAS rampaging through Brinsford?" Abel shook his head. "I don't trust him."

"Nor me, from what you two said. Maybe we could ask him to ring us about a problem?" Rob held up his phone. "But I'd rather he didn't have my number."

"He's got my name already." Abel picked his up. "Ferryl?"

"I do not trust him, but I dislike the church on principle. My kind and theirs do not agree."

Kelis held out the card. "Here. You do it."

Abel called the number, and a very polite voice told him the Archbishop was not immediately available. "Please tell him the young man he met outside Castle House wishes to discuss a problem. Discuss, not ask for physical help."

"I understand. Someone will call."

Abel turned off the speaker. "Now we wait. That bloke didn't seem very interested."

"He answers phone calls from people who think they have problems. Sort of a 999 for the church. They'll have people phoning because they want to know the vintage of the communion wine." Rob shrugged. "It'll go on a list, someone else will look at it and cut out the worst, then it goes through four more before they'll bother anyone important."

"I do not believe that man handed that card out to many people."

"Good point Ferryl, but it certainly isn't a direct line." Kelis turned to the game files. "We may as well get on with this." She jumped a mile when Abel's phone struck up with 'People are Strange' because an unknown number had called.

After answering Abel put it on speaker in time for the others to hear,

"Have you opened the house?"

"Maybe that is his phone." Kelis put her hand over her mouth as she realised the Archbishop would hear her.

"Not quite, but using that number and Castle House has my attention. What do you wish to discuss?" Creepio Mysterio didn't have a sense of humour.

"The house is still sealed. We have a bone glyph, taken from a sorceress who attacked us. We do not want to activate it, but cannot destroy it without possibly killing someone. Can you help?"

"How did you…?" Creepio sounded startled. "We should speak face to face. It would be best if I saw the item. Would tomorrow be convenient?"

"We'll be at school. Tomorrow evening?"

"Where is this item? Is it safe?" Now Creepio sounded much too interested.

"Yes, it's inside Castle House grounds. Thank you for the cross over the food at school." Abel shrugged at the rest. He didn't like the bloke but fair was fair.

"I'm pleased they paid attention. Tomorrow evening, seven p.m. outside Castle House?"

"No need for God's SAS, we don't want collateral." Kelis shrugged a sort of apology for interrupting. "I just want that clear."

"Is that the witch, or is she the sorceress now? No God's SAS, Kelis." He chuckled so he had a sense of humour after all. "God's SAS, I might use that. I will see you tomorrow." With that the phone went dead.

"We must be very careful. He wanted to know where it is. Perhaps he wants to steal it." Ferryl's voice suddenly had a very nasty edge. *"I hope he tries."*

"No we don't because if the whatever guarding Castle House wins the battle it won't stop in the garden." Abel turned his phone off. "That's where we'll be before he arrives, inside the garden. Then if he brings heavies, the collateral won't be one-sided."

*　　*　　*

The following day dragged, for three people anyway, until they were home and had eaten. Rob and Abel called for Kelis, but instead of going to a Tavern meeting as her mum assumed, the three set off over the fields. They came into Castle House gardens from the rear, through the spooky wood, just in case the Archbishop had arrived even earlier than them. The next hour, waiting for their appointment, wasn't the most comfortable, but Ferryl kept them occupied and warm. She turned the time into a lesson in either creating very faint heat glyphs or counter blasts to stop the cold gusts of wind.

As his wristwatch ticked off the last few minutes, Abel dug up the glyph while Rob and Kelis kept watch. He left it in the little silver box Kelis had brought from home so that none of them ever had to touch the bone again. Dryad Chestnut's and Ferryl's warnings about never activating the spell worried them all. Abel held the box and the three of them watched from behind the trees and bushes as, on the dot of seven, a car drew up.

"Vicar Creepio Mysterio," Kelis breathed as the man with a priest-collar climbed out, followed by another man, the driver. "He must be the GSF, God's Special Forces."

"Stop it." Rob chuckled. "He might be here to hold the Archbishop's coat if there's trouble."

"Don't get too near them, especially the second one. He carries something. I will only speak to Abel while they can see us." Ferryl pulled in her creepy-phone attachments.

Abel raised his voice. "Hello. Only one of you, please. We'll meet you at the fence."

"Please keep whatever is in there in check. Otherwise my friend will respond." At a nod from the Archbishop the second man walked back to the car and half-sat on the bonnet, arms folded.

Abel, Kelis and Rob came out onto the grass, walking slowly towards the repaired fence so they'd arrive the same time as the churchman. "We're a bit worried, because of what your friend brought. Do I still call you vicar?"

"Please. It is a little less formal. Are you Abel or sorcerer, since this young man appears to be a warlock at least?" The vicar stopped a good metre from the fence and waited, eyes on the box Abel carried. "The bone glyph is in there?"

"We are all still training, carefully as you advised and I'm sure you already know who Rob is." Abel held the box out a little. "I have been told you might want to take this, so I'm a little cautious. We really do want to destroy it."

"So why did you cut it out? More to the point, how did you three hold down a sorceress long enough to do so?" His eyes narrowed. "You four, since no doubt your invisible friend is here."

"Be careful when explaining. Not too much detail, and not my name."

"By helping each other and being very lucky." Abel explained briefly, but without really saying who did what and simply referring to Ferryl as our friend. "Once we had the glyph, we found out roughly what it does. Be really careful with magic near it."

"If I may use my cross? Will the house react?" The vicar took out his cross and this time Abel could see the faint glow straight away.

"Put the box on the fence post, but resting in your hand. Warn him that if he activates the glyph while you hold the box, he will be the victim. Ask Rob and Kelis to stand behind you with a hand on your shoulder, so he cannot pull you or the box out of the protection." Ferryl sniggered. *"If he extends magic into the garden to pull all three of you, run away very fast and we'll use the glyph on the survivor."*

Abel passed that instruction on to Rob and Kelis, including the warning about running away, then rested his hand on the fence post. "You heard what I told my friends?" The vicar nodded. "Do you want the box opened?"

"No thank you. I believe the warning and have no intention of trying to touch it." The vicar's hands moved just a little, tendrils crept out from the cross and Abel's hand itched just before a slight chill touched his flower. The vicar's eyes narrowed and the itch and chill increased, but only a little. His eyes opened in alarm, and he took a step back. "That is a trap! Whatever is in there is aimed at the church!"

"No!" Abel shouted because the other churchman stood straighter, holding one hand aloft as if poised to throw or cast a glyph. "It attacked me and I'm not church."

"The trap must be for anything using magic, not magical. The sorceress lied. She definitely came for you or your friends, not the dryads."

Abel continued in a quieter tone, as if the pause had been to collect himself. "You have answered a question. The sorceress came for us, not the dryads. Someone has been testing our defences, and now we are sure who." Abel sighed. "Can you tell us how to get rid of the thing?"

"Even knowing she came for you and might come back, you would still like to destroy it?" The vicar smiled faintly, recovering from his brief alarm. "I knew there must still be someone, or three someones, with principles. How refreshing. I really wish I could oblige. I could take the box and place it somewhere very safe?"

"No." Rob spoke before Abel could answer.

Kelis's hand tightened briefly on Abel's shoulder. "Not a chance."

"The church would keep trying, and would find a volunteer to risk activation. If the volunteer survived, they would have another weapon."

Abel forced a smile. "All my friends agree. This is as safe here as anywhere else. My mystery friend has no principles and already wanted to keep it to greet the sorceress."

"Please hide it well, because you are unlikely to need it quickly. The sorceress will not be back." The vicar's smile seemed quite cheerful. "I haven't been completely open."

"Surprise surprise," Kelis whispered.

"Be ready. Watch that other one."

"I know the sorceress, or I do after hearing your story. The church heard of a fight between three sorcerers and a sorceress. She had a very potent glyph torn from her bone, and her Shades were destroyed. That weakened her and the three either killed or enslaved her, bound her, it is hard to get details." The vicar looked over the trio he could see, slowly. "Your phone call made me wonder if you were the sorcerers. Now I know you damaged her badly, and the other three simply took the chance to finish her off."

"Where? We can't find any sign of a sorcerer, apart from this?" Rob shrugged at Abel and Kelis. "Sorry, but he should know."

"In a city, the same as all the other sorcerers. That's where the money is. Now look, you've got me gossiping." The vicar looked along the repaired section of fence. "Nice job. So is the strengthening of the barrier spell. If that is all, I'll be off."

"Yes. Sorry to drag you out for nothing." Abel wanted to keep on the right side of the vicar, even if Ferryl kept muttering about him wanting to steal the glyph or get to her.

"It gave me a chance to check the house, and assess you three. Congratulations, the village is looking much neater." His little smile widened. "Have you found out yet how little food the thanks of your neighbours will buy?"

"They don't know." Abel grinned. "A public service. Perhaps it will catch on?"

The vicar actually laughed. "Not a chance. Try to get apprentice witches and warlocks and you'll soon find out. Those attracted to magic like the power, and therefore the wealth."

Kelis laughed. "We'll have to look for a different business model. One that makes protecting villages profitable."

"Let me know. It might work with the poorer churches." The vicar gave a little bow. "Please tell your friend I understand the message in the fight. Not too many people would recognise the attack in time to survive, let alone actually tear out a glyph like that. The church will give such knowledge the respect it deserves." He glanced at the man by the car. "Please do not call too often. Some people are already nervous about anyone who can walk into this garden." With that he turned and walked back to his car.

"Marvellous. I had another million questions." Kelis took her hand off Abel's shoulder and as he turned she tried to copy the vicar's voice. "Please do not call. People are nervous." Her voice reverted. "Nervous? I nearly wet myself when he jumped back! Though after that I really do vote for burying that thing very deep."

"Not too deep. The sorceress might not come back, but he might, and now we know it works against church magic." Ferryl sounded really pleased with the last part.

"But we don't want to use it. Do we?" Rob sounded confused, and

Abel could sympathise.

"You might prefer using the glyph to letting the house defences wake up." Nobody had an answer to that, and they walked back and re-buried the box without speaking.

They did plenty of talking on the way home, mainly about why the sorceress had tested and targeted them. Ferryl still thought she, or maybe a witch, had sensed the magical discharge when the Bound Shade and guardian were destroyed and Abel freed her. Hopefully what happened to the sorceress would frighten anyone else off, especially if the nearest sorcerers were thirty miles away. Rob came up with another very good reason. "You heard Archbishop Vicar Creepio. People are nervous about anyone who can get into Castle House gardens. The people might include sorcerers, not just church. Maybe I really should buy a baseball bat." For once Rob didn't smile after saying that.

*   *   *

Abel still checked the traps in his garden, but only caught a couple of hoplins after Halloween. He hoped the sorceress really had been the one testing, and anyone else had been frightened off. The damaged maple tree seemed to be recovering now, with both a growth glyph and a protection mark on the nearest fencepost. Putting the magic in the post had been laborious the first time. Abel, Kelis and Rob all contributed a little then waited until their levels recovered. Abel asked about leading a few fruit bushes to the post, so they could keep it topped up, and sparked another memory in Ferryl.

In the woods behind Castle House, Ferryl showed Abel how to drain magic from the root of a mature tree. The glyphs for feeding the barrier could be adapted to put magic into any object, such as a fence post. Rob and Abel filled the occasional protection post and hammered them in here and there around the edges of the village, because Dryad Chestnut had been right. The wooden posts held the magic for a long time.

To start with, Abel used the little kitchen knife to cut the glyphs in the posts. The plastic handle had warped with the heat so Abel daren't put it back in the drawer with the rest. Experimenting proved that would repel smaller magic creatures for about three metres all round. The main restriction turned out to be topping them up once driven into the ground.

The three of them daren't top up too many or they would have never had any magic reserve of their own.

The three of them had scrounged every suitable length of wood they could, for if they could find a better way. Carving the glyphs and the Tavern Hex became much easier when Kelis had found an electric chisel in her dad's garage. It had an attachment that cut a neat groove, ideal for the job. She sneaked off to use it during the week when her dad wasn't at home, and carefully cleaned up any mess. Once they could work out how to keep them full of magic, or Ferryl found a way in her wits, at least half the village could be protected.

Meanwhile the willow dryads were still safe, and happy, and quite talkative even if they weren't very knowledgeable. Dryad Chestnut stayed taciturn because he claimed that he still didn't trust sorcerers. Just in case he changed his mind, Rob and Abel dug up two very young trees in the wood behind Castle House and took them home. They were planted in big pots, ready for potential dryad baby passengers. Neither Rob nor Abel fancied dragging the filled pot back to the wood, even in a wheelbarrow. Rob told his parents the trees were a school project, and had so far got away with it.

The first half of December crawled by, as it always did with Christmas looming. Trimmings finally appeared at school as did a rash of end of term tests. To make sure everyone did well every teacher set extra homework, which dampened the Christmas spirit a bit. Abel tried to lift them again by taking the other two into the wood to choose a Christmas tree each. There were plenty because the barrier spell stopped people going in there.

Not big trees because they had to be carried or dragged out, but then Ferryl turned the expedition into a lesson. She taught them to carry the trees on cushions of air using continual air glyphs. The trees ended up by the road where they could be wheeled home in barrows, but first all three trainees had to pick the leaves, twigs and muck off each other. The air cushions had blasted debris from the ground all over the humans, much to Ferryl's amusement since the mess didn't touch her. The real fir trees arriving in Rob's and Abel's house were appreciated by both families and saved them a few quid. Abel's tree kept Kelis amused. She came round to help decorate it because her Dad didn't believe in all that nonsense and had thrown hers out.

* * *

Less than a fortnight before Christmas, Abel sat in his room trying to complete his homework when his mark tingled really strongly. Moments later a really strong surge, sucking and almost painful, shot through his flower. "Kelis." He scooped up his jacket and headed for the door, already calling her on his mobile.

Ferryl came in from the garden and caught up halfway down the stairs, flowing into her tattoo. *"What is happening? You nearly left without me."*

"Not likely, you fly faster than I run. Kelis might be in trouble. I felt her through my tattoo." Abel called into the living room to let Mum know Kelis wanted him, and raced off down the street. "It might be Henry." According to the phone, Kelis's mobile wasn't connected which made no sense.

"When did you start feeling people through your mark?"

"Just Kelis, and always." Abel saved his breath for running, and anyway Ferryl seemed to be talking enough for two. Most of it had to do with her promises being pointless when fools left a clear opening for an attack, right through all her defences. When he ran up to Kelis's gates, Abel could clearly hear shouting, screaming and furniture or something similar smashing. Her father's car parked in the driveway, on a Thursday, explained the rest.

Abel dialled 999 without any hesitation and reported attempted murder of multiple persons, and send an ambulance with the police please. He held up his phone for the woman to hear the crashing and screaming after explaining how far away it was, and inside a house. They'd need an ambulance if that was Kelis screaming, because Abel would be hurting her dad very badly. Maybe he wouldn't get the chance, because Ferryl understood now. *"Let me blast the gates open, then the door, and we can stop him right now. I can bind him to Kelis and she can teach him respect."*

Abel wanted to agree, but if the police found broken gates and doors they'd be more interested in the vandal. Worse, if Abel and Ferryl got to him and he survived, Kelis's dad might even blame everything on Abel or a mystery intruder. At the moment the noise had stopped, after another savage pull on Abel's flower. He could still feel Kelis's tingle now and then so with luck it was all over.

After a moment's thought Ferryl could help, though Abel had to gesture rather than speak because the 999 woman wanted to keep him on the phone. Smoke rose from the box by the locked gates, and they swung open. Now the police and ambulance could drive straight in. Abel sent a fire glyph into both back tyres of the car and Kelis's dad wouldn't be driving away. Ferryl got into the swing of it and the small glass panel on the front door shattered outwards onto the stone slabs. *"Now the police can get into the house."*

Abel could now hear a man's voice shouting at the little bitch to come out here, so maybe Kelis had hidden? *"I can give him something else to think of. Something noisy."* Abel held up his phone to catch the sound as a big window on the front of the house blew outwards. *"We had better have a reason, now I can reach inside."* A big carved wooden chair followed the glass onto the lawn. Mr. Ventner ran into the room, looked out, waved a fist at Abel and ran back out of sight, while Abel described it all to the woman. She kept telling him to stay away, probably a good idea since Ferryl wanted Mr. Ventner to attack Abel. *"Then there will be no rules except no killing. I can pull out bones and keep him alive to watch. That hurts, really hurts and won't kill him straight away, and your hospital might be able to keep him alive afterwards."*

Abel felt a stronger tingle, and held the phone under his arm to muffle his very quiet voice. "If anyone starts screaming, we'll go in. If he's hurting Kelis or her mum you can do something really painful but not obvious, and I'll help." Abel wasn't standing outside and listening to that.

"I hope he tries to hit you." The sheer anticipation in that would have stopped Kelis's dad in his tracks if he'd heard it.

At least the tingles from Kelis's mark reassured Abel she must be conscious. The ranting inside had been joined by more splintering noises by the time the police car hurled around the corner into the driveway. Abel relaxed because four coppers had come in a proper patrol vehicle, not one bloke in a panda car. They rushed in through the broken window when Mr. Ventner didn't answer, and a full-blooded fight broke out inside.

The ambulance crew were spilling out of their vehicle when the coppers more or less carried their struggling prisoner out. From their torn uniforms and the two who were limping, the police were going to have their own list of complaints. Another police car arrived behind the ambulance, and two of the occupants were WPCs.

The woman on the phone said thank you and told Abel he could hang up now, so he did and called Rob. Abel moved a bit closer to the house, too close. "No sightseeing. Who are you?" The copper pointed at the gates. "Why are you in here?"

"I phoned 999 for you lot and the ambulance. I came inside the garden because if the screaming started again, I was going to go in and try to do something." Abel was busy explaining to the copper when the stretcher came out of the door. Abel didn't think it could be Kelis because he'd felt her touch her tattoo, but even so it came as a huge relief when she walked out of the door being helped by a paramedic. One of the WPCs quickly moved in to help.

"Kelis!" She looked up and smiled, a very tired, worried smile. Abel put a hand over his tattoo, and for the first time tried to push out towards her.

"*Don't...*" Ferryl's objection died half-said. Kelis glanced at her arm, startled, then a big beautiful smile broke over her face for a moment and Abel blew her a kiss. Her smile stayed long enough to blow one back, then worry swept back in and Kelis hurried after what had to be her mum.

"Your girlfriend?"

Abel stared at the policeman and tried to concentrate. "Kelis? No. She's my best friend, one of them. The other one will wish he could have got here in time." Glancing back, Abel could see Rob outside the gate but police tape now stopped anyone else coming in.

At least the copper seemed willing to give Abel a bit of time to gather his wits. "I'll wait a minute until she's left."

Abel took the chance to ask how Kelis and her mum were, and the copper must have been feeling sociable. Either that or he thought telling Abel that Kelis seemed to be walking wounded, not too serious, and her mum wasn't critical, would be reassuring. By the time he was done talking the ambulance set off with Kelis and her mum inside, and most of the village were stood near the gates. The cop car followed with Mr. Ventner sat in the back, hidden under a blanket. Rob looked worried until Abel gave him a thumbs-up.

The wait before answering questions turned out to be a good thing, since Abel had time to think about why he'd been at the gate of his not-girlfriend, near enough to hear the noise. Claiming he'd gone for a walk to clear his head of some difficult homework got an odd look, but the policeman wrote it down. With a little smile, Abel wondered if the copper thought Kelis had been sneaking out to meet him. The rest wasn't so bad. Abel explained the gates were unlocked when he pushed so he came nearer, and the 999 woman insisted he didn't go further.

"A good thing. He might have hurt you. I'll see you home." The policeman put away his notebook and turned towards the gate.

Abel pointed. "That's my mum, but thanks anyway." As Abel left another van full of police arrived and began to either question people or put tape around the area.

*　*　*

Abel's tattoo tingled a lot overnight and the next morning. *"That will have to stop."*

"Not yet Ferryl. Kelis will need the reassurance. She felt it outside the house, so this lets her know we're thinking of her." Abel touched his mark and gently pushed magic.

"Once Kelis is home, it must stop. The connection, you drawing the ward, didn't seem active so not too dangerous. Now you tell me it is an open link, permanently connecting you in both directions. That is a weakness, an open channel past your ward to your inner self. It is a weakness for Kelis as well if you are killed or captured, maybe bound." Ferryl sighed. *"I understand, but this really is dangerous for both of you. What if the sorceress glyph had struck Kelis? You would be sucked in as well, unable to defend her. So would I."*

"All right, I get it. But not yet." Abel felt the tingle as Kelis replied, so she'd got his message. Friday seemed to last forever, because word had spread so half the school asked after Kelis and neither Abel nor Rob had an answer. At least Seraph, Henry and the other seraphims seemed to realise tempers were short and didn't make any remarks. Abel and Rob hurried home, but their parents didn't know any more. The hospital was being non-committal to non-relatives, and the workmen who turned up to board up the door and window on Saturday knew nothing. The strange hiatus continued across the weekend, with Rob and Abel messing about with a bit of magic practice, but unable to concentrate properly.

Sunday evening Kelis came home in a car with a stranger. Abel's mum found out from Mrs. Turner, phoning to find out who it was. Abel had no idea when Mum asked. When his phone rang Abel didn't recognise the caller number. "It's me, Kelis. My phone is broken and I couldn't find your mobile number until I could get home." She sounded embarrassed. "Can you come over please, you and Rob? I want you to meet my aunty, and explain I'll be safe going to school on the bus with you two. She wants to take me in the car."

"Do you want me to phone Rob?"

"No, I'll do it." She giggled which came as a big relief. "Or he'll accuse you of trying to cut him out. See you soon?"

"I'm going to collect Rob now, so get on with calling."

Abel and Rob walked down to the Green, and on to Kelis's house, almost in silence. Neither knew what this aunty wanted to know, but if Kelis wanted to ride to school on the bus they'd do their best.

*   *   *

The gates still gaped wide open, and the glass and chair still littered the lawn. The car had been removed. Someone had swept up the glass from the front door, which opened even as Abel lifted his hand to knock. Moments later both Abel and Rob were being thoroughly hugged by Kelis.

She stopped and stood back, blushing a little. "Sorry." Though the half-glance behind might mean sorry because her aunt was watching.

Abel still stood staring at her bruised face and black eye when Rob replied. "You'll have to make up your mind sooner or later, Kelis. Dump Abel and concentrate on me, it's the sensible choice."

A happy smile broke on her face. "What, a Glyphmistress with a sweaty barbarian? The shame of it." She turned. "Aunty Celia, this is Abel and this is Rob. My best friends."

At least Aunt Celia, a stout, cheerful woman, didn't seem worried about Kelis having her friends in the house. She took them into the kitchen, allegedly the tidiest room at the moment, and found them a drink of cola while she explained. Aunt Celia would be looking after Kelis until her mum came home, or made other arrangements. Kelis flinched at that, and again when Aunt Celia pointed out she'd be keeping undesirables out, but at least Rob and Abel didn't seem to be included. Ferryl kept quiet so she didn't have any ideas though she connected Kelis via spooky-phone to reassure her. Any more trouble and Ferryl would be here faster than Abel could run.

Rob and Abel were accepted as school escorts, as long as they called in to collect Kelis and brought her home again. She wasn't to walk through the village on her own, which seemed odd. Kelis didn't seem to be objecting, so the pair went with it. They soon left, following the not terribly subtle hints from Aunty about how tired Kelis must be. Abel suffered the cross-questioning from his mum, repeating that he didn't know until she gave up. He assumed that Rob suffered the same problem.

The gates were still open on Monday morning, which really seemed weird. Kelis came out the door as Abel and Rob walked down the drive, and almost trotted to meet them. "Phew, free at last." She giggled. "Not that bad, but Dad is out on bail and Aunty Celia is a bit paranoid. She thinks he'll snatch me, which would be the first time in my entire life he ever showed any sign of wanting me."

"He'll need an army, and will have to climb over many bodies."

"He can't have you, and Ferryl agrees. You're our Glyphmistress." Abel smiled but Kelis looked very serious and glanced back.

"I might have made a mistake. He came home a day early, really drunk because some deal went bad. He kept drinking then started on Mum, the usual insults, twisting arms and slapping." Abel and Rob stared but kept quiet; Kelis never mentioned what her Dad actually did even if they'd guessed. Kelis never noticed, just ploughed on. "This time he didn't stop, he got worse, throwing things and really punching her. I tried to stop him, push him with magic when Mum fell down, and he hit me. He doesn't usually punch me." Kelis stopped and sighed. "It's about time I told you two. I nearly lost the chance because...." Her voice tailed off.

Rob nudged her shoulder. "We guessed some."

Abel grinned. "Ferryl wanted to do really bad things."

Kelis giggled briefly and then her face straightened. "So did I. Mum got up and tried to stop him hitting me, and he went crazy. He knocked her down again and started kicking her." Tears started to trickle down her face. "I lost it. When I could get up again I concentrated. I put my hand on him and pushed, really hard. With a glyph." Her attempt at a smile didn't last long. "No control."

"I felt it." Abel gestured at his arm.

"You did? Oh." Kelis put her hand on her arm. "I put my other hand on here first, to concentrate." She stopped, looking from Abel to Rob with her eyes wide in wonder. "I threw him, Dad, right across the room, into the wall. It hurt my arm, but knocked Dad out. I'd landed on my phone and broke it, the house phone had been ripped out of the wall, and Dad started to stir." She shrugged. "I helped Mum onto her feet and sort of half-carried, half-dragged her upstairs to my room and started piling up furniture. I used a wind glyph to help carry Mum so maybe she saw that, but I didn't care just then."

"I heard him telling you to come out."

"Yeah, as if that would work. Mum passed out again, and I could hear Dad downstairs, yelling and breaking things. He started on the bedrooms then realised my door wouldn't open. He started beating the door down, then left for a bit for some reason."

"Probably Ferryl busting windows for when the police arrived."

"She did? Thanks, Ferryl. I just kept hoping he'd pass out from the booze, or someone had heard the noise and reported it to the police. He came back and started again and the door split but the furniture stopped it opening. Maybe the wind glyphs helped it to hold. I thought he would be through any time, so I kept trying to get calm enough to really floor him with a glyph. Then the police arrived."

"I called the police when I heard the noise." Abel shrugged. "I wanted to come in but the emergency woman said no. I knew you were still all right." Abel touched his arm, without letting Rob see, and Kelis smiled. "Ferryl really wanted to come in, which might have been a problem."

"We could have hidden the body in there." Kelis nodded towards Castle House as they walked past, and didn't seem to be joking. "I wish I could have taken Mum there. The barrier would have stopped Dad."

"I reckon the police will deal with it now. They were looking a bit battered when they brought him out." Abel left it at that, because the TV kept on about how many abused women wouldn't prosecute so maybe Mrs. Ventner wouldn't.

"Oh no, that's the least of his worries. Mum is mad as hell, and if she looks like backing off I'm going to set into her." Kelis sighed. "All the times he's hit her, and she's finally got mad because he punched me." Her face hardened. "Well I'm mad about him kicking Mum, and now I can fix him." For once Kelis didn't laugh as she lifted a hand and said "Glyphmistress!"

"No need. I'm sure Ferryl can sort that out if necessary while you are sat someplace with fifty witnesses."

"Please?"

"Ferryl wants permission. She wanted to pull out your Dad's bones, because I wouldn't let her kill him." Rob and Kelis stopped to stare at Abel's arm. "She swears it won't kill him, but it will hurt. Apparently intensive care might save him afterwards."

"Wow. I don't ever want Ferryl mad at me." Rob shook his head. "She seems to be a lot of fun most of the time," he chuckled, "except when clobbering Wolf Shades."

"May I talk to them now? I didn't want to before, in case I gave Kelis bad ideas."

"I think she's got some already, but you can explain alternatives."

With the little mist tendrils Ferryl could talk to them on the bus. The other students stared at Kelis's bruised face, but apart from saying hello didn't speak and left the three of them alone. That seemed to be the general reaction at school. Everyone, including the teachers, obviously wanted to know the whole story but didn't feel they should ask. Even Seraph seemed to be struck dumb, a definite improvement, and several of the seraphims said hello without the sneer.

Kelis decided that someone's parent would know someone in Brinsford, and the whole village had seen her dad dragged off and her mum on a stretcher. Some sort of story would spread, so best to make it the truth and at lunchtime Kelis gave their table the gist. Dad hit Mum,

189

police, Mum in hospital, Aunt visiting to look after Kelis. Everyone told her they were sorry, and Una offered her sword for if Kelis's dad came back, once she'd got a sword. Kelis hadn't said her dad hit her, but the bruises told the story.

Kelis's Aunty Celia had been busy. By the time Kelis came home from school the glass had gone from the lawn, replaced by a skip full of broken furniture and at least a couple of splintered doors. Two cleaners, not the usual ones according to Kelis, were busy in the house and Abel could hear hammering from further inside. Once again Aunty Celia invited Rob and Abel inside for a few minutes, and thanked them before they left. Halfway home Abel felt his tattoo tingle, and sent a reply. *"That has to stop."*

"You can fix it when Kelis's life is fixed."

"I am trying to work out how to." That definitely gave Abel food for thought. Ferryl didn't know how to stop the bond, or how to fix Kelis's life?

*   *   *

The week dragged by with almost everyone being kind and Seraph still keeping quiet. Since she usually held Henry's reins that kept him in check as well. Thursday evening Henry couldn't keep quiet any longer, or maybe he'd just waited until nobody else could hear him because he caught the three of them in an empty corridor. "About time. Let's hope it knocked some manners into you. What happened to this?" Henry raised a hand and waggled a finger, a sneer matching his mocking tone.

Both Rob and Abel took a step, but they were too late. Kelis lunged, her hand landed on Henry's chest and Abel felt a tug through his flower. Henry slammed back against the wall, his breath leaving him in a whoosh and eyes wide in shock. Kelis had grown upwards even if she stayed really thin, and now she looked down at Henry and murmured something before turning on her heel and walking away, face serene.

"You can't threaten me like that!" Henry lunged off the wall, his hand reaching for her and rage spreading across his face.

Abel snapped. His hand came up and a wind glyph, *"Well controlled"* a little voice complimented him, knocked Henry's hand wide. Two more stopped Henry's shoulders, so he lost balance as his legs kept going for a

190

moment and then staggered backwards.

Abel followed, catching hold of the hand Henry had stretched out to catch Kelis. "Not a brick Henry, one finger." Abel concentrated and launched the glyph from his palm into Henry's hand, then let go.

"Really good control." Ferryl sounded eager, almost savage and Abel realised she was poised, hoping Henry attacked.

Instead, Henry spun away, his face losing colour as he cradled his hand and stared down in disbelief at his ring finger and the completely un-natural kink in the bone. Abel followed, keeping his voice low because a small group of students had just come round the corner. "Enough, Henry. If you raise a hand to my friends again, I'll do that to your elbows and knees. This costs you three weeks out of the rugby team, next time you'll never play again." Henry didn't answer. He stared for a moment then staggered away, elbowing the group aside.

"I wish I'd brought my bat." The other two looked at Rob and burst out laughing, but he looked indignant. "Well, there's Glyphmistress throwing Henry about, then you snap a finger like a twig and threaten ruin. I feel a teensy bit useless."

"So do I. I'm supposed to be the protection."

"Ferryl is complaining as well."

Rob looked at Abel's shoulder and smiled, then frowned and turned to Kelis. "What did you say? He went crackers."

Kelis had her serene smile back again. "I told him if he ever gave any of us any crap again, I would shove his ribs through to his spine and leave him to drown in his own blood. I'm done with taking that sort of thing from anyone." It crossed Abel's mind that letting Kelis discuss punishment with Ferryl might have been a mistake.

"I will talk to her." Even as Abel relaxed a bit, an amused Ferryl continued. *"That is too crude. A Glyphmistress should kill with style."* Abel kept quiet on the bus, then tried to explain restraint to both of them as they walked up the lane and Main Street. He wasn't sure either Ferryl or Kelis were convinced, even with Rob pitching in, but both agreed to not dismember anyone without talking to Abel or Rob first.

Kelis's parting shot, "Unless someone throws a punch," didn't sound encouraging. Aunty Celia came to the door and invited Rob and Abel in, which ended any discussion.

*   *   *

Henry stayed clear after that, and from the lack of reaction from Seraph probably never mentioned how he broke a finger. The pupils were more interested in Christmas than a broken finger. Abel, Rob and Kelis were invited to the Tavern party in town but declined. Kelis didn't fancy going anywhere, her Aunt wasn't keen on Kelis going anywhere, and now both Rob and Abel wanted to make the most of their time with her. According to Aunty Celia, Kelis's mum would be best off selling the house once the divorce came through, and moving somewhere without bad memories.

Kelis didn't want to leave, and now Abel and Rob found out she'd been moving all her life. After a year or two her dad would sell up and buy another house, usually in some remote village but within commuting range for his business. Now there were no secrets, Kelis admitted it probably happened whenever neighbours noticed the arguments, or black eyes.

Kelis definitely cheered up when she found out her mum would be home for Christmas, though Aunty Celia would be stopping for a while to look after her. Once Mrs. Ventner fully recovered, Kelis, Rob and Abel were at least half-convinced the "For Sale" signs would go up but kept hoping. Ferryl suggested keeping Mrs. Ventner too ill to move but all three vetoed that, and using a glyph to bind Kelis's mum to the place, unable to leave. Though now she knew such a glyph could be made, Kelis wanted to know how. She fancied using one to keep Henry bound to the school toilets, but finally agreed that wasn't fair to the other students. Abel wasn't sure if Ferryl really couldn't remember how without her wits, as she claimed, or just didn't fancy letting Kelis loose with the knowledge.

*   *   *

Kelis's mum, Jessica, or Jess as Aunty Celia called her, came home two days before Christmas. That evening Abel's mum answered the phone, then called Abel downstairs. She looked baffled. "It's Mrs. Ventner. She wants us round there at Christmas." Her eyes went to the little freezer where the tiny Christmas turkey, or turkling as she'd christened it, waited to be defrosted. "For dinner, and some sort of party? Do you know about this? She's asking Rob's mum as well."

"Kelis never mentioned it. We can have family Christmas if you want Mum, but it'll save all the cooking." Abel grinned. "They've got a dishwasher so it'll save me some work as well."

"If you're sure? It's not like we're a big family now, you and me, and you're a bit past Santa." She put the phone back to her ear. "Thank you very much, Mrs. Ventner. This party, how are we supposed to dress?" Abel saw his mum relax, so nothing dramatic, then she laughed. "I'll bring it."

After some more listening his mum rang off and Abel grinned "Does she want the turkling?"

"No, my dressing gown, the bath robe Kelis wore at Halloween. She'd like to see it." She shook her head, baffled. "She seems very happy, all things considered. Oh damn. A present. What can we take?"

"Sprouts?" Abel laughed. "It's Christmas Eve tomorrow so she can't really be expecting anything."

"I suppose I can take the marzipan fruits?" She looked unhappy, but Abel knew Mum would be getting a box of hard centred chocolates Christmas morning and would be scoffing them.

"Just enough for one each from the sounds of it. Better than taking the Christmas cake." Abel meant that. He'd offer Kelis and Rob some when they came round, but his mum made a really mean fruit cake and didn't stint on icing or marzipan. Better yet, Mum didn't eat much if he let her pinch some of the marzipan from his. "Otherwise I'd have to buy you another slab of marzipan for Christmas."

"That's what that present is? It had better not be. She said not to dress up, but we'd better posh up a bit." Mum laughed. "We can't posh up a lot. I'll ask and see what Rob's family are wearing."

"We won't need posh. Kelis reckoned her dad trashed the wardrobes when, you know, he went crackers."

"How much did you know, before? You should have said."

"We didn't know, not that it was that bad, honest. Kelis wouldn't talk." Abel shrugged. "I offered her a settee if necessary. So did Rob."

"Settee? She'd have got your room. You could have had the settee. I'm off to find out what on earth sort of party frock I'm supposed to wear." Abel watched his mum heading down the road. From what Kelis had said, her mum might have to borrow a frock. Maybe Aunty Celia had sorted it out? He took out his mobile to ask Kelis.

"Don't dress up! Mum doesn't want posh, fancy, anything like that. She's had enough of that." Kelis sounded really happy, bubbly. "It'll be great. This is to thank you for looking after me. She's been laid in hospital planning and Aunty Celia must have been helping. There's a caterer bringing in food by the truckload, and they're taking over our kitchen Christmas morning. Mum can't do much, but right now she's poised to point and criticise while I get some more trimmings up."

Abel dived in when she stopped for breath. "She's all right then?"

"Her arm is in a pot and she's on lots of tablets, but not as many... The doctors say there is probably some concussion working its way out, she's still wobbly and sleeps or rests a lot. Don't worry about Dad because he's been lawyered even if the slime ball has got bail. If he turns up he gets HM lodgings." Her voice hardened. "Or maybe a Glyphmistress."

"She needs tuition. I could go and direct her?"

"Ferryl says wait until she gets there. As a Glyphmistress you should show restraint."

"Restraint, hah!"

"Restraint? Finesse, yes, but a Glyphmistress under attack has no restraint."

Abel still hoped he could avoid serious bloodshed, even if he knew he probably wouldn't. "Call me first, right? You'll see him coming."

"OK, but he won't get near Mum again." Abel ignored the threat in that because it seemed fair enough. He managed to get Kelis back onto the coming meal, and her mum being home, until she rang off because Rob would be burning out his phone trying to ask the same questions.

*   *   *

Neither Rob nor Abel saw Kelis on Christmas Eve because she spent the day either running back and forth to town in the car with her mum and aunty, or preparing for Christmas Day. Her texts and phone calls were brief, but happy, which is what really mattered, and Abel kept in touch in a way through flower power tingle-phone. Ferryl didn't object too much, probably because she could also feel the sheer joy coming through the contacts.

In the evening, while his mum caught up on watching her recorded TV programmes, Abel finished off his presents for Rob and Kelis. He'd made them plastic figurines of a Glyphmistress and a barbarian, or at least adapted them. No such figures existed, but once she knew Abel wanted something unique for his friends, Ferryl had come up with the idea. Originally she'd wanted to start with clay, but Abel knew his modelling limitations and a bit more about modern materials.

The two figures had started life as a model of the Hulk, and one of a sorceress or maybe elf that probably came from a chess set before ending up for sale on a market stall. Abel's carefully hoarded cash had been just enough for the two decent-sized if battered figurines when his mum took him to Stourton for Christmas shopping. Abel thought they were done a couple of days ago, but Ferryl turned out to be a perfectionist. He started picturing the glyph, the old wooden lolly-stick poised in his other hand. *"Careful. A tiny, tiny heat glyph, just enough to make it malleable without burning. Then the wooden tool and a tiny puff of air to cool it at the perfect moment, to look as if the wind caught the hem."* Ferryl and Abel considered the figure for a little while. *"I believe that is enough. They look enough like your friends to show who it is, and yet like the characters in your game to show what they are. I still believe the sorceress should have a red and black robe."*

"That is such a cliché, and anyway Kelis looked terrific in that white dressing gown of Mum's, like a real Glyphmistress." Abel looked at the slim figure, arm raised to cast and hair blowing back, the cloak fluttering to show a light blue lining because Ferryl insisted it had to be different to the outside. "Kelis will be a good sorceress, not like the ones in stories."

"But white shows bloodstains, it's impractical. Imagine the state of that after dragging a troll out of her lair, or blasting a pack of hellhounds apart. Though you don't have hellhounds now, not even enhanced war hounds." Ferryl sniffed dismissively. *"Kelis will be a true bloody-handed sorceress when she masters her glyphs."*

"No she won't. She doesn't like blood," Abel sniggered, "or slime." Though privately Abel did wonder, if something upset Kelis enough.

195

Ferryl must have thought the same. *"I will drive your ribs through to your spine and leave you to drown in your own blood."*

"Good sorceress, in white. No point in encouraging her."

"I wish I could be sure of the animating glyphs, but I just can't remember. We could bind something small, a mouse or a Hoplin, and use it to animate them? One for each?" Ferryl sounded a bit too keen.

"Bound Shades? You want me to give my friends Bound Shades for Christmas?" Abel shook his head. "Not only that, but a miniature Glyphmistress and barbarian racing around the place would be hard to explain." He put the wooden lolly stick down. "At least Kelis will be able to explain to her mum since she wants me to bring the whole game folder, drawings and everything."

"If they are to remain statues, we are finished. May I wrap them, please? Your paper is beautiful." Abel let her. Some trivial things, such as wrapping paper, really seemed to blow Ferryl away, whereas cars weren't that wonderful except for the speed. While she wrapped, Abel watched with definite pride. The reshaping had been slow, delicate work with just heat, wind and a lolly stick. The colour had been another minor glyph Ferryl remembered, a useless one she pointed out. Abel finally mastered it, even getting the green out of the hulk plastic and hitting a decent skin tone. Abel wasn't sure if being able to change the colour of more or less anything, permanently and without dye, would ever be useful but it certainly taught him control.

Despite the bit of sleet in the rain tonight, not reindeer and sleigh weather, Abel walked down to Castle House once he'd done to sit on the stone slab for a while. He'd used quite a lot of magic in the finicky work on the models, and didn't want another sorceress catching him with his levels down. As Ferryl had noticed, he recovered faster sat on the slab while it seemed to make no difference to Rob and Kelis. Ferryl spent the times Abel visited the slab either checking the boundaries or dancing with the wind if the weather gave her plenty of gusts as partners. Sometimes Ferryl spent time inspecting the glyph on the bone from the sorceress, at a distance without touching. In her wind form she could do that without digging it up.

*   *   *

Abel and his mum opened presents from each other on Christmas morning, and she agreed that the chocolates meant the marzipan fruits weren't such a loss. Abel's present, a pair of short boots "because if you will insist on wandering about outside in bad weather, trainers aren't really weather-proof" would be perfect for a different reason. Abel could keep the little knife in one, because it really had come in handy that night.

Rob's family knocked on the door and the two families went together, as arranged, all of them wondering exactly what was waiting. Rob and Abel weren't worried, because Kelis sounded too happy for there to be anything that might cause a problem. Everyone began to wonder about their dress when a smart young woman took their coats and showed them through to the huge lounge, but the sight of Kelis in her usual holiday jeans and blouse soon relaxed them all. Her mum greeted them all with a big smile, sat in an armchair and wearing a fluffy dressing gown with one arm cut off for her plaster cast.

Mrs. Ventner, "Jessica, or call me Jess," seemed delighted by the marzipan fruits. "We've been getting in lots of goodies, but we haven't any of these. Somebody didn't believe in wasting money on all this nonsense at Christmas, so we're making up for it." She waved her good arm around at the loops of decorations. "Kelis and Celia did their best, but I'm not up to it." The tall, slim woman didn't look up to much at all, very pale and shifting now and then in some sort of discomfort. She kept rubbing her arm above the cast, so that must bother her as well.

When everyone found a seat Kelis gave out her presents, and she'd bought Abel a folding penknife "because you never know when one might be useful." Kelis must have been thinking about that night, because she'd bought one for Rob as well. The two little figurines for Kelis and Rob set the adults off, and they all wanted a look.

"Kelis has been talking about these. Did you bring the robe, Mrs. Conroy?"

"Christine, Chris usually. Yes, though it doesn't look like that." A flurry of less formal introductions led to all the Mr. and Mrs. being dropped.

Rob's dad leant forward to inspect Rob's barbarian. "I've seen a few pictures, but this is different. It even looks a bit like Rob, if he'd got muscles like one of the Copples. Is Roughly Hewn a description?" He looked at the other. "Kelis Glyphmistress is her actual name, so have you been rechristened Roughly?" He tried to glare at Rob but couldn't keep the smile back. Before long all the pictures and game rules were being passed around and commented on. A blushing Kelis had to put on the dressing gown and pose dramatically, arm out to strike something or other down. She wouldn't bring a hair drier to create a wind for her hair, in spite of Rob suggesting it.

Somehow everyone seemed to get really involved, and Abel found himself explaining the magical system and creatures, assisted by Rob and Kelis. Even Rob's big sister, Samantha, seemed to get interested. Melanie, his thirteen-year-old 'baby' sister really got into the swing, wanting to know why none of the characters had a young sibling, called Melanie or possibly Mel. Ferryl offered to create a wind for Kelis, or show everyone the brownies and pixies in the room. She'd sent out her little mist connections to Rob and Kelis so all three kept smiling at the same time.

Eventually another well-dressed and very polite young woman told them Christmas dinner was ready, and everyone went through into a huge dining room. Rob, Kelis and Abel hung back for a quick round of mutual congratulation and pride. Rob's family and Abel's mum had known about the game, but not the details. Now they'd seen the whole thing, and despite some teasing nobody had ripped their idea to shreds. There'd been a few looks at Abel's shirt sleeve when the pictures of Ferryl Shayde went round, and Abel thought Melanie would try for a look when she got the chance.

Christmas Day turned out to be one long party, to a greater or lesser degree. Not the loud music, crazy hat and dancing type, and definitely not the boozy type, just a group of people being happy talking together. Dinner started out looking very formal, a massive carved wood table with big wooden chairs around it and a half ton of assorted cutlery and glass arranged across the top. Mrs. Ventner, Jessica, soon stopped the formality, asking for extra cushions for anyone who needed them and removing half her cutlery. "It's not as if we have to impress some customer today, is it?"

The meal meandered. Abel sort of expected the staff to be like they were in the few restaurants he'd been to, hovering to scoop up his plate and get the pudding served. Not this time. Despite some of them taking their time to finish, everyone had their plates cleared at the same time, and in spite of delays the next course came in piping hot. John, Rob's dad, found himself volunteered as turkey carver, and Abel mentioned to his mum they'd found where the turkling's dad went, unless this was an ostrich.

After everyone announced themselves thoroughly stuffed, they all went back into the lounge. Jessica didn't seem in any hurry to send anyone home, turning on a TV for anyone wanting to watch. Melanie lost interest in the game when Kelis showed her another TV in a smaller sitting room where she could look through an entire catalogue of programmes and films. Kelis came back, and beckoned Abel and Rob. "Just going to the library Mum."

"Good. Have fun, you three." Abel shrugged to his mum, he'd no idea what it was about.

*   *   *

The room definitely fitted the description; three walls of tall bookshelves, all full, with a big window in the fourth wall. Kelis sat in a padded chair, and twirled it around with her arms out wide. "Welcome to Bonny's Tavern, the original and best." She laughed at their faces. "We can have this room. Completely. Mum says make a bonfire if we don't want the books. Dad never let anyone in, possibly because there's a section there that opens. Behind the books used to be enough booze to stock a real Tavern, or maybe float it."

"Really?" Abel noted the complete absence of magical creatures in here. "Already protected?"

Kelis swung open a section of books to show the Tavern sign propped up on the counter behind, a big version carved into a sheet of wood. She brought it out and put it on a picture hook. "I hid it so I could do the big reveal. Mum doesn't mind how much I use that electric chisel." Her face sobered. "She's really on a sort of high, doing everything he hated, but sooner or later she'll come down. We'd better make the most of this place because Aunty Celia still thinks Mum should leave and I don't think she's sure herself."

"Our settee is still there." Rob laughed. "Not really up to the standard of the ones here."

"My mum told me she'd throw me out if Kelis needed a bed, make me sleep on the settee." Abel suffered a mixture of accusations from Rob that he'd only said it to get Kelis to move in, and Kelis claiming it was a bid for Rob's settee. Abel countered by insisting he really wanted the chair Kelis still twirled around now and then.

"*Please roll up your sleeve.*" Abel did, and after a moment Ferryl asked, "*Will this truly be the Tavern?*" Ferryl had been very quiet, so now they all stopped larking about to answer.

"Yes, Mum said so."

"*A home for all of us, the characters? Including Ferryl Shayde?*"

Kelis answered very quietly, possibly because Ferryl sounded nervous, tentative, which wasn't usual. "Until we move. For a long time if I can persuade Mum to stay. You can even come here without that lump, if you need some space."

"*Nobody gives me a home. Not once they see me, know what I am.*" Both Rob and Kelis gasped as Ferryl left her tattoo, because they'd never seen her shimmery wind form. The vague shape moved around the room, never the same for more than a few moments. "*Thank you.*" She flowed back into the tattoo, and her voice became stronger, more like her usual self. "*Time for a party.*" Her tattoo exploded, literally, into a frantic firework display before balloons and streamers slowly settled over her cat-form.

"Is this why you wanted all the files? We can come here every Tavern night, instead of to our bedrooms." Rob sat on the floor. "I'll want to bring a cushion, or one from in the lounge."

"This is instead of my bedroom. Mum told me that regardless of your house rules, she wasn't having dozens of young men trooping in and out of my bedroom at all hours." Kelis giggled. "Dozens?" She finally stood up from the chair and opened the fridge under the counter to show it stocked with soft drinks. "Mum's idea of hilarious because Dad kept it full of booze. Drink anyone?"

"I'm stuffed, thanks." Rob dropped into the chair. "That's better. I'm not sure where you sit."

"Come on, we'll raid the office." Abel and Rob shrugged at each other and followed her out. With a wave to her mum, Kelis led them past the lounge. "Just raiding the office, Mum. We need a few things for the Tavern."

"Help yourself dear. If anything you want is screwed down, wait until the workmen come back to take it out properly." Rob and Abel exchanged glances as they followed Kelis to a room at the back of the house. Both Kelis and her mum seemed to be on some sort of high.

"Look. Four more chairs. They are supposed to be for meetings, but he never had many. You can take the big chair as well if you want, but I'm *never* sitting in that!" Kelis went to the glass table and licked her fingers before smearing them along it. "He used to get really uptight about the cleaner leaving a fingerprint on this. I'm surprised Mum hasn't put a hammer through it."

By the time they'd moved the four chairs, and emptied a cupboard of office stationery, Abel at least had begun to wonder if Kelis might put a hammer through the table. *"I could teach her real control with that table."* Kelis had just smeared it again, she did so every time she went past. *"With practice she could melt little holes, or even write a curse in it. If he really did like the table, the curse should work."*

Abel dropped back far enough to speak privately, since Ferryl had stopped using the mist connections while they moved furniture. "Both of them, Kelis and her mum, have a lot of anger to get rid of. Let them get through it without doing something they might be sorry about later."

"It doesn't have to be permanent. Boils, piles, ulcers. Rotten teeth? Septic ears! They are painful, smelly, visually disgusting, embarrassing and almost impossible to cure. I just want to say thank you for my home." Ferryl sniggered. *"Kelis might not be sorry even afterwards."*

"No. Please."

"All right, because otherwise you'll use that name."

"I haven't for ages." Abel thought a moment. "I haven't needed it."

"I'm being good. It really is difficult and irritating." Ferryl's mist connections reached out and cut off their privacy.

*   *   *

When the party ended everyone went home together, laughing and joking even as Abel and his mum turned up their own front path. Once inside, all the joking suddenly stopped. "Abel, I need a serious talk to you. You aren't in trouble, but this might take some time. Would you like a drink?"

Abel stared at his Mum, baffled. "Not really thanks, I'm bloated."

"In that case we may as well get comfy." Once they were settled in the living room, Abel watched as his mum almost started to speak several times. Finally she took a deep breath and pulled out one of the sketches of games creatures, a thorny. "Where did you get the idea for this?"

"We've been building the game and the creatures for ages, Mum. I'm not sure."

Even as he spoke Abel could see Mum didn't believe him, but he couldn't figure out why. Not until she whispered, "I've seen them. Things like those in the game, some of them. A long time ago." Her voice strengthened, though she looked really worried. "It can be fixed, the hallucinations. It takes time, and lots of counselling."

"How did she stop seeing them? That is not possible."

"You saw things then stopped seeing them?" Abel wasn't confirming he did see anything. He didn't fancy counselling.

"Yes." Her eyes and voice dropped. "Not really, but you'll learn to ignore them because they aren't real." Abel wanted to hug his mum because right then she looked frightened, and ashamed, then he gave up on fifteen-year-old hang-ups and did.

"It's okay Mum."

"Tell her." Abel considered it, but Ferryl claimed that adults finding out about magic usually went crackers. They couldn't handle it the same as younger minds. *"She already knows, and thinks she is crazy. It is well hidden, this knowledge, or I would have seen it."* A tinge of amusement touched Ferryl's voice. *"I didn't pry too deeply because of how worried you were."*

Abel decided to test a bit first. "Are there less of them lately?"

"You believe me? You see them?" Abel kept his face straight and didn't answer, trying to make up his mind. His mum didn't wait. "They all went away, finally, and I thought that after twenty years I was cured. Then some came back. I've been wondering about more therapy."

After hugging her again, Abel went for it. "You don't need therapy Mum. I got rid of them. You complained about the mess so I let the good ones back in."

"Should I explain?"

"I'll try to explain Mum." Abel hoped Ferryl understood the hint in that and kept quiet. "I can see them. You remember Halloween?" She nodded, eyes wide, so Abel ploughed on. "We really did go out on a creature hunt and drove most of the nasty ones out of Brinsford."

"Rob and Kelis as well? What are those things? Is that game real, all the characters?" She frowned. "Good ones, and nasty ones?"

"No Mum, it really is a game but the creatures are accurate. The game really will tell you which ones help with housekeeping, I promise." Abel set into explaining, or halfway anyway. He had no intention of explaining Ferryl Shayde, magic, or glyphs, though he showed her the Tavern hexes cut into the tops of the doors where she wouldn't see them. Eventually both of them were too tired to keep going. Abel suffered a proper mum-hug before bed, and she seemed happy enough going up to bed.

Boxing Day morning Abel found his mum in the kitchen, happy and smiling and looking straight at Pictsies hunting along the skirting. "What are they after?" She sighed. "I've never dared to even look at them, not properly. I remember slimy ones."

"Pictsies hunt bugs, sort of super-spiders without webs. Some of the slimy ones will clean up stains, allegedly, but we don't like them." Abel laughed. "Kelis freaked about them, more than the rest."

"There seem to be less stains these days. Washing machines are noisier but look better than creatures."

"Is there a way to get rid of them at work? Some people seem to be left alone, but my workspace is covered in them. There are bigger ones in the car park, but none go near my car now." Her eyes opened wide. "You protected my car? How?"

"If you'll let me make you a Tavern sign, Mum, I can give you one to clear your workspace. You can have more for the washroom and wherever you eat. The creatures are also frightened off by anything religious, like a properly blessed cross or people who go to church every Sunday." Abel launched into another explanation. The next few days were interspersed with little sessions like that, where Abel explained a particular creature or mark to his mum. He had to explain the marks on the post near her tree when she spotted them. On the plus side, his mum wanted the hex, the Tavern mark, properly carved into every window frame when Abel explained that worked better.

"You should tell her, all of it."

"Nope. Mum's happy. She's relaxed and cracking jokes about creatures, not pretending not to see them in case she gets locked up as being a nutter." Abel still wasn't sure his mum could handle the Glyphmistress or dancing tattoo part yet.

"Chris is not stupid." As usual Abel flinched at Ferryl using Mum's real name. *"She will look at the Tavern hex, and the creatures, and wonder what else is true."*

"Then I'll tell her more."

"Introduce us?"

"Mum will go absolutely barmy if she finds out I let you out from under a stone and then brought you home." Abel still wondered why he'd done that so quickly. Abel also worried Mum might push a bit harder about who or what Ferryl Shayde might be. He still didn't want details, because it might be gross and he needed his tattoo.

"You will have to tell her in the end." Abel didn't have an answer to that. Though perhaps he could see that point coming sometime in the future when she started asking about the creatures in the garden. He wasn't sure if Mum was being fooled, or just happy and didn't want to ask how her son suddenly knew all about an invisible world.

*   *   *

Abel thought the day had come when Mum called him and pointed into the cupboard under the stairs. "Explain that, please." Abel looked past her, knowing full well what she could see. He used this cupboard to feed the brownies, pixies and pictsies.

For a moment he hesitated, but the creatures were obviously clustered around their saucers of sugar and milk. "These are trapped in the house, so a bit of extra energy helps them. They are all good ones Mum, honest."

"I know, I took that list of yours to work and photocopied it, and I'm trying to learn it. There are some missing, creatures I see in town." She laughed, to Abel's immense relief. "There again, I don't know the name of every bird and insect I see in the fields. Why did the lights stop?"

"Probably they just seemed to glow because it's dark under there." The creatures were gradually edging away into the shadows, away from Abel. They treated him as dangerous, but not his mum.

"Chris sees the magic in them. Sooner or later you must tell her. Before she sees you cast a glyph."

Abel settled for warming one of the saucers of milk, explaining to his mum that pixies preferred that. Two days later he found the saucers on the sideboard in the living room. His mum didn't think the food should be in that dusty old cupboard, and anyway she liked watching them. Abel didn't try to explain it wasn't their food, or he'd have to go into the creatures gathering magic.

*   *   *

Kelis, or her mum, insisted The Tavern became the permanent home for all game planning. Rob and Abel were told the code for the gates once they'd been fixed, and were always met by smiles and greetings from both Mrs. Ventner and Aunty Celia. Partly, Kelis finally admitted, because her mum remembered something about that night. Not clearly, just that Kelis had somehow knocked her dad down and got them both away. Kelis explained about Abel and Rob teaching her some self-defence against bullies at school, and thought her mum visualised some sort of Judo. She'd offered the library at least partly as a thank you, though she also enjoyed turning it into a playroom with soft drinks.

Abel barely needed the code for the gates because they were open more often than closed. The occupants of the other four big new houses along one side of Brinn's Lane usually kept themselves fairly private, even if they weren't as fanatical about it as Mr. Ventner had been. Now several used the season as a reason to pop round and say hello. The rest of the village usually stayed clear of the posh types in the new houses, even if some of the village houses probably cost as much. Now they, and even a few of those from the council houses, dropped by once word spread they'd be welcome. Some were just nosy, but regardless of why they came most of them brought something, a few home-made buns or something similar.

Kelis nearly choked laughing when she told Rob and Abel about Stan visiting. He'd brought a fresh hare he'd allegedly fallen over out on a walk, and advised them to hang it for a bit to get it to taste right. Unfortunately, neither Kelis's mum nor Aunty Celia had any idea where to start with skinning or dressing it so the hare went to the butcher in town before coming back sliced and diced. Now Aunty Celia lived in dread of Stan turning up again because handling a warm body had freaked her out.

Although she tried to persuade them, neither Aunty Celia nor her mum would let Kelis take the security cameras off the trees in the garden, even to fasten them on poles. As a result, the dryads in her garden still wouldn't talk to Kelis. The three young willows by the bridge remained quite chatty, for trees. Rob still didn't quite trust dryads, but had taken on the job of approaching any he could find along the nearby field boundaries. So far none of the dryads that would talk trusted him enough to consider a bargain. Abel warned him that Henry would start complaining about trespassing, but Rob seemed quite eager. That left Abel hoping Rob would remember control if Henry tried to get physical.

Coming Together

Two days before New Year, Abel and Rob still hadn't worked out their costumes for the official opening of the Tavern. Kelis had her own robe now, one very similar to both the bath robe and the one on her figurine. Rob's "one leaf floating" text message puzzled Abel, because Rob had already managed semi-hovering and could disturb gravel. After the next message, "Come quickly" Abel went outside and met Rob coming up the street.

"One leaf floating?"

"An email." Rob looked stunned. "I sent a text to Kelis and she's waiting for us."

"Not from Kelis?" Abel realised. "An email? Has one of the Tavern betas been in touch? What's the matter?"

"The email came to Ferryl Shayde. Remember, when we gave out instructions to calm themselves until they could float a leaf, to find out if they had magic?"

"Yes, in the game. You used your domain for the email address because you'd got spares." Abel stopped. "Someone actually made a leaf float?"

"Possibly. Petra sent the message to the right email address, exactly as the game instructions told her to. She wanted to be a cat-sorceress, Ferryl Shayde, because they all think we made her up. It might be real because she added "Help, I'm frightened." Rob tugged at Abel's arm. "Come on."

"One of the Tavern players, from the game, has discovered magic? Wonderful. Now she can guard her own village." Careful enquiries among the betas had already shown nobody knew of any witches or warlocks.

"No, she'll be scared witless when she sees all the magical creatures." Rob stared so Abel explained what Ferryl said.

"Her email didn't mention creatures, just floating a leaf."

Kelis waited with her front door open so Abel and Rob shut up until they were all safely in the library. Between them, he and Rob brought

Kelis up to date. Kelis seemed more excited than worried. "Did you email back?"

Rob grimaced. "Only to wait, help will be coming. Where does Petra live?"

"Briarley. About six miles by road, or four across the fields which I'm not even attempting in this weather. The mud will be knee deep." Abel looked from one to the other. "What can we do anyway?"

"I cannot go. I promised to protect you, and that is too far away." Ferryl sighed. *"I might make things worse."*

"We can go and see her. At least take her some Tavern hexes to keep the slimies off her clothes, and we can clear out any globhoblins, thornies, that sort of thing." Kelis headed for the door. "I'll ask Aunty Celia to give us a lift."

"Blimey, do you think she will?" Rob stared after Kelis.

"You know what Kelis told us, her Aunty Celia feels guilty because Mr. Ventner is her brother. Even so I'm not sure about this. We can try our parents?" Abel slumped a little. "Mum has just settled down with the TV to catch up on the soaps, so she won't be happy."

"Explaining why it's so urgent will be fun. Dad's had a drink so no chance there. I could suck up to Samantha, if Dad will let her drive his car?" Rob shook his head, "but I've no idea what to bribe her with."

Kelis interrupted them. "Ready in ten minutes, but she has to be back in an hour for Mum's therapy. Rob, you'd better let Petra know."

Abel pulled out his phone. "I'd better get the okay from Mum. Why are we suddenly haring off to Briarley?"

"Tell your mum that Petra has just had a brainstorm about the game. After all, she really has." Kelis stopped smiling. "This is not going to be fun, is it? I don't know what I'd have done if the leaf had suddenly levitated and I hadn't had the talk first. The creatures really will freak her."

"She's seen pictures, and even knows which ones to avoid. Hang on, Mum's answering." Abel suffered through the teasing about his game and a stern warning to be back for tea, and rang off. "I'm clear."

"Me too." Rob raised his phone. "Petra must have been waiting for a reply, she's answered my email already. 'Please hurry. I'm freaking.' That's fairly restrained."

"*I cannot teach her control in one hour. She must learn to avoid danger while she trains. That will encourage practice.*" Ferryl seemed decidedly upbeat. "*Now Petra can wear her cat suit with pride. Wait until the other betas hear.*"

"They'll run a mile, call us liars, or have hysterics and want us to prove it now, right in the school canteen." Abel sighed. "Remember, nobody believes in magic."

"*I believe this is when one of you usually says oops.*"

∗   ∗   ∗

Unfortunately only Ferryl could speak silently on the trip, and none of the humans could answer. The three of them listened to a happy litany of how Petra could improve her village, become the witch or maybe the sorceress, and benefit from all that had been worked out in Brinsford. As the car swept past the first houses in Briarley, Ferryl's tone changed. "*Oh no! Petra might be in danger. I hope the priest here knows of the agreement, or he may denounce her.*"

"Priest?" Abel spoke without thought because he couldn't even see a church as yet.

"*Look. Very few magical creatures, and very little litter because there are no thornies. The church here must be well attended. Yes, I can feel it, an itching telling me to leave.*"

"I can't feel it." Rob kept his voice very low, while the other two shook their heads.

"*I can, but not as strong as other times.*" Ferryl cheered up. "*I can bear this. There are some good things about being a tattoo.*"

Aunty's voice from the front seat interrupted. "This is the place, Kelis, according to the satnav. Nip in and find out how long you'll be." The three of them went, after thanking Aunty Celia for the ride, and she drove up the street to park.

"Thank God. Oh, boys, never thought of that." Petra glanced over her shoulder. "I can't take you pair to my room for privacy." She looked around. "I'll get a coat." Seconds later she came back, pulling on her fleece. "Is this real? Is there a real Ferryl Shayde, and Saint Georgeous, and all the others? I've been calling myself Ferryl Shayde and dressing in fur, I won't grow real fur and ears, will I?"

"Magic is real, but most of the characters aren't. You'll stay as human as we are. Me and Kelis anyway, we've always wondered about Rob." The silly joke brought a smile at least.

"Thank God. So what is it, some sort of Far East mystic meditation thing? I've been holding my Tavern mark when I meditated before playing for weeks. It felt really nice, calming, even though I thought the whole thing was just some bullshit way to settle all the players down and start the game. That funny feeling, the calming, flowing sensation got stronger then ping, the leaf fluttered up and away." Petra whirled round, jabbing Abel in the chest. "It scared me shitless. Not the first time, but the second. The first might have been a draught. You could have told us!"

"We didn't expect it to work unless someone had already done some magic by mistake. We wanted to warn those what they'd got into." Abel frowned. "The meditation instructions never mentioned holding a hex, or your warding mark."

"The first beta to find out might have been an accident. Warren told me the stroking helped, but someone else might have told him. The town Tavern started it, all meditating together before a meeting." Petra put her hand to her arm where, presumably, she'd drawn her ward. "We've all got hexes now, I think. A couple have them tattooed on. Just how real is this, the game?"

"It's a hex when it's on a car or door, and a warding mark on skin. Do you want to talk to Ferryl Shayde?" Abel couldn't think of a way to shut Petra up long enough to explain, but that did it.

"Tail? Ears?" Her eyes opened wide, "All fur and whiskers? She really has an email address?" Petra looked around furtively. "Can she make herself invisible? Is she here?"

"Hold out your hand and close your eyes." Abel had just remembered how Kelis and Rob reacted to that tendril of mist, invisible to the non-magical. "Ferryl Shayde, please say hello to Petra, our new apprentice."

"Hello Petra. The game is not a game. It is how the real world is. You will see me, but not right now. Is your family religious? Do they go to church?"

"What? No, but the neighbours do. Mum and Dad go to the church fete, that sort of thing. Does it matter? Oh crap, is this a pact with the devil? I'm not selling my soul, or even renting it out."

"No devils. Some sorcerers probably qualify, but any who claimed to be the real thing were killed very quickly."

"Abel, why are we connected by creepy-string? Is it you talking in my head?" Petra had opened her eyes, which were now fastened on the connection coming out of Abel's coat arm.

"That's a sort of mental telephone line to Ferryl Shade, and I'm the telephone exchange." Abel shrugged. "I have to make a living somehow."

"Idiot." Petra reached out carefully and tried to touch the connection but her finger passed through it. She watched as more mist came out of Abel's sleeve and Ferryl connected to Kelis and Rob. "Spooky. Can you hear me down that if I just.."

Rob smiled. "Whatever you said, no, but I'm guessing you said think it."

"No, I thought do a cartwheel."

"I cannot hear thoughts."

"Whew. All three of you can do the leaf thing?" All three nodded and Petra scowled. "Swine, all of you. How many others?"

"You are the only one who emailed." Abel gave her a potted explanation, concluding with "So you did really well to imagine the glyph well enough."

"Ah, the imagining thing. It's hard, so some of us started using a bit of charcoal or lipstick, or a pen." Petra looked embarrassed.

She looked startled at Abel's sigh of relief. "That explains why you managed. It takes a lot of control to manage using imagination. That's why only someone already magically active can do it."

"We'll need an extra line in the rules, pointing out it has to be imagination or the meditation won't work." Rob looked pale at the next thought. "Otherwise we'll be buried in magic users freaking about what's crawling through lunch." He rallied, glancing round, "At least the magical creatures won't bother Petra because the church protects the area."

"You'll be grossed out when school starts again." Kelis shuddered. "I had things crawling over my clothes and dinner to start with."

"There aren't any around here now, or not many anyway." Petra's eyes opened wide. "Can anyone do magic, or just a few?"

"I've no idea about everyone, but many can once they discover how."

"Brace yourselves for trouble because now most of the betas are holding the hex, the Tavern ward, to keep them calm to meditate. Well, we thought meditate. I've no idea how many draw the symbol." Petra rolled her eyes. "Suckered. When do I find out the good stuff or if I'm truly doomed?" She might have been trying to joke but the quaver in her voice told the truth, Petra was terrified.

"Mostly good, sometimes gross, but you aren't doomed. A couple of days training would help." Abel looked helplessly around. "We never considered anyone actually managing it."

"Two days would be enough. If you work all day, every day, you will be able to drive off a Globhoblin. It might be easier if you leave home."

Abel sniggered. "Ferryl has an odd idea of adulthood."

"You could visit me?" Kelis shrugged and grinned. "I'll suggest using the guest suite. It was for important clients, so Mum might like the idea of one of my friends messing it up. Otherwise you can doss down in my room, or on the floor of the Tavern." Abel wasn't so sure, but it was the best they had. Petra definitely looked puzzled but Kelis just smirked. "I'll explain later. Can you come and visit?"

"Hellfire, you're serious? I can ask. Mum and Dad will want to phone your mum first, or maybe deliver me. Maybe not deliver me, you don't look like white slavers." Petra shook herself, rallying. "What will I need?"

"Bring the cat suit. Kelis can wear her Glyphmistress robes." Abel smiled. "Two days means New Year, if your parents and Kelis's mum agree."

The first truly happy expression swept over Petra's face. "Really? I'm sold."

While Petra went indoors to start convincing her parents, Kelis phoned her mum. It didn't take long. "Mum says okay. She'll get fresh sheets put on and organise smelly girly soap, pretty towels and all that. I told her it's for a Tavern meeting and training."

Rob and Abel looked at each other, astonished. "It'll never last." Rob shook his head. "I know she hates the bloke, but even so…"

"I'd better explain to Petra about Aunty Celia and not talking out loud on the way back. Ferryl, will you explain the creatures in the fields on spooky-phone and why Petra can't talk about them?" Abel snapped his fingers. "Pad and pen!"

Kelis patted her pockets and produced a marker pen. "Why?"

"That's how I talk to Ferryl at school sometimes, she reads my notes through my eyes."

The phone call, where Mrs. Ventner explained to Petra's parents about the New Year's party Kelis would be hosting for star Tavern members, did the trick. Abel couldn't get his head round how Kelis's mum seemed to be going with it all. Now Petra's parents agreed, with a comment that it would probably be livelier than anything in Briarley. Better still, without Petra at home they could go into town for New Year themselves.

Petra brought a pad and pencil, and Ferryl answered questions on the way back. The number of creatures in the fields freaked Petra, but quietly since the voice in her head had the answers.

* * *

When the four of them arrived back, Kelis's mum didn't sound bothered, just curious. "That was short notice."

Kelis answered. "Petra just found out about the calming, and it freaked her a bit."

Abel stared at Kelis, then switched to Mrs. Ventner because the answer hadn't puzzled her at all. "Fair enough." She smiled at the group. "It might have freaked me if my daughter hadn't explained. Being pumped full of painkillers and tranquilisers might have helped as well." Mrs. Ventner put her hand to the top of her broken arm, above the cast, and smiled. "Now it means I need less medication, which must be a good thing. You'll be all right dear, Petra isn't it?" Petra nodded, speechless. "Don't worry. It will be a great comfort sometimes. What character do you play?"

"Cat-sorceress, Mrs. Ventner."

"Ferryl Shayde? I'm Jessica if you like, though this pair can't seem to manage it. Would you like a cuppa? There's soft drinks in the tavern." A few mumbled replies to say they'd be fine with soft drinks, and all four made their escape to the Tavern.

"It'll be a great comfort." Abel glared at a decidedly shifty-looking Kelis.

"My daughter explained?" Rob's glare joined Abel's.

"You two didn't know?" Petra stared at all three.

"I can explain."

"Drinks, sit, and then an explanation." Three nods answered Abel.

This should be interesting, at the very least. Chris, then Jessica, so much for secrecy. When do Rob's family join us?"

*   *   *

Kelis kept silent until they'd all found a seat, then took a deep breath. "I couldn't think of anything else."

"You told her about magic? Your mum can see magical creatures? Will she want to learn magic?" Abel shut up, because he really should let Kelis answer at least one of those.

"Adults don't take to magic very well. Finding out at a late stage can send them mad."

"My mum hasn't gone mad! She doesn't know about magic." Kelis looked and sounded really defensive now, all trace of the Glyphmistress gone. "Dad hurt her, really bad, and he frightened her." A flash of her alter ego returned, "There were things all over the hospital ward! Nothing came near because of my mark, but the nurses wouldn't let me stay!"

"It's all right Kelis. Really. We're not mad at you. Not even Ferryl." Though Abel could feel his tattoo pacing.

"I am angry, but not at my apprentice. Why are hospitals not warded? Even poorhouses had hexes when I went in the hole."

"Hole, what hole?

"Later, Petra. Part of the two days." Rob grinned. "One small part and possibly not the weirdest."

"A varied but intensive magical world induction course." Petra shrugged at their looks. "My dad designs and runs induction programmes. He'd have a ball with this."

Abel chuckled, because Petra probably would. "Though first, what exactly did you do, Kelis?"

"Showed Mum my Tavern mark, or rather the flower." Rob mouthed a silent 'later' as Petra opened her mouth to ask. "I explained. Even then I think she only let me draw one on her arm to stop me crying. A Tavern hex." A fit of giggles interfered with the next bit. "She stroked it like I said and jumped a mile. The staff, the nurses, they wanted to clean it off and she wouldn't let them."

"What about the burning? Mine really felt hot." Rob touched his waist.

"If it burned when I did it, Mum can't have felt it with the rest. She has a broken arm, for a start." Kelis waved her hands, indicating the room. "Now you know why she wants to know all about the Tavern, and wanted us to have this. Also to stop the dozens of boys of course."

"Didn't the doctors or nurses insist on cleaning it off? They more or less scrubbed the skin off me to inspect my leg." Rob glanced from one to the other.

"Mum told me they tried and she went barmy. Told them it was her only link to me, it had to stay. Cried on them. She can be quite devious, my mum." Kelis lost her smile, and sighed. "She's had to be, for years."

"Not anymore." Abel hoped he'd understood. "So she can't see creatures, and she's not trying to float a leaf or anything like that?"

"No, Mum thinks it's some sort of Zen thing, meditation aid." Kelis smiled at Abel. "Protect, soothe and ease the pain. That last part seems to mean inside and out, Abel. A lot of intent for a few lines, Glyphmaster."

"More impressive, the intent passes to all the others. Perhaps because of belief. Strange. My memory says there is a reason, but not what." Abel waited and sure enough Ferryl finished with, *"I need my wits!"*

He smiled at Petra. "Time for the first part of your induction. Ferryl Shayde is right here." Abel rolled up his sleeve.

Petra giggled. "The infamous tattoo! No wonder your mum went barmy. Oh."

The tattoo turned her head, winked, and in a blur wore the pair of leather shorts and top in the Tavern drawings. Ferryl turned around with a sweeping bow. *"Hello Petra. I am Ferryl Shayde, rescued by Abel from a deep dark hole. I have promised to protect him as well as I can, and teach magic."*

Petra tore her eyes away and stared at Abel. "You let a genie out of a, a, a whatever? You idiot." Her eyes went back to the tattoo. "Though I can see why a guy might."

Abel cut off the laughter, though it continued in his head. "Time for the real story. She didn't look like that. Remember when we came back after the holidays, the story about my broken hand, well...."

* * *

Petra spent the next two days in a daze, and usually exhausted. The exhausted came from continually using magic, because Ferryl wanted to keep her levels low to reduce the risk of blowing gravel through the ceiling. Rob spent a good while at Kelis's, encouraging Petra because he still wasn't that good so he didn't seem as intimidating to her. Abel spent even more time round at the Tavern, talking or practicing with Kelis while Ferryl Shayde taught Petra.

Unfortunately due to training Petra, and the distraction of that and the bombshell about Kelis's mum, Abel forgot he needed a New Year costume. When he remembered, midday on New Year's Eve, Ferryl refused to magic him into a cat-sorcerer again because Petra had brought her cat suit. Petra still wouldn't give a full description but confirmed she had clothes, unlike the original. The original still fascinated her, even after touching the tattoo briefly. Rob claimed he had improved his Halloween version of Roughly Hewn, but wanted a new name. Kelis Glyphmistress already had both name and costume.

Petra come up with the solution. "I'll need a bodyguard."

"Ferryl Shayde usually fights for herself."

That didn't deter Petra. "But she always has another with her. Her Shayde Warrior. The town Tavern have been on about that and Warren even has a costume, some sort of ninja with magic." She slashed with the edge of her hand then wiggled the fingers on the other. "A combined magic and skills character, so it's very hard to work up through the levels."

"What does a beginner dress as?" Abel remembered the bit about Warren wearing judo gear. "I could tie the belt off my dressing gown round my head, or try and find that necktie?" Abel looked down. "Wear pyjamas?"

"The head thing is out, you'll strangle yourself. Not pyjamas. Leather!" Kelis grinned, "Which Ferryl can provide if you wear shorts and a shirt."

"How?" Petra stared as Abel appeared to change into leather trousers and back to jeans. "Brilliant, he can match mine, please, Ferryl?"

"But he'll need weapons. Have we time to paint wooden ones?" Rob looked at Kelis. "Has your garage got silver paint for blades?"

"I have a strange and allegedly useless skill." Abel waggled a finger. "Paint will not be needed." A few hours in the garage carefully wielding the least damaging of the cutting equipment in there, and Shayde Warrior had a dozen knives and swords with improbably curved or wriggly blades. Petra spent most of the time trying to float sawdust and off-cuts of wood for practice, but really wanted to learn the colour change. Her mum insisted on buying Petra clothes in shades of yellow and orange, and Petra hated them.

* * *

As night fell on New Year's Eve the four of them gathered in the Tavern. Abel's mum had gone to a big party in town because she didn't have to keep an eye on him, and Rob had been given an overnight pass to sleep in one of the four guest rooms at Kelis's. The four all robed up after a late tea, dinner as Mrs. Ventner called it, and started the real party.

Abel arrived first, in a pair of beach shorts and a shirt as instructed, which looked really stupid with his socks and boots and all the wooden weapons tied on with bits of string. He felt better when Ferryl made the string look like leather, and the shorts denim, but the final transformation awaited Petra.

Rob had tried really hard. An old pair of jeans torn off at the knees and an old tee-shirt torn off short looked more Hulk than barbarian, but the big papier-mâché club got the message across, as did the papier-mâché helm built onto a bicycle helmet. Abel loaned him a wooden sword and dagger for his belt. They'd both expected Kelis to be here at the same time since she only had the robe to put on, but she kept them waiting.

Rob had started wondering if Kelis and Petra were having trouble with the cat-suit when Abel heard both of them coming.

Kelis came in first, to complete silence for a moment. "Don't you like it?"

"Yes. It's just, crikey Kelis. Makeup?" Rob spluttered a bit, which gave Abel a chance to gather his wits.

"It's great, Kelis. It's just that the makeup makes you look older. Sort of haughty, wise, all-knowing." He bit off the beautiful bit because this was Kelis. "A real Glyphmistress." Her eyes were made up to look wider, not quite slanted but upturned and her makeup gave Kelis really high cheek bones. With her hair caught back off her face but flowing down her back, the robes and makeup suited her tall slim figure.

"Behold the Glyphmistress. Red and black would look even better."

Kelis lifted her chin and poised her hand to cast. "Tremble, mortals."

Rob cowered convincingly. "Oh definitely. How will your mum feel about you raiding her makeup?"

"Petra did this. Is it all right, not too much, tarty or anything?" While Rob and Abel reassured her Petra knocked on the door.

"Have you pair recovered? Can I make my entrance now?"

"Mind what you say. She's a bit worried about it." Kelis hissed that quietly before raising her voice. "Come in Petra, they are both suitably prepared."

Petra looked apprehensive, standing just inside the door and looking from face to face. "I'm pleased I didn't go with shorts, not after seeing Ferryl in a pair, but now I'm worried about the skirt. Is it too short?"

"Not really. After all you're dressed in head to toe fur anyway." Otherwise, Abel thought, the answer is yes. Too short and with a tail coming out of a split at the back.

"If fur is enough, why do you make me get dressed?" As everyone looked towards Abel's arm Ferryl continued, *"though the clothes suit Petra Cat-sorceress."*

"Nice costume. Does the tail wag?" Rob looked fascinated.

"A dog's tail wags. The only way to move this is…" Petra wiggled her hips and the tail swayed. "I wanted the electric one, but this suit cleaned me out. Look, matching shoes and gloves with claws."

"Good makeup as well, are the whiskers stuck on?" Rob moved his head. "No, just painted."

"Now you know what the delay was, makeup for both of us." Kelis opened the bookshelf and fridge. "Drinks?"

"Definitely. Nice match Abel." Petra giggled. "They would be, what are you really wearing?" Abel looked down at leather knee-length pants and a leather vest under his weapons, with shin-high moccasins on his feet. The leather matched Petra's perfectly.

"I might try a skirt like that, but not tonight." Ferryl's tattoo threw off a big black hooded cloak to show her leather shorts and top. *"Are we playing the game first, or music, or TV? I haven't been to a real party for two hundred years."* After a brief pause for staring the four of them picked drinks and snacks, and the five of them played music, the Tavern game, and even Monopoly though both Ferryl and Abel cheated. Their plastic houses kept changing colour to the more expensive ones. Everyone assumed Ferryl fixed her dice throws as well, but couldn't prove it.

An hour before midnight Kelis turned the TV on, and they laughed at or joined in with the songs and acts at the televised party. The four humans tried to dance like those on the TV, which turned out hilarious, while Ferryl Shayde twisted and contorted in ways no human could. Rob ended up dancing mostly with Petra, because they'd started playing catch the tail after she'd lashed him with it by mistake. When the New Year chimes started Petra stopped dancing. "New beginnings. You should kiss me, for luck."

"My first proper New Year kiss? You know, from a real girl?"

"Really?" Petra put her arms round him. "Pucker up." When they parted she started laughing. "Blimey. The girls will have to watch out once you get a bit older." A little half-smile hovered on Petra's lips. "Especially the way you stroke a girl's fur."

"I didn't!" Rob blushed. "All right, but only on your back. It felt really soft, you know, under my hand and here." He half-pointed at his bare stomach. "Sorry." His eyes narrowed. "It's not me that should be answering questions. Those two have only just finished, unless they're going for seconds?"

Abel barely heard Rob, and really did wonder about seconds. From Kelis's eyes she felt as surprised as him, and he wondered if she'd felt the lovely soft glow that came out of his flower. It certainly turned a peck into his first kiss, and scrambled his brain. "Kelis?"

"Mmm? Maybe." Kelis sort of shook herself a little. "Must be magic."

"Felt like it."

"You two?" Rob rolled his eyes. "I knew I should have found leather pants. She's obviously a sucker for the bad boy look."

Kelis held Abel's eyes for long moments before turning to answer. "He's not wearing leather, idiot. It's just magic."

"So is that why you two are still holding hands?" Petra giggled. "Magic?"

"Oh." Abel looked down, looked up into Kelis's startled eyes, and they both blushed and let go. He tried for a laugh. "Of course it is. I'm completely entranced by the Glyphmistress. Putty in her hands."

"Putty? Yeuk. Cold, clammy. I think not. Now if I can just remember how to reverse the glyph, otherwise you are doomed, Shayde Warrior." Kelis laughed and went to her seat, picking up a drink. "I'm surprised I managed to get an enchantment past your guardian."

"*So am I.*" Nobody else reacted, so the mist connections were selective if Ferryl wanted them to be. "*I warned you about this connection.*" She must have felt Abel tense because she laughed. "*No you fool, it isn't a spell, or it's an old one that doesn't need glyphs. You two are connected, right down to your bone. That is why sorcerers sometimes bind a young woman in a certain way, or a sorceress traps a man.*"

"I'll have to ask Ferryl to try and break it." Which came as near as Abel could to admitting to a problem out loud.

"*I am trying to find a way. I believe it can be done, but both of you will have to be willing.*" From the way everyone turned to look at the tattoo, Ferryl switched back to public broadcast for the next part. "*That depends on what the Glyphmistress decides to do with him. A bit of humility might do my apprentice some good.*" The moment passed as Rob and Petra joined Kelis in thinking up humiliations for her new slave.

220

The four of them went through to the lounge to wish Kelis's mum and aunty Happy New Year. Mrs. Ventner announced she felt ready for bed and the rest took the hint. In the corridor Rob smirked and nudged Petra. "Hey, Kelis, do you want your bodyguard to walk you home? You could check on his enchantment?"

Petra giggled and Abel blushed, because that meant to her room, but Kelis grinned. "I might, then Abel can bring you back a teddy bear. Something furry for you to cuddle tonight." The four of them parted amid spluttering denials from a bright red Rob and Petra waving her tail towards him as a goodnight fur-fix.

* * *

Petra stayed an extra day, or until New Year's Day afternoon, so that she could go and meet the willows. On the way Rob, Kelis, Abel and Ferryl recounted the great Halloween creature hunt, the willow trying to charm sweets and magic from Rob, and then the attack by the Shades. The sombre mood after that evaporated immediately when Petra, forwarned, offered all three trees a chocolate.

"You really did!" She stared at the faces on all three trees, and then the creatures emerging. "You really asked the dryads the answers to those questions!" Petra looked at the wrinkled creatures. "There's still some betas complaining your game doesn't have the dryads of legend. How did one of these try to charm Rob?"

Abel offered a sweet. "Please show Petra how to charm a human, that one." He pointed to Rob.

"I must be touching my tree." The dryad moved back a little and the head and shoulders turned into a young woman with long hair, the roots on her upper limbs becoming fingers. "We were told this is attractive, that a human would touch and we could steal some magic."

"I'm devastated. I thought it was my fur, but bark does it as well?" Petra laughed at a very embarrassed Rob. "I promise not to tell anyone else, or not yet." She offered more sweets and inspected the Tavern hexes on the trees, while one dryad showed her a male head and shoulders. "I can see how the legends started. May I?" She touched the hair, tentatively. "Close, maybe not quite right but on a moonlit night. Crikey."

Eventually Petra had to tear herself away and go home, chauffeured by Aunty Celia again. Not for much longer, another week and Kelis's aunty would be going home though there would be staff coming to the house every day for a while yet. Petra took ten small Tavern hexes, carved into wood, so she could protect anywhere she wanted. At least her house would be safe because of the church, but she worried the gym club and swimming baths might be infested. Quite rightly, as phone calls over the next couple of days confirmed.

At least Petra's personal Tavern mark repelled creatures, which even Ferryl hadn't been sure of without Abel or Kelis activating it. Once again Ferryl claimed she knew the reason, if she could just find her wits. Petra would design her own personal ward but Ferryl warned her to wait until Abel could be there before applying the mark, in case of problems. Petra agreed to wait, but insisted that any of the betas who could distinctly feel the magic sensation down their arms should be let into the secret, now. She wanted them warned, because finding out about magic on her own had badly frightened her.

Rob and Kelis still claimed they didn't want another ward, because both theirs were unique when applied. Privately, Ferryl told Abel she wasn't sure another mark would take on Kelis.

*   *   *

Two days before going back to school Storm Jeremy blew in off the Atlantic, lashing Brinsford with rain all day before rattling windows and setting off car alarms all night. While Abel debated going out to inspect the magicked bushes for damage, or waiting until another blustery shower passed, his phone rang. Rob sounded really worried. "One of the trees the other side of the field has blown down, one I've been visiting. I can see the dryad in plain view, and I can see Tyson too. He can't see the dryad, but what happens if Tyson cuts up the tree and carts it away?"

"If the tree dies, or is destroyed, the dryad either finds another or dies. An old dryad will need a large tree."

Abel passed that on, adding "I'll call Kelis. We're on the way."

When Abel and Kelis arrived, both puffed from a run across the fields, Rob pointed at the fallen Sycamore tree. "I came over when Tyson left but the dryad won't talk to me. It keeps going round and hiding behind the tree."

"Let me try." Ferryl's wind form seemed to have no trouble with the blustery weather, soon disappearing behind the fallen tree. A little later the dryad peered suspiciously over the top of the trunk. Ferryl soared, then swooped back into her tattoo. *"It is vulnerable and fears death or enslavement, or both. At the moment the magic in the tree still protects it, but the tree is already dying and you know what Dryad Chestnut said. Magic drains quickly from wood."*

Abel raised his voice. "Hello dryad. You heard what my friend Rob offered before in return for some magic. A safe home for your young to grow. But now we will not ask a price, we will take any young and find them trees."

"Too late sorcerer, even if that is truth. I have no young, and it is too early in the season to ripen any. I will die too soon, when my tree does."

Kelis chipped in. "We know of empty trees, mature ones."

"Liar. Any adult tree has a dryad." The dryad pointed a twig at Rob. "He told the same lie."

Abel smiled. "What about the trees behind the barrier at the back of Castle House?"

"Behind the barrier? You mean the Dead Wood? No dryads can live there." The dryad rustled its twigs, agitated.

"You can with this." Kelis held up the white pebble. "I no longer need it."

Even as Abel stared, wondering, Ferryl cut in with *"I told the barrier to let her cross, and Rob as well. Carrying a glyph is inconvenient when you have said they can pass at any time."* Another surprise, Abel hadn't known he had to give permission before people had free access to the garden.

The dryad came right out into view. "Let me see the stone."

"Even Chestnut has better manners." Kelis threw the pebble anyway, and the dryad's twigs shot out to neatly snatch it from the air. "Good job that isn't a snare."

The dryad shot her a startled look, then inspected the glyph on the pebble.

"That is a bad idea. It can draw the glyph now, and enter anyway. We

223

will have dozens of dryads."

"If this one cheats, change the spell a little bit so the glyph doesn't work." Abel murmured very quietly but the dryad looked straight at him.

"Cheat? Alter the spell? So it works. Now I wish I had young. I cannot go that far." It looked across the expanse of ploughed field and the adjoining one, and the tops of the trees on the far side. "Dryads have very little magic of their own. I would need a large tree filled with magic to sustain me, too big to carry."

"How big? Will a chunk of this one do?" Rob eyed up the broad trunk. "We could cut a piece out for you."

"Cut it! This is my tree!" The dryad subsided again. "But my tree is dying, so the magic is leaking away and even half the trunk would not hold enough for such a long trip."

Rob persisted. "But how big a piece if it is absolutely stuffed full of magic, and doesn't lose it?" He glanced at Abel and Kelis. "The fence posts? We filled them."

"We can burn off a piece of wood, big enough for the dryad, small enough to carry?" Abel saw the dryad shiver at the word burn. "Can we supply enough magic?"

"We cannot carry enough magic with us, not to keep replenishing the dryad and also power the glyphs to carry the wood."

With a sigh Abel faced the dryad. "We can put enough magic into a smaller piece of wood, but it will run out too soon and we will take a long time to recover our magic. Too long."

"Why not take magic from these unguarded trees? If they really exist." The dryad looked suspicious again. "I thought you were sorcerers, or at least witches and warlocks."

"We are only trainees. How do we regain our magic using a tree?"

"If I tell you, you will swear to take me to a tree large enough to sustain me?" The dryad looked at its tree. "Even so, I do not know if I can leave my tree. We have been together since we were both saplings. A dead piece will not be the same."

"Pull off a shoot and grow it. Then your tree doesn't die." Rob shrugged. "Mum does it with some plants. When it's big enough you could move back in."

"Oh no." Kelis pointed. "Too late." A pickup truck bounced along the edge of the next field. As it grew nearer Kelis sighed. "Henry and Tyson. Wonderful." She smiled, "Unless one of them swings, so it's self-defence?"

"Restraint, Glyphmistress. They'll just tell us to leave because we're trespassing. This is Copples farmland." Abel didn't expect much restraint if either of them tried to hit her, but didn't think they would. Though even if Abel argued about the trespassing, nobody could rescue the dryad with Henry standing here.

The real problem turned out to be much worse. Once Tyson parked up Henry reached into the back of the truck and hauled out a big chainsaw. "Tyson noticed a tree blown down, so we thought we'd come and get the firewood before some thieving git nicked it." He looked at the three of them with a sneer. "So if the trespassers will sod off, we'll get on with it."

"The tree will lose the magic much quicker if it is cut into pieces. Then the dryad will die before we can find more wood for it to ride in."

Abel turned his back on the brothers, speaking quietly. "We can't stop them."

"We can."

"Not without causing a big ruckus and being prosecuted for trespass. They'll get the coppers if we argue." Otherwise Abel would have tried, but he couldn't do much about the law.

Rob nudged Abel and raised his voice. "We aren't trespassing. Right to roam, Countryside Act. This land isn't exempt so we can wander all over it, and we've wandered here." He grinned at Tyson and Henry. "Why don't you go home and ask your dad?" Rob turned to Abel and Kelis, lowering his voice. "Mum knows I've been searching for all the local mature trees, but not that I'm asking dryads of course. She worried about me trespassing while crossing the fields and made me check the law." He turned back to raise his voice so Henry heard the rest. "It's a pity the landowner's idiot sons don't know the law."

Abel rolled his eyes, because he knew Rob wanted the Copples to take a swing. Rob still complained occasionally that he owed Henry, big-time. Instead of fighting, Henry sneered and pulled the starter on the chainsaw. "Watch out then, because that means you also have the right to sawdust and flying splinters."

Kelis turned to Abel in a silent appeal while the dryad cowered among the leafless branches, invisible to the brothers. "We can't stop them, Kelis. It's their land." Abel wiggled a finger a little. "I'm tempted to fix the chainsaw but it might blow up. We're stumped unless it conks out."

"Good idea. Back in a moment." Ferryl poured out of her tattoo and flew across the gap to the pickup truck, detouring around the brothers. She hovered around it then disappeared under the bonnet, reappearing soon after with a slightly singed gremlin! It shot a look of pure malice at Abel and scampered across the ground to Henry, climbing swiftly up his trouser leg. Ferryl flowed back into her tattoo.

"How did you know?" Abel wouldn't be heard over the chainsaw as an oblivious Henry cut off small branches.

"I remember the hex on that vehicle from when we were working out why some are never activated. You told me that is a cheap make and when I just checked, the hex isn't working. This is a farm with lots of machinery so there will be gremlins. The rest is luck." Ferryl sounded triumphant. *"The gremlin will be very angry after a singeing and threats. It will make a very good job of the saw."*

As Ferryl finished speaking the chainsaw coughed and smoke began pouring out of it. "Turn it off you idiot. What did you do?" Tyson snatched the machine as soon as it stopped, trying to see what was wrong. Oil dripped down his clothes. "You bloody fool, you've left the drain plug loose." The metal plug dropped free and oil gushed briefly.

"I didn't. It was fine." Henry turned to the three grinning faces. "Don't laugh too much. I don't know what this tree means to you, but I'll cut it up by hand if I have to."

"Come on, there's another chainsaw back at the farm, or you can have a go with an axe if you're that keen. I'll hold your jacket." Tyson scowled at the spectators and threw the chainsaw into the back of the truck. As he got into the cab, the gremlin climbed over the top and after glaring at Abel, slipped under the bonnet. Tyson gunned the engine and roared off along the side of the next field, heading home. Before he'd gone far, the engine started coughing and spluttering.

"A very angry gremlin. The machinery on that farm will have a terrible few days."

Ferryl had trouble staying connected with others out in the open because of the wind so Abel passed that on, adding, "But hopefully the pickup will get out of sight."

"Probably, or they'll walk home and won't be back for a long time. The gremlin will want to get to the farm before wrecking the engine, so it can start on the rest."

"Now it's down to the dryad, and how big a piece of wood it will need." Abel turned to where the creature had now come out of the branches, looking much more hopeful. "Dryad, I promise on my name, Abel Bernard Conroy, to find you a mature tree with no dryad inside and allow you to move in. Now how do we get the magic?"

"That does not truly bind a human to keep your word, but I must take a chance." The dryad hesitated. "Dryads do not usually take chances." It looked from one to the other. "Cut a glyph as if draining magic to power a spell such as a barrier. Can you do that?" All three humans nodded. "This time cut through the bark into the live wood. Create the same glyph on your limb, your hand, and place it over the cut glyph. You will be able to draw magic. Please do not take too much from one tree."

"There are a lot of big strong trees. We usually hide the draining glyphs under the bark on roots, to power the barrier." Though Abel still couldn't do that on his own, without Ferryl helping.

"For this the glyph must be available on the outside and reach right through to live wood. It will heal up eventually, once you stop stealing magic." Dryad shouldn't sound so bitter, considering the reason.

"I should know how to get magic that way!"

"I know, it's in your wits, somewhere." Abel really wanted Ferryl to find her wits, or read the ones she'd got, because they sounded like a magic encyclopaedia.

Kelis had already moved closer to put a hand on the fallen tree. "How big a piece, dryad? Abel can cut it, and put the rest of his and Ferryl's magic into the piece. Rob and I can fill it up and start moving while he takes Ferryl and gets topped up because Abel can run fastest. We get a twofer with Ferryl."

"I hear and obey, Glyphmistress." Abel moved towards the tree as the dryad reluctantly showed them a suitable section.

Rob laughed. "Blimey, still under the spell?"

Abel and Kelis grinned at each other and she pointed dramatically and snapped her fingers. "Hurry up, slave." With Ferryl advising and the dryad cringing, Abel burned off a chunk. The green wood didn't catch fire, the sap spitting and hissing as the heat glyph worked through.

The slave laughed when he'd finished. "That will give Henry a headache, trying to work out how we managed to burn a lump out of the middle of the trunk." Abel and Ferryl poured magic into the hunk of timber. "It's going to take a hurricane to lift."

"Not now. May I take control of both hands please, while we have some magic left?" After getting permission Ferryl created a ball of wind to protect one hand, and put the other under it, palm down. *"The bottom one pushes straight down, while the protected hand stops either one being crushed. The protection is a wind glyph on top of a reverse wind glyph, at different angles and pulled in tight."* She wriggled both Abel's hands into the soft earth under the chunk and the glyphs strengthened, lifting it clear of the ground. *"No actual weight on your hand but this will be expensive in magic. We could not do this at Christmas without draining everyone, but now that doesn't matter."* The wood wobbled. *"We will need two people to keep it steady."*

"Then you'd better get off and get topped up. Shoo." Kelis turned to the dryad. "Let us know when you can move in."

"Hang on." Rob snapped off a shoot and tucked it in his belt. "Ready." As soon as Ferryl agreed Rob and Kelis had the protective wind glyphs right, and Abel had given all the magic he should, Abel set off running. The running away practice finally came in handy.

*   *   *

Tree magic felt lovely, cool and fresh, pouring into Abel's hand just as the dryad had promised. Ferryl promised to work on a way to create a store, once she could remember or work out how to do it. For now, Abel's magic 'battery' couldn't hold any more. He ran back as fast as possible and as soon as he took the weight, Kelis borrowed his penknife and set off running. Ferryl compensated for Rob tiring, and they continued their slow clumsy way until Kelis came back wearing a big smile.

"That tree magic feels lovely." She patted the piece of wood. "Thank you, dryad."

"He will not answer, because it uses magic."

"Be careful taking over. If you get it wrong the tree scrapes through the glyph barrier." Rob showed Kelis a skinned knuckle. "Does it matter which tree?"

"A big one, that's all. If we only take a bit from each they'll all recover quicker."

"I'm more worried about how fast I recover." Kelis frowned, concentrating on the glyphs. "I'll need a long sleep after this."

"It's a pity the trees won't recover as easily." Abel felt guilty somehow. "How long will they leak?"

"We can heal the trees straight away, now I have thought about it. The same glyph you drew across the grass in Castle House garden will work, and use very little magic."

"All that crawling about, those lines in the dirt, were a glyph?" Abel tried to imagine a pattern to all those swirls and lines.

"Yes, drawn very large. Why do you think the grass and bushes recovered so quickly?" Abel didn't have an answer, though he really did feel better about healing the trees. He'd had visions of them bleeding magic for days, even if it didn't work like that.

An hour later they all agreed about a long sleep though as Kelis came back from topping up they could see the target tree, a Sycamore because dryad wanted the same species. It had been very tempted by an oak, but didn't feel comfortable switching. Rob ran off to top up but when he came back he hesitated before trying to take over. "Can you make it, Abel?" He showed his skinned knuckles. "You and Ferryl are a bit more precise than I am."

"We've got plenty of magic left for this stretch." Abel glanced back at a shout over the fields. "You could slow up Henry, because that's who it'll be. We can hide this bit of tree once dryad is home safe." Abel chuckled.

"Henry won't come into the wood anyway."

"The wood will rot to nothing if we drain every last dreg, or rot enough so it cannot have come from the fallen tree." Ferryl sang a few words, sounding a lot like Kelis when she'd made the first ward. *"Because I can do magic."* All three laughed because this close together Ferryl had connected up.

"So can I, so I'll go and tease Henry." Rob held up both hands. "I promise not to deliberately provoke him, but only because we don't want too many people looking at that burned tree." He jogged off with a happy smile.

"One last effort?" Kelis's smile showed the strain as they staggered into the wood. "Close enough?"

"Next to the tree. Dryad may be weak, despite us topping up the magic in the wood."

Ferryl must have been right because dryad seemed to stumble moving from log to tree, disappearing without a word. Abel picked up the shoot from against the trunk, where Rob must have propped it. "We'd better plant this. I hope it grows."

"It will." Both Abel and Kelis jumped as a long, slim, definitely woody hand plucked the shoot from Abel's hand. They looked up to see a rough face in the sycamore trunk. "This tree is strong, filled to the brim. Already I feel better, and have plenty of spare magic to keep this alive." A small hole opened in the tree and the dryad slotted the shoot partly inside before the bark closed up to hold it. "Once I am fully recovered, I will find a place to plant. Does it matter where?"

Abel swept a hand around. "Choose a clear spot, near enough to protect until it is strong enough." He looked up at the face. "Are you comfortable? Does the barrier bother you?"

His answer briefly gleamed white inside a hole in the bark, before being sealed away. "I will keep your glyph safe." The face became much more human-looking. "I thank you. You may take one of my seedlings to tell the other dryads you speak truth, once one is strong enough."

"Brilliant!"

"We can protect the village." Abel and Kelis turned to each other, then their arms were round each other and Abel's second kiss felt just as nice as the first. Maybe better, and possibly longer.

"Oh yes, go and annoy Henry, Rob. I should have known you just wanted a chance to pounce on the poor girl." Rob stood with his hands on his hips, trying hard to look indignant.

Kelis blushed. "I just wanted to make sure of the spell."

"From the look of Abel, it took the first time. I suppose I'll have to put up with this behaviour from now on? I thought you would have stopped another enchantment, Ferryl?"

"They told me to close my eyes so I did. What happened?" Ferryl laughed. *"Will I have to close my eyes very often?"* Ferryl sounded a little bit tipsy, she'd been that way since her first top-up from a tree.

"Maybe?" Kelis smirked. "A Glyphmistress does not give up her captures too easily."

"Maybe? A lot more than that, considering you're still clutching his sweaty paw." Rob broke up laughing. "I wish I had a picture. You pair look priceless, like you'd been caught swigging your Dad's whiskey or something. Petra wanted to bet Abel would kiss you again before we went back to school, but I'm not that much of a sucker."

"When was this? Have you been stroking her fur again?" Abel didn't think they'd had much time to talk but wanted to distract Rob because yes, Kelis still had hold of his sweaty paw.

"No, she's too old for me and I'm definitely too young for Petra. There are telephones. Petra finds me easier to talk to about magic, because I'm still learning. Have you two topped up your magic, or were you too keen to get to the snogging?" Rob held up his hands when Kelis glared. "All right, I'll be good. Eventually." He kicked the log. "What happens to this?"

"We drain it of magic."

A shoot grew from the sycamore and connected to the log. Moments later the log visibly aged, drying and cracking, and the bark crumbled off.

Abel shrugged. "Or dryad will. Come on Kelis, let's get topped up." It wasn't until they went to cut the glyphs either of them realised they were still holding hands.

"I warned you." Ferryl sniggered. *"I don't suppose you'll both agree to*

break the connection, not yet?"

Abel didn't want to ask Kelis, but worried a bit that he should. He'd had the same lovely warm tingle again from his ward when they'd kissed, and hoped that wasn't some sort of magical love charm affecting her. He still couldn't decide after going home to get changed out of his wet clothes, and when the three of them met later Kelis seemed cautious, unsure. They didn't hold hands or kiss, but Abel for one definitely thought about it quite a lot.

*   *   *

Abel slept really well, but still felt stiff walking down to the school bus the next morning. The other two felt as bad, so the magical lifting didn't take all the strain. Once at school, break and lunch became a whirlwind because Petra arranged for Abel, Rob and Kelis to team up with her and break the news to four betas, the ones who were getting a strong reaction from their meditation. Once all three explained that the tingle really could be magic, Petra fluttered a bit of paper over her hand to prove it. All the betas agreed to close their eyes to talk to a real Ferryl Shayde, but opened them again though this time the spooky-phone stayed invisible. Finally Petra and Rob explained training and what a pain it would be. Petra kept smirking at Abel and Kelis, but didn't actually say anything.

Talking about how the Tavern would develop now and if the betas were that or a coven kept the three of them occupied on the way home. Pandora's Box had been opened, because all four of those betas were now determined to make a leaf flutter at least. Somehow Stourton and the surrounding villages would have to cope with a sudden outbreak of magic, even if everyone agreed to keep it a secret. The bit about adults being driven insane ensured that, nobody wanted to send a parent barmy.

Halfway up the lane Kelis and Abel ended up holding hands, while Rob grinned at them. He turned away and covered his eyes at Kelis's gate, because tonight there wouldn't be any Tavern so Abel wouldn't be seeing her. The pair looked at each other for a moment, until Kelis smiled and whispered, "Is the enchantment still working?"

"Yes." Abel tipped his head up, Kelis bent hers and that lovely warm feeling flooded through the mark. "Did you feel that? The mark?" Abel had to ask before Ferryl said something.

"Yes, but Ferryl said no intent, so I think it might just be a sort of bonus." They were stood very close, talking quietly so Rob didn't hear, so Abel tried for another bonus. Kelis giggled afterwards. "I'd better go in. I'm sure the net curtain twitched."

"Will your mum mind?"

"I doubt it. Not out here in broad daylight. If you start banging on windows at night, or dozens of boys troop in and out of my room, she'll probably object." Kelis raised her voice. "We'd better let Rob get home, or he'll be growing roots like a dryad."

"As long as you bring me plenty of honey, it's a viable career choice. No homework for starters." Rob laughed at them and set off home, and Abel caught up.

"Me and Kelis. Are you okay with it?"

"Real girlfriend and boyfriend stuff? Crikey. Though I always thought you'd be a sucker for a pretty face." Rob shook his head. "I'm heartbroken and eaten up with jealousy of course."

"I'll buy you a teddy bear to cuddle."

"I'll steal one of Melanie's, she's got dozens." Rob raised a hand in goodbye and headed to his own house.

"*Very strange. I never have been able to understand human emotions, even when in human bodies. He would have liked to kiss Kelis, but is happy that you did. Very strange.*"

"Like you say, you don't understand." Not that Abel did either.

* * *

Kelis understood, or had made up her mind the next morning. When Rob and Abel collected her from home, she put out her hand to Abel once they were through the gate. She held hands until the bus arrived at school, and under the table at break and lunch, and on the way home. The teachers came down hard on anything more than hand holding at lunchtime in the school itself. Abel still worried a little bit, but Kelis didn't and at her gate she told Ferryl to cover her eyes and put her arms round him. After another goodnight kiss, Abel stopped worrying. Somehow, after a few days of teasing from Rob and at school, everyone moved on.

Rob's teasing eased off because he'd got a real problem at home. Both his sisters were interested in the game, and had started asking about coming to Tavern meetings. He'd persuaded them they had to learn the rules first. That meant Rob sitting with them playing the game with dice, which definitely ironed out a few small glitches. Luckily both of them had other interests, and Rob hadn't mentioned leaf floating. He really couldn't handle that, not yet, and hoped they'd both get bored.

The Taverners wouldn't be bored. Despite dealing with the sorceress, an increasing number of magical creatures were invading the village. Not so many of the thornies or anything smaller, because the gradually increasing number of stakes bearing hexes kept those out. The trespassers were hoplins in pairs, globhoblins, and even the occasional skurrit. Other creatures were still rooting in the bins, leaving litter in the middle of the village, but even Ferryl couldn't catch sight of the culprits.

Her guardians, who now included almost every cat in the village, weren't very specific in their reporting. There were intruders, and sometimes a cat could chase them off or catch them. Other times the cat's food had been taken, or mice were killed. That annoyed the cats more than anything else so Ferryl couldn't get them to concentrate on what else happened.

Henry had found ways to be a nuisance again. He still wouldn't challenge any of the Taverners, but he'd seen them driving in stakes. He couldn't possibly understand the reason for them, but still pulled a few up here and there. As a result gaps were made and a few of the larger magical grazers made it through as far as the Village Green. A shower of twigs and lashing branches soon drove them off when one tried to browse on a dryad's tree!

At school Henry started a campaign of little niggling annoyances. He had realised none of the three were going to use waggy finger in public. A steady stream of small paper darts, bits of gravel, small pebbles, erasers and the occasional pencil assaulted Kelis, Rob and Abel. In addition, they soon learned that every time the car taking Henry to or from school passed them, he'd throw something. All three became adept at using small wind glyphs to deflect the missiles without disturbing other students or books and papers. Ferryl claimed the practice made them more efficient magic users, but still wanted to burn Henry's arm off at the elbow.

The rest of the seraphims, and all the fifteen and seventeen-year-old students including betas and apprentices, were too busy for much teasing. The teachers had started on the run-in to the exams for all of Abel's year, cramming in extra work and homework to make sure everyone would end up with decent grades. There wasn't much discussion about the Tavern despite an undercurrent of excitement as first one, then another, made their leaf flutter. At weekends the phone calls flew back and forth trying to make plans for half-term, a real meeting, with everyone who had managed magic so far.

Meanwhile, Una really did want a sword once her leaf fluttered and she saw the magical world. Where she lived wasn't near a church, or any other hexes, and she almost had to wade through magical creatures. Kelis more or less took over her dad's tools in the garage to produce a steady stream of carved wooden Tavern hexes. With Ferryl supervising all three became adept at activating the wooden squares inscribed with the shield and flower, before distributing them among the trainees. Warren found that his home area wasn't so bad with a distinct line across his road, halfway along, that the creatures were reluctant to cross. Investigation showed that the line circled a church, just as Vicar Creepio Mysterio said.

Petra practiced as much as possible, and now her leaf stayed above her hand even if it danced frantically. She kept smirking and saying she would be finding a signature move once she'd got it right. Several of the others claimed progress, but Ferryl couldn't judge very well because they only met at school. Some people already wanted to know what came next, when could they throw other glyphs? The original Taverners were really pleased they hadn't followed Ferryl's suggestion and put real glyphs in the game.

Three weeks into the school term Kelis met Abel and Rob at her gate with a huge smile and a kiss that left Abel breathless, or more than usual. "Mum says we can have a meeting here! All the Tavern, anyone who wants to come. She'll put on nibbles, either Saturday or Sunday."

"Everyone?" Rob tried to calculate how many belonged now, because the original betas had now confessed to recruiting a few more pupils, friends and siblings. "Bloo.. curses, Samantha and Melanie will want to come! Well Melanie at least. Will your mum want to come, Abel?" Abel's mum had finally got over her embarrassment and admitted seeing creatures, to Rob and Kelis at least. She couldn't really avoid explaining the saucers of milk and sugar on the sideboard.

"No, she doesn't know about magic. I've considered a Tavern mark for her, but if Mum's already seeing creatures?" Abel shrugged.

"She will take to magic very easily, but I am still not sure if it will be good for her. Adults really do go crazy if they start as adults, though in a way Chris has always been aware."

Abel had no intention of trying anything Ferryl couldn't be sure about, not on his mum. "It's not worth risking. We'll stick to everyone who can float a leaf or at least flutter it. We can have a proper training session, and sort out warding marks for those who have decided on one." Abel wondered how many that would be, six he thought or possibly seven if Sarah, another town beta, fluttered her leaf by then. "Saturday, because there's no bus on Sunday. That's if the ones in the villages can get to town and then out here."

"In costume?" Rob hesitated. "No, not to travel but they can all bring them. Then we'll decide."

"They can all meet me properly, and the willows by the bridge. Those three are particularly friendly and only need a few sweets to encourage them." Ferryl really liked that idea. Nobody had met her at school because they couldn't guarantee privacy.

"If Henry decides to give us grief we can all wave fingers, nine or ten of us." Rob smiled happily. "Or if we catch him pulling up stakes, POW, one grease spot." He still wanted some payback for the beating, but Henry kept his aggravation at a distance.

*   *   *

At school Ferryl connected to the magic users one at a time to ask, and Abel soon discovered a problem. As soon as he could get Kelis and Rob together for a quick private word, he told them. Rob almost exploded. "More? Ones we don't know? Who? How many?"

"Calm down and hush. I'm not sure yet. Una looked downright guilty and said some others, because she couldn't stand the thought of them eating dinner that had been trampled." Abel glanced round. "Warren's enrolled his older brother, he's nineteen and has some news about other places in town. It's all quick remarks, because Ferryl's connection is only one-way."

"*They would not like me listening to thoughts. The wards would hurt us both. I would only get past them because of my link to Abel.*"

"We invite anyone and everyone who has activated magic, and count up at Mum's. I'll apologise to her afterwards." Kelis squeezed Abel's hand. "She's still grateful for you two looking after me, and the ward. She uses it to get to sleep, to stop her nightmares."

"It would help if we have some sort of number first. Just ask everyone that, how many have fluttered a leaf, and if any drivers can help with transport?" Abel shrugged. "Then Kelis can at least give her mum a vague idea."

"*I will pass the message so they can just give you a number without names or explaining.*"

By hometime, the three of them had another problem, though they had to wait until the bus dropped them off in Brinsford to talk properly. "Sarah took the last five wooden hexes." Kelis pulled a face. "We'll have to make more."

"*She's done it, the leaf, and can see creatures?*"

"Yes, and doesn't need the intro from you and Ferryl." Kelis nudged Abel. "Someone told her and she'll leave the spooky voice in her head until the weekend, please. Though she is terrified because there's others out there, magic users."

"*Witches or sorcerers?*" Ferryl sounded really wary. "*We must find out, and where their territories are.*"

"Just a man in the park feeding pigeons. Sarah sees him on her way home most days, but last night Sarah could see creatures." Kelis stifled a giggle. "He isn't just feeding pigeons, he's talking to what sounds like a dryad from the description and throwing something to it. Though Sarah says the other creatures weren't avoiding him. He kept swatting them off."

"*We'll get her warded at the weekend, but she is to keep well clear until then. After that she can approach him, carefully. Perhaps another of the town Tavern can watch over her?*"

"That's another thing, Justin and his sister Rachel have Rachel's Tavern in their front room at home, but Warren has his own as well. It's sort of exploded. At the beginning the betas roped in extra help because after all, The Tavern is only a game. Now it isn't, and oops doesn't quite cover it." Rob shrugged, and looked up at the big iron gates. "I'll leave you two here so I don't have to suffer all the embarrassing soppy stuff."

"Never mind, just think how many might turn up in fur."

Rob stuck his tongue out at Kelis and set off home singing, "Just wanna be your Teddy Bear" in a very bad imitation of Elvis.

"Embarrassing soppy stuff?"

"Like this? Close your eyes, Ferryl." Kelis bent her head.

"Oh, that stuff. We'll get a lot of teasing this weekend, unless you want to stop while the rest are here?" Abel would have crossed his fingers, but his hands were holding Kelis's.

"No, they sort of know anyway." Kelis smirked. "I can show the girls the power of glyphs. Is it still working?"

"Oh yes, though you could check again?" On the way home Abel thought about that second check, and tried to work out if the 'magic' might be getting stronger. He didn't want to ask Ferryl because she'd advise breaking the link to find out.

*   *   *

Kelis's mum didn't seem fazed by having seventeen young people in her house on Saturday, just happy that Kelis seemed to be making friends this time. Kelis explained to her mum she didn't usually make friends because in a couple of years Dad would up sticks and move. The reaction came as a shock, as Kelis told Abel and Rob at the Tavern meeting that night.

"Mum's going to think about that, me making a lot of friends. She confessed to thinking about selling up because Dad is already fighting the divorce settlement so money might get tight. It's a big house to maintain but now she'll consider either keeping it, or selling and buying a smaller one in Brinsford." Kelis sighed. "She's really impressed by how many people talk to her in the village."

"So my home is safe?"

"You have a home with me anywhere I live, Ferryl." Abel smiled. "Even after you move out of my arm. Life wouldn't be the same without you nagging now and then."

"I'll persuade Mum to donate a settee." Rob frowned. "You don't need a settee."

"If we have a new home, you can have a home there." Kelis jabbed Rob in the ribs. "You just want Ferryl because she's furry."

"Is it a crime?" Rob laughed, "Yes, probably. Hey, Mum, meet our new lodger. She's just like any other girl under the fur."

"Or the bark." Abel stopped teasing at a thought. "We'd better get in some sweets for the willows."

"We'll take some honey. My trees are being snooty so I can spare a jar and the willows have never had any." Kelis's smirk died away. "I should ease off on my sudden craving for the stuff if money is a problem."

*　*　*

The first Taverners arrived at ten o'clock on Saturday, and by eleven Kelis's mum had let them spread into the dining room for the overflow. The food had been put out there, stacks of packets of snacks, bowls of nuts and crisps, and plates of little sandwiches, well beyond the usual definition of nibbles. When the last recruit puttered up the drive on an old scooter, twenty-three people including Abel, Kelis and Rob were sat or standing around the big table.

Kelis looked at the crowd, shocked into almost a whisper. "Where did the six extras come from? Can Ferryl talk to everyone at once?"

Yes, but not until they are ready to hear voices.

"I'm a bag of nerves. I don't know half these people!" Kelis took hold of Abel's hand, let go at a raised eyebrow from Una, then stuck out her tongue and took his hand again.

Able tried to smile. "Nor me, so we'd better get introductions over first. It's a good job we nicked all the pads and pens from the study."

"Redistributed. Everyone's name, who told them about magic, and what they've managed so far." Kelis looked around the sea of faces. "It'll take ages. I'll ask Mum for the cushions off the settees because we won't have enough chairs, even using the dining room."

"Who is in charge? Who runs the Tavern? Sorry, I'm Eric, Warren's brother. I started off helping him beta a game, and suddenly I'm overrun with magical nasties." The tall, dark-haired youth with glasses shrugged. "Or I'm not, because Warren drew this mark on me, a hex, and they scurry away. The thing is, I haven't really seen any organisation so far."

"On a person it's a ward to protect you, on an object or building a protective glyph or symbol is called a hex. I'm Abel, this is Rob, and this is Kelis, and we aren't organised. The game is our idea, and was only a game. Then I found out about magic."

"Someone should write this down, for any new recruits." The girl with short cropped blonde hair looked alarmed. "I'm Shannon. Don't ask me to write, and I'm hopeless at typing."

"Tape it, then we'll sort typists or data entry out later." Abel didn't even see who that was, but everyone seemed to agree.

Sarah put up her hand, as if in class. "Can we hear about magic first, because that's why we're here."

"All right. Here we go. The two local bullies decided to have a go at me....."

* * *

After most of the room finished telling Abel what a fool he was, and how lucky he'd been, he introduced Ferryl Shayde by rolling up his sleeve. That shut them all up, then produced a storm of questions that Ferryl answered, eventually. Kelis and Rob roped in a few helpers to collect cushions and dish out drinks from the library fridge. Meanwhile Abel acted as a Ferryl spooky-phone exchange. They had all drawn the wind symbol on their palms, but promised to stop doing so when Ferryl explained they'd need the skin clear to use different glyphs in time. According to Ferryl, drawing an imaginary glyph with a finger would work now they'd all mastered directing their magic.

As the guests finished filling out their names and details on a lined pad, each one went through to see the actual Tavern and the large wooden sign. About a third had no ward on their skins, just a wooden hex in their pockets to keep creatures away. Ferryl explained that an indelible drawing on skin gave better protection against binding.

That led to a discussion about the differences between Tavern and

Church protection. Five people with drawn wards had been confirmed at church and Ferryl announced their God's mark still remained as strong as ever. All five still prayed, and were relieved that the magic made no difference so it wasn't inherently evil. That puzzled the cropped blonde, Shannon, roped in as a beta by Una despite her going to a different school, a church school. "Can I be religious and a sorceress?"

"That's what a Paladin is, I think? Saint Georgeous is definitely a holy sorceress." Kelis turned to Abel. "Ferryl?"

"Most such sorcerers, magic users who were also believers, joined the church. Bishops were probably at sorcerer level, but the church did not admit women unless they became nuns. As a result, most women could only become witches or sorceresses outside the church. Perhaps bad or good depends on the sorceress, not religion or magic." Ferryl sounded as if that might be a new idea to her as well.

"Do we, the religious ones, even need a Tavern hex or mark? After all, the creatures avoid us anyway." This young woman had a silver cross on a chain around her neck, and now pulled a wooden hex from her pocket.

"Vicar Creepio said the christening marks or a cross frighten magical creatures but if they overcome the fear, they can still hurt you." Kelis nodded towards Abel. "I saw something try to bite Abel, and his ward stopped it. He didn't get a scratch."

"The ward works, because on several occasions it has turned icy cold and deflected magic." Abel tapped the flower, now showing because everyone wanted to see Ferryl Shayde. "Mine is a tattoo to look at, but it goes down to the bone and is stronger than any drawn symbol."

"A cross or a wooden Tavern hex irritates the magical creatures, but does not actually harm them or protect the person. Not unless the cross is on a church, or charged with a specific spell, or is a magical talisman such as the churchman carried. Someone like Seraphim but with real intent could affect a person carrying a cross or a wooden hex. They might even bind someone marked at church because that is an ephemeral symbol. Magical protection must be a permanent mark on the skin, or to the bone for true protection, and preferably a unique personal ward."

Looking from the silver cross to the wooden hex, Shannon frowned. "So the cross and the hex are the same."

"No, the hex is charged with magic, so it is stronger. Maybe a priest could put church magic into a cross?"

"Does anyone go to confession?" A cautious hand went up. "You could ask if magic is considered evil or good." Rob smiled to take any sting out of the next bit. "Since most of us appear to be the ungodly."

"I asked. There is no magic, just God's miracles." The young man who came with Petra, a neighbour of hers, looked confused. "I carried on meditating because it really is peaceful, sort of like prayer can be sometimes. When the leaf moved, I asked again. The church does not believe in magicians. The only magic is God's, the magic of faith." His brow wrinkled in thought. "I suppose that explains why the cross keeps the creatures away but so does the hex."

"What about creatures? Mark, isn't it?" He nodded and Shannon shrugged. "I daren't ask at school, because there aren't any."

A smile finally appeared on the young man's face. "The Father thinks I'm imagining the creatures. I'm supposed to say Hail Mary until they disappear." A ripple of amusement went round the group because they could all see faeries flying past the window.

"We met an Archbishop who definitely knows all about magic and uses some version of it, so don't worry. Maybe the vicars, priests, that sort of person, don't know?" Kelis swept her eyes across everyone there. "We should all try to find out who does know about magic."

"Meanwhile, are you going to keep developing the game?" Justin, the fifteen-year-old beta who had started a Tavern with his fourteen-year-old sister Rachel, looked decidedly guilty. His sister suddenly looked really worried. "It's just that my cousins live the other side of Leeds and when we went on holiday together we showed them the game. There's seven of them, with their friends, and they're forming their own Tavern."

"My cousin is beta testing and said he knew people nearby who would be interested. I've no idea how many but he lives in the Pennines near Sheffield." More and more confessed to including friends and family until Abel called a halt.

"We either stop the game now, and just stick to magic, or try and work out how to deal with magic users popping up all over." Abel scowled. "I'm not keen on the second option."

"I am. We visited my aunt in Hull last weekend and her house is overrun. I left a hex in the kitchen behind some tins." Petra shrugged. "I'd like to know how to fix one into her wall, permanently."

"There seem to be creatures everywhere there's no church protection, so somebody has to do something about it." Justin looked defiant. "A few more Taverns will help."

That roused a storm of mainly agreement until Shawn, the nineteen-year-old who had arrived on the scooter, managed to quieten everyone down. "I hardly know anyone here, but you seem to cover a good part of Stourton and most of the nearby villages. None of us has seen any sign of a sorcerer protecting an area like Abel and his friends have tried to. I don't want my parents, other relatives or friends to have those things wandering through their houses. To fix that we've got to organise. Who is in charge?"

"I vote for Ferryl Shayde, on the magical side." Eric, Warren's big brother, loved meeting the moving tattoo.

"I can't!"

"Why not?" Abel thought that had to be the best idea yet.

"I have promised to protect Abel Bernard Conroy for ninety years, and teach him magic as safely as I can. How can I watch over all these others?"

"Not watch over, not directly. If you are teaching Abel, will you also advise us please, Ferryl Shayde?" Eric sounded very respectful, and looked directly at Abel's arm as he spoke.

"You truly wish this?" The round of agreement left little room for doubt, everyone wanted the only honest-to-something sorceress to be teaching magic. Abel did wonder if it had occurred to them Ferryl wasn't exactly a person, but they were all talking to a tattoo so maybe. *"As long as it does not interfere with my promise to Abel, I would be honoured."*

After the cheers died down, Abel asked the other question. "What about the actual game?"

"Market it properly. Is it patented, or trademarked?"

Abel, Kelis and Rob stared at Shawn, until Rob answered. "No. We just made it up, and wanted to test it. We sort of talked about making our fortune, once we left school, but we've got no money to do anything about it yet. We're fifteen." The last bit came out a bit plaintive.

"You can get a patent at fifteen, and probably a trademark. Otherwise some elder brother or sister or parent will look at what little Jonny is playing and say hmm, that's interesting. Next thing guess who makes a fortune?" Shawn shrugged. "They won't have a blind idea about magic, which really will mess everything up. That Ferryl Shayde email, for instance, whose is it?"

"Mine, Dad bought me a domain." Rob grinned. "I wanted to be a games designer."

"That means the email and domain are under your control, which is a relief. How much do trademarks and patents cost?" A flurry of consulting phones led to it being between hundreds and thousands of pounds. Eric didn't seem bothered, and pulled out a wallet. "Here, first donation. Forty quid. Worth it to know I'm not going to burn the house down experimenting. I'll pay in more when I can."

Shawn pulled out his wallet, looked inside, and grimaced. "I can manage twenty until payday?"

"Fundraisers! We can wash cars and cut grass."

"Baking, I make a mean iced bun."

"Boot sale, I've got old toys."

"Hang on, we'll need a proper bank account, all that sort of thing." Shannon looked around, then through to the library. "Will your Mum let us use this as a business address, Kelis?" She wasn't put off by Kelis's hopeless shrug. "Ask her and I'll pick Dad's and Mum's brains for how to set it up." A big smile broke over Shannon's face, "Fair exchange for their daughter not being taken by the dark side."

"You'll need people over eighteen to front you, to make a legal contract. Reliable people." Eric grinned. "People who know that, fifteen or not, you can fry them into a grease blob if they cheat you."

"I like him."

"Will your mum stand for another meeting, Kelis? We'll bring the food." A sea of hands agreed that the Tavern should meet in a fortnight, if Mrs. Ventner would agree. Various people promised to bring crisps, buns, cake and assorted snacks. Some more discussion agreed the next meeting would be in three weeks, the Saturday after half term, because several people already had arrangements for Valentine's and the holiday. If Kelis's mum wouldn't agree, any member with a big enough room at home would work on their parents.

Meanwhile everyone would look out for signs of magical influence that wasn't church. Sarah would approach the man in the park, but not until she had a ward, a real one down to the bone. A good few flinched at that but Ferryl wouldn't allow anyone to really advance in magic unless they created their own ward, and several flourished drawings. Sarah had a drawing, but didn't look convinced.

To drive home the warning, though they didn't realise that, the entire group trooped off down to the willows. At first most of them joked about going to talk to the trees. Once everyone assembled, Abel threw a sweet in front of each tree. "Greetings, willows. Please show us your pretty human faces."

A round of startled and complimentary comments followed as the beautiful faces with flowing hair showed, one on each trunk. Several visitors gave Abel some stick about making dryads ugly in the game, until he threw down more sweets. "Please show your true-faces. If you show your true selves, Kelis has brought real honey."

"Truly? Real honey? What does it look like?" All the complimentary comments were forgotten as the slim but wrinkled shapes sporting twigs quickly moved out of the trees. Abel explained about these three, that they were very friendly for dryads, and started to tell everyone why.

"Let the dryads tell them why. It will convince the doubters that there really is danger."

The sight of the dryads, and their version of the confrontation with the two Bound Shades and sorceress convinced all the visitors. The dryads did not know exactly what spells and glyphs had been used, but they had seen the flows of magic raging around Abel and the Wolf Shade, the casts by Kelis and Rob, and the physical attacks and result. All three were obviously frightened and relieved. They were also ecstatically happy once they had the honey, and claimed it lived up to expectations.

Abel confirming that his ward had gone icy cold, and Kelis agreeing hers was very cold, further convinced the trainees. Rob confessed the sorceress had ignored his wind glyphs up until he whopped her pet with an enchanted rounders bat. That added a bit of hilarity but the message went home; bad things are out there, and a proper ward can make the difference in a tight spot. Abel's recital of what had happened to the wounded sorceress underlined just how deadly magic could be.

By now everyone wanted to see real magic, not leaves and dust dancing. Kelis and Abel tossed sticks and stones about by magic and burned little sticks out of the air, before Ferryl gathered dozens of tiny pebbles using a cloud of glyphs. After the descriptions, everyone wanted to see Ferryl control thrown sticks, and they all threw a stick or stone. Ferryl's glyphs seized each one and diverted them unerringly into a shape drawn in the mud.

Petra topped it off with her own new party trick, her signature move, learned while she practiced wind glyphs. She held her hands apart and threw two wind glyphs at each other, producing a loud clap out of thin air. That impressed everyone more than the acknowledged magicians' tricks. Better yet, it encouraged the new apprentices and they promised to spend long hours practicing control.

Even after all the warnings about pain, nine people went into the library, one at a time, and burned their ward into the bone. Kelis gave them plenty of ice from the little fridge to try and numb the pain and Abel gave each one wadded tissues to bite. Each person carried out the warding alone with only Ferryl's wind form present, to help them concentrate and also protect everyone's modesty. All of them were warned they'd use the ward to help with magic, so everyone chose somewhere they could touch through clothes in public.

Sarah finally plucked up courage because that man in the park worried her. Even then she wanted time to learn much more about magic before approaching him. Meanwhile Sarah would take note of exactly what he did, and a couple of the nearest apprentices would also have a look. After the story from the willows, none of the apprentices wanted to approach a magical stranger.

*   *   *

A dazed Kelis, Rob and Abel waved the last car off, the majority having already left on the seven o'clock bus into town. The Tavern really existed now, and one hundred and thirty-four pounds in donations in a drawer in the library sort of proved it. At least four recruits were convinced they could prise serious money out of parents, though some would be for fancy dress. Petra parading her Cat-sorceress fur, Una her Robyn D'Ritche with long boots and Kelis her Glyphmistress left the male attempts like Warren's Shayde Warrior admitting defeat. Most of those present promised to come up with something for next time. A round of boos greeted Abel's seeming transformation, despite Ferryl claiming that magic wasn't cheating.

"They all seemed very well behaved. A bit happier than our usual visitors, weren't they?" All three jumped as Mrs. Ventner spoke just behind them. "That game of yours is more popular than you told me. I thought you were only experimenting."

"We were Mum, but now I think it's all turned serious." Abel felt Kelis's grip tighten. "Could we have another meeting please, in three weeks? We haven't got anywhere else."

"While we have the house and the money for the food, the more the merrier."

"It'll be cheaper next time, Mum, they'll be bringing food. Crisps and buns, that sort of thing."

"That is very thoughtful." Mrs. Ventner looked puzzled. "There didn't seem to be many in fancy dress? All four of you had one at New Year."

Abel laughed, he had to. "There'll be more costumes next time, after seeing the Glyphmistress."

"Yes, I noticed that had an effect on you at New Year." Mrs. Ventner's voice became much more serious. "I think there will be a lot of interest from some of the young men after seeing Robyn D'Ritche and Petra as Ferryl Shayde. Perhaps it really is a good idea to have your meetings here, where I can keep an eye on you. How old were those people?"

"From fourteen to nineteen but it's all about the game. They are all betas. The most advanced betas." Abel had trouble getting his head round the next bit. "According to them there could be a hundred playing beta versions of the game, spread out across half the country."

"You'd better make sure you've sorted out all your characters and rules in that case. If they all want to meet you'll need a marquee on the lawn, though I will insist on no alcohol. Could I have a picture next time, please, of everyone in costume?" That came out a bit embarrassed then as all three stared at her Mrs. Ventner continued, with a definitely wicked smile, "I'd like to let a few people see a real party in that dining room."

"Yes Mum, and you know I won't stand for alcohol." Kelis blushed a little. "The costumes aren't that shocking."

"Not the costumes, even if they are a little bit startling in real life. I meant a group of happy smiling young people, and especially sober ones. Enough about my little hang-ups, has the furniture survived?" She winked at Abel. "I hope the Glyphmistress has a cleaning up spell."

"I have." Kelis flourished her arms. "Clean up, slaves."

"We hear and obey."

"I really do have a glyph, but it would blow everything out of the room including the furniture."

Adios Amigos

Walking back past the Green after cleaning up the debris at Kelis's house, Rob and Abel turned at a familiar voice, Dryad Chestnut. "With all those apprentices, I thought you would have dealt with the goblins."

"What goblins?" Abel looked around because according to Ferryl, goblins were visible even to non-magical people.

"In the churchyard. They are chewing the roots of the trees there."

"Why didn't the dryads say?" Rob shrugged at Abel's look. "There's five lovely big trees there, but the dryads kept sending me away."

"They are church trees and not supposed to speak to the ungodly, but the church has left so they are unprotected. Now the goblins come out at night and search the grass for any sweets the human young have left. They take chances, and get there before we dare." The last part sounded downright indignant.

"Now we know why Dryad Chestnut is annoyed."

"More to the point, how come we've only ever seen one goblin? The one I squished."

The dryad seemed amused. "Goblins hide from humans, and keep well away from glyph users. Why didn't you clean out the churchyard at the same time as the rest of the village?"

"I've no idea. We never thought of it." Abel shrugged. "We've always respected it as private, because there's graves in there. Some of the churchgoers still go in there to cut grass."

"I kept clear because churchyards won't let me in, but it is strange one of you didn't at least think to check."

Abel thought one of them might have. "Rob, did you go inside the churchyard to talk to the dryads?"

"No, now I think of it. I even nipped into Mrs. Turner's garden, next door, to get to one tree. That's weird." Rob turned towards the church. "Weird enough to check on right now."

"Too true. Thank you, Dryad Chestnut. I'll leave a few sweets here next time I come past." Abel giggled. "Even if I've been answering your questions." A creaking noise startled Abel for a moment.

"That is dryad amusement. Either that or preparation for an attack, which is why most people are cautious around dryads." The humour in Ferryl's voice turned to caution. *"I may not be able to enter the churchyard. Even if we can, I will not try to talk to Rob in there as the spooky-phone might be attacked."*

"We'll wait outside and send Rob and his bat in first."

Rob grinned at that and set off, though he waited before going underneath the archway covering the gate. "I'll wait until Ferryl has sussed it out."

"The lych-gate is warded, or was, but the church magic has faded. Some of those glyphs are telling us to walk by, ignore the churchyard. They probably don't affect anyone bearing a cross. There are also remnants of something similar to the sorcerer's barrier, just a hint that non-believers are not welcome. Passing through may irritate me but with your mark to hide behind, I will be safe." Ferryl's laughter echoed in Abel's head. *"This will be a new thing, after all these years. I have never been inside a churchyard."*

Abel passed that on and Rob opened the gate, waiting on the other side. For the next five minutes the three of them wandered around among the overgrown gravestones and tangled grass and small bushes. Around the back several graves were kept very neat, and the area nearby had been trimmed to keep the grass down. Rob stopped to look at the inscriptions. "Only four graves still looked after, out of the whole churchyard. It's sort of sad."

"If there were more, I could not come in here. The church wards, the crosses, are still working on these graves. The families must be enough to keep them working." Ferryl sounded sombre, hushed, and almost reverent. "There is true power in prayers."

"What was that?" Rob pointed. "I watched the faerie going past, and as I turned I'd swear that gargoyle moved!"

"That one?" Abel sent a small glowing glyph at the ugly stone creature in question, perched up on the edge of the church roof. He hoped to flush out anything hiding behind it, but instead it morphed into a goblin!

"Don't do that! It's dangerous."

"It wasn't very hot." Abel inspected the green, fat-bellied, spindly-legged creature, then glanced around. If something that size had been nibbling roots, the ground should look as if manic badgers had been at work.

"That has not been digging. I am trying to remember how many types of goblins there are." Ferryl sniggered. *"Ask this one. The hot glyph really frightened it."* Abel remembered his lessons, goblins were very flammable.

"Sorry about the heat, I thought you were stone. Who has been chewing on tree roots?"

"I'm supposed to look like stone, because humans can see us. Why don't you know about ratlins? Even a hedge warlock should know." The humanoid goblin turned into a stone gargoyle again except for the mouth and eyes, this time a squatting toad-like creature.

"We are trainees. I've only seen one like you." Abel skipped over squishing it. "We came here because of the tree roots."

"Typical. We have been here forever, since soon after the church closed, and nobody noticed." The stone head turned to glower at the rest of the churchyard. "We have been safe in here, but those greedy little rats wouldn't listen. I told them, stick to bushes and the flower bulbs in the gardens nearby but no, they get greedy."

If ratlins ate flower bulbs these bigger ones must take something more substantial, which worried Abel. "What do you eat? I thought magical creatures only took a little bit of real food?"

"No, I told you goblins eat more which is why they are too solid to hide. Did I tell you?" Ferryl sounded frustrated and Abel cut in before she started ranting about her wits again.

"You eat a lot, don't you? The dryad said sweets from the Green, so what else?" Abel took a breath and calmed down a bit. The gargoyle turning into a goblin had shaken him, because the church had gargoyles all over it and several more on old graves. "I'm sorry, it's just that I didn't know about the turning to stone thing, otherwise I wouldn't have used fire."

"It is just a seeming, not real stone, which is why the fire is dangerous.

This is the best way for us to hide, out in plain view but now I suppose we'll have to move. Unless you are having a party." The goblin didn't seem too happy about a party.

"Why a party?"

"The stories have been passed down. Many goblins died like that, at sorcerer parties." The creature brightened a little. "Maybe you don't need us since fireworks became popular?"

"That's it! Sorcerers used goblins at feasts. The guests were allowed to shoot burning arrows at them for amusement. Sometimes the goblins were hung over a flame for a while, so they would explode when hit instead of just burning. Hobgoblins could be very dangerous if they were hot enough." Despite Ferryl sounding happy about remembering, Abel flinched at the mental picture.

"We, my friends and I, wouldn't burn you for fun. We might not even throw you out if the ratlins leave the trees alone." Abel got back to his original question. "What do you eat?"

"Usually what the humans leave outside at night. We can gang up to fight off the foxes, and you chased off the globhoblins so things have been a bit better this winter." A long tongue came out and licked its mouth. "Cat food is delicious. Dogs eat all of theirs up straight away."

"Cat food, discarded sweets and half-eaten pizzas? There isn't very much of that in Brinsford and I can see a lot of gargoyles, so what else?" Abel started to worry, because the goblin looked definitely shifty.

"We open the big bins with discarded food inside. Humans throw away some amazing food." The tongue slurped again. "Especially at Christmas. We don't need mice or rats for a week or more afterwards."

"You eat mice and rats?"

"Sometimes hoplins and thornies, but we need solid food as well as magic. We really can stay?" The creature scowled. "We can't stop the ratlins chewing roots. They hide in tunnels."

Abel thought about it. "Explain that if they continue, we will find a way to shift them. We'll think about leaving you alone, the gargoyle types, though if you stay there will be rules. No litter for starters. I'd wondered about there being so much even after we chased the thornies out."

The goblin looked shifty but didn't deny littering. "Maybe, but we need the food from the bins. We can stay here?"

"If you pick up any litter you find when you are hunting food, stay hidden, and leave cat food alone." Rob shrugged at Abel. "I'm not sure how much of that suggestion came to you by spooky-voice, but I've got the gist. I'd rather not be putting food out for Rusty just so this lot can nick it."

"*I agree about the cat food. The goblins are being very cautious because my cats have not seen them. There are many complaints about food being taken, but I thought foxes must be to blame. Goblins explains why you have no rat problem in Brinsford.*" Ferryl sighed. "*The goblin has been very careful to only mention ratlins and itself. How many others are there in here? Not Hobgoblins or we would see signs, but I can't remember all of them.*"

"How many sorts of goblins are in the churchyard?" The creature eyed Abel, obviously trying to decide how much to give away, so Abel killed a small fae with a fire glyph. "I wouldn't want to hit one by mistake."

"Just us, ratlins and batlins. We are all goblins, but humans like to give us different names. Batlins eat faeries, fae, bugs and birds. Not many birds, because the feathers can cause a blockage." An ugly grin appeared. "A blockage can be very dangerous for goblins. We try to vent gas as quickly as possible, and away from flames."

Abel smiled at that, he had to. "What about pixies and the other helpful creatures, do goblins eat them?" That started a proper discussion, and Abel found out the goblins encouraged pictsies to keep vermin out of the church corners where batlins couldn't reach. Because the church had no human residents, these goblins had encouraged a small tribe of brownies to move in and keep the place dusted. As they talked, almost a score of gargoyles turned into little pot-bellied humanoids and came to join in. Some of the other gargoyles opened their eyes to watch, not always easy to spot as darkness closed in.

Eventually Rob pointed out they'd better get home, though even then a dozen hopeful goblins followed to the gate. Abel hoped the ratlins saw sense, because these creatures seemed fairly harmless and would keep the nastier pests out of the churchyard. Rob wanted one for his garden as a stone ornament, and even promised to leave table scraps near it. On the way home the pair of them composed a long text for Kelis to explain. Her answer didn't take much typing. "Not fair. I want to see!"

*   *   *

It wasn't goblins that excited Kelis the next morning. "Mum wants a real party at the next Tavern meeting, a birthday party, a double if you don't mind." She squeezed Abel's hand. "My birthday is on the Sunday anyway and yours is only ten days earlier, the day we break up for half-term. Would you mind? I've never had a real party with people I know, friends."

"Families as well? Because Melanie is really pushing to come to Tavern meetings and if she sees the wards she'll know why I've been stalling." Rob sighed. "She gave me hell about the last one, and I've no excuse for her not coming because she knows Kelis and also plays the game." A little smile touched Rob's lips. "What about your mum, Abel?"

"Mum will probably want to come, if only to help Kelis's mum out." Abel grinned. "She'll steal the marzipan from the cake."

"I'll steal the cake if your mum brings one." Rob made a big production of licking his lips. "Two birthday cakes? Forget the party, just leave me in a quiet corner with the confectionery."

"A birthday cake? I never thought of that. He never let me have one. Will your Mum bake one, please?" Kelis danced in a circle. "I'll give her all the ingredients. Or I could try, with fire glyphs?"

"Do you all like cinder cake?"

Even Kelis didn't fancy that, so Abel would ask his mum to bake Kelis a birthday cake. He hoped she'd say yes, because usually Abel and his mum ate the rest of the Christmas cake for his birthday. "Sixteen candles of course, though I'm not sure Mum's got thirty-two for two cakes."

"We can keep enough ratlins to make up the numbers? For Abel's cake of course, because he's gross already." Rob cowered. "Hey, no fair. How come both of you are hitting me?"

"Because you mentioned burning ratlins on a cake? Yeuk." Kelis smiled happily. "Though you two will be taking me to see goblins today, or there will be real trouble. Do they need treats, like a dryad?"

"Don't start that or you'll be shipping in pizzas by the vanload. There are a lot of them." Rob frowned. "I've no idea how many, or how many ratlins or batlins. What on earth does a batlin look like?"

"Or a ratlin. A goblin crossed with a bat or rat? They must be called that for a reason." Though Abel agreed after a short argument that wasn't necessarily true. It wasn't until later Abel realised Ferryl had kept quiet. He asked her once they were alone and Ferryl seemed very down. She couldn't taste cake, and couldn't remember batlins or ratlins, and felt useless. Eventually Abel managed to get her cheered up, and even attempting animated tattoo versions of a possible batlin or ratlin.

*   *   *

The Taverners met a batlin straight after dinner, because Kelis wanted plenty of time to ask questions. Batlins were goblins, little fat-bellied green humanoids, until they opened their wings. Kelis thought they looked like cartoon bats, a jolly joke demon or vampire with really bony and leathery wings. Even Ferryl agreed she might have seen them and thought they were bats, if the creatures flew about in the darkness. The batlins weren't really conversationalists, being more worried about staying in the church tower. Once they'd agreed to Kelis's demand to leave butterflies, finches and robins alone, the three who'd agreed to talk flew back into a hole in the boarding over the church window. The original goblin, or maybe another, reported that they'd passed the message to the ratlins but none of the burrowers had answered. Abel repeated that they'd got until Saturday, one week.

Abel's mum agreed that a birthday party with the Taverners would be a great way to celebrate, especially if she got to meet them all. Abel confessed they could all see magical creatures, and were learning to deal with it without therapy or counselling. *"Chris will realise how they all deal with it when she sees their wards. Some are not at all shy about showing their marks. Chris will see the creatures avoid Jessica, and the two will talk and maybe wonder how you deal with creatures."*

"I'm not risking sending my mum or Kelis's crackers."

"What about Rob's sisters? They may want to play the game when they meet Taverners their own age. Samantha will like the fancy dress."

"Stop it. This is all getting out of hand. We've got to slow it down somehow." Abel thought hard. "We've got to get a board game out there, one with dice so people concentrate on that instead of floating leaves."

"In that case you had better get it all completed before the meeting. If I understood properly, Shawn and Eric are both old enough to get the legal part organised. Perhaps you should concentrate on that instead of your bound woman."

"Kelis isn't bound, or my woman!" Abel really hoped the first bit was true. He resorted to his last defence. "It's not serious. We're only fifteen."

"Until the party. After that, is Kelis a girl or a woman? Break the link."

"If Kelis agrees." When Ferryl didn't answer, Abel took a deep breath. "I'll ask after the party."

"If you say so."

* * *

During the week an undercurrent of excitement ran through school with those in the know exchanging looks and smiles. As a big plus magical creatures were more or less banished inside the buildings, and now it would take a major offensive by the cleaners to remove the plethora of hexes. Despite the amount of homework the phones were busy at night, though most investigation had to wait for the weekend.

On Saturday morning Abel talked his mum into taking him into town, where he bought a Valentine's card, a proper one. He looked at it for a long time when he came home, really worried. It was big and covered in hearts and flowers, nothing like he would have dreamt of getting mere weeks ago. "This is getting serious."

"You could block the connection?"

"Can I? Are you sure it's the connection?" Abel sighed. "I think it's growing stronger. I'm too young for this. Kelis is too young." He sighed again. "Though we are both too old for me to risk this being just the mark."

"So you'll really ask her this time? If she burns in her own ward, and I burn out this connection, that will stop any leakage either way."

"Maybe."

"Which means you won't really mean it, and the connection may not

be broken. Why can you not understand? If that Wolf Shade had taken you, Kelis would have been taken as well." Abel didn't answer. *"Worse, if it had taken her first because she wasn't protected properly I could not have defended you, or myself."*

With that card in front of him Ferryl's warning seemed more certain, more serious this time, and Abel firmed up. "I'll ask tonight."

"Stop worrying. You might still want to give her the card afterwards."

"But Kelis might not want it." Which would prove he'd been influencing her, which Abel didn't want to think about. "Keep quiet until we've been to see the goblins. Kelis may as well have some fun this afternoon."

*   *   *

When Abel led Kelis and Rob into the churchyard he knew there must be a problem. The church had hardly any gargoyles which meant a lot of goblins must be hiding. "Come and talk to us, goblins. We will not burn you. All we want is an answer."

A round, bald green head peered out from behind a gravestone. "What if you don't like the answer?"

"From the ratlins? That's not your fault." Kelis sniggered. "It might be bad for the ratlins. Abel told me they eat flower bulbs and I really like daffodils and tulips."

"You can't get to them." The goblin came further out from behind its gravestone. "The ratlins say you cannot reach them in their burrows."

"I can explain their mistake."

"Please ask one to speak to us, or show us a ratlin hole." The goblin didn't answer, just thought a moment then beckoned and headed off between the overgrown graves.

"I'm not going to be in a good mood after scrambling through those creepers." Kelis started forward but Rob jumped in front.

"This is what a barbarian is for." He used his penknife to cut a long thin branch from an elder bush and started beating a path. "I hope that goblin waits."

The goblin did, or at least it came back for them several times before pointing to a neat round hole in the ground near the churchyard wall. "This is a ratlin hole. I have called, but they will not answer." The goblin shrugged. "The holes are all connected and they don't come out very often."

"Just to dump litter." Torn crisp packets and other bits of rubbish surrounded the hole. Abel, Kelis and Rob waited, but eventually Ferryl had waited long enough.

"*We should send a message. No goblin likes heat, so perhaps a small heat glyph blowing through their tunnels will get a ratlin's attention?*" Ferryl waited as Abel suggested that and the other two agreed. "*If I could use your right hand, please? Drop a small heat glyph into the hole, and I will catch it in a small puff of wind.*" Abel did as asked, and the glyph dropped to the entrance then suddenly shot inside.

Within a minute a small, green, muddy and very annoyed face peered out of the hole. "Fire is dangerous!"

"You didn't answer. That wasn't hot enough to harm you." Abel let that sink in for a moment. "We want to talk to you."

"Apprentices? We have nothing to say. We like it here and you cannot move us." The little face, thinner than the other goblins, bared a row of little sharp teeth in a grin. "If you use fire that will burn the tree roots. That one there has been asking the dryads for help so you will not do that. They would never speak to you again."

"*The dryads are not speaking to Rob now, nor are they helping. Even if the other dryads are upset, the one we rescued will send out seedlings eventually. They will show the rest we can be trusted.*"

Ferryl couldn't pass that on by spooky-phone, not in the churchyard, but Rob agreed with her once Abel explained. "I know whose idea that is. The church trees are useless to us anyway."

"I don't like it, but maybe the dryads will realise it has stopped the tree roots being eaten. They may forgive us in time." Kelis shrugged. "But if not, then Rob is right anyway." She glared at the little green face. "So let your little friends know. We will burn you out if you don't agree to leave tree roots and flower bulbs alone." Kelis pointed to the litter. "No more rubbish. You put it in bins, and you can get food from the same place."

The ratlin looked from one to another. "No. We have tunnels all over here, so you can't blow fire down every one. We'll dig more now, across the gardens so you'll never find us." Voices from deeper inside the tunnel behind the little creature, and from the bushes either side, agreed.

Abel waited before answering, and sure enough Ferryl had a solution. *"If you do not mind scorching the tree roots, the ratlin is wrong. It will take very good control of wind, but that is my speciality. Ask the goblin if his kin will hunt down ratlins on the surface, and show us all the holes. In return they can stay, as can the batlins. If you agree?"*

Abel passed it on, and the goblin didn't hesitate. "If you will allow us to live here, protected, we will help." It bared decidedly larger teeth at the ratlin. "Usually ratlins laugh at us and hide underground. We will see if they laugh with their tunnels full of fire." The ratlin didn't answer, it disappeared into the hole and everyone could hear little feet scampering away.

"Collect your kin, and show us the holes. Stand clear of them because fire might come out, but be ready in case ratlins try to run back into the village." Abel bent to shout down the hole. "We will start from this end. We will not chase any ratlin that leaves the churchyard and the village."

Even when 'their' goblin had revealed every ratlin hole and told Abel the rest of its kin were ready, he still couldn't be sure how many goblins there were. An awful lot of glimpses of green scuttling about suggested at least thirty, and at least that number of gargoyles were missing from the church. "Ready?" Kelis squeezed his hand and let go to raise both hers. Rob nodded, concentrating on one hand to get better control.

The three stood shoulder to shoulder over the first hole, so Ferryl connected to them all. "Remember, lots of tiny, very hot glyphs. Try to let them float down so I have time to catch each in a puff of wind and send it down the hole. The wind will preserve the glyph until it hits something living, a root or creature. Abel, please start."

Abel dropped a hot glyph, trying to keep it slow, and his right hand started moving. As soon as Abel's glyph dropped, Kelis dropped one, then another, then Rob, and Abel had another ready. Each glyph only took a little magic, so the three of them kept up a continual stream as the shrieks of ratlins and the excited shouts of hunting goblins spread out among the graves. Puffs of smoke came out from some of the nearby holes, and one of the church trees rattled branches.

"Next hole." The trio moved to one that still smoked just a little, and continued dropping glyphs. As they moved from hole to hole, and down the back of the church, the noises and smoke spread in front of them. By the time just over half the churchyard had been cleared, a goblin reported ratlins fleeing over the church wall. *"Keep going or some will stay and hide."* Abel flexed his fingers and wondered if the others were starting to feel the strain.

"We'll need to top up from a tree after this." Kelis shook her hands, then started casting glyphs again.

"I'll need splints for my fingers. At least I'm only using one hand at a time." Rob smirked. "There are advantages in being incompetent."

"Tree magic will make you feel better. Keep out from under these trees, because the dryads are annoyed." Sure enough, small branches flew towards the trio if they came near the big church trees. Kelis blew them aside and went back to her heat glyphs.

Eventually a very satisfied looking goblin reported smoke from every hole, and no more ratlins were coming out. "Batlins are following the survivors and will tell you if any stay in the village." Another three goblins appeared, peering hopefully from around bushes and gravestones. "May we stay now?"

"Yes, but you've got to keep hidden. Don't let the rest of the villagers see you." Even as Abel spoke all the goblins in sight turned into stone ornaments, then back again. "Fair enough. If you clean up the ratlin litter we'll bring you some fresh food, or fresh enough." Abel didn't think goblins cared about sell-by dates. He turned to the other two. "I don't know about you pair, but I need to hug a tree."

"I'll bring them some pizza. There's some frozen ones at home that neither of us will ever eat." Kelis shook her hands. "My fingers are nearly numb." Not too numb to hold Abel's hand on the way to Castle House garden for tree magic. Abel savoured the walk, remembering it for after.

The three of them chose a big strong tree each and split up to cut their glyphs. "Ooh, that feels better." Abel stretched luxuriously as the fresh, bright magic flowed in.

"Tree magic seems purer, in some way. Remember that and don't let too many dryads in."

"Ferryl says to keep some trees without dryads, because tree magic is better."

"She's right." Kelis whirled, her arms out wide. "I feel a little bit like drunk would be, I suppose." Her twirl ended up in Abel's arms. "I feel really happy." When the two of them parted, after much too long, both stared at each other in some sort of shock. "Maybe it's the tree magic." Kelis barely whispered, a hand going to her lips.

"Certainly magic." Abel couldn't think too straight because that had been wonderful, mind-blowing. Much too much, something warned him. The connection had to go. Abel kept that to himself as he walked back into the village holding hands, and mercifully Ferryl kept quiet.

Rob turned off to Riverside Close, leaving Abel to walk Kelis home, with a parting, "I'd probably starve to death waiting until you pair finish."

Kelis giggled. "He might." Her face sobered. "What happened?"

"Too much tree magic? That really did feel different." The two of them walked to Kelis's door.

"Different, or just more? We aren't full of tree magic now?" Kelis bent her head as she spoke and Abel lifted his for the only reply.

It took Abel three tries to talk afterwards. "More. Definitely more. Is it too much more, Kelis?" He smiled. "Not for me, for you. I'm still firmly enslaved."

"Or am I?" Kelis sighed, but a happy sigh. "It isn't a terrible fate. Maybe once more so I can decide, later?"

Walking home after that last kiss, Abel really did try to decide if the magic might be to blame. Though either way he now knew the connection had to go, because he had to find out.

"I suppose that means you won't be asking now."

"Yes I will. More so now. I've got to know."

"That makes a change. Humans are very good at finding reasons for doing something they enjoy, regardless of the consequences. I hope you have enough willpower to go through with it." Abel didn't answer, because

he also hoped he had enough willpower. He couldn't think of much else through eating tea, and until he could finally head to Kelis's for the Tavern meeting.

*   *   *

Kelis might have been psychic, or had also been thinking hard. No sooner had Abel murmured that he wanted to talk to her than she asked Rob to give them a few moments alone in the library, for embarrassing stuff. As the door closed behind Rob, Abel took a deep breath. "About the feeling, the warm one inside."

"When you kiss me? Or when I kiss you because I feel something really scary-nice that scrambles my brain." Kelis took his hands, then let go. "I'm worried, especially after this afternoon. What happened?"

That was all Abel needed. "I don't know, but I'm worried as well. We are both too young to feel like this, I think. I still don't believe I'm influencing you, but we'll never be sure while we are connected."

"Can Ferryl fix it? Sorry, Ferryl, can you fix it?"

"Yes, but you must both have intent. Abel must truly want to break the connection, and you must want that enough to burn in a proper ward, to the bone. Not Abel's mark."

"I've already drawn one of my own. I've had it for a while, but kept putting it off. What happens if we still feel like this?" Kelis smiled, sort of wistful. "Some books describe that sort of feeling when people kiss, so it might be real."

"That's in books, not real life." Abel tried to smile back. "If it still happens, we'll deal with it." He bit off pointing out that wouldn't be a terrible result. "What happens if you hate me afterwards?"

"Not hate. I liked you before the mark, or we felt the tingles. Hah, I even kissed you, on the cheek." Kelis sighed. "Intent. I can have that, because I want to know if the mark is affecting me, or you."

"I want you to be safe. Ferryl reminded me, again, that if the Wolf Shade had taken me, it would have taken you as well." Abel shuddered. "That's frightening enough for me to mean it." Without another word Kelis went to get the ice, and Abel wadded tissues to bite on. Kelis brought a drawing out of the desk and sat memorising it with the ice on her arm.

When she put it down, she came to stand in front of Abel.

"One last time." Her little smile seemed uncertain. "For comparison, and for memory."

Afterwards Abel didn't think the kiss helped his intent because the whatever from this afternoon hadn't worn off. He ruthlessly crushed how much he liked the feeling. "Ready?"

"Ready." Kelis poised her finger on the outside of her upper arm, the opposite side of the bone to where Abel had drawn the flower.

"*Ready.*" Abel and Kelis bit on the tissues, and Kelis brought her finger down.

It didn't burn Abel as badly as he'd feared. In fact it felt like a wrench, something being pulled free or breaking off before the heat. Kelis hissed in real pain, and clasped her arm for a moment. She turned that arm towards Abel. "Did it?"

Abel looked at the shape, a double circle filled with curved lines, almost Celtic, and a downward point like a spear or arrow head, all straight lines towards the point. Kelis had coloured her tattoo in shades from pale pink through to dark red. "*Everything protected in two circles, with the point outside to strike at any who threaten. That suits our Glyphmistress. Can you feel anything?*"

From her lack of reaction, Kelis didn't hear Ferryl so Abel didn't answer directly. "That's lovely but I wouldn't want that point aimed at me. I felt the connection break."

"Is the flower gone?" Kelis raised her arm.

"Yes." Abel frowned. "It was indelible marker."

"I haven't had to renew it for a long time. I'd sort of hoped it would stay, but not connected." A tear appeared in the corner of Kelis's eye and she scrubbed it away. She whispered "time to test" and leant forward.

When they parted, Abel answered the question in her eyes. "Very nice. Definitely addictive, but no warm feeling." He hoped Kelis still found kissing addictive, but thought crossing his fingers might be a bit obvious.

"Yes, definitely a nice kiss, but no flood of warm to scramble my head. That really must only happen in books. The trouble is that now I don't know if the kiss felt nice because of all the practice and memories. We should have a clean break until we know." Kelis didn't seem overjoyed, but Abel recognised the determination in her voice and face which settled one thing. The little something Abel thought he felt when they kissed wasn't a link, it was his heart breaking. Which seemed a bit melodramatic, but Abel thought he might be justified.

At least that thought allowed him to smile at himself. "You can kiss Rob to compare? He might give up on fur if he kisses a Glyphmistress."

"Yeuk, the barbarian? I think not. I haven't got a candidate, or not until we have the next Tavern meeting." Kelis smiled brightly. "After all, it's my birthday so I can demand kisses all round." She poised one hand to cast a glyph. "It'll have to be someone magic or I might end up binding another sucker."

"I agree. You have a very strong will."

Kelis looked startled. "Really? Magical and properly warded then." She hugged Abel, quickly. "If we still wonder in a month or two, we could find a quiet place and try again?" The laugh that followed definitely sounded too bright and forced. "Come on, or Rob will be wondering himself, about just how embarrassing we're being."

"We should tell him why. Otherwise he'll think we argued and give me hell for upsetting you." If Abel had thought it through he would have realised Rob would give him hell anyway, for making the link in the first place. At least Rob and Ferryl ganging up to berate him got Abel, and Kelis, through the rest of a very short Tavern meeting. Afterwards Abel felt strange leaving with Rob, after just a wave goodbye to Kelis.

Abel spent an hour in his bedroom drawing a homemade Valentine's card for Kelis. Bearing in mind how much Kelis disliked slimy creatures he did his best to draw a green snail laying a trail reading 'Please be Slime' in a slimy-looking font. Two days later, on Valentine's Day, Kelis immediately guessed who drew it and called him gross. Kelis's card from Rob had a teddy bear in a collar, offering the lead with 'I just wanna be' above its head. Kelis sent Abel an anonymous one which showed a sorcerer in a pointy hat trying to dance with the tree, while a pretty dryad looked on disgusted. Her speech bubble said 'Tree's a crowd.' Rob's had a barbarian sucking his thumb and cuddling a teddy bear in a skirt.

*   *   *

The next few days until half-term were really odd, for Abel at least. Their table, the geeks and betas, all noticed but most of the other students didn't notice because Abel, Kelis and Rob still sat together. Abel missed Kelis's hand. He thought about her a bit too much, trudging around from lesson to lesson with his head down, lost in memories. The lessons slipped by, not really registering, and Abel ignored the occasional complaints when he bumped someone because he hadn't even seen them. He kept going round and round everything in his head. Yes, the warm thing ended but he still really liked kissing Kelis, and he felt something. At least Ferryl must have realised he didn't want her interfering, and kept mostly quiet.

The last day before half-term Abel walked into the wrong person, Mr. Beresford, earning himself some extra homework. Abel complained to Rob and Kelis, but without conviction. He didn't really care, because he'd probably spend the time in his bedroom anyway. He still couldn't work out if he'd feel better spending time with Kelis, hoping she'd change her mind, or would it be best to keep out of the way. Then she might miss him. Mr. Beresford had an office in the sports hall, so after collecting his extra work Abel mooched along the back of the school towards the bus. Everyone else would be coming out of the front so he went round the building, because right now solitude suited him. Except that around the corner he found Jenny, the star of the Acro team.

Jenny stood leaning against the wall, hugging herself with her head down. Abel wondered what might be wrong but on catching sight of him, Jenny spun away and almost ran around the next corner. Abel heard her scream above the squeal of brakes and the sounds of a crunch and clanging metal. He started running, but skidded to a halt as he came around the corner. A lorry loaded with scaffolding poles and planks had buried its back corner in the school wall, spilling about half the load. The driver got out, turned around looking baffled, and went off out of sight frantically calling someone on a mobile.

"*Quickly. Look, there!*" Abel's hand jerked without volition and pointed, and he saw a hand sticking out from between the planks!

"I'll call the ambulance." Abel dropped his school bag, fumbling for his phone.

"She'll die. Quickly, lift the planks. Then you can call." That made sense, so Abel ran to the planks and put both hands under.

"No, you'll break your hands. Remember moving the tree." Abel put one hand on top of the other and pushed on the glyphs. *"A surge to lift, toss them up then a wind glyph to blow them away. Hurry, and she lives!"* As he smacked the planks away and they scattered across the lorry. Abel wondered how he'd explain that but now he could see half of Jenny, and the amount of blood. She coughed weakly and blood dribbled from her mouth as he reached again, glyphs scattering planks and metal poles.

"She needs an ambulance."

"She needs me! Hurry, carry her round the corner out of sight."

"What! She'll die."

"She's dying now. I can save her if you are quick enough." Abel couldn't argue about Jenny dying so he picked her up, wincing as her arm flopped at a totally un-natural angle. His stomach churned at the sight of her foot, crushed into a shapeless mess of flesh, bone and black leather shoe. Even as he carried Jenny round the corner, Abel could see blood spreading across her torn blouse and skirt.

"Quickly. Save her Ferryl. What do I do?"

"Hold her head up a little bit more. One moment." Abel managed to raise Jenny's shoulders so she was more or less sat on one arm with the other round her and her head nearly on his shoulder. Ferryl's mist tendril shot out, connected, and Jenny's eyes jerked open. She closed them again, blood bubbled from her lips and she started shuddering. *"It is done. Kiss her."*

"No!"

"I have to be inside her to save her. She has agreed. Do it! You promised!" Jenny's eyes opened again and Abel could see pain and pleading in there, while her good arm tightened a little and she tried to raise her head. Abel braced himself, then ducked and kissed her quickly.

He meant to be quick. Instead his lips clamped onto hers and Abel tasted blood. He couldn't move as he breathed out, and out, and out, long after every last gasp should be gone. His head spun and his ears roared, but as Abel's grip loosened Jenny's tightened, holding him firmly in a real lip-lock. He felt his legs give way and tried to stay up, but couldn't and sprawled on the concrete. At least that broke the hold, and Abel dragged in big breaths as hard as he could.

Abel looked up, head still spinning, to see Jenny stood above him. "Thank you. Debt paid." The words bubbled out in a red froth but already the bleeding had lessened, and Jenny's broken arm straightened and flexed as if testing. She turned, limping away but already straightening a little more.

"Jenny, are you....? What are you doing here?" Abel shook his head, fighting to gather his wits because that sounded like Henry!

"What is it?" Seraph's voice this time. Abel groaned and rolled onto his hands and knees, turning his head to look at Seraph's pointing finger as she continued. "Why is there blood on his mouth? All over him?"

Unfortunately Henry had an obvious answer to that. "The pervert must have tried it on with Jenny. She's covered in blood. Luckily she must have knocked the little wimp down. I should...."

"Oh no, Henry. We'll let Jenny deal with this, or the law at least. Come on, let's see how poor Jenny is." Seraph turned away.

"But you just told Jenny..." Henry's voice faded and Abel used the wall to clamber to his feet. His legs were wobbly and he felt as weak as the proverbial kitten.

"Ferryl, what happened? Did you save her?" Total silence answered. "I'll use the Pung name. Answer me, Ferryl." Still nothing, and his tattoo didn't move. Worse, it felt empty, like when she flew off. But why fly off when Henry might have...? Abel finally connected the dots, Ferryl had taken Jenny over. She'd possessed Jenny, and Abel had helped! He groaned, and straightened.

Abel looked round but except for voices round the corner the only sign of life was the bloodstains on the concrete. He staggered to the corner and stared at the back of the driver, two workmen and a teacher arguing about the crashed lorry and the planks strewn all about. There didn't seem to be enough blood, but he hadn't really stopped to inspect it at the time. Abel scooped up his schoolbag and limped past behind the arguing group, wondering where he'd banged his knee.

Abel staggered onto the bus before it left and made his way to his seat trying to hide the blood. From the way Kelis stared at his face, the quick wipe with his sleeve hadn't been enough. "What happened? Ferryl, tell us, please."

Abel leaned in close to whisper and Kelis flinched away. "She's gone."

At least Kelis kept her voice down. "Who? Ferryl? Will she be able to catch up with the bus, because we're off any second." Sure enough, the driver started the engine. "Is that your blood? Are you hurt?"

"No. Yes, I'm hurt but not much and not blood. That's Jenny's blood."

"Jenny's? On your face and," Kelis and Rob both inspected him, "all over you." Kelis's voice hardened. "How did you get her blood all over you, and where is she?"

"Maybe in hospital. There was an accident. Ferryl has gone." Abel stopped and took a deep breath, then tried again. It didn't help that anyone close tried to eavesdrop, and the rest were staring at the blood all over him and now the bus seat. He settled for a very quiet "Ferryl got me to pick her up and used my breath to move over into Jenny. She's supposed to heal her."

"You kissed her, Jenny? You got blood on your face kissing her?" Rob screwed up his face in disgust, then glanced round to make sure nobody had heard.

"Ferryl took over. By the time she'd gone, I'd more or less passed out." Abel glared at those leaning closer. "Later, when we get off." He turned towards the window, scrubbing at his face again.

*   *   *

Kelis had been thinking on the way, because as soon as they were walking up the lane she rounded on Abel. "What was the deal? How were you supposed to supply a body for Ferryl? I thought she meant body, dead, not someone alive! Does that mean she just grabbed the nearest available when she felt like it?" Kelis stopped, her face ashen. "Does that mean Jenny's dead?"

"I don't think so. Jenny stood up and I saw her arm un-break itself, then she limped off on what should be a crushed foot." Abel shook his head. "I wish I knew what it meant, Ferryl going into her. If she's still

Jenny she'll remember me picking her up and carting her off." Abel paused, wondering just how much would be Jenny, and what she'd think of what happened.

"Then trying to kiss her. If Ferryl's really taken over she'll explain. Something." Kelis shook her head. "I have no idea what explanation covers this." She sighed and passed Abel a tissue. "Clean your face properly. Did Jenny actually die, stop breathing?"

Abel hesitated, then plunged on. "Not unless she died right then. You didn't see her Kelis. Blood from her mouth and the side of her head, and her clothes were torn and the bloodstains were spreading as I watched. Her arm bent all wrong and flopping about with blood coming out, and her foot. Her foot had been crushed. Not broken, I mean gone, mashed into her shoe." Abel stopped and hung his head, hands over his eyes. "Even if she'd lived, she'd have been crippled. No more athletics, gymnastics or Acro. I wish I could forget that, her foot. And her eyes, Kelis, she knew."

"Knew what? You'd sold her body?"

Abel winced from Kelis's cutting tone. "No, Ferryl connected, spoke in her head, and Jenny's eyes opened. Pain and pleading, I swear she wanted saving."

"Or she was pleading for you to stop Ferryl, you bloody moron." Rob scowled. "How come you never asked, about taking a body?"

"It just never came up, what with everything else. Neither of you asked." That sounded feeble even to Abel and sure enough...

"Because we assumed you knew! Though now I think about it you're right. We just accepted the whole thing, magic and Ferryl. I thought it was because of the game, but maybe she bewitched us?" Kelis sighed. "You are an utter and complete idiot, Abel Conroy. If Ferryl is in charge, you'll get away with the blood and the rest. If not? At least you'll know before school starts again because plod will be beating down the door."

"Thanks. I knew you'd cheer me up." Abel didn't even try to hide the sarcasm.

"Well ten years for molesting a road traffic victim might be better than what Jenny got." Kelis stopped and almost whispered the next question. "How old is Ferryl, Abel?"

"Hundreds of years, she came here with the Danes and speaks Latin and Greek." Abel shrugged at the two stares. "How do you think I did so well at the holiday project?"

Kelis barely scowled at him beating her by cheating. "So how many years will Jenny or her body be trotting about with a passenger? Hundreds? A thousand? Until the body finally conks out?"

"Twenty years!" Abel finally smiled. "I remember, Ferryl told me. She usually offers to cure a fatal illness in return for twenty years, and promises to leave the body in top condition. That means Jenny can't be dead." His shoulders slumped. "I turned it down, and the gold." Abel skipped the women under the circumstances.

Though Kelis wasn't letting go. "Why, apart from you not having a fatal disease? What's the big catch?"

"Grand theft schoolgirl. Ferryl will be the driver, not the passenger. I had to negotiate to get Ferryl as a rider without reins or spurs. Ow." Abel turned to glare at Rob, rubbing his shoulder.

"You deserve that at least. Jenny has to watch someone else driving her about for twenty years?" Rob shook his head.

"That or wake up in twenty years. She'll be thirty-six, with no idea what Ferryl's done with her. You stupid idiot." Kelis thumped Abel on the other arm.

Abel gave up trying to rub both arms. "Better than dead."

"We'll have to wait twenty years to ask Jenny that." Kelis looked at Abel's arm, the one with the tattoo. "She's really gone, Ferryl?

"Yes, the tattoo feels empty, more so than when she used to fly. Maybe it isn't there, and then I'll have to get one done or Mum really will ask questions." Abel sighed. "I feel tired, drained."

"Drained? Has your magic gone with her?" Kelis flexed her hand and a small wind glyph picked up a few leaves. "Try."

Abel tried, and couldn't even rustle them. "I've got no magic left." He tried again but couldn't feel the familiar flowing sensation. "It's all gone, Ferryl stitched me." He groaned, his head going down again as that sank in. "Oh great. The mighty sorcerer, watch him wave his hands. Looks like protecting Brinsford and training the Taverners is up to you two. I'll fetch the tea."

"Maybe not totally stitched. You still know how to do magic." Rob pointed back towards Castle House. "Steal some magic from a tree, as a dryad would put it. If that works, Ferryl just used a lot saving Jenny."

"But definitely stitched anyway. She's supposed to be protecting you for another eighty nine years." Kelis looked around. "Nope, no magic guardian. We'll come with you, since your bodyguard has run off."

Even when the tree magic flooded in and he could work glyphs, Abel still felt completely flat. All he wanted to do was sleep so he limped off home, begging off a Tavern meeting tonight. He felt depressed, let down, abandoned, deserted, cast off like a worn shirt. Ferryl had taken the first chance to leave despite all the fine words about training and ninety years protection. Maybe it shouldn't have hurt so much, but he'd trusted her and betrayal cut him to the quick. Abel really didn't fancy school in five days. Even if Jenny recovered he'd have to watch her bouncing around with the Acros, while he knew who she was and couldn't say a word. Where did that leave the Tavern? Could they survive without their only real sorceress and how did he explain where she'd gone?

*   *   *

Abel begged off the Tavern meeting with Kelis and Rob the next day, claiming a badly wrenched knee. It hurt, but he hurt more inside. First Kelis, then Ferryl. His tattoo mocked him, flat and dead looking though he'd expected it to disappear with her. At least he'd been spared having it really tattooed on, but somehow that didn't seem like a plus. Abel's flower wasn't the same either, now he'd lost the link to Kelis. He could still feel his magic, but never the tingles he'd got so used to.

Rob calling round to tell him the other Taverners wanted to know what had happened didn't help. "There are some very strange questions, Abel. Seraph hasn't wasted any time. At least half the calls I've got have heard some version of you assaulting Jenny, either after her accident or you injured her."

"I didn't assault her!"

"You walked across the yard and got on the bus looking like Freddy Krueger, covered in her blood. Since I've no idea what sort of injuries Jenny has now, if any, neither me nor Kelis can reassure anyone." Rob threw up his hands in exasperation. "You could at least answer calls and emails. That's not exactly helping, is it?"

"Yeah right. I'll tell them the last I saw she'd started dying, just before I kissed her and she walked off." Abel sighed and sat on his bed. "Forget it Rob. It's not your problem, or Kelis's. It's a good job Kelis got rid of me."

"You can't let Seraph spread her lies! You've got to at least speak to people, Abel."

"No I haven't." Abel waved towards his phone and laptop, both turned off. "See? They'll all believe what they want so sod 'em. You and Kelis sort out the Tavern. You're both better than me anyway."

"No we aren't. Your magic is way ahead of ours."

"Not without a magical tattoo to help. You've learned properly so you two take on the Tavern. I'll just wait and see what happens." Abel turned his back, lying down on his bed. "I'm going to sleep now. Maybe when I wake up it'll all be over, or plod will have arrived and I'll know the worst."

"You selfish.... All right, if that's how you feel. I'll let Kelis know since you haven't got the decency to even answer her calls." Rob waited, then stormed out when Abel didn't answer.

*　　*　　*

When even his mum started to ask what the problem was, why he didn't go to the Tavern, and had he fallen out with Kelis, Abel hid away from her as well. At least in Castle House gardens only two people could reach him, and Abel took care to avoid the cave and stone slab. He didn't fancy sitting there anyway, remembering Ferryl Shayde promising to help and protect him. For the first time he really considered her name, and what it might mean. She wasn't a Shade, he didn't think, though maybe that shimmering meant a ghost? He'd never truly asked, and now he'd never know. Even now, Abel didn't want to think too hard about Ferryl maybe meaning feral. A Feral Shade sounded really nasty, and he'd put it into a sixteen-year-old schoolgirl.

The third day of the holiday Abel plodded along the edge of the field and wood at the rear of Castle House, to avoid the road and any villagers. Abel turned into the wood, avoiding the stretch with the dryad or the creature would want to talk. He paid absolutely no attention to anything else, still churning his own problems over and over in his mind, until a familiar voice interrupted.

"Hello squeak. I've been watching and your friends aren't around, are they? Did they finally get sick of you?" Henry came out from behind a big tree inside the wood and while Abel tried to work out how he'd overcome the barrier, strolled forward. "Seraph said leave it for the police, but I reckon you've earned a bit of real pain first."

Abel raised a hand. "Don't do it Henry. I'm not in the mood."

"That won't work. I've got a defence against. Against." Henry frowned. "Whatever that is." Abel threw the glyph, a tight air one at Henry's leg but the youth walked straight through it! While Abel tried to come to terms with that Henry threw a punch. Abel tried to avoid it, but Henry's fist hit his shoulder like a club, spinning him round. Abel tottered, trying to keep his feet and Henry swung again. Abel went down, rolling away from a kick and firing off a really hard, concentrated wind glyph that had no effect at all. He scrambled away as fast as possible and stood, rubbing his shoulder.

"Defence against what, Henry? Who gave you it? Seraph?"

"Not her, she doesn't know about, about, this stuff. Stuff against waggy finger. I'm going to stomp you, then I get." Henry paused, his face screwed up in concentration before it suddenly cleared. "Everything! I get everything. Claris said so. She drew this." Henry pulled his shirt open to show a glyph painted across his chest. Abel didn't hold back with his glyph this time, but Henry didn't even stagger when the hammer of wind hit. He closed quickly and Abel moved away, favouring his bad knee. Running wouldn't work, injured like this.

"Back off now Henry, or the gloves are off. I mean it." Henry threw a branch and Abel knocked it aside with wind. His magic worked, but not on Henry. Abel fired two tight glyphs at the ground right under Henry's toes, and the burly youth staggered but recovered and ran forward. Abel tried a trap, like those in the bushes behind the house but Henry snapped it and lashed out.

Abel got an arm in the way, staggering back again before using growth glyphs, the ones for making grass grow. He poured them into the brambles under Henry's feet and the plants writhed up out of the ground in a thigh-high thicket. "Smartarse." Henry tore and kicked, ripping the briars and creepers apart though the thorns cut deep gashes in his hands. "You can't keep it up for ever." Abel couldn't but how did Henry know? Abel hurled a succession of tight, hard glyphs at Henry's legs, head and torso, without effect. He ducked one thrown branch, but another hit his bad knee and pain lanced through him. Henry pounced forward, then ducked and put up a hand to avoid a dead branch coming from off to one side. A storm of twigs arrived next and Abel saw blood trickling down Henry's face.

Abel glanced over in time to see the dryad hide behind a tree. He cudgelled his brain, fighting the lethargy that had smothered him since Ferryl left. Non-magic hurt Henry, but he wasn't strong enough to fight Henry like that. Abel threw glyphs at the ground again, digging deep but this time Henry strode over the hole. Henry leapt forward, and Abel stumbled, once more taking the punch on his arm but again he went down. He put both hands down flat and blew himself up and back as Henry's foot swung, sort of flying clear.

"Getting tired already, squeak? You aren't so bloody cocky now, are you?" Henry kicked a small branch aside and clenched both fists. "I'm gonna beat you senseless, then, then…" Henry hesitated a moment, looking confused, then his face cleared again. "I'm gonna beat you senseless." Abel struggled to his feet again, pain finally getting through the lethargy so he could think. He had to slow Henry but couldn't manage a stronger trap because his magic levels were already dropping. He'd put too much into some of those wind glyphs and the growth ones.

Abel glanced back and there were several large trees he could use, but his strongest glyphs weren't working anyway. Though Henry had to kick to break the magical trap, so it had an effect. A smile, or maybe a snarl, showed briefly on Abel's face. He knew where to get more magic than any human could hold. Some last shred of common sense tried to avoid blood and possibly bodies, because Abel didn't have a Ferryl to tell him if this would be safe. "Last chance Henry. I really mean it."

"Last chance for you. Then I've got to visit Kelis to explain what a big mistake she made, threatening me!" Henry picked up another branch and swung it like a club but Abel used wind to blow up a blinding wall of leaves and twigs. Abel used the wind to push himself backwards, then blew up another storm of twigs and leaves. With Henry unsighted, Abel picked up a thin branch, running magic down it to draw a large magical trap on the ground around him. A very weak one, because his levels really were down. Abel moved back, blowing more leaf litter and using the moments when Henry couldn't see to draw a connecting line from the circle. He glanced back, then repeated the procedure with a couple of tiny fire glyphs at Henry's eyes.

The fire glyphs had no effect except causing Henry to duck, blink and shout "More tricks, squeak? None of them work now." Henry concentrated and started wading through the leafy assault with a snarl on his lips.

The delay gave Abel chance to reach a huge beech tree. "My apologies tree, but I really need this." Abel cut the glyph deep, wishing he had time to grab some magic himself, but Henry had just stepped into the circle.

Even the leakage as Abel connected the tree to the circle gave him a lift. It raised a howl of frustration from Henry, because he couldn't get out! A simple garden trap, but powered by a whole tree! Henry battered at the invisible barrier, tried to go back, and then tried to throw a branch. That flew through because it had no magic and Henry stopped, staring. Abel moved forward. "If you want to use this fancy stuff, Henry, there's tricks to deal with it. Now calm down and tell me who really gave you the glyph." Abel felt sure it hadn't been Claris.

Henry's lips moved, saying something and Abel moved nearer but couldn't hear except the last words, "Knock him out." Henry bent forward and started retching. He dropped to his knees, coughing and choking, and then his throat bulged. One last convulsion and something gushed out of Henry's mouth, something too big to be in a person's throat. It landed and writhed, and Abel tried to make sense of it. He shouldn't have been distracted, because a blow to the head picked him off his feet! Abel shook his head, put both hands palms down, and blasted himself up and back again.

Once his head stopped spinning Abel could see that Henry had charged out of the circle, face convulsed in rage. Now he headed straight for Abel to hit him again. At least the blow had finished clearing Abel's head, got him thinking straight. Just to check he threw a small branch at Henry and the big youth caught it and tossed it contemptuously aside. Abel limped backwards, looking for the right sized piece of wood and crouching behind it. No time for finesse, he used both hands under the log to blow it up towards Henry, putting up with the scraped fingers. As Henry raised his hands to catch the wood, Abel brought both palms up and hit the missile with a double blast.

Abel ended up on his backside, again, because of the sheer effort he put into the push and the backlash through his weakened arms. Henry had expected to knock the thick branch aside, and when it accelerated there simply wasn't time to dodge. Despite his muscles the youth screamed as the wood struck, splintering as it shattered against his outstretched hand and arms. Abel sat a moment, getting his breath back because Henry had finally gone down despite his glyph. Remembering the protection glyph got Abel to his feet again because he had to break that now, before Henry recovered.

Abel opened his penknife, but didn't need it to cut the glyph. As Henry rolled onto his back Abel could see that pieces of the wood had lacerated the glyph and Henry's chest. It had been designed to stop magic, but nothing else. "Get away from me." Henry glared. "Your tricks still won't work." He held up a hand to threaten Abel, then paled when he tried to clench his fingers. Henry glanced down at the protection glyph, spattered in his blood. "Tricks won't work" he mumbled, trying to clean it with the edge of his hand. "No! She said, Claris said." Henry looked up at Abel with dawning horror in his eyes because his hand had wiped a path right through the glyph, destroying it!

Abel raised his hand and waggled a finger. "That's right Henry, it's broken. I warned you. Now what's that thing in the trap?"

Henry glanced at the trap, eyes wide. "It told me, said things. Get you, knock you out. It promised, things." He looked back and forth in panic. "Get me out of here. I can feel eyes. There's things watching. Get me out of this wood!" The last came out almost as a scream and he tried to get up, then screamed properly as his weight came onto the other arm. Abel winced as he took in the distinct kink half-way down Henry's forearm.

Abel realised the barrier spell had got to Henry now the glyph had stopped protecting him, but simply hadn't got the energy or magic left to help. "You got in here Henry, so now you can wait." He turned away. "Welcome to my playground, you stupid shit." Henry didn't even reply to that, and as he limped painfully towards a lovely big oak tree Abel could hear the youth still demanding Abel got him out, now, before the things arrived. "I'm sorry, oak tree, but I've got something to deal with and need help."

"The tree will not mind, as long as you kill that." The dryad kept a good distance, pointing to the creature still writhing and pulsating inside the magic trap.

"I think you can bet on that. Thanks for the branch."

"My tree is too far away so that is all I could manage. I wanted to warn you, but you didn't come past." The dryad moved back close to his tree, but continued to watch the creature in the trap. "Blood magic, very bad."

Abel relaxed, letting the magic from the oak wash through him. "Not for long." He healed the glyph and limped to the trap. As he came closer Abel suddenly felt a strong urge to release the creature, to help it, and his ward flashed to icy cold. "Nice try. No sale." Abel turned to the dryad. "Fire or wind?"

"No fire in the wood please. A big club works. Dryads drop branches on anything smelling like that."

"Air it is." Henry had shut up, squinting as if he couldn't quite see the dryad. He turned to Abel even as Abel scraped through the feed to the trap and dropped it. The long red bag covered in thin wriggling tubes reared up at one end as if it looked at him. Abel raised both hands and punched two tight balls of wind, powered by all that lovely strong oak magic, straight through the glyph burned into it. The creature splattered, bubbled, and rapidly disappeared except for what looked a lot like blood staining the ground and nearby vegetation. Abel limped to the beech he'd used for the trap, topped up again and healed the glyph. "Thank you, tree."

When he finally got to Henry, the youth couldn't do much more than babble. He was terrified of Abel, possibly the dryad or whatever he could see there, the spatter where the creature had died, and a squirrel that ran up a tree. Abel reverted to lifting him with wind blasts because both arms throbbed from Henry's punches. So did his cheek, head and shoulder, and pain jabbed through his knee with every step. Henry yelled and screamed a bit, but Abel didn't think the wind did much more damage before getting out of the wood.

"Where's your phone, Henry? Either that or give me your Dad's number. I can't carry you." Abel considered slapping Henry. It probably wouldn't get an answer, but he still fancied it. It crossed his mind Rob would be mad as hell he'd missed this, and he'd definitely want to take a swing. Abel actually had his phone out to ask Rob if he'd like to come over when he realised that he wasn't quite rational. "Come on Henry. I'm not staying once it gets dark." He wasn't leaving Henry here either, because dryad kept glaring at the youth and after all Henry had cut its old tree up.

Now they'd come out of the wood Henry gradually recovered his wits, or some of them. He still seemed very confused about the whole thing and kept saying if he caught Abel he'd get everything, though Henry couldn't say what he'd get, or who told him. Henry ranged from denying the creature existed to retching over the memory of it going down his throat or coming back up. He'd confirm kissing Claris, and then he'd start retching over the thing in his throat. By the time Abel got the phone number he felt sure Claris needed help, or possibly a mercy killing.

Henry seemed at least as worried by his injuries as all the other stuff by the time his dad came bouncing over the field in a 4x4. The youth would probably freak out again when the pain wore off, because Henry could definitely see some magical creatures now and kept flinching. "You two been fighting again?"

"Yes, Mr. Copples."

The farmer looked Abel over, then his son. "You whipped him properly this time. I told him when you cracked his cheekbone, lay off, that lad is tougher than he looks." Mr. Copples helped Henry into the cab, then opened the back door and beckoned to Abel. "Come on. I'll give you a lift home, unless you need the hospital as well?"

Abel considered telling him to stuff it, or finding something sarcastic to say about how it hadn't seemed to matter when Henry won. Instead he shrugged, got up and climbed into the vehicle. "No hospital thanks."

"I'll tell Tyson to lay off." Mr. Copples chuckled. "I can't afford to have him laid up as well. I reckon this one has learned his lesson, haven't you, son?"

The "Yes Dad" sounded resigned. Henry kept his head down, possibly to avoid looking at the thorny rummaging in the glove compartment. Abel amused himself trying to work out ways to squish it without Mr. Copples seeing it, but gave up. Instead he thanked the farmer, tottered up the path and let himself in.

Abel's mum heard him come in and called him through. Resigned to a good ear-bashing, Abel didn't expect to find Rob in the kitchen. "Your friend has good news for you." She stared at Abel. "You probably need good news after whatever happened to you. Those Copples boys? That's enough! I'm going to bend that man's ear properly. He thinks he owns this village!"

"You'll find him at the hospital, with Henry. I won." Dead silence followed that, so Abel got the worst over with. "He's got at least three broken fingers and probably a broken arm." Still no answer. "Mr. Copples gave me a lift home and says Henry and Tyson will leave me alone now."

Eventually Rob spoke. "Will they leave me alone as well?"

"He didn't say so." Abel finally began to smile, because he knew what came next.

"Good, I'd hate to miss my chance." Rob smiled happily. "It'll have to be four broken fingers or break both arms, or I'll never hear the end of it."

"Steady on you two." Abel stared because his Mum giggled! "Let the poor boy heal up first, and maybe Kelis will want a go as well. Coffee, Abel?" He nodded. "You'd better tell him Rob."

"Good news Abel. That accident Jenny got into? She's all right so it can't have been too bad. Una says she saw Jenny and her family in town, the whole tribe, and she's got bandages and a sling and a bit of a limp. Jenny waved to Una, which came as a bit of a shock." Abel relaxed. Jenny had made it, presumably, and that had to be Ferryl waving so she'd got control. No police, and hopefully the end of Seraph's rumours.

Abel drank his coffee, talked a bit more, and pointed out he might have won but it wasn't a bloodless victory. After a shower he laid on his bed feeling sharper, more alive, as if he'd finally come out of a bad dream or at least a really deep sleep. Even if the circumstances might not have been great, Jenny would survive. His tattoo still felt empty but at least Ferryl wasn't bound now, in any way.

There would be problems dealing with the Tavern, this whole new magical world, and whoever had sent that thing for him, but he'd got friends and a safe haven at Castle House. He actually felt a bit proud, because he'd fought Henry and that creature without any help from Ferryl. Maybe he hadn't relied on her as much as he thought. Perhaps he could keep going with the Tavern, because Rob and Kelis had magic as well. That's if Kelis would talk to him after shutting her out like that. He'd certainly killed any chance of persuading her to kiss him again. So he'd lost his shy magical friend and his girlfriend, but that wasn't the end of the world, was it? Abel had nearly convinced himself by the time he fell asleep.

THE END

The next book in the series

A STUDENT BODY

will be coming soon.

Players

Brinsford - a small village in rural England, eight miles from Stourton

Consists of:

Main Street - with pub and small shop

Brinn Lane - off village green, leads to a small bridge then up valley to local farms

Riverside Close - a dozen council houses

Castle Road - road from village to main road half a mile away

Residents:

Abel Bernard Conroy - 15 - lives with widowed mum

Christine Conroy - 40 - Abel's mum, has part-time job

John Tyler - Rob's dad

Terri Tyler - Rob's mum

Rob Tyler - 15 - Abel's best friend

Melanie Tyler - 13 - Rob's sister

Samantha Tyler - 18 - Rob's sister

Jessica Ventner - Kelis's mum

Kelis Ventner - 15 - Abel's best (only) female friend

Stan - local pensioner and reputedly poacher - has a shotgun

Mr. Copples - local farmer

Henry Copples - 15 - local bully

Tyson Copples - 18 - Henry's brother - bully with crossbreed dog (Cuchelain) Cooch

Stourton - Town eight miles from Brinsford

Stourton Comprehensive - local secondary school

Seraph Courts-Pederson - 17 - wealthy young woman who manipulates the rich, influential, athletic and good-looking to form an elite, the seraphims

Laurence Sperrick - 17 - seraphim - minor nobility but not wealthy, attends local comprehensive - he is an Acro dancer

Jenny Forester - 16 - seraphim - Acro dancer

Diane Forester - 14 - Jenny's sister

Claris - 17 - seraphim - likes the rugby players

Arabelle - 16 - bubbly redhead, one of the seraphims - Acro dancer

Petra - 16 - game beta lives in a village

Warren - 15 - game beta in town

Eric - 19 - Warren's brother

Una - 17 - game beta in town with character costume

Sarah - 15 - beta in town

Justin - 15 - beta in town

Rachel - 14 - Justin's sister

Shannon - 17 - beta at church school

Shawn - 19 - friend of a friend of a beta

Mark - 17 - friend of Petra's - devout Catholic.

The Tavern - proposed new board game - becomes

Bonny's Tavern because there are lots of places called The Tavern

Game Characters: Players choose their own names when adopting a character:

Saint Georgeous - Paladin, severe but beautiful. Innate magical defences

Roughly Hewn - Barbarian adventurer - buys charms and spells to hang about him

Robyn D'Ritche - female mercenary, scruffy inebriate, part-owner of the Tavern

Bonny - Barmaid - part-owner, half-sister to Robyn

Champ - Bouncer - ex-pugilist

Ferryl Shayde - half-cat sorceress

Shayde Warrior - fighter-mage trained in magic and weapons

Abel's Magical World

Ferryl Shayde: a sorceress, trapped until she almost faded and cannot survive except in a host.

* * *

Magic: a power that permeates the air, but cannot be utilised in its raw form. All living creatures absorb magic but plants are unable to dissipate it. Trees are the greatest natural reservoirs of magic, if old enough. Animals from insects to elephants will dissipate any surplus in an uncontrolled fashion, unless they are sentient and learn to utilise glyphs and store more.

Glyphs: patterns drawn or etched on solid objects or in air or water, used to control magic and give it specific purpose. The strength of a glyph depends on the magic put into it, the medium it is drawn on, and the intent of the wielder. Glyphs in metal are the strongest, scribed in air the weakest.

* * *

Gods: possibly originally sorcerers who have learned how to draw magic from worshippers using a symbol or mark. Their power grows with the number of prayers, but old gods act quickly to crush young ones. Eternal as long as one worshipper still lives. Legend claims that the glyphs were stolen from the first God

Sorcerer or Sorceress: advanced glyph wielder who has learned how to prolong their life either with magic or at the expense of other living creatures. They are usually wealthy, living in a well-guarded home and keep a wide area clear of any large or particularly dangerous entities.

Witch or Warlock: minor magic practitioner who sells charms and hexes, and removes or creates curses. They have a normal lifespan, usually training a replacement who will also support them in old age. The profession is dying out in the countryside and smaller towns due to the current disbelief in magic and magical creatures. There are fewer paying customers to provide a living so apprentices prefer to take up other jobs.

Bound Servant: a being branded with a mark allowing a glyph wielder to control them completely. Will ignore pain or injury, hard to kill because partly protected by brand.

* * *

Creatures Visible to Humans

Dryad: creature that utilises the magic gathered by trees to protect its home tree and prolong both their lives. Gnarled, bad-tempered, rude creatures, they can manipulate magic to create a veil to hide their surroundings or to change their appearance. Will trade answers to questions in return for honey.

Blood Leech: old blood magic remnant that survives by possessing a human and feeding on fresh blood. Prefers pale skinned hosts to shed excess heat. Wear dark glasses because their eyes show red around the pupils. Most find a willing victim, usually promising a fixed period of possession and the curing of otherwise fatal illness. Once vacated the discarded husk looks young and healthy but is barely alive and infected with a seed. If it finds enough fresh blood, the abandoned host lives and another Blood Leech is created.

Goblins: the well-known greenie of legend comes in various sizes such as batlins, ratlins, Hobgoblins, and Stonelins. They eat too much real food to remain invisible, some resorting to posing as gargoyles or garden ornaments (Stonelins) to escape notice. Have been hunted almost to extinction because they are very flammable if their skin is punctured, making them a severe fire hazard. Some sorcerers use captives as entertainment at feasts, heating them slowly until they explode.

* * *

The following are invisible to normal human sight, unless the human is awakened by magic.

Free Spirit: semi-sentient fragment of a force of nature that has absorbed a fraction of the life magic from a dying entity. A ripple in the water, a flame or a puff of wind can become alive though not really thinking, and will persist if it finds enough magic to feed on.

Wild Spirit: Free Spirit that becomes sentient, deliberately hunting for magic and becoming stronger. They usually start by killing insects or fish eggs for their magic, but can grow enough to learn glyphs and threaten humans. Relatively weak unless they can possess flesh. Are destroyed on sight by most magic practitioners.

Skurrit: pack hunter. Long thin low-slung body with a variable number of short legs and clawed feet, all covered with long, matted, dirty brown fur. A light brown bald tail and a nearly bald head and snout each about 40 cm long. Tiny red eyes in a small skull, with a long thin pointed snout containing several rows of sharp teeth.

Globhoblin: warty, globular creature up to the size of a football with multiple legs ending in clawed feet. Will drain magic from the maggots and other life in discarded food but prefers to prey on the helpless like kittens, hamsters, and baby animals as well as small wildlife. Will also prey on drunks or the ill, using a stinger to draw magic. Easily killed by weak glyphs or banished by hexes.

Gremlin: tiny, vaguely human-looking creature whose skin and carapace look somewhat like a toothless old man in overalls. They live inside any type of machinery, including electrical equipment. They cause malfunctions so that angry or frustrated humans touch the object, and the Gremlin can feed from the leaking magic.

Thorny: prickly creature the size of a mouse, prefers fruit but will absorb magic from most human food and especially the flies and insects attracted to it. Infest canteens and rubbish dumps.

Hoplin: little creatures looking like a miniature armadillo hopping like a kangaroo, with a mildly venomous bite. Hunt in pairs that can kill rats, mice or a kitten to drain magic. Useful for dealing with infestations of rats and mice.

Faerie: rough-skinned creatures in shades and patterns of brown, with long, thin horny wings and a variety of limbs. Absorb the magic in grass or leaves, or sometimes fruit. Eat a little to help remain solid, which leaves tiny blemishes. Too many on one place can kill grass or leaves.

Fae: similar looking but a little larger than faerie, and prey on them. Some hunt small insects and are harmless to humans while others have stings and can be dangerous. Their natural magical food supply is sucked like mosquitoes from larger magical creatures that browse on the magic in plants.

Fairies: prefer wilderness, living on magic leached from plants especially flowers, many are bright coloured which makes them vulnerable to hunters such as fae.

Pictsies: like to live with humans and their pets where they hunt lice, flies, insects and spiders.

Pixies: live with humans. Live on the magic leaking from the residents of 'their' house or left on clothes, removing dandruff and loose hair.

Piskies: live in gardens, in stock pens, or in the wild. Like jokes.

Brownies: good ones are fanatically tidy. Live with humans if possible and tidy up dust, cobwebs, pet hair, but will leave if humans are either too tidy so there is no food, or too scruffy. If the humans are too untidy, the brownies may become angry and will trash the house before leaving.

A profusion of other small creatures exist, hunting the magic from anything from fleas up to rabbits or small dogs. They also hunt each other, and there are magical prey creatures that 'graze' on the magical energy in plants such as grass. Cats and dogs can see them but not clearly, just enough to avoid them or fight back. Some are beneficial, but if aware most humans prefer to stop most from fluttering, crawling, hopping or slithering into their homes.

Allegedly Extinct Species

Skoffin - Icelandic creature - breathes fire and turns prey to stone before consuming.

Dragon - many types, now all hunted and killed.

Aryadne's Hound - man/spider hybrid created by Goddess Aryadne to serve her. Live in caves, eat carrion, four spider legs and rear and four spider-like arms on humanoid torso. Died out when she faded.

Created Creatures

Guardian: very hard to kill without magic. Usually a stone statue, the construct is charged with magic and set to guard. Once triggered the magic will animate the stone regardless of any weathering or damage. The animating glyph is carved in the centre of the stone block, a very skilled magical task, and impossible to reach without destroying the vessel.

Bound Shade: a creature with its spirit captured at the moment of dying and used to keep a semblance of life. Usually controlled by burying a glyph deep inside it, or imprisoning the spirit within a tattoo on the Shade's master or mistress. The Shade will then obey direct orders from the glyph-maker or if sent on mission or left as a sentry follow imprinted instructions, guarding an area for instance. While torpid a Bound Shade needs only a little sustenance, but once roused it must feed on the living.

Pungh Hmmshtfun (Old Hebrew dialect)

Spiritus qui Furabatur (Latin)

Koška Smerti (Russian)

Braeth Huntian (Old English)

Ferryl Shayde - name currently used by a faded sorceress

Review

If you enjoyed this book, please share a short review with us on Amazon, Goodreads or the platform of your choice. Help other readers discover new authors.

Vance reads each and every comment you post and loves to hear from his readers.

VANCE HUXLEY

Vance Huxley lives out in the countryside in Lincolnshire, England. He has spent a busy life working in many different fields – including the building and rail industries, as a workshop manager, trouble-shooter for an engineering firm, accountancy, cafe proprietor, and graphic artist. He also spent time in other jobs, and is proud of never being dismissed, and only once made redundant.

Eventually he found his Noeline, but unfortunately she died much too young. To help with the aftermath, Vance tried writing though without any real structure. As an editor and beta readers explained the difference between words and books, he tried again.

Now he tries to type as often as possible in spite of the assistance of his cats, since his legs no longer work well enough to allow anything more strenuous. An avid reader of sci-fi, fantasy and adventure novels, his writing tends towards those genres.